A Rainbow
Murder Mystery

Praise for the Ben Candidi Mystery Series

Biotechnology Is Murder (2000)

"Nifty, light-hearted and deadly."

— Edna Buchanan, *Garden of Evil*

". . . a potent mix of science, business and crime."

— *Publishers Weekly*

"Dirk Wyle . . . is a sure winner. His character Ben Candidi is just finishing his Ph.D., but Ben packs more punch per square inch than most veteran detectives . . . a timely plot with larger than life characters with which the reader has an immediate affinity. Ben Candidi is the young Jack Ryan of the biotechnological world."

— Shelley Glodowski, *Midwest Review*

"Dirk Wyle seems to know more about science and bio-tech thrillers than Robin Cook or Michael Palmer . . . a winner."

— Norman Bogner, *Honor Thy Wife*

". . . a very well written and clever second addition didi series. Dirk Wyle is able to paint a vivid picture world. . . . Halfway through this book, I reached happily lost track of time and had to remind mysel followed through with a stunning ending that felt plete."

—Andrea Collare, *Charl*

". . . a combination of white collar crime medical mystery. . . . Ben Candidi doesn't carry a gun o He's witty, complex and a very different sleuth."

— Lane Wright, *Mystery Books Review at About.com*

"Against the backdrop of this intriguing mystery, the author takes us on a tour through the Byzantine world of high finance and biotechnology."
— *Charles Ouimet in the H.M.S. Beagle*

". . . Wyle writes a heck of a good novel . . . keeping the reader hooked as he proceeds."
— G. Miki Hayden, *By Reason of Insanity* and *Pacific Empire*

"An exciting tale of murder and mayhem generated by the greed of the pharmaceutical industry. . . . As the tale unfolds the reader learns a great deal about the workings of basic and applied pharmaceutical research, the patenting process, and escort services available in Miami. The book is technically accurate and exciting."
— Ronald K. Wright, MD, JD,
Chief Medical Examiner Emeritus, Broward County, FL

"Science and exotic murders combine with America's favorite Gen-X detective to offer a perfect read for the educated mystery lover curious about the biotech industry. Highly recommended. Another movie script prospect."
— Arno F. Spatola, Ph.D., Pres. & CEO,
Peptides International, Louisville, KY

"Dirk Wyle has woven often overlooked but important aspects of patent law into a due diligence investigation overlaid with murder. Time is always of the essence in such investigations and facing a deadline Ben Candidi is prodded to winkel facts from unwilling sources to provide his expertise, information related only to patent law and base a significant portion of his investigation on it."
— Arthur R. Crawford, Esq.,
Patent Attorney, Nixon & Vanderhye PC, Arlington, VA

"Fun reading. . . . The characters are very well drawn. One quickly conjures up an image of each. . . . The Oxford/Cambridge pathologist and the video gadgeteer are welcomed when they reappear . . . [in the second novel]."
— Stephen J. Morris, Ph.D.,
Professor of Molecular Biology and Biochemistry,
University of Missouri-Kansas City

"Great characters, good logic and memorable twists."
— Tom Gasiewicz, Ph.D.,
Professor of Environmental Medicine,
University of Rochester

Pharmacology Is Murder (1998)

"... Wyle skillfully pairs the tone of the hard-boiled mystery with the intricate scientific detail common to the medical thriller. The result is an excellent whodunit. . . . a first-class mystery that combines elements of Michael Crichton, Patricia Cornwell, and even Edna Buchanan."
— *Booklist* Mystery Showcase (American Library Association)

"... one fine debut mystery, combining scientific method with a quirky, humanistic scientist/detective and resulting in the perfect compound ... inventive, intriguing, and, most importantly, evocatively drawn. If you like a puzzle, you'll love this one."
— Les Standiford, *Black Mountain*

"Dirk Wyle fuses Miami's cosmopolitan setting with academic intrigue, scientific discoveries, romance and murder to create a unique read. . . . this book delivers. . . . Wyle explains scientific jargon and theories in clear layman's terms, mixing investigations with in-depth character studies to explore all aspects of the crime." — Devorah Stone, *The Quill*

"... a good solid interesting mystery in the traditional style of literate storytelling. . . . very smooth and intelligent."
— Sharon Villines, Archives of Detective Fiction

"... so easy to pick up and so hard to put down!"
— Reviewer's Bookwatch

"... written for the intellectual who loves mysteries ... characters well presented." — Under the Covers Book Reviews

"Wyle demonstrates a breezy style, a flair for drawing vivid and memorable characters with just a few deft strokes. . . . I've found myself thinking about it and admiring it in retrospect over an over again."
— Joe Lofgreen's Detective Pages,
Judged **Best First Detective Novel** of 1998

"... step into the scientific world, the Mensa Society, be led down a heady path of suspense, and witness in our main character an emergence of love and vulnerability."
— Linda Tharp, *The Snooper*, Snoop Sisters Bookstore

"The reader is amazed at the author's ability to create tension, introduce a little love-making along the way, and tell a good mystery story."
— Kathie Nuckols Lawson, BookBrowser

Titles in the Ben Candidi Mystery Series by Dirk Wyle

Pharmacology Is Murder (ISBN 1-56825-038-X)
Biotechnology Is Murder (ISBN 1-56825-045-2)
Medical School Is Murder (ISBN 1-56825-084-3)

DIRK WYLE

Medical School Is Murder

A Ben Candidi Mystery

Dirk Wyle

Rainbow Books, Inc.
FLORIDA

Wyle, Dirk, 1945-
Medical school is murder / Dirk Wyle.
    p. cm.
ISBN 1-56825-084-3 (alk. paper)
    1. Candidi, Ben (Fictitious character)--Fiction. 2. Pharmacologists--Fiction.
       3. Miami (Fla.)--Fiction. I. Title.
PS3573.Y4854 M4 2001
813'.54--dc21   2001031956

Medical School Is Murder © 2001 by Dirk Wyle
(http://www.dirk-wyle.com)

ISBN 1-56825-084-3

Publisher
          Rainbow Books, Inc.
          P. O. Box 430
          Highland City, FL 33846-0430

Editorial Offices and Wholesale/Distributor/Retail Orders
          Telephone/Fax: (863) 648-4420
          Email: RBIbooks@aol.com

Individual/Retail Orders
          Telephone: (800) 431-1579; Fax: (914) 835-0398

Cover and interior design by Betsy A. Lampé

This is a work of fiction. Any similarity of characters to individuals, living or dead, is purely coincidental.

All rights reserved. No part of this book may be reproduced or transmitted in any form or by any means, electronic or mechanical (except as follows for photocopying for review purposes). Permission for photocopying can be obtained for internal or personal use, the internal or personal use of specific clients, and for educational use, by paying the appropriate fee to

Copyright Clearance Center
222 Rosewood Dr.
Danvers, MA 01923   U.S.A.

First Printing 2001
Printed in the United States of America.

Dedication

This novel is dedicated to all the career scientists who panned the streams until they went bust, yet never jumped a colleague's lucky claim nor tried to pass off fool's gold for the real thing.

Author's Note

In common with legal thrillers, courtroom dramas and other forms of white-collar detective fiction, this novel contains examples of authentic professional dialogue. Business and scientific terms are limited to those found in *Webster's New Collegiate Dictionary* and are explained in the novel within their immediate context. No specialized knowledge is required to solve the murder(s). Have fun!

Acknowledgments

I would like to thank Betty Wright, my publisher, for her unshakable belief in my work and for her suggestions on its fine-tuning. I am also deeply indebted to Betsy Lampé for imaginative cover design and for tenacious promotion of my work.

I also thank the many readers who have written and e-mailed their reactions to *Pharmacology Is Murder* and *Biotechnology Is Murder*, the first two novels in the Ben Candidi series.

The present novel benefited from the early-stage critiques of Yvonne, Ed, Charlie, Ira, Harrison, Robert, Karl, Gisela, Carlisle and Douglas, a Spanish lesson from Raul, information from Alan, and from the comments of Duane, Suzy, Gregg and Chris.

ON THE POTOMAC   1

The phone call put an end to a four-month dream. The phone call caught me lounging in the cockpit of the *Diogenes*, my nomadic home. I was enjoying a glass of wine and the rays of the setting sun while my mate prepared dinner. A pair of mallards dipped their wings, rounding our masts and continuing their descent into the marsh grass lining the Potomac River.

What could be more idyllic than working at a good job during the day and living close to nature at night? My commute was less than two miles. In fact, I could almost make out my office building, the United States Patent and Trademark Office, just beyond Washington National Airport.

The next bird to fly over our masts was not so charming. But the thunder of an occasional Boeing 737 wasn't bad enough to drive us to a spot farther down the river. Our spot was perfect. It was a nearly perfect circle whose radius was equal to 50 yards of anchor line and whose center could be anywhere we decided to lower the 40-pound CQR.

A glance towards the Jefferson Memorial was a reminder that Ben Candidi, with his newly granted Ph.D. in pharmacology, had scored three out of three on Thomas Jefferson's list of essentials: Life, Liberty, and the Pursuit of Happiness.

Yes, after 30-some years of Life, Ben Candidi was finally achieving sustainable Happiness.

A sweet, buttery smell wafted through the companionway. I leaned forward for a peek at Rebecca who was down in the galley frying crab cakes on the alcohol stove. Her black ponytail quivered as she stretched her slender body over the dinette table, balancing on one knee and a hand. Her hips tilted, her spine flexed and a shapely leg extended in counterbalance as she reached into a deep storage locker under the cushions. She retrieved a small bottle of salad dressing, reversed her stretch, turned nimbly and rose to face me. "Dinner will be ready in about ten minutes, Ben." A twinkle of her olive-green eyes and a broad smile on her narrow face told me she was aware of being admired.

"Looks great, Rebecca. Everything."

And everything *was* just great, like an endless vacation — until the phone call put an end to it.

The vacation had started four months earlier, when, on a rising April tide, we unhitched dock lines and motored our 36-foot *Diogenes* past the cruise ships and out Miami's Government Cut. We hoisted canvas up the main and mizzen masts, and sailed north with the Gulf Stream, rounding Cape Hatteras and popping into Chesapeake Bay. Here, on the Potomac, we dropped anchor.

For the last few months we had lived professional lives in Washington, D.C. Every morning, Monday through Friday, we climbed into the dinghy and rowed ashore. Rebecca walked to the Metro station and took the Green Line to George Washington University. For me, it was a walk to the Patent Office where I was in on-the-job training to be a patent examiner. And at the end of the day, we returned to our floating apartment for peaceful evenings.

Our weekends began on late Friday afternoons when we hauled anchor and headed downriver towards Chesapeake Bay, usually with a boatload of friends who encouraged us to sail onward for the whole weekend and then welcomed us as Washington houseguests when Sunday evenings transformed into Monday mornings. Yes, the *Diogenes* spent many a workweek tied up at far-flung marinas until we retrieved him on the next Friday evening for a new install-ment of the party — Patuxent River, Annapolis, Patapsco River, Baltimore, all the way to Havre de Grace — East Shore, West Shore, so much to explore. But the arrival of September put an end to our sailing parties.

And the phone call put an end to the vacation and to my career at the Patent Office.

Well, the vacation would have ended anyway. September is the back-to-school and get-down-to-business month. Early Septem-ber brings the first chilly evenings, reminding us that October is around the corner, followed by a cold, wet November and a bone-numbing

December. January might even bring snowstorms. Now was the time to start looking for a dock with electricity. Yes, September is the month of reality checks.

My reality was that I loved Rebecca Levis deeply and would never let her go. I'd known that since we'd first met. That was several years ago when she was a med student and I was a Ph.D. student doing research in pharmacology. This new advocation had rescued me from a 6-year downward spiral towards the life of a boat bum. Five years my junior, Rebecca has always known what she wanted to be — a doctor. After graduating from Bryan Medical School in Miami she accepted a fellowship at George Washington University School of Medicine. This would allow her to pursue a major passion — evaluating medical treatment for developing countries. I still don't completely understand her program — that consortium arrangement between the World Health Organization, the State Department and the National Institutes of Health. But I've always understood that I love her. I completed my Ph.D. at Bryan the same month and followed her here.

I never questioned the decision to follow her. Rebecca was the perfect girl — the soul mate I'd been searching for all my life — a bright-spirited, witty, athletic and beautiful girl in her slender sort of way. We were perfectly matched in physical type, height, temperament, philosophy, ideals, and everything else that counts. And concerning all the rest, we were open-minded, always ready to step in and protect each other's blind sides. Our partnership was destined to last a lifetime, and I would do anything to keep it that way.

I'd been lucky to get that trainee position at the Patent Office. It was a well-paying job for a guy with a recently earned pharmacology Ph.D. The job was secure, intellectually challenging, and exciting at first.

But the phone call put an end to my career at the Patent Office and took me away from the woman I loved. It forced me to question my assumptions.

Actually, I had set for myself a long-range professional goal. A high-paying, four-day consultant gig a few months ago had whetted my appetite for work in technology transfer. And I figured the Patent Office job would be good experience for a later career as a technology transfer consultant. Play my cards right for the next couple of years, and I'd be able to command big bucks for my appraisals of technology companies being offered on the auction block.

But thinking back on my dissertation, it was a shame to give up laboratory science. There's really nothing to beat the thrill of inventions and discoveries made in your own lab. The problem is *getting* your own lab. It's a damn imperfect world. Making a career in academic laboratory research would be too hard, and the reasons had nothing to do with natural talent. The odds were simply were against me, and against everyone else. Too many Ph.D.s were already out there, chasing too few positions at research universities. To get my own laboratory, I would have to spend the next four years as a post-doctoral slave in someone else's laboratory. What a hopeless grind! — a category of endeavor that I've spent my life avoiding.

My problem was that academic success had come to me too easily. It arrived in early childhood and followed me all the way through college. The teachers identified me as a "boy genius." Gold stars and A's came my way without requiring much effort. I never had to grind. Yes, it influenced my personality. But hell, I wasn't cut out to be a mill horse. Life is too interesting to wear blinders and strain in the harness day *and* night. Yes, you can call it a streak of laziness. You might even call it fear of failure. Sure, it probably adds up to a character flaw.

And that's why the phone call was so upsetting — the phone call that ended our vacation, ended my career at the Patent Office, took me away from the woman I loved, reopened old wounds and almost got me killed two months later.

Rebecca's crab cakes smelled awfully good. A cool breeze was rolling in from Foggy Bottom as the setting sun cast shadows over the Potomac Valley. In my long-sleeved sweatshirt, I was prepared.

Or so I thought when the phone rang.

Rebecca called up to me, "Can you get it?"

Our cellular phones were a necessary part of our live-aboard lifestyle. I reached into the cockpit's side pocket and grabbed the correct one and called down, "Got it. It's mine anyway."

The voice on the other end was deep and jocular. "This is a blast from your recent past." It was Dr. Rob McGregor, my old friend and erstwhile dissertation advisor from Bryan Medical School in Miami. "Are you still giving the molecular genetics people a hard time with their patent applications?"

"No," I laughed, and gave him the long answer. "I'm just making the DNA jockeys include a convincing statement of utility. Can't give them rights to a DNA sequence if they can't say what the corresponding protein does. Can't call it an invention if you don't know what the hell it does. And we make them prove it, too. Can't give them a patent if they can't show how it's useful." This must have been the third time we'd replayed this question and answer.

Rob chuckled. "So Old Ben Candidi's still crusading to make sure everyone is being useful." In these conversational warm-ups, Rob often reminded me of a bear pawing around, sometimes friendly and usually clumsy. Had he forgotten what he was calling for?

"Well, Rob, I hope I'm still useful to *you*. You did look at the manuscript attached to my last e-mail message, didn't you?"

"Yes. That will make the fourth publication we squeeze out of your dissertation. Not bad."

"Right, Rob. I worked hard in your lab. Now you just send up the graphs for publications number five and six, and I'll work up the manuscripts. I'm trying to be *useful*. Trying to get you six publications from my dissertation. That will keep things going for a while, won't it?"

"Right. Should be able to keep singing your praises through next spring. That's when I'm going to the FASEB Meeting." He was referring to a big annual conference that draws over ten thousand biomedical scientists from all over the country. "When I see the old gang, I'll be able to tell them that you're still doing *real* science."

Real lab bench science, as opposed to phoney Patent Office science?

That was just Rob; there was no changing it. Sometimes he'd take a clumsy swipe for no reason. Hell no, I wasn't going to give away my option to do "real science." Not yet, anyway.

"Come on, Rob! You've got to be careful what you say about me at that conference. I worked my butt off for those papers. I'm still a world expert on calmodulin-activated protein phosphatases." These were important enzymes that can keep a stimulated cell from running out of control. "If you drink too many cocktails with those guys and start saying Candidi's not doing real science . . . *you'll throw all my hard work away.*"

"Okay. All right. I was just kidding."

"You just be careful. They have to think I'm still slaving away."

Yes, slaving away in an endless cycle of experiments, writing papers and writing grant proposals so I could do more experiments. If they found out that I've jumped off the merry-go-round, they'd never let me back on again. "You understand? I don't want to throw away my option to be an academic scientist. Not yet, anyway."

"Who are you talking to?" Rebecca asked.

I stuck my thumb over the tiny microphone hole before answering her. "It's Rob. Can't you guess?"

I removed my thumb. The line was silent for so long that I was afraid Rob had heard me anyway and was insulted.

And that was when I asked the question that broke the four-month spell. "What else can I do for you, Rob?"

"I called to bring you sad tidings, but also an opportunity." Rob had a way of making outdated expressions sound hip. "You remember Peter Peterson?"

Yes, I remembered that goofy old professor — always ready to talk science at the drop of a hat. He always found a reason to stay late to do another experiment, too. I pictured the tall, lanky, absent-minded, third-generation Swede ambling down the hallway.

"Yes," I said to Rob, off-handedly. "Pete Peterson, from the Physiology and Cellular Anatomy Department. White hair, crew cut. Always in the lab, even Saturdays and Sundays." The thought of my own Sundays spent in the lab must have angered me. "To quote an old fable, he loves science like the horse pulling the milk delivery wagon loves its route. Hitch it up to the carriage for a Sunday ride, and it goes back to delivery route. He'll probably keep working until he drops dead."

"He just did. Heart attack."

"Damn!" My right hand shot to my sternum and made a sign of The Cross. When you were brought up as a Catholic, certain things remain life-long reflexes — guilt included. "I'm so sorry. I didn't mean it that way . . . Did it happen in the lab?"

"No. It happened last Wednesday night. They found him around midnight, floating face-down in that canal by the med school."

"Wagner Creek?"

"If that's what they call it. Must have happened when he was sitting on the fence by the canal, smoking his pipe. Right next to his apartment building. You used to live there. You must have seen him."

"Yes, but we didn't talk much."

"Anyway, let me get to the point. I talked to his chairman, Harold Boyle. Got him to agree that maybe you could take over Pete's grant! It's got two years to run."

I sucked in my breath. "Harold Boyle said I could take over Pete's grant?"

"Yes, and you could direct Mildred Goodman, Pete's career technician. I planted the idea in Boyle's head. I started by talking about his department's moral obligation to Mildred. I reminded him that nobody on his faculty was interested in Pete's research. Got him agreeing that Pete's work is outside the scope of physiology and has nothing to do with anatomy. Hell, physiologists aren't really interested in oxidative damage to cells and free radical chain reactions."

"That's true."

"I told Boyle about all the manuscripts coming from your dissertation. One thing led to another. I told him that if he could keep the project alive, his department could keep its share of the grant's overhead money. I said you'd be a useful guy to have around. You might be able to help him with his calcium movements in adrenal glands. I offered the bait and he nibbled."

"Good thinking." I said it with enthusiasm but felt ambivalence. "Can't let soft money go to waste."

I'd probably given the words "soft money" a sarcastic intonation. Federal grant dollars are called "soft money" because of their annoying tendency to go soft on you. The money from a three-year grant is just fine, but there's no guarantee that you can get a new grant at the end of the third year. It's a lot better to be living on "hard money" where your salary is paid from the normal operating funds of the medical school.

Rob continued with his pitch. "Of course, the soft money would let us renew our collaboration. Free radicals and oxidative stress probably affect the protein kinases we've been working on. We could do some more work together."

Yes, we probably could. And Brer Bear was starting to sound more like Brer Fox.

"Thanks, Rob. It sounds interesting. Tell me about the financials."

"You will be paid what the grant was contributing to Pete's salary — forty thousand dollars a year."

"Not bad."

"Yeah, not bad for *you*." Rob told me Pete had been making only $55,000, which is not much for a full professor at the end of a 40-year career. Then Rob gave me an earful of bureaucratic babble, describing the grant's financial categories and the "overhead payments" that came with it.

After Rob finished, I summarized. "So I'm being offered two years at forty thousand dollars a year, payable in soft money, but secure for the two years. A chance to do research using my own ideas for two years. And then, maybe I'll be able to carve out some space and get my own grants. But after two years, no guarantees."

"Right. And maybe you'll be grateful and do some more cellular control experiments with your old *Doktorvater* . . . meaning yours truly. That's the deal. You going for it?"

"Have to talk with Rebecca. I'll call tomorrow, Rob."

"Yes, you do that. Because we've got to land this thing before other people start drooling over the money. Because tomorrow afternoon at five-thirty, you and I and Boyle are going to have a conference call. We're going to pin it all down. Think it over carefully. You're getting two years of salary and a toe-hold for a permanent position. Don't blow it, buddy." (Click)

There it was: an offer of two protected years with good pay to launch a career in lab research — a career that I'd all but written off. A chance to start up a lab research career without having to endure four years of post-doctoral serfdom. A chance to make scientific discoveries on my own. I swallowed hard.

Rebecca emerged from the galley and handed me two plastic plates. The crab cakes were sitting on a mound of yellow rice garnished with sliced cucumbers and curlicues of carrot. With limber grace, Rebecca climbed to the cockpit and sat on the bench across from me.

"What did Rob want?"

I could answer her first question, but not the ones to come.

THE ALGEBRA OF EMOTION

Rob's offer — his challenge, really — had caught me flat-footed. I took refuge in the crab cakes. Took a couple of bites and vocalized my approval.

Then I swallowed hard. "Rob called to say that Peter Peterson just died. Rob's offering me his job."

"That's what I thought I heard. You have a job offer." She said it neutrally. Her gaze was placid and sympathetic. The setting sun sparkled in her dark-green eyes — eyes that could convey so much meaning, and extract it, too.

I didn't want eye contact. I needed time to think. Damn. Where was a thundering jet when you really needed one? Why couldn't the ducks swim over and offer some cute distraction? I mumbled something and took another bite. Did I want to make a try at academic laboratory science? Would two well-financed years be enough to get me started? "I think we need to talk about it," I said, finally.

"I understand. How do you *feel* about the offer?"

Rebecca has a lovely voice — high-pitched but not squeaky, expressively and honestly modulated, and always self-confidently feminine. Like a heroine in a turn-of-the-century operetta, she can deliver a wide range of feeling in a natural soprano register.

Sitting across from her, I must have sounded like an adolescent tenor. "Rebecca, it's hard for me to describe my feelings until I have thought it through."

"Just talk to me about it." Her voice cracked in mid-sentence, like a cold shiver. "Tell me your thoughts as they come to you. Don't worry which way your thoughts will lead you."

I threw a glance her way. She was still in shorts and T-shirt. The sun was now below the hills. Soon, the cold air would penetrate the fabric and harden the delicate nipples of her small but charming breasts. She drew up her legs and hugged herself at the knee.

I was glad for an excuse to go below and bring back her sweatshirt. While helping her put it on, I kissed her cheek. She returned the kiss, lightly. I returned to my side of the cockpit.

Rebecca reached back and removed the band holding her ponytail. Slowly, she rocked her head from one shoulder to another, in a slow yoga motion that loosened tension in her neck and redistributed her shoulder-length hair. She can be so serene when problems come rolling in. She went back to hugging her knees at the chin. The pose suggested a contemplative mood, but also created fascinating contours where her thin, shapely legs join her broad, flat hips.

Now, the two ducks were quacking in the water below us. They always came begging in the middle of dinner. I tossed them a couple scraps of French bread. Winter was coming for the mallards, too. All four of us had decisions to make.

I described to Rebecca the scenario that Rob had laid out. The job would pay $7,000 more than I was earning at the Patent Office. While Rebecca ate, I described Peter Peterson's work on free radical damage and the cellular effects of antioxidants such as vitamin E. As I spoke, something unexpected happened: Ideas started hatching within me — ideas for extending Dr. Peterson's work into the areas of cancer, arthritis and stroke. Rebecca listened intently and asked an occasional question until I had talked myself out. By then the crab cakes had grown cold on my plate and the sky was dark.

Behind a row of trees, the Jefferson Memorial had taken on the yellow glow of a warm campfire. The Washington Monument was spotlit like a rocket on a launching pad. The Capitol dome shone like an alien spacecraft in a Spielberg movie. I looked down again at the water. The ducks had retreated to the reeds.

I ate my last bites and Rebecca took away the plates. She brought back two cups of hot tea. "I understand what you're saying, Ben. I know how you feel about taking a post-doctoral fellowship in someone else's lab. This offer will save you four years of post-doctoral work and you will get your *own* lab. Rob's offering you a jump start for an independent research career!"

"That's true." It was, but the words came out unenthusiastically.

The scattered city light revealed a frown on Rebecca's narrow, fine-featured face. "But you don't sound happy about it, Ben." Her next words came out ever so cautiously. "You must still have negative feelings about making a career in academic research."

Rebecca can read my emotions like a magazine. She knows me better than I know myself. That must of irked me just then.

"I don't want to be a slave to the soft money system — writing grant proposals to the National Institutes of Health for the rest of my life." The bitterness of my words surprised me. "I love science, but I hate . . ."

"Yes, Ben, I know how you hate that system. I remember you calling it a forced labor camp without bars. I know that there's not enough money to go around. I know that only one in seven grant proposals is funded. And I remember you comparing the review committees with the death list committee in a Nazi concentration camp . . . with the inmates making out their own death list."

"It was an ugly analogy. I'm sorry."

But Rebecca continued with clinical detachment. "And I remember how you compared the NIH bureaucrats managing those committees with concentration camp guards."

"Yeah, bureaucrats with 30-year-stale Ph.D. degrees!"

Like a skilled psychotherapist, Rebecca had unlocked a lot of my emotions in a short time. She laid in a pause before resuming. What would she get me to say next? That I was turning into a bureaucrat, myself?

"But you aren't happy working in the Patent Office, either."

"How can you say that?" I tried to make my reply sound neutral.

"Because you don't look happy when I kiss you goodbye in the morning. And at night you don't talk about your work — not like you used to talk about your protein phosphatase research."

Uncanny, how she could peer into my psyche.

My answer came quickly in the tone of an older brother. "Rebecca, the Patent Office work was very interesting when I was first learning the rules. Now that I've figured out the rules, I'm putting more energy into broadening my understanding of biomedical science."

"But now it isn't making you happy."

Damn!

"A lot of those patent applications are junk science," I continued, "but you can't reject them like when you're reviewing a scientific paper for a journal. You can only reject *claims*."

"I don't think you'll be happy as a patent examiner. Or as a patent attorney, either."

Rebecca was working through the logic of my emotions with the tempo and rigor of a college instructor presenting theorems in Algebra & Geometry 101. And I felt so stupid, not being able to keep up.

"No, I don't want to be a patent attorney. But working in technology assessment would be okay."

"Like that four-day consulting job you did for that venture capitalist?" This was a challenge, but she said it gently.

"Yes," I said, with enthusiasm. "The consulting job for Dr. Broadmoore that paid me twenty-four thousand dollars — for four days of work." The guy had hired me as a scientific bloodhound to sniff out a biotechnology company he was going to buy.

Rebecca did not match my enthusiasm. "The job that paid you twenty-four thousand dollars to risk your life?"

Now *that* was just 20-20 hindsight from the cushy vantage point of the psychotherapist's chair.

"Look, it was a raggedy deal. Three people took some serious shortcuts and paid with their lives. It was a big gamble, with twenty million dollars on the table. That sort of thing doesn't happen every week."

"Thank goodness." She shook her head. "If the consulting jobs come only once in a while, you won't be able to count on them for making a living."

"Not right now. But I will in a couple of years. I'm building a reputation as an expert in technology evaluation. That's why this Patent Office stint is good."

"Will your reputation be that much better if you spend another year and a half at the Patent Office?"

Her manner was quiet and her logic was ruthless.

"Probably not. But, Rebecca, I want to be with you." My voice cracked.

Now it was Rebecca who was looking down on the water. "Another year and a half at my fellowship won't help me that much, either. I know many of the people on the grant committees, already."

Her fellowship was a desk job, evaluating information on the cost-effectiveness of different types of medical treatment in developing nations. Her real goal was to do field work in those countries. She wanted to develop new health care paradigms.

"Rebecca, even if I take the job, I do *not* want you to quit your fellowship just to be with me in Miami."

"Not right now, but I could quit in six months. There are plenty of emergency rooms in Miami where I can work until a grant comes through." A Mona Lisa smile was growing on her face. "Back in

Miami, you can help me with finding Latin American connections."

"Yes, I could help you with the Latin American angle."

Fine, but nothing was decided. We were silent for several minutes.

"Ben, I have just one question. Imagine your dream job — the kind of a job that would really make you happy."

Oh, hell! I'd have to admit it.

"I'd like the chance to make scientific discoveries every day — but without having to write grant proposals . . . and without having to deal with a lot of bureaucratic hassle."

"Would the Miami job give you that?"

"For the first two years, it would."

"Suppose everything worked out well in those two years. What would you have then?"

"I'd have a patentable medical discovery that would make the world beat a path to my door. If it was really good, I could command money from government *and* from industry."

"Ben, I really believe you. You take to science like a duck to water. Now, would it be worth two years trying? To know if you could come up with a medical discovery?"

"Yes." It was true. But I felt the throbbing of old emotional wounds: my disdain for the grind and my fear of failure.

"And what if the discovery doesn't come to you like magic?"

Damn it! Had she been reading my mind again? Would she remind me that independent discoveries might not come as easily as straight A's?

"You're right. I'd have to hedge my bet, using some of my effort to build a consulting practice. Or maybe at the end of the two years, I'd fold my hand, cash in my chips, and go for a regular job in the pharmaceutical industry. When you work for them, you don't have to worry about grants."

We said nothing for several minutes. My tea had turned cold. It was Rebecca who broke the silence.

"I'm glad you have a plan. I want you to be happy. I know how important it is to keep your brain in gear. And I know how you hate regimentation."

Rebecca was actually thanking me for opening up my inspection ports and letting her play analyst. Yes, my brain is excellent at figuring out Nature's marvels. And my brain usually works okay when dealing with other people. But my brain is the world's stupidest when it comes to analyzing myself.

Okay. Thanks, Rebecca, for giving me a soft kick in the butt. And while I'm at it, thanks to Old Dr. Geoffrey Westley for the kick in the butt that saved me from turning into a boat bum back in the days when I was working as a cocaine analysis technician in his Miami-Dade County Medical Examiner's Office. Dr. Westley had fired me for my own good and sent me to the pharmacology program at Bryan Medical School. Thanks to him, I met Rebecca and got a Ph.D. degree.

Emerging from my thoughts, I noticed that Rebecca was studying me. "My fellowship isn't perfect, either, Ben. I took it to help make policy. But all those people are really thinking about is protecting their comfortable lives in suburban Maryland. Sometimes, I feel like they're turning me into a bureaucrat!"

I didn't mind hearing that from Rebecca's lips. Occasionally, her dedication to Third World medicine had irked me. I'd sometimes found myself wishing she would choose a more lucrative medical specialty to speed our payments on her $65,000 of student loans. The M.D. degree can be a real financial powerhouse once you fire it up.

The stock market was doing well, but we weren't in it. But I never said anything like that to Rebecca.

"Talking this stuff out has been good for me," I told her.

"I'm glad. Your job offer sounds worth considering. You can do bench science eight hours a day, and then you could do consults on the side."

"Exactly. They wouldn't mind if I popped out for a week or two to do a consult."

Rebecca was picking up enthusiasm. "Two stable years should be long enough to build up your consulting practice. And maybe you will make a big discovery. All the while, you'll be helping science — saving Dr. Peterson's work from going to waste."

The girl had a lot of sense. She put it all together so well.

Her eyes searched mine. "And the work *is* important to health, isn't it? Diet, nutrition and ageing?"

"I guess. But Dr. Peterson's research seminars were pretty disorganized. It might take a lot of work to tidy things up."

"Good. Then you can help human health and his legacy. It will be good for you, too, to try out your ideas — like what you just told me about a possible role of anti-oxidant vitamins and 'redox potential' in programmed cell death."

"Yes," I said, cautiously.

"Maybe this is a good piece of luck. A boost for your enthusiasm. Like when Dr. Westley advised you to go into the Ph.D. program."

"You've got a point."

I probably said it with a sigh. If left to myself, I would go back to my old dilettante habits — spending a lot of time on things that interest me but have no practical consequences.

"Rebecca, what would *you* do if I go back to Miami?"

"I'll wait a few months for you to decide if you really like your job in Miami. If you like it, I'll cancel the second year of my fellowship."

Six months of separation. No use saying it.

Rebecca didn't say it either.

"Go down there and try it out, Ben. If you like it, I'll follow you."

My words came out in torrents. I gushed about how we'd learned and loved together, and had become life-time partners. "Like Canadian geese. Like those ducks! Except we're joined at the hip."

She laughed. "And in the bank account."

I moved to her bench and put my arm around her. She hugged back. "Oh, Ben. I love you so. And I need you to keep me on track."

"You mean I need *you* to keep me —"

Her kiss cut short my exclamation. Our embrace warmed our bodies from the chill of the night air, and our deep, thirsty kisses warmed our souls to face a frigid world. For a long time, all was quiet but for the gentle lapping of water against the hull, the distant quacking of the ducks and the occasional roar of a jet engine.

Finally, Rebecca pulled back a couple inches and looked me in the eyes. "Tell them 'yes.' The move won't be so hard. You can stay in the apartment."

Then I moved back a couple inches along the bench. "But it's sublet to Barbara."

"We sublet only half of it. She's only paying half the rent, you remember. And we have all our things in our bedroom."

"You're saying I should go back there and live with her!"

Barbara was a fairly attractive girl.

Rebecca broke into a smile. "Sure. She's an old friend. I trust you with her. And she's practically engaged to George."

"But . . ."

"But nothing. Everything will be fine. Saves us worrying about hunting an apartment here and moving up all the books and furniture. Let's face it, Ben, we're not ready to live permanently in Washington."

"Well . . ."

". . . where you can't sail the *Diogenes* in the winter," she added brightly.

"Right. What are we going to do with the boat now if I . . ."

"I'll look for a good dock with electricity and deep water where it won't freeze."

"But I hate to think of you living aboard in the cold."

"If we could do it together, I can do it alone."

"But . . ."

"Or maybe I could have the *Diogenes* hauled and put in dry storage. Don't worry, Ben. Just leave it all to me."

I thought it through. She was giving me permission. She was cutting me some slack, but was not cutting our bond. I kept thinking.

"Ben, you look so sad."

She kissed my cheek at the wrong moment.

"Don't cry. Life goes on. You remember what we said to each other the night we decided to get married?"

I remembered that night like it was yesterday. "That we would be married in synergy, not in hindrance."

"And we decided that you would back me up when fate gives me the lead, and that I'll back you up when you get the lead. This is your lucky break. Go for it, Ben! I'll take care of everything else."

We kissed until my tears became hers, and hers mine. Joined at the hip, we moved from the cockpit to the main salon, where our hips joined in other ways. As we gave our bodies to each other, our souls entwined in an ever-tightening knot that could only be loosened by sleep.

Rebecca's last whispered words were, "Don't worry Ben, I'll take care of everything."

The 737 sped along the Potomac then pointed its tail to the runway and its nose to the sky. While acceleration and gravity tugged on my back, I looked through the port window, down on *Diogenes* floating at the edge of the lonely marsh. I didn't give up looking until we ascended into a thick layer of clouds.

The outside world became a milky sea of microscopic water droplets whizzing by at three-quarters the speed of sound. Through this sea we banked, turned and twisted, changing altitude as ground controllers vectored us away from Washington and steered us clear of incoming- and cross-traffic. The pilots were competent; I was in good hands. Like the advertisement said, it was time to kick back and let the airline take care of me.

Actually, everyone had taken care of me. Rob had taken care of me. He had handled our conference call so adroitly that Boyle was actually thanking us. The next morning, I received a faxed letter appointing me "Research Assistant Professor." Rob had greased the skids and maneuvered me into the position, and Boyle was only too happy to get back to his experiments.

The Patent Office had taken care of me, too. They were so understanding. Yes, Dr. Candidi, we understand that this out-of-the-blue offer from Miami is a great opportunity. Yes, they agreed, it is unusual for a young fellow to be offered a position and a laboratory. Of course, your experience here will be very useful to Bryan Medical School. So many universities are confused about what is patentable and what is not. Of course, you should make your experience known to your university's technology manager and patent committee. Offer to give them a briefing. And, you did find it a useful and interesting experience here, didn't you?

Yes, gentlemen, my experience has been interesting. The Patent Office is to be congratulated on its training program. Like you were saying, there are many ways that a knowledge of patent law can be useful, besides being a patent lawyer or patent examiner. When I get settled in Miami, I will write your organization a letter of appreciation. Of course, I will send you a copy.

What did you say? No, I didn't know that I had two weeks of

accumulated vacation. Sure, I'll go right over there and sign the papers. I really don't have any open files right now, but I will go over my work with Examiner Chaudhary . . . Well, thank you, too!

And Rebecca had taken good care of everything else in the last couple of days.

"Don't worry, Ben, I've worked everything out. Barbara finally answered my page. She's been working mostly on a night schedule. She said your moving back is fine. She's going to shift her utensils to one side of the kitchen so you can bring our stuff out. Now, I want you to eat right. I don't want you going back to that canned camping slop that you were subsisting on when I first met you . . . when you were living on the *Diogenes* off Coconut Grove. Now remember — fresh vegetables and fruits every day."

"Now wait a minute," I'd protested. "Don't you remember my shrimp scampis? You said that was how I won your heart."

"You cooked it for *me*, Ben. I'm talking about what you will do for *yourself* when I'm not looking after you. You be careful with your heart. I don't want you eating unhealthy foods. And don't wear yourself out trying to get that lab organized by the end of the first week. Are you listening?"

Rebecca was starting to sound like her mother.

Yes, they had all taken care of me.

I looked out the window. We were now high above the clouds. The State of Virginia was nothing but one continuous woolly carpet. Far to the left was a long indentation, probably an effect of Chesapeake Bay.

I pulled out a magazine but fell into contemplating the hairy backs of my hands. Fell into contemplating my situation, too. Here I sat, dressed in my blue blazer, charcoal slacks, penny loafers and Oxford cloth shirt with button-down collar but open neck, flying down to Miami to brass it out as a "research assistant professor." And something was making a pit in my stomach.

The captain announced 30,000 feet. A couple rows ahead, a pair of flight attendants were working their way towards me with the drink cart. The blond one flashed me a nice smile, which I returned. Her smile went beyond professional courtesy. I might be a couple inches short of the masculine ideal, but certain girls are attracted to me. Physically, I'm a mixed bag. You could say my face is attractive, but my teeth aren't perfectly straight. Nature put my voice in the high tenor range, which is probably less masculine than baritone or bass. A long time ago, I decided to just be myself. I never play the macho.

The flight attendant and I exchanged smiles again when she asked for my drink preference. After she moved on, I stared into the bubbles in my Seven-Up, lost in thought. I would have to work hard in Miami. This opportunity couldn't be squandered. I would learn to deal with the bureaucratic hassle and petty medical school politics. More importantly, I'd have to become a mature scientist, ready to design experiments, analyze data, write papers, write grant proposals, and collaborate with physicians. I'd take my ideas on anti-oxidant vitamins and programmed cell death and I'd run with them. And all the while, I'd be on the lookout for possible inventions. As Dr. Westley would say, I would "have a real go at it."

But I'd have to watch myself. I have a tendency to fall into lazy, self-deceptive traps where I need a kick in the pants — like when Dr. Westley kicked me out of my job and into the Ph.D. program in pharmacology at Bryan Medical School.

Maybe I was being too self-critical. I've always risen to the occasion before — like when I carried out that undercover operation at Bryan Medical School, which was Dr. Westley's real reason for sending me there. Yes, I'd tested the Old Boy's theory of murder and came up with the right answer, too. I'd figured out which prof had murdered the Pharmacology Department's chairman with which poison. And I'd told Dr. Westley how to prove it — which he eventually did — in court. Rebecca never knew about this because Dr. Westley had sworn me to secrecy.

But I didn't get through the investigation unscathed. After the prof was arrested, a couple of med school security officers did a clandestine investigation on *me*. And one day, off campus, things turned nasty. My memento of that day is a three-inch scar which I wear on the top of my head, obscured by thick, black Italian hair.

For a second time this week, a dark thought came over me. Could this secret history come back to haunt me as a "research assistant professor"? I thought for a while. No, there shouldn't be a problem. Bryan Medical School had a new dean, and the offending security people had moved on.

I let out a deep sigh. My new job should work out fine. I'd just have to keep focused and avoid getting mired down with a lot of bureaucratic hassle.

My thoughts gravitated to the man I was replacing. I remembered Pete Peterson as a tall man, probably six foot three, who wore rumpled shirts and tennis shoes and walked around stiff-backed and hunched forward. He had short gray hair, crew cut if I remembered right. His large rimless glasses weren't always clean. I remembered him speaking with a deep unmodulated voice and expressing himself with jerky hand movements which were very distracting but never threatening. His science was solid but not spectacular.

A few times, I'd seen Dr. Peterson overwhelmed by fits of enthusiasm. And a couple times in seminars, I remembered him disagreeing with the speaker and expressing himself in embarrassingly plain language. I had chatted with him once at a Christmas party given by the Physiology and Cellular Anatomy Department. He displayed a friendly, almost rural, sense of humor. He capped off almost every statement with a goofy laugh.

But we had never had another full conversation, although I had seen him many times by the fence at the side of the creek near our apartment building, smoking his pipe. He seemed like a good guy who would listen earnestly and would never betray a confidence. Now I felt bad for not having gotten to know him better.

The flight attendant roused me from my thoughts. "Sir, would you like a roast beef or tuna salad sandwich?" She smiled down at me in an unmistakably personal way.

"Uh, roast beef."

"I could have guessed it. Keeps the hair on your chest."

After she moved on, I noticed that I did have a couple of buttons open. The hills and dales of the cloudscape glided below as I ate. Then I fell asleep while thinking about the job.

The pressure change in my ears woke me up. We were making our way through a mushroom garden of cumulus clouds over the blue Atlantic. Ten minutes later, the pilot dipped the right wing. When he straightened out I saw the south end of Miami Beach. Then came the mainland. Through the port window, I made out *Dade County General Hospital* and Bryan Medical School, not be confused with the more prestigious *Jackson Memorial Hospital* or the University of Miami School of Medicine, which are also located along the glide path.

Half an hour later I was in the back seat of a cab together with my necessary possessions from the *Diogenes*: one duffle bag, one diving bag full of clothes and my attaché case. It was a two-mile ride, due east, along the Dolphin Expressway. The cab exited on 17th Avenue, passed my apartment building on 12th Avenue and turned into the medical center.

I got out, shouldered my gear and trudged along the crowded aluminum-covered walkway that led to the 11-story building. At the entrance, in the "air lock" space between the two glass doors, I was detained by the guard for lack of an I.D. badge. I had to search for my driver's license while entering employees stumbled over my bags.

I headed for the underutilized elevator in the center of the building. This took me past the labs of the "Project to Cure Stroke." The labs were packed with scientists who had been hired in response to a big wad of benefactor money. There was talk of breaking ground for a new building. The hallways were covered with "posters," a form of scientific presentation consisting of charts, graphs and figures thumbtacked on a six-by-four foot corkboard. Close to the elevator, four people were discussing a scientific poster. I apologized while squeezing by.

The elevator was slow to come, leaving me little to do but observe the foursome. The man in front of the poster was obviously the scientist. He had a white shirt and tie and did most of the talking. He waved his hands over the figures, looking nervously from one man to the other.

I recognized this as a delicate situation involving the transfer of money. The semi-bald man wearing the casual suit and receiving the most of the scientist's attention just had to be a benefactor. The dark-suited, semi-confident man standing next to the benefactor would be either his lawyer or financial advisor. The third man was also dark-suited but less confident. He was hovering on the side of the display like it was a renaissance painting protected by an ultrasonic anti-theft device. Occasionally, he took a small step forward to interpret the scientist's words or to add an assurance. He could only be the med school's "project development officer," the guy who's responsible for making sure the benefactor gives the money.

And now I was receiving mistrustful glances from the two well-dressed chaperones.

Hell, guys! Do you think I'd be dumb enough to interrupt a scientific discussion important enough to attract suits? I just wanted to get past you with my bags.

The elevator delivered me to the fifth floor where I found Rob plodding around the lab. The tall, heavy-boned Canadian Scotsman greeted me with a deep-throated "welcome" and a bone-crunching handshake. "Park your stuff in my office."

I did. He followed me in and pulled a picture I.D. badge from the center drawer of his desk. "You remember this?"

It was my old photo I.D. badge they had given me when I first came to Bryan as a student. It showed a younger, hipper version of myself, shot in quarter profile and revealing three inches of ponytail.

"Thanks Rob." I clipped it onto my blue blazer, backwards so the picture wouldn't show.

We went straight up to the office of my new boss on the sixth floor. His secretary advised us to try his lab. And that's where we found Harold Boyle, Ph.D., Chairman of the Department of Physiology and Cellular Anatomy — hunched over his computer in the corner of the lab.

Rob pushed me towards him and said, "Harold, here's Ben Candidi, your new Research Assistant Professor and expert on free radicals and oxidative damage."

Boyle glanced up from his computer and turned not more than five degrees in my direction. He didn't get up. He didn't extend his hand, either, although Rob had moved me close enough. Boyle glanced for a second at Rob and said, "Glad to see you again." Then he turned back to his screen. "Have you taken him to the lab?"

"Not yet." Rob hooked his high-hanging butt on the edge of the lab bench and stretched his legs forward, like we were going to have a long scientific discussion.

No, it wasn't time for a discussion. But it was time for me to pay some form of homage to the bearded introvert. "Complicated diagram that you are working on," I said, referring to an array of labelled circles, squares and triangles on his computer screen.

"Yes, and it's not just a diagram. Not a cartoon. It's a *computational model*." He emphasized the point with a contraction of facial muscles that fuzzed his eyebrows and creased the field of protective hair between cheek and upper lip.

"Yes, I remember your seminars. Positive and negative feedback on intracellular calcium movements in cells of the adrenal gland. Nice work."

"Which demands a lot of time."

No, Brother Philosopher, I will not disturb your circles.

"I agree. I'm anxious to go to Pete's lab. Rob can take me over there."

Boyle leaned back in his chair but did not remove his eyes from the screen. "Pete's death gave us some problems, because there wasn't any responsible person to take care of this thing. He didn't have any students or post-doctoral fellows. Just his technician Mildred Goodman, who's been with him for as long as I can remember."

Boyle was speaking slowly and quietly, and I wasn't going to interrupt.

"When Pete didn't come in, we didn't think anything of it at first. Then his lawyer called and told us the news. He said he got in contact with Pete's niece — she's the only family he has left. I'm told his apartment was quite a mess." Boyle's eyebrows twitched then set in a frown. He fell silent.

"A mess?"

"Magazines lying around."

"Magazines?"

"The wrong kind."

"Did his niece tell you that?" I couldn't imagine Pete's lawyer saying such a thing.

"No, I just heard it mentioned at the chairmen's meeting with the dean, yesterday."

I decided not to ask what kind of magazines were "wrong" and how the chairmen of the other departments would happen to know about them. It would be best to let this interview die a natural death. I'd wait for Boyle to dismiss me.

But he didn't. "Pete was a good professor, although he did get sidetracked."

"Sidetracked?" I wasn't trying to argue, but I had to know what he meant.

"Yes, sidetracked — getting into med school affairs that weren't productive of research. Shouldn't forget what we are getting paid to do at this med school." Eyebrows twitched again.

"How was he sidetracked?"

"Let's just say he was too much of an iconoclast."

Iconoclast? Smasher of icons? Crusader against established beliefs? Well, if Dr. Peterson was an iconoclast, then Dr. Boyle was a misanthrope — a guy who might worship icons but distrusts Mankind. Sure, Boyle had a reputation for leading by example, putting in 16 hours a day in the lab. But his was a pessimistic leadership style. I remembered him making brilliant observations in seminars. After getting everyone excited with his ideas, he'd look down at the floor and grumble into his beard that his ideas probably weren't right, anyway.

Rob kept quiet. After a long silence, Boyle sighed. "Anyway, Ben, I didn't need any faculty meeting or dean's approval to make this temporary appointment."

It was nice that he was resolute on this point, but why had he brought it up in the first place?

Boyle frowned at me for a second, then shifted his gaze to Rob. "You just make the most of it. You have the run of Pete's lab. Just make sure you do a good job of retrieving his research. I don't want to be forced into second thoughts about the decisions I've just made." Why was he looking at Rob while talking to me? Why wouldn't he meet my eyes? Why would he be having second thoughts? What the hell was going on? And if there was something wrong, why didn't he come out and say it?

I started having second thoughts, myself — about coming here. Started feeling sick.

Rob said it was time to go, and began to move out. When we reached the door, Boyle called out, "And Rob! Maybe Ben can deal with the thing Pete's lawyer was talking about. We wouldn't want to destroy any important history."

He didn't look up from his monitor.

"Sure thing," Rob called back.

I held back my question until Rob and I were out of earshot. "What the hell is this thing with Pete's lawyer?"

"Beats me, but I didn't want to say so."

Seeing the lab did make me feel better. Career technician Mildred Goodman was in her late 40s, a little on the plump side, and slow moving. She was also slow talking, but everything she said was precise and well thought-out.

In the middle of our conversation, she looked to the side, took a breath and shook her head. "Dr. Peterson was a great man," she said, sadly.

I waved goodbye to Rob and leaned against the lab bench. "Tell me a little about how the two of you worked together. Did you talk about the experiments once a day, or more often."

"He would give me general instructions. I would bring back data . . . We would analyze it together. Sometimes, he would give me new instructions then and there. Sometimes he would think it over."

"So he spent most of his time in the office."

"Yes, analyzing data and reading scientific literature. And he had some *special projects*."

"Could you tell me about them?"

She sighed and shook her head. "There's not much I could tell you about them."

"Can I move into his office?"

"Don't ask me. You're the boss."

"Can I use his computer?" A guy's computer is a little more personal than his desk.

"Yes. It is in good shape. Just two days ago, two men from Network Services came and gave it a going over. You have a network connection, now."

"What's that?"

"It's a connection to the central computer. It's also supposed to get you out to the Internet. I don't know much about it. Pete never used it."

In the corner of the lab was the entrance to Pete's office. It was just big enough for a metal desk, a couple of file cabinets, his swivel chair and one guest chair. There was no window. Most of the wall space was hung with narrow boards that sagged with the weight of books and scientific journals.

Mildred gave me a key. Now I had my own lab, fully equipped and with a career technician — a turn-key operation. And I had the responsibility for putting a lot of Federal money to good use.

After grabbing lunch at the Burger King across from *Dade County General Hospital*, I spent the afternoon in Pete's office, reading up on his science. He had three unfinished manuscripts. Good. I would complete the work and send them out for publication. I checked the manuscripts against the articles he'd published over the last five years and learned a lot of science along the way. Around a quarter to five, Mildred asked permission to leave for the day. I gave myself permission an hour later. Called at the apartment first, and got no answer. Barbara was probably on a 48-hour shift.

With my two bags and attaché case in hand, I trudged across the medical center plaza towards my apartment building, the Medical Towers. It is on the far side of the enormous Metrorail station that sits on tall columns and straddles 12th Avenue.

The Medical Towers building was an okay place to live if you weren't particular about your neighbors. Several of its floors were converted into light-duty outpatient clinics and administrative offices. A Burger King is conveniently located on the ground floor.

Our residential section occupied one side of the building. Had to squeeze through a checkpoint to get to the elevator serving us. I introduced myself to the guard at the desk, showing him my med school badge and apartment key. The elevator took me to the 10th floor, which is six floors above the integral parking garage. Knocked and got no answer. Let myself in and went to Rebecca's and my room. Our trusty bicycles were still leaning against the wall, waiting for us all these months. A bike is the ecologically sound way to get around. Moving in didn't take much effort. Just took the four cardboard boxes off the bed. Kept opening them until I found the one with the sheets and pillows. Made up the bed. Hung up my jacket.

I went back to the kitchen, left Barbara a note and headed downstairs. Was it the lure of the outdoors or a morbid attraction to the spot where Dr. Peter Peterson died?

4 WALK ON THE WATER

Wagner Creek, the place where Peter Peterson died, comes within a few dozen feet of the driveway that serves the side entrance of our building. There, the creek is lined by enormous slabs of boiler plate bonded at the top by a ribbon of concrete, and looks more like a canal. On its seaward path, the creek snakes between the Medical

Towers and *Zion Hospital*, then turns south under the shadow of the elevated Metrorail Station.

The architects of both buildings had done their best to accommodate the creek while safeguarding patients and hospital personnel. A wooden fence lines the creek; a covered pedestrian bridge crosses it. On the other side, they provided benches where people can sit and contemplate the water.

Of course, Wagner Creek doesn't flow like a creek, except in a long, heavy rainstorm. As I stood looking at the water, a Styrofoam cup floated by in the northward, inland direction. That meant the tide was flowing in. I looked to the eastern sky. Yes, the moon rising above the massive Metrorail platform.

How many times had I traced the creek's northward course, searching for its headwaters? Near the enormous air-conditioning units at the northeast corner of the hospital, the creek jogs diagonally and crosses under the driveway. There it loses its boiler-plated wall, and the water is only a couple feet deep. Tree roots clog its channel and land crab burrows pock its eroded banks. They also pock the backyards of the 1940s era bungalows. But nobody walks in those backyards. The houses serve as offices for temporary nursing services and high-volume, low-budget criminal defense lawyers.

A couple of blocks farther north, the creek passes under 16th Street and through a patch of meadow along the high metal fences of the VA Hospital. There, it looks like a creek and even nurtures a stand of cattails. On the other side of 17th Avenue, it snakes through a saw grass jungle that was once a citrus grove, then meanders through the grounds of a high-rise housing project, and then passes an automotive battery shop and finally ducks under 20th Street — never to reemerge.

I walked to the fence where Pete Peterson used to sit and smoke his pipe. It was one of those chest-high, flat-topped, widely spaced, cross-braced wooden types that you see in horse country. I leaned against it and looked once more into the water. Tracing the creek's seaward path was a lot easier. It runs parallel to 12th Avenue for a block, then jogs left and disappears under 14th Street. On the other side it passes a medical arts building until it disappears under the tall embankment of the Dolphin Expressway.

Although narrow and modest, the creek is still a haven for

wildlife. I remembered getting off my bike to help an ailing cormorant that had strayed into the middle of the 12th Avenue and 14th Street junction. She looked so pitiful and out of place, standing in the middle of the pavement with head cocked high like a proud but destitute old lady, trying to look over car hoods to get her bearings. A couple of Hispanic men climbed from their dilapidated truck and helped me shoo her to the safety of the traffic island. Everyone else was honking their horns.

Maybe the cormorant sensed their anger, too. She used her last quantum of strength to take off and fly under the expressway overpass. Narrowly, she cleared the top of an oncoming semi-trailer. I prayed that she would find the Miami River. Maybe she would follow the seagulls to the Southeast Fisheries when they throw out chum.

The interface between Nature and commercial man is fragile.

On the other side of the expressway, I once saw a manatee grazing on the creek's aquatic weeds — in the shadow of the oil-stained concrete deck of a County equipment yard. Nature's wonders are fragile — like the 1920s clapboards with chickens and fighting cocks in the yard — fragile like the old two-story frame houses with bay windows and copper turrets — fragile like the week-to-week existence of the Hispanic immigrant families who populate the neighborhood — fragile like the economics of the small boatyards lining the creek where it broadens and joins the Miami River.

Fragile, like my toehold at Bryan Medical School. Quite a gruff reception Boyle had given me that afternoon. Was that why I was meditating on the survival of old houses, birds and low-budget lawyers in this cheap neighborhood? Better start thinking about your own survival, Candidi. Toughen up. Better hit the ground running, tomorrow.

But maybe the ground was uneven. What had Boyle meant about "being forced to have second thoughts" about my employment? What was I to make of his veiled warning to not get "sidetracked" like Pete?

"Hi." The voice came from over my left shoulder. It was the guard who manned the front desk.

"Off duty?"

"No. The other guy just relieved me so I can make my rounds."

"I'm just standing here, watching the tide roll in . . . wasting time."

"Yeah, like in the song."

We talked a little. I told him about taking over Pete Peterson's job. I mentioned that Pete had drowned in the canal.

"Yeah, that was the old guy that died last week. I guess it happened on my shift, but like I told the cops, I didn't see anything happen that night."

"Did you see Dr. Peterson at all, the night he died?"

"Yeah, I saw him. Could have been the last one to see him alive . . . or that old lady, anyway."

"What was he doing?"

"What he was always doing, every time I seen him. He was sitting on this fence, right about here, smoking his pipe and looking at the water like he always did."

"And then?"

"And then I went around the building to make my rounds, and when I come back he wasn't here. And she wasn't here either."

"What was the old lady doing?"

"She was there, talking to him."

"Do you know her?"

"No, never seen her before."

"And when you came back, she was gone."

"Yeah."

"And that's all there was to it?"

"Yeah, like I told the cops. I felt real bad about it when they discovered him in the canal that night. I mean, if he had fell when I was there, I would of gone in and rescued him. But the way it went down, I didn't know nothing."

It was time to call it a day. I went up to the apartment, set the alarm on my digital watch, and had a good night's sleep.

The next morning I hit the ground running. Mildred was already hard at work around 9:00 a.m. when I walked into the lab carrying a bag of doughnuts and a Styrofoam cup of coffee. She didn't need any guidance from me. She had a whole week's worth of experiments to finish. That was fine with me: I spent the first week getting organized.

My first project was to e-mail Rebecca. Pete's computer did have a cable connection to the med school system, but his Microsoft

Explorer program wasn't set up to work with it. After two hours of fiddling with it and making phone calls to the med school's Unix guys, I gave up on the cable connection. I called up my old Internet service provider. Within 15 minutes, we had an account set up and a modem connection running. I inaugurated the service with an e-mail to Rebecca saying I loved her and missed her already.

My next project was to stroll down the hall, reading the name cards at the doorways of my fellow faculty members. After a few days of getting settled in, I'd go around and introduce myself to all six of them. Academic politics can be as important as your lab experiments. And getting on the right side of the administrative staff might be still more important.

At the departmental office located at end of the hall, I introduced myself to the secretaries and administrative staff. The chief administrator, Olga Hernandez, was about 65. She had fled Castro's Cuba as an adult. She was friendly enough in a matronly way, but wouldn't say much about Pete or his lab. She did volunteer some advice on ordering supplies and keeping accounts on the grant. She showed me how to read the "Report 70s."

"Now you watch your accounts like a hawk," she admonished, squinting a little like a hawk herself. "Central Administration might bill you for a lot of things if you don't watch out."

Next, I went back to the lab and asked Mildred what she knew about Pete's accounts. Luckily, she had kept her own set of records on the grant. And it all turned out very simple because our only expenses were for chemicals and rats, and for Mildred's and my salaries.

The only irregular expenses I noticed were for a computer expert who had worked part-time six to eight months ago. Mildred said the guy had worked on the Windows set-up. When I asked what else he did, Mildred rolled her eyes and said the two had some sort of "extracurricular project."

I spent the rest of the day studying Pete's three unfinished manuscripts. The first one was titled, "Protective Effects of Melatonin Against Lipid Peroxidation in Perfused Rat Liver." It had some medical relevance because melatonin acts as a "sleep hormone" and is being sold in health food stores as a "natural sleeping pill." Pete's work suggested that melatonin also had vitamin C-like antioxidant effect.

Pete's second unfinished manuscript was less relevant to human health. He was studying the effects of chemicals which I didn't recognize — a toxic effect of pentachlorophenol and a protective effect of dithiolethione.

And the third manuscript seemed pretty confused.

I spent most of the next day going through Pete's file cabinets and reading articles by other scientists on "anti-oxidants" and "free radicals." I already knew most of this story of the "good guys" and the "bad guys." Anti-oxidants like vitamins C and E, and so-called phytonutrients like flavenoids and carotenoids are the good guys. They fight off renegade oxygen molecules and "free radicals" which are the bad guys. The bad guys can cause a lot of cellular damage if allowed to go around unchecked.

Towards the end of the week, I knew the subject well enough to lecture medical students. I could explain how a successful oxygen attack will break an unsaturated fat molecule into free radicals and how these critters can go on to attack other molecules, multiplying and attacking the cell's machinery. I could tell them how plants manufacture vitamin E to neutralize the renegade oxygen before it can do much damage. I could even quote them the minimal and maximal anti-oxidant doses of vitamins E and C.

Of course Great-Grandmother already knew this in the practical sense: She said to always drink orange juice and eat whole grain bread, grapefruit and plenty of carrots. But people like to rediscover things; now the active ingredients are called "dietary supplements."

While I familiarized myself with the intricacies of free radicals, my super technician worked hard in the lab. That's what Mildred was — a super-technician who didn't need much help in setting up new experiments. And she was pretty good at explaining the old ones. Sometimes the old girl took her time answering, but the answers always came out well-phrased and factual. She was perfectionist, that's all.

I spent a lot of time going through the black ring binders that sat on the narrow bookshelf over Pete's desk. They contained his publications, about 90 in all. His work wasn't anything earthshaking, but it wasn't bad either. Pete's only bad habit was a tendency to exaggerate the importance of his work in the discussion section of his papers.

On Thursday evening of my first week, I placed a credit card call to Rebecca using Barbara's phone. There was no reason to activate my cellphone down here. I told Rebecca that things were going well. She wanted to know about my work routine and how I was getting along in the department. I couldn't bring myself to tell her about the negative vibrations from my new boss or the strange things he had said about Pete. Instead, I told her about my ideas for extending Pete's work into *apoptosis* — the new "hot research topic of programmed cell death."

Just before we came to an end and said our I-love-you's, Rebecca said, "Say hi to Barbara for me."

I said, "Will do, but I haven't seen her yet. She's either pulling long shifts or spending all her free time with George."

"I see," Rebecca answered, sounding both surprised and relieved. So was I.

Late in the next afternoon I was congratulating myself for a job well done on both fronts — bureaucratic and scientific. And I said, "Thank God it's Friday!" Then Mildred laid a big surprise on me. She "reminded" me of a memorial service for Pete. It would be that Sunday at the First Unitarian Church. I called up the church and got the time — one o'clock in the afternoon. I got the feeling that Mildred would be attending, but that it would be too complicated to go together.

But that memorial service made my life complicated anyway.

5   MEMORIAL SERVICE

That Sunday morning I locked my bike in the pine and scrub undergrowth, far enough from the windows to not distract the congregants. Removed my blue blazer from the rat-trap carrier and put it on. High in a nearby Dade County pine tree, a woodpecker was tapping persistently. Occasionally, the roar of a semi-trailer broke the tranquility.

The First Unitarian Church sits in the pinelands by the Palmetto Expressway. It is a modern structure with a hemispherical concrete roof supported by flying buttresses, with ground-level doors and windows. I have never been able to think of it as a church. Maybe it's because the sanctuary faces west. Or maybe I have attended too many of Ira Sullivan's Saturday evening jazz concerts in their sanctuary. Since it lacks an altar, you couldn't call it a sanctuary anyway. It must be my upbringing: Once a Catholic, always a Catholic, if but a lapsed one.

In the breezeway, between their meeting hall and the church offices, a catering crew was setting up a luncheon. Noon was approaching and the eleven o'clock service was winding down with the last hymn. They went through four verses.

When the doors opened and people came out, this lapsed Catholic was surprised by the Unitarian dress code. A lot of men and some women were wearing shorts. The most frequent male ensemble was long pants and a polo shirt. Some wore long sleeves. I saw only one man in a suit and tie — a slightly built, medium-height sixtyish guy who was standing near the buffet, apparently overseeing the caterers. I took him for a leader of the congregation.

While drifting through the crowd, I exchanged greetings with a sixtyish polo shirt guy. He had lots of hair on his chest and none on his scalp. I said something about having not visited a Unitarian church for a long time.

"Well, you ought to come more often. You just missed a good sermon on Sartre, Camus and Existentialism."

"Yes, I know you Unitarians are very intellectual."

He smiled and laughed. "A thinking man's religion with an ethical man's taste." He was obviously quoting something.

"I can agree but I don't understand."

"No, you wouldn't. It was a cigarette slogan. You're too young to know. 'A thinking man's filter with a smoking man's taste'."

At my mention of Pete's memorial service, he looked to the buffet and then towards the sanctuary. "That won't start 'til after the luncheon that Pete's giving us. And the luncheon won't start until they get done with Reverend Kominsky at the Talk-Back. Some people would rather argue with him than eat."

I thought back to my boyhood in Newark and tried to imagine anyone contradicting our parish priest right after his sermon.

I asked, "Did you know Dr. Peterson?"

"*Doctor* Peterson! Yes, he never let any of us forget his degree.

Like me, teaching math at Miami-Dade Community College with only a master's degree."

His loud mention of Pete's name got the attention of an old woman who was standing nearby. She reacted with a tight-lipped frown, and then threw me an appraising glance.

The math instructor looked towards the buffet, again. "But Pete was a good friend — a good member of the congregation. Sure rather have him here than at Woodlawn Gardens Cemetery."

"Is he already buried there?"

"Yes. Interred without ceremony in the mausoleum. The way he wanted it, Ted Walden told me." He nodded in the direction of the man with the jacket and tie. "A little superstitious for a guy who was so rational and ecological. We Unitarians don't make much of bodies after we die." He glanced at the buffet, now quite impatiently. "Tell me, how did you know Pete?"

I told him about taking over Pete's research and he asked a lot of questions. All the while, the tight-lipped old woman was moving in closer. A couple of times I smiled in her direction, to draw her into the conversation. But she just hovered a couple arm's lengths away and never returned my glance. Probably in her mid-seventies, she was thin, gray-haired and small-boned, but agile. As our conversation shifted to teaching mathematics, the old lady drifted out of earshot. I asked who she was.

"Oh, that's Annabelle Pemberton."

"Was she a friend of Pete's?"

The math instructor's laugh echoed across the breezeway. "No, you couldn't say that. She fought with him all the time about science. They used to get into real emotional arguments. Even in front of everyone."

"In front of everyone?"

"Yes. She's very active in animal rights. Pete was a vivisectionist. Told everyone he was working on rats, and that he would work on cats and dogs if his experiments required it. And she organizes protests against medical schools!"

"You said they argued 'in front of everyone.' Did they have a personal relationship?"

"I don't know. And I don't think either of them knew, either. Love-hate relationship, maybe. There were stories about them carrying on at the Southeastern conference. But that must have been ten years ago."

I couldn't help smiling — at the thought of a love affair sparking between an old bachelor and a spinster at an adult summer camp. I imagined it slowly resolving into a decade-long, love-hate relationship revolving around the imperatives of science versus animal rights.

The math instructor snagged a tall man who had just emerged from the sanctuary. "Reverend Kominsky, I want to introduce Dr. Ben Candidi. He knew Pete. He's taking over Pete's work."

Reverend Kominsky had a large hand and a firm grip. "Glad to meet you," he said in a gentle, low-pitched voice. He was two heads taller than me. His gaze was so steep and sunken that I could hardly see his eyes behind his rimless glasses. "Maybe you can say a few words about Pete at the service. In fact, I would like you to meet Ted Walden."

But the introduction didn't take place. Another parishioner rushed to remind us that it was already twenty minutes past noon, and could Rev. Kominsky please announce that the buffet was open and please ask everyone to stay for Pete's memorial service.

Most of the congregation did stay for the buffet and about half of them stayed for Pete's service. Annabelle Pemberton didn't stay, although she seemed interested in the food. And Mildred did not show up. When I saw her the next morning, she explained that the service conflicted with mass at her own church.

Around ten minutes before one o'clock, I grabbed a program leaflet from the table by the door, and took a seat on the right side of the sanctuary, about a third of the way back. The room was slow to fill up, and most people sat half-way back. I didn't recognize anyone from the medical school.

A good-looking woman walked down the center aisle. At first glance, she didn't seem that much older than me, but closer scrutiny put her age in the mid-forties. She wore a close-fitting velvety, charcoal-colored dress. It fit well with her straight, shoulder-length blond hair and soft, china-white skin. The way she walked to the front in those high heels reminded me of a 1950s Marilyn Monroe movie, except that this woman's curves were less pronounced and she didn't sway. When she took a seat in the first row, I figured she was a relative.

Up front, the floor was elevated three steps to form a platform. After a few minutes, a choir of four women and three men took places in a semi-circular arrangement on the back of the platform. Ted Walden was one of them. Next to him sat an old, dark-haired man, hunched over in a wheelchair. His face told me that he had suffered a series of minor strokes. At a baby grand piano, to the side of the platform, sat a woman with a sympathetic face. The program identified her as Sally Pyle.

On the front page of the light-green program leaflet, a phoenix bird rose from a flaming chalice. Towards the front of the platform stood a stone chalice resembling the one on the leaflet. Rev. Kominsky approached the chalice and lit it. A flame grew. It must have had a wick floating on oil.

The reverend announced the first hymn, Morning Is Broken. What a strange choice: I had always thought of it as a Cat Stevens song. But it began to make sense as the small choir led us through the first verse. The man in the wheelchair sang with a beautiful tenor. I guessed that he had loved music all his life.

Reverend Kominsky gripped the sides of the lectern with his heavy hands and read several paragraphs from a Thoreau essay about living in harmony with Nature. Then he choir sang a haunting song: Robert Frost's "Choose Something Like a Star" set to music. This little fellowship had a lot going for it. It was like a Mensa chapter with heart.

Then came the eulogy. Rev. Kominsky pushed his rimless glasses closer to his face and ad-libbed the first few seconds. He said that Pete had never married. Pete came from a small family which was being represented by his niece, Carole Peterson Vandoren, who had come down from Michigan. Clearly, she was the blond in the first row.

Reverend Kominsky read his notes with fluency and conviction, but with heavy eyes that lifted only occasionally from the page. When uttering combinations of words evoking feeling, he always glimpsed to the right.

"Pete never talked much about his past, but we know a few things. Born and raised in Grand Rapids, Michigan . . . answered his country's call after Pearl Harbor . . . and served in photo reconnaissance in the Pacific Theater, leaving the Navy as a chief petty officer when the war was over. He was an avid student, who chose chemistry, and then biochemistry. It was natural that his spirit of inquiry led him to Unitarianism while he was in college."

He looked into the congregation, seeking affirmation.

"For Pete did have an unquenchable thirst for knowledge . . . and an insatiable need to share his knowledge with the rest of us."

The reverend ended that statement with emphasis; the congregation responded with a gentle ripple of laughter.

"Pete was always there. Always ready to explain his science to us. Always ready to get into a discussion or even an argument."

Some smiled and others chuckled.

"But we must never forget that Pete was a true practitioner of liberal religion, who believed deeply in humanistic principles and—"

Rev. Kominsky turned to the choir.

"— who, in death as in life, made profound contributions to the welfare of the Unitarian-Universalist Society and to this church."

Ted Walden nodded. Carole Vandoren shook her head.

"And now has come the hour for us to remember him. Now is the time allotted for you, his friends, to offer your words of remembrance."

The reverend looked to the congregation. I glanced around and registered a scattering of blank stares. Was nobody ready to say a thing? The reverend looked down on Pete's niece and said, "It is only appropriate that Mrs. Vandoren be given the first opportunity."

The invitation caught her by surprise, but she quickly got to her feet. "My memories of him were as Uncle Pete who used to write me letters and send me Christmas presents and birthday presents." She spoke with a cultivated voice, in the middle of the female range. "And sometimes he would come for Thanksgiving dinner. It was too bad that Daddy and Pete didn't get along. My mother told me it started when they were teenagers. But Uncle Pete was always nice to me. I remember how he was always interested in science. He used to send me the Science Newsletter and Things of Science, and he was always interested in what I did with them. And I guess . . . I guess . . . I *know* that I'm going to miss dear old Uncle Pete a lot more than I ever guessed." She sat down quickly as if fighting back tears.

The reverend smiled benevolently into the congregation; I saw no volunteers, only bewilderment. Up front, Ted Walden squirmed in his seat, as if he might raise his hand. But the reverend didn't notice him.

Rev. Kominsky turned his head in my direction and beamed down on me through smudgy glasses.

"We are most fortunate to have with us Dr. Ben Candidi who has worked with Pete, and who is carrying on Pete's scientific work. Dr. Candidi, could you say a few words about Pete Peterson and his science?"

I wasn't prepared for this. I got to my feet and half-turned, trying to face everybody.

"I knew Pete as an acquaintance . . . as a scientific colleague . . . before I went to Washington."

Inquisitive looks and blank stares. *Ben, you are confusing them.*

"And when he died, I gave up my job at the Patent Office to pick up his work where he . . . left off."

What an unfortunate turn of phrase.

Inquisitive interest. Too much of it on me. My voice sounded like it was coming through a tin can telephone.

"Pete's work in the early 1960s showed something that most medical scientists didn't suspect. We all know that oxygen is a good thing — we have to breathe it to stay alive. We need it to burn carbohydrates and fats to get energy. What Pete's work showed is that oxygen can also be a *bad* thing."

Thank God. Now you've got them on your side.

"His work showed that oxygen can be bad when it reacts with *unsaturated fats* in your body. It can act like a . . . renegade . . . starting a *chain reaction*, breaking the fats into fragments. And the fragments break into more pieces. Other scientists showed that these fragments — we call *free radicals* — can attack delicate proteins that control cellular function."

Okay, they're listening. But the reverend is fidgeting, probably worrying that you're going to give a biochemistry lecture.

"Years of free radical attack alters the *elastin* molecules in our skin, and our skin loses its elasticity."

For some reason I was staring at an old lady. She was looking back, sympathetically.

Focus on Pete, silly. You've got to talk about Pete.

"Many scientists picked up on Pete's early work. Some carried it on. Some carried it away. And some found new effects that even Pete couldn't understand — that the cell has special enzymes for fighting rogue oxygen — that these enzymes can't work when the cell is low on energy. They discovered that the most dangerous time in a heart attack is when the drugs start dissolving the clot and when oxygen-carrying blood flows into the oxygen-starved tissues."

Sure, you've got them charmed, but this is supposed to be a memorial to Pete. Find a gracious way to end this speech.

"The important thing is that Pete dedicated his life to knowledge, and that he did his part to solve the puzzles that are holding us back."

I laid in a pause for emphasis. It had been a strong statement — the best thing I could say about Pete's life work without embellishing the truth. As I looked around the auditorium, I saw many examples of what I had just described — glaciated and palsied faces, recovered heart attacks and strokes. Everyone was looking back at me . . . as if . . . as if I'd opened the door of knowledge and the gilt rays of heaven were shining over my shoulders.

Thank God, my voice was no longer thin and wavery. It was throaty and moist. So were my eyes.

"And on those Sundays when Pete got into discussions — and even arguments — at the drop of a hat, it was his love of *all* useful knowledge that he was sharing with you."

I sat down quickly to keep from saying a word too many and spoiling it — by breaking into tears. I always get emotional at funerals, even for people I don't even know. I'll never come to terms with the finality of death.

Rev. Kominsky addressed us softly. "What a wonderful end for a long life so fully lived — to have your work carried on by an intelligent young man who can explain the meaning of your life work in a eulogy. I am certain that many of you have much to add."

Pressure was building behind my eyes and cheeks. How cruel, the ironies of Life: A man struggles a lifetime to leave his mark and it is washed away in one cycle of tide. It took a stranger to say a nice word about him.

I looked at the floor, thinking of the goofy old man with his pipe, and the infrequent rewards of science. I thought of the unfairness of it all. I was sickened by the thought of his carcass as food for my scientific life.

But my ears were reporting a miracle. The congregation, one by one, were coming down to the river, offering anecdotes of remembrance of Pete — of the time he had rushed out to repair the broken pipe in the church kitchen that threatened to flood the auditorium in the middle of the Easter service — of how he had tutored a teenaged parishioner out of a failing grade in math — of being surprised to see him on the local news — and of the culinary merits of his entry in the chili contest at their Tex-Mex party. A man in the middle of congregation stood up and read a biography of Pete in the form of a poem — a "Lifeline," he called it.

Ted Walden stood up and said he was not only Pete's friend but also his lawyer, and that he had never known a more dedicated Unitarian.

The reverend announced the final hymn: Amazing Grace. They sang it briskly, in Scottish rhythm, although some congregants did ramp up on the whole notes and hold them too long.

The reverend extinguished the chalice then walked up the center aisle, indicating that Carole Vandoren was to follow him. He signalled the same to me. I used the outer aisle to make my way to the back. The reverend formed us into a receiving line, starting with me and ending with Mrs. Vandoren.

Many people said many nice things as I stood there, moist-eyed, shaking their hands. Slowly, those bits and pieces formed a clear picture. They were expressing gratitude for my interpretation of Pete's life. This young, dark-haired stranger had solved the enigma of Peter Peterson.

I waited around the breezeway as people said their goodbyes and drifted off to their cars. Then, just as I walked towards my bike, someone called out. "Dr. Candidi!" It was Ted Walden.

At close range he seemed less formal than when sitting on the platform with the choir. His suit was just a rumpled, loosely woven sports jacket worn over a pair of dark slacks. His tie was also loosely knit. He introduced himself and shook my hand. "I would also like to thank you for standing up and saying those nice things about Pete."

"It wasn't much. I know only his scientific work."

"Your personal observations were so kind." So were his eyes, regarding me behind tortoise-shell framed glasses.

"But, I must tell you that I really didn't know him well."

"What you said was most appropriate. You have great presence of mind."

I had been looking down at his shoes: brown leather topped

and thick rubber soled. Pretty low-key for a Miami lawyer. I looked up at his face. "Thank you. I just felt that something had to be said."

"I understand. And you are taking over his scientific work?"

"Yes, I'm taking over his grant and completing his scientific work."

"In the course of which you will probably learn a lot more about him."

What was his angle? I gave a straight answer. "Yes, probably. Hardly a day goes by without my learning something new about Pete — from our colleagues and from things I find in his files."

Mr. Walden asked me many leading questions about Pete's science. He used every opportunity to learn about me: about my undergraduate studies at Swarthmore ten years ago and about my recently earned Ph.D. His questions were almost intrusive. He wanted to know if I did a lot of reading, if I had read any scientific biographies, and if I had taken writing courses at Swarthmore.

Finally he asked, "Do you have a word processor?"

"Yes."

"Dr. Candidi, I must now speak to you as Pete's lawyer. As his scientific heir, you are involved in Pete's last will and testament."

"How so?"

"I am not completely sure, at this moment. The question is under review." He must have caught my searching look, because he rephrased quickly. "What I meant to say is that I need the evening to think it over . . . if you could bear with me."

"Sure."

He handed me a business card. "Could you come to my office tomorrow morning? At 10:00 a.m.? It has to do with his will, which we are reading at 11:00 a.m."

"Sure." Any guy with enough honesty to correct his evasive language will get the benefit of my doubt.

I pedaled my bike through that sprawling suburb called South Miami and through that well-manicured, Italianate city called Coral Gables. Must have been lost in thought because the bike seemed to be steering itself. It hung west through the northern Gables, then took me into Miami's Little Havana section via S.W. 8th Street.

Then it steered me through the gates of Woodlawn Gardens

Cemetery. The ride past turn-of-the-century gravestones and the Somoza mausoleum stirred memory traces of my first date with Rebecca. Once again, I locked my bike in front of the big mausoleum built like a Romanesque cathedral. As Rebecca and I had walked down its white marble halls, I'd read and interpreted names on the vaults. Gave her a snow job on local history. Today, my steps were taking me to a new section with more recently occupied vaults.

After five minutes of searching, I found the inscription I had been looking for:

> "Peter S. Peterson, Ph.D., WW II
> veteran, scientist, and crusader for
> what is right."

I had to chuckle. Pete had taken care of everything — a free lunch for his friends and a definitive statement on his life. He had staked his claim for immortality.

The next morning I would discover that he had staked a claim on me.

6   IRON WILL

A bike ride to Ted Walden's office was a pleasant way to start Monday morning. It was a straight shot down N.W. 12th Avenue, over the drawbridge crossing the narrow Miami River, through Little Havana, and to *Calle Ocho* (our name for Southwest 8th Street). I detoured one block west to the Bay of Pigs Memorial and paused a few minutes under the Eternal Flame.

My destination was a dozen blocks farther south, in a sturdy, mostly Hispanic residential neighborhood. Ted Walden's office was on a tree-lined boulevard named Coral Way. The buildings are low-rise commercial and the trees are high-rise ficus. They were planted on the median strip, all the way to Coral Gables. It might be fairer to say that the trees planted themselves. Like most things that successfully take root in Miami, ficus trees pick their own spot and do a good job of taking care of themselves.

On the south side of Coral Way, one ficus was taking care of itself next to Ted Walden's building. Walden's boxy, 1950s vintage, two-story residential duplex was hopelessly overgrown. In fact, its stuccoed walls were obscured by the tree's braided trunk. Thick branches hung menacingly over the building's shallow-pitched roof, framing it like a gnome house. The tree had probably started in the southwest corner and had walked its way up the side yard. In a few years there would be no room left in the front yard.

Walking is the right way to describe how these critters grow. First they put out a lateral limb. Then they start dropping "air roots" — dark-brown coils of dangling monofilament that grow downward. Once they touch the ground and take root, the coils thicken and stiffen into a new trunk which cross-braces the parent tree and sprouts lateral limbs of its own. In this way, the tree keeps moving six feet a year in the direction of greatest opportunity. It reminded me of how Bryan Medical School expanded around the medical center.

Ted Walden was either a great nature lover or a hopeless procrastinator. Too late for corrective tree surgery: Ficus trunk was fused to the back corner of the house. And the concrete stairway leading to the upstairs, probably a residence, was littered with ficus berries. On the roof was a piece of broken limb, six feet long and several inches in diameter — pruned by the last windstorm, no doubt.

I pushed my bike through Walden's front gate, and locked it to a downrigger trunk extending from the concrete wall. I walked to the front door and let myself into a hardwood-floored reception area that was probably once a living room.

I was greeted by an elderly secretary who looked very Miami Beach and sounded very Brooklyn. Had she been part of the congregation at Pete's service? She pushed a button on an ancient fabric-covered intercom, announced my arrival to Ted Walden, and then resumed typing in a chaotic rhythm. Her machine was an old IBM ball-style Selectric. Every keystroke produced a sharp clack that echoed off the hardwood floor and plastered walls.

The reception was organized around a coffee table that sat on an oriental rug. I sat down. Picked out a National Geographic but didn't get into it. The morning sun shown through the open windows — four-paned, steel-framed and vertically hinged. In another hour they would have to crank them shut and turn on that big air conditioner mounted high in the wall. Then the room really would be noisy.

Ted Walden came out in shirt-sleeves to greet me. I doubted that he was a native Miamian: good enunciation and no sun damage to the skin. His 60-year-old face was pale and with only a few wrinkles.

"Nice neighborhood," I said. "Nice house. Probably built in the 1950s."

"Very close! Built in 1948, as a residential duplex. I like it so much that I live here — upstairs. It's very convenient to the courthouse. Actually I take the Metrorail there."

"Good choice. The Vizcaya Station can't be more than three blocks away." We made small talk about why they call his neighborhood the "Roads Section." A jog in Biscayne Bay forced the old City Fathers to distort their orderly grid of streets and avenues with some diagonally oriented "roads."

Ted Walden's office had once been an oversized bedroom. There was enough room for an unpretentious desk and a pair of visitor chairs. A Seminole rug was tacked to the inside of the door. After he shut it behind me, the rug absorbed most of the typewriter's clacking. Our conversation would never reach the reception but Walden spoke softly, anyway.

"I wanted you here early. Dr. Peterson's niece . . . if I may speak in confidence . . . Mrs. Carole Vandoren isn't going to be happy . . . although she has probably guessed there won't be much in this for her . . . Still, she may be surprised as to how little. She is coming at eleven o'clock, which leaves us less than one hour."

His manner was informal and friendly, more like a college professor than an attorney.

"I still don't understand how this involves me."

"I touched on it yesterday. You have taken over Pete's laboratory. So you will know a lot about his professional life — which was the biggest part of his life. Pete's will contains a request that I, as his executor, commission a writer to write his biography. So I thought you could help in . . . gathering material."

I didn't have time for that and I told him so with a shake of the head.

"He set aside twenty thousand dollars for the writing." Walden stated this matter-of-factly.

The money got my attention. Rebecca and I could use it. How nice of Walden to politely ignore my shake of the head! Walden looked down to refer to a document on his desk. "He set aside ten thousand dollars for printing, and another three thousand for sending copies to newspapers, libraries and senior members of several scientific societies that he belonged to."

The thought of posthumous vanity publishing brought an involuntary smile to my face. Walden noticed but ignored it politely. He looked out the open window where a hairy, fist-sized clump of ficus air root dangled, obscenely, like the scent hairs of a male buffalo. So that was why the room's light had such a brownish cast!

"I thought you might consider taking on the project. You would only have to produce the manuscript. My office will handle the business details of publication, et cetera. Just as my office handled all other affairs such as the details of his interment at Woodlawn, his memorial service and all his remaining business affairs."

"I have done some writing," I offered, then stopped to think for a few seconds. "I was doing a photographic history of Miami before I . . . rededicated myself to science. I guess I know something about writing biographies. I have read enough of them. I've read one for each of the great men that I admire. But I didn't know Pete very well. But of course, you knew him quite well."

"We didn't know each other well. I knew him as a Unitarian, but I didn't know him well personally."

"At any rate, I know less about him than you. I'm not exactly sure how to write the biography of a regular person. I mean, I've read biographies of famous people like Thomas Edison, Clarence Darrow and Charles Lindbergh. Famous people generate a lot of newspaper clippings that you can go by."

"There are a lot of newspaper clippings of Pete, too."

"But he isn't really famous."

"He doesn't have to be. We just need a *balanced story* of his life."

"And this is specified in his will? Maybe you can show me the passage."

The lawyer handed me a thin document, indicating the passage by the placement of his thumb.

XI.   <u>Publication of my life story</u> The preliminary

title will be "My Crusade." Or maybe we should call it "Conscience in Babylon," "Crying Shame" or "The Shout in the Forest." It will tell the story of my life, and will describe my great work which should be accomplished soon. I have been keeping a diary which should be a great resource and other resource material, including my proofs, can be found in the file drawers in my apartment. The summaries can be found on my computer (which you should remember belongs to me and not the school) in my office at Bryan Medical School. The book should be at least 150 pages, except that if newspapers ask for serialization rights and the author wants to make it longer he can.

The next paragraph specified the author's payments and his instructions for free distribution. "However, if my story makes the big time, and the publishers offer more than $20,000, the author and the Unitarian Church will split the excess and the royalty which should be 15%, or whatever it can get."

I looked at the last page where it was signed and dated, one year ago. The question rattling inside my skull might blow the deal, but I had to ask it anyway. "Was Pete mentally balanced?"

"Yes, although he did exaggerate." Ted Walden was so tactful.

"I would like to consider the project."

"Thank you. Of course, you would not be bound to use Pete's suggested title . . . or to adopt his tone, either. It could be that . . . how shall I say? . . . that death robbed him of his greatest accomplishment. So you should feel free to put *everything* in proper perspective — scientifically and personally."

Ted Walden was an honest man. What other explanation could there be for a lawyer who is smart but not rich?

"Thank you. I would like to take the job. But can I have until tomorrow for my decision?"

"Certainly. I will wait for your call."

He was so patient and low-key.

"Is there anything else in Pete's will that I should know about?"

"Yes, although it will not require any effort from you. There is a section about classifying and storing his papers for ten years."

Walden leaned over his desk and indicated four lines in the will. It read:

"Rationally disposing of my books (except for my Clive Cussler series, that belong to my scientific crusade) and my personal effects so that they will have the greatest usefulness to the greatest number of people."

Walden said, "He appointed his niece, Mrs. Vandoren, for this, and provides fifteen thousand dollars to pay for the work. I am supposed to pay her only after it is done properly. It is apparently his last attempt to teach her something, or to make her jump through another hoop, depending on your point of view."

He said these words neutrally. He made eye contact ever so lightly.

"Does she get anything more?"

"The information is privileged, but only for half an hour more. So I'll tell you. The answer is 'no'."

"Does he have any more relatives?"

"No. His brother, Mrs. Vandoren's father, died eight years ago. Of course, Pete's mother and father died a long time ago. As you learned yesterday, the brothers were not close. As you also probably noted yesterday, Pete's relationship with his niece was quite limited.

"So who gets the remainder of his estate?"

"Unitarian-Universalist Society. He was a dedicated religious liberal."

"Well, I guess they could use another twenty thousand dollars."

"It is more like six hundred thousand dollars, but, again, this is confidential."

At the mention of $600,000 I sucked air. Mr. Walden noticed.

"Pete lived a simple life. He saved and invested in mutual funds." Walden looked at his watch. "Mrs. Vandoren will come in a few minutes. For appearance's sake, I will have to ask you to take a seat outside. I shall read the will before both of you, the two of you being the only interested parties."

"But I do not have any official standing."

"No, but I want you here when the biography project is mentioned. I will say that you have agreed to consider it. And I also want you here as . . . as an informal witness and as a buffer."

"Is there anything more I should know?"

"Mrs. Vandoren is moderately rich and quite spoiled. Her husband . . . her *second* . . . has a lumber yard and construction business in Traverse City, Michigan. It is some sort of summer resort area on the northern part of Lake Michigan. Considers herself upper-class. Sort of a big frog in a small pond." His rendering of the opinion was matter-of-fact.

I went back to the reception room and played Walden's description against my memories of Sunday afternoon: a good-looking girl from a North-Central state. She had that natural openness of face and a prim, self-confident sexiness that they pick up in Sorority houses of big public universities like Michigan State.

My estimate was verified a few minutes later, when Mrs. Vandoren walked in. I nodded to her but she didn't recognize me. Too self-absorbed. Her dress was quite similar to yesterday's, but this time it was red velvet. It matched her red lipstick and reminded me of St. Valentine's Day.

Carole Vandoren waited impatiently before the secretary's desk, shifting weight from one foot to another, while the old girl got Mr. Walden on the intercom. Mrs. Vandoren's high heeled shoes provided a lot of cleavage between the big toe and neighboring toe. And the cut of her lapels presented a lot of the other type of cleavage. She sat down across from me. I nodded to her again, and, after getting no reaction, pretended to read the National Geographic. Slowly, she figured out who I was. Her light-blue eyes studied me but she said nothing.

Walden came out and greeted Mrs. Vandoren. "And, of course, you remember Dr. Candidi from yesterday. He is the heir to Dr. Peterson's *scientific* legacy."

"Yes, I remember," she said in a detached sort of way.

Walden focused all his attention on Mrs. Vandoren while ushering us into his office. "Was your stay in the apartment okay?"

"It was, after I got it cleaned up. I know you said you had it straightened up. But it needed a thorough cleaning. I had to call a 24 hour maid service just the same." She reached into her purse. "Here is the bill. And they still couldn't get rid of that muffy pipe smell. I really should have stayed in a hotel."

Walden smiled, like he could take this in stride. "Maybe today's proceedings will remind you of an episode from Masterpiece

Theater — a pipe-smoking deceased, a lawyer reading the will, and a good-looking next of kin."

"Flattery will get you nowhere," Mrs. Vandoren said, seeming half-pleased. "Why don't you do me a favor, and just read the part that involves me. I can read the whole thing later."

Mr. Walden agreed. He thumbed through the document, cleared his throat, and started reading. As we descended into the ceremony of reading the will, Carole Vandoren sank into her chair. She sank deeper still when we got to the part about her earning $15,000 on the condition that she sort Pete's personal things. For his part, Pete had furnished an explanation. "I hope she may learn to place value on scholarship by classifying it."

Mrs. Vandoren smirked when Walden read the part describing "the greatest good of the greatest number of people" as the distribution principle. And as Walden read Pete's final statement expressing the hope "that she will finally appreciate the value of science," she got mad.

"He never gave up on those silly 'Things of Science,' even in death. Those stupid rocks, moths, butterflies and fools gold samples that came every month. And I always had to be a good little girl and write him a nice thank you letter each month. Burrrr!" She shook her head like she'd been doused with cold water.

The room was silent. "So is this all the monetary consideration I get?"

"Yes."

"Who else is getting his money?"

"He specified a set-aside to publish his biography, and the remainder will go to the church — half to the First Unitarian Church, and half to the Unitarian-Universalist Society."

"Then I will protest. I will get myself a lawyer, and have it overturned."

"I should advise you that will be most difficult. The will was properly drawn, and the church will defend its rights. Many members of the congregation would be willing to testify as to his purpose and to his soundness of mind."

Mrs. Vandoren looked at me, searching for support, then glared at Mr. Walden. He continued. "Your Uncle Pete's purpose is clear. I will quote from the document, 'This is my ironclad will'."

Carole Vandoren wrinkled her brow. "How am I supposed to

classify his junk for the greatest good for the greatest number of people? Should I give all his clothes to the Salvation Army? His furniture too? The books could go to a store in Miami Beach."

I imagined her throwing out all Pete's stuff with a vengeance. She stared at Walden, petulantly.

Walden did not rise to the bait. He waited a few seconds, then answered in even tones. "That would be acceptable for his clothes, and maybe for some of his furniture. But by no means for his books. And certainly not with his personal papers, which you must make available to Dr. Candidi, who will be writing his biography."

Mrs. Vandoren cleared her throat and looked at me. For a few seconds, I was afraid she would make a scene. I simply looked at Mr. Walden and nodded my head, gently.

She cleared her throat in dismissal. "I'll think about it. Give me a day to go through that muffy apartment and see how much there is to do."

"Yes, you have custody of the apartment for now. You must allow Dr. Candidi access to the apartment during the day to look at your Uncle Pete's papers."

"Yes, of course." She thought for a minute. "Did the will say anything about paying my travel expenses, since I am supposed to be working in his apartment."

"No, but I think that payment of travel expenses would be reasonably justified if you are willing to do the work spelled out, and if you agree with the provisions of the will."

"Okay, I will call you tomorrow."

I told Mrs. Vandoren that I lived in the same building. Gave her my phone number and we exchanged apartment numbers. Pete's apartment was on the 18th floor. Mrs. Vandoren said I could ring the bell between nine and five.

Ted Walden saw us both to the front door, but told me, with a glance, that he still wanted to talk. I fumbled with my bike lock until Mrs. Vandoren drove away in her rental car, and then returned.

"I just wanted to thank you again, Dr. Candidi. You were a calming influence."

"No problem. Glad to help."

"There is one other way you could help me. Pete drove a 1956 Oldsmobile. Kept it in good condition. It must be parked in the garage of his building. Could you take a look at it and give me some idea what it is worth on the open market?"

I agreed.

I rode north on 13th Avenue, retracing this morning's route and also retracing its events. Had to stop at the 12th Avenue bridge when it went up. A couple of tugboats were pulling a mid-sized freighter between its lifted halves.

I kind of liked this Ted Walden, even if he didn't have enough sense to hire a Cracker with a chain saw to protect his building. Maybe an Albert Schweitzer style reverence for life comes as part of the Unitarian philosophical package.

You can tell a lot about a person by observing how he treats plants, animals and old people. Like keeping that 80-year-old lady on as a secretary. Or maybe he was just satisfied to practice a low-key style of law, generating $4,000 a year to pay the taxes on his building and a few thousand more as a modest salary for his secretary. Maybe his quiet patience bespoke a higher purpose.

The cars started inching towards the gate arm as the halves of the bridge began to lower. While reflecting on the guy who was making me $20,000 richer, a strange thought came to me: He was so nice that I'd completely forgotten that he was a lawyer.

The next guy I had to deal with was much less agreeable.

DECANAL DISAPPROVAL   7

I had just settled down in the lab working through a six-inch pile of Pete's mail, most of it junk. Then the phone rang.

"This is Lizzy-Mae from the dean's office." It was a Southern voice that sounded old. "Dean Weisburd would like to see you in fifteen minutes."

"Okay, Ms., what did you say your name is?" I might have sounded cocky, but I found the invitation too brief and abrupt.

Her answer was also minimalistic: "Lizzy-Mae." Apparently she thought it was enough of a name — like Madonna or Cher.

"What does he want me for?"

"He wants to talk to you." Apparently she thought that was enough of an explanation.

Fifteen minutes was an uncomfortable lead-time: too short to do anything useful and too long to be kept guessing. I remembered the last time I'd been invited to the dean's office — to an interrogation. That was several years back, when I was a student. The invitation had come from the previous dean, Dr. Alcibides, about five years ago. I had completed my job for Dr. Westley — the clandestine investigation of a prof in the medical school. Dr. Westley had acted on the information. Then, a couple of weeks later, Dean Alcibides had summoned me for an interrogation about why I was studying pharmacology at Bryan Medical School. I passed his test, but he may have remained suspicious.

Now I started worrying. Could the old and the new deans have compared notes on me?

My feet knew the way: down the fire stairwell, along the narrow first floor hallway, past the guard station and deeper into the building. My nose remembered the rodent smell escaping from under the locked double doors that guarded the building's "veterinary core" and its associated elevators. And I remembered the strong plastic smell after passing through the double doors to the administrative office suite called the Eisenhut Pavillion. The spongy plastic floor-covering material crackled with every step.

I passed a lot of doors marked "Private." They were separate exits for the dean's conference room, for the dean's office and for the dean's secretary. The final door was marked as the reception. I opened it and walked into his anteroom — actually the anteroom to his anteroom. How could anyone work all day in a room without a window and daylight like those two receptionists? I announced myself to one and was told to have a seat. She picked up the phone and punched in four numbers. I sat down and picked up a magazine on health care management. Heard a muted ring through the open doorway of the next room. In a hushed voice, the receptionist told Lizzy-Mae that I was there.

It would have been a lot simpler for her to have taken a couple steps and told Lizzy-Mae through the open doorway, but they obviously had their protocols. From where I was sitting, I could plainly see the old girl diagonally through the door. I also heard Lizzy-Mae calling the dean to announce my arrival, also in a hushed voice: "Mister Candidi is here."

Through the diagonal, I inspected this important woman who had the power to strip me of my Ph.D. She looked like she sounded: mid-sixties or older, short, thin and small-boned, with pulled-back gray hair and a taut, uncomfortable face.

It was probably unfair to be critical of the old gal, but it wasn't unfair to be curious. After a few minutes her phone rang and she carried out a hushed conversation. As it wore on, she began speaking loud enough for me to listen in. It was girl-talk, probably with a daughter, communicated in loping Florida Cracker rhythm. It was something about how the relative liked her new job. She ended on a serious note:

"Now, you mind yourself, you hear now."

A few seconds after she hung up, she got a beep from the dean's office. She picked up, said "Yes, I'll tell him," then hung up and punched four numbers to get the receptionist and tell her to let me in. The setup reminded me of a retro nightclub where everybody has an art deco telephone on his table.

As I entered her room, Lizzy-Mae threw me a feral glance. No question about it: We were natural enemies. She crept around her desk to open the dean's door. "Doctor will see you, now."

It always irritates me when they say "Doctor" instead of "the doctor." The expression's probably older than Calvin Coolidge — about as square as you can get. As if dropping the definite article would put "Doctor" on the level of God! So what did we have here? A Doctor's little Angel who would do anything for Doctor? Would she offer him in sacrifice her prettiest granddaughter?

Then I remembered hearing that Dr. Weisburd had kept the same secretary for the last 20 years — that she'd moved with him up the ladder. So here she was. And what had two decades of doctor-glorification done for this Cracker woman besides giving her a permanent frown?

I walked past a coffee table, sofa and stuffed-chair arrangement, and up to the desk where Dean Weisburd was sitting. Obviously, I had been carrying the wrong thoughts into the room, but the dean didn't seem to notice. He kept me waiting for a long time. Funny, how closely he resembled his predecessor — Mediterranean features, gray hair in a rounded cut, bright tie and Oxford cloth collar set high on the neck, the whole thing framed by the white shoulders of a clinician's jacket. Finally, he looked up and stared at me for a long time.

I said, "You wanted to see me? For something?"

Dean Weisburd glanced to the visitor chair, indicating I was to sit. He also glanced down at his watch — bright gold with a diamond-studded dial and bright gold band. The same wrist bore a loose-fitting gold link bracelet. "No particular reason. I just wanted to get to know you."

That was fine with me.

"I must say, Dean Weisburd, that I'm glad to be here."

He let down his wrist. The bracelet slid to the watch band, half dangling over it. "Of course, I signed off on your temporary appointment, although I didn't know much about you."

He spoke so smoothly it was almost hypnotic.

What kind of crap was this? Boyle had said that a chairman doesn't need to consult with the dean to make a temporary appointment of Research Assistant Professor. I was about to say so. Stopped myself, just in time.

Think before you act, Ben.

This was obviously a male dominance thing — like I saw on a Discovery Channel show about African Wild Dogs. This guy was saying, "Take a good sniff, buddy, because I'm the alpha male."

And never in my life have I given in to raw domination.

Hopefully, I hadn't shown anger. I worked hard to maintain an intelligently attentive demeanor and I said nothing.

Dean Weisburd searched my face as he talked. "But despite what anyone might say, let me be the first to say that it may be good that you are working on this salvage effort, given . . . and I am only summarizing what I have occasionally heard from others speaking in various capacities . . . given that there had been some concern about Dr. Peterson's science."

"Concern?" It came out like a knee-jerk reaction. I just couldn't help it.

Dean Weisburd's eyes hardened. "Yes. Concern about the quality of his science." He spoke so smoothly.

It was becoming a vicious circle: The more I resisted, the stronger he would insist. How could I break the cycle without giving him the last word?

I shrugged my shoulders. But Dean Weisburd just stared at me, as if demanding agreement.

I had to say something. "Dr. Peterson studied antioxidant agents and how they ensure the maintenance of critical cellular functions. There can't be any question about the need for new knowledge in this field." It was a good medical science answer and I'd leave it at that.

"He was working alone."

"So?"

"Without students or post-docs."

"So?"

"With students and post-docs in the lab, results are automatically verified."

Boy, had he gotten that backwards! Students and post-docs make most of the mistakes. The profs uncover the mistakes when the data doesn't make sense. But it would be no use arguing with this guy about generalizations. I went for the human approach:

"Dr. Peterson's technician is very good. Mildred Goodman is a career technician. She is a good churchwoman, too."

Now it was my turn to search Dean Weisburd's face. His attempt at a benevolent smile was as genuine as a three-dollar bill.

"It is well-known in this medical school . . . and, in fact, at all medical schools . . . that technicians cannot be relied on for oversight." He spoke like he was conducting a disputation.

"You are talking like there was a problem. Was there a problem?"

"There was some discussion of it."

His upward glance to the left suggested that he was probably making this up as he went along.

"By whom?" The question had to be asked.

His eyes narrowed and settled on me. "It would be inappropriate for me to tell you who has said what, but you should be reassured that in bringing up this subject . . . and I bring it up only for the sake of the best interests of this medical school and for the numerous colleagues who have worked so hard, both at the bench and in the clinic, to make this a great medical school . . . and for the sake of Dr. Peterson himself and for the memory of his *early* contributions to this school, which . . . let me be the first to say . . . were rock-solid."

Yes, the guy really did speak in paragraphs — in one continuous stream. He had mastered the art of filling the room with meaningless phrases, slithering from one assertion to another, and filling his gaps in logic with vague quotations from unnamed people.

Blame it on the anti-authoritarian spirit I picked up at Swarthmore, but questions popped out of my mouth. "What sort of shortcomings were these people talking about?" I couldn't stop myself. "Sloppiness? Fabrication of data? What?"

No, Ben, blame it on yourself. Ben, you're a quirky guy with a lot of rough edges.

"It would also be inappropriate for me to say. I will only advise . . . and please take this as friendly advice . . . that you should be careful in your interpretation of his notebooks and files."

Holding the dean's gaze was as painful as looking into the sun.

"I will. This is an on-going project. I will be repeating every major experiment anyway . . . Just as if we had new students and post-docs in the lab."

Surprisingly, the guy didn't seem happy after I caved in.

Dean Weisburd shook his head and looked down. "What I do know is that the man always stirred up hornets nests of controversy. He was always speaking out of turn on everything — animal rights, sensitive topics like gene therapy, and gamma ray sterilization of food. Certain people in the school had to go to a lot of trouble to contain him so that the public wouldn't get the wrong ideas."

His gaze returned to me. "When a person exercises bad judgement in these areas, it may be indicative of bad judgement in other areas. There have been cases — in other universities — where an older professor with eccentricities has to be retired, and the grant money given back for ethical reasons. If Dr. Peterson's work came into question, we might have to consider a similar course of action."

He laid in a pause to see if I was accepting his pretzel logic. My heart was pounding.

I responded with a nod of the head. The dean continued. "So my advice is to work intelligently and carefully. You might be able to salvage some of his work. If I see that you are exercising good judgement, this would be helpful in case your chairman decides to recommend that we switch you to a tenure track."

Quickly, I tried to think of a way to tell Dean Weisburd that the Patent Office people thought my knowledge would be useful to the med school and had even suggested that I give a lecture on patenting. But Weisburd had already picked up a letter from his desk and was making a show of reading it.

"I'll consider your advice." It was all I could to say and I received no reply.

As my feet took me past Lizzy-Mae, past her two handmaidens, down the tacky hallway, past the guards and out the front entrance, I held a conversation with myself. You blew it, Ben. That interview was the worst thing that could happen to you here. You should have kept the Patent Office job.

I didn't go back to the lab right away. I walked south tracing the path of Wagner Creek to the Miami River. Crossed the drawbridge and took the long way back on the other side of the river. Reentering the building required an act of willpower. I went straight to Rob McGregor's lab. He was working at the bench, transferring gels between two Tupperware containers. Rob was such a happy camper.

He paused in the middle of the operation to size me up. Purple stain was dripping from the postcard-sized gel that hung from his tweezers like a piece of Italian pasta. Actually, it looked more like a stiff slab of purple Jello.

"How you making out, Ben?"

Somehow, I couldn't tell him about the interview. "The lab work's going along fine. Mildred's a good tech, and Pete had her loaded up with experiments. Everything looks good. Probably five manuscripts in the works. I should be able to talk to you about collaborative experiments in a week."

"Great." Rob continued his operation, dropping the gel into the container of clear solution and then probing in the dark purple solution of the other container to fish out another gel.

"What proteins are you separating on those gels?" I asked.

"I'm probing the secrets of cellular suicide. Checking whether phosphorylation dissociates the apoptotic transducer protein from its receptor. Using a variety of kinases." He was transferring the slabs with the gusto of an Italian pasta chef. Chef Boyardee.

"Deciphering the signals leading to cell suicide," I echoed.

"Yes, we should find some interesting free radical effects on those regulatory enzymes." I tried to forget the interview and pump enthusiasm into my words.

When the last gel was in the box, Rob put it on the rocking platform. He set the timer for 10 minutes and then studied me. "So what brings you here, Little Britches?"

Rob had gotten into this thing of calling me Mougli when giving me advice, like I was the orphan in the Jungle Book who couldn't survive on his own. In response, I had always answered him as "Baloo." But today I didn't feel like playing games.

"Thought you could fill me in on Dean Weisburd. Is he a dangerous cat in the jungle? Anything like his predecessor, Alcibides."

"Hard to say. Hasn't shown his claws, yet. Some people say he knifed Dean Alcibides in the back to get his job. That was three years ago. But others say they've been playing it as a two-man team all along. Officially, Alcibides is now his consultant. Unofficially, he's doing behind-the-scenes 'efficiency studies' on all the clinical departments, and rolling a lot of heads in the process."

Rob leaned his backside against the lab bench, uncomfortably close to a couple of drops of purple stain.

"Dean Weisburd didn't seem to like Pete," I said.

"Do cats like dogs?"

I waited a bit, but Rob didn't volunteer anything. "Thinking about those five manuscripts, was there ever any scuttlebutt about anything being wrong with the data in Pete's papers?"

"Hey, you've been here long enough to know. We used to visit those Physiology and Anatomy seminars. Don't you remember? All kinds of people said he had all kinds of things wrong with his papers. You remember the arguments that flared up in seminars about the interpretation of his data."

"Yes, about the *interpretation* of his data. You expect a lot of disagreement on that. No, I'm asking whether anyone said there was anything wrong with his *actual data*."

All the while, Rob had been gazing into the rocking Tupperware box where the sloshing clear liquid had been leaching stain from gels, producing a clear background but leaving arrays of purple bands. Those purple bands showed where the protein molecules were. Each band had a protein of different molecular weight. Before our eyes, the gels were developing like Polaroid photographs of an over-sized bar code.

Rob turned and looked at me like my last question was complete nonsense. "You saying that Pete's data isn't reproducible?

You talking about fraud? Like Pete took out a purple Magic Marker and drew a band on one of these gels?"

I could have used Rob in the interview with the dean. "I was asking if there was any scuttlebutt."

"Hell no, there wasn't any scuttlebutt. And there shouldn't be any. The guy was a straight arrow, and Mildred's the best long-term tech in the whole school." Rob continued poking around his gels. "Who's been telling you that?"

Somehow, I couldn't find the strength to render a blow-by-blow account of the morning's interview. Maybe I was afraid of the truth. How shameful to return to Washington with my tail between my legs.

"Rob, I don't know that anybody ever questioned Pete's intellectual honesty. But I got the impression the dean was talking around the question . . . like it was an issue . . . when he had me in for a . . . get-acquainted interview, this morning."

"Don't worry about it. Weisburd was probably just gnawing on your tail to make you squeak, like he does to everyone else around here. I hope you told him the right thing."

"The right thing?"

"I hope you told him you're already busy writing a bunch of grant proposals."

"No, he didn't give me any chance. Now why would I have to tell him I'm going to write a lot of grant proposals?"

"So he can be assured that you'll be bringing in a lot of overhead money."

"Overhead money?" I groaned the words.

"Hell, weren't you listening to me when I was talking to you on the phone last week? This place is a soft money paradise, and it only works when everybody's churning out grants to keep Administration happy. Now tell me, Little Britches, how much is Pete's grant bringing in?"

"About one hundred thousand dollars."

"Wrong! It's actually bringing in two hundred thousand dollars. You're just thinking about the one hundred thousand dollars of usable money for salaries, rats and chemicals. You also should be thinking about the extra one hundred thousand dollars that Administration is getting."

Rob went on to tell me that Administration gets about $33,000 in inflated "fringe benefit" costs and another $67,000 in overhead costs. "That's what Administration is interested in. That's their profit for what they call their investment in us. And that's what you have to maximize."

Okay. Rob had just told me the facts of life. From now on I'd have to start thinking of myself as a cash cow.

"Sure Rob. I'll do it. I have some good ideas for a Florida Heart Association grant. And I hear they aren't too hard to get."

"Wrong agency, Little Britches. They don't pay any overhead. A grant from them won't make the dean happy. It's likely to make him mad, actually. He'll say that Administration would just have to make up your missing sixty-seven thousand dollars somewhere else. Stick with the Feds. Put in for an NIH grant, even if the odds are impossible."

"Sure. Next time I see the dean, I'll promise to be a good cash cow for the Administration."

"But don't oversell yourself. To his way of thinking, what we produce is *goat* milk. Basic scientists never get big enough to be cash cows. If you want to see a real cash cow, take a look at the Women's Health Study at the clinical annex building. They've got an annual budget of four million dollars from NIH. That means two million dollars for doctors and nurses salaries and all those high-priced disposables they stuff the dumpsters with after every round of patients' visits. And that means another two million dollars for Administration. You get it?"

"Yes, I get it." And I was getting mad. Rob had just told me one fact of life too many. "I also remember our colleague Gordon Taylor making fun of their High Fiber Versus Low Fiber Diet Longitudinal Study for slowing bone loss in post-menopausal women. He said it was 'a questionnaire-driven outpatient study completely devoid of intellectual content.' He wondered out loud if they were testing whether fiber binds and delivers calcium in the gut, or whether it just gives a more perfectly formed stool!"

It was a perfectly good joke for scientists and Rob had laughed at it before. But this time he didn't think it was funny. "Taylor might have said that to you when you were a student, Little Britches, but he's not saying that to the dean today." Rob looked at the over-sized timer clock on the lab bench in front of him. "You gotta excuse me. These are quantitative staining experiments. Got to pull these puppies out at exactly the right time, or my most important band will get bleached out."

I thanked Rob and went back to my desk, Pete's desk. Okay, Weisburd hadn't singled me out for a flailing: He pulled that kind of stuff on everyone. Okay, I'd be a good cash cow and write a lot of NIH grants. Okay, his talk about problems with Pete's data was just his crude way of getting a handle on me.

I worked on an e-mail to Rebecca. I'd promised her one every day. We had decided to save money by keeping our long distance calls to a minimum. It was easy enough to write about getting $20,000 for Pete's biography, and how we could use it to reduce the debt from her tuition loans. But writing anything about the medical school was hard going.

After sending the e-mail, I worked on Pete's unfinished manuscripts. But I couldn't get into it; the fraud question kept gnawing on me. Then I remembered a newsletter I'd thrown out with the junk mail, a few hours earlier. I fished it out of the waste basket — the newsletter of the Office of Research Integrity (ORI) of the NIH in Washington.

OF FRAUD, SCRAMBLED EGGS, AND FOOL'S GOLD   8

The format was familiar; I had read copies of this Federal newsletter before.

CASE SUMMARY
Charles Z. Graben, M.D., Ph.D., University of . . .
(UUMS)
Based on a report from UUMS, information obtained by the Office of Research Integrity (ORI) during its oversight review, and Dr. Graben's own admission, ORI found that Dr. Graben, Assistant Professor of Medicine at UUMS, engaged in scientific misconduct in biomedical research supported

by a grant from the National Institute of General Medical Sciences of NIH. Dr. Graben cooperated with UUMS's investigation.

Specifically, Dr. Graben presented to the UUMS Stroke Research Group (1) a blank autoradiographic film, which he represented to be a Northern blot, as evidence that he had conducted an experiment that he had not done, and (2) a photographic slide representing a Western blot analysis that he had falsified by using a computer to duplicate three sets of bands to misrepresent protein kinase treatments at different times and by misrepresenting the identities of two bands in one of the sets. He also falsified data from experiments with tumor necrosis factor and with transforming growth factor beta. These falsified data were included in the publications listed below.

Dr. Graben accepted the ORI finding and entered into a Voluntary Exclusion Agreement with the ORI in which he voluntarily agreed, for a 3-year period beginning July 31, 1999, to exclude himself from any Federal grants, contracts or cooperative agreements and to exclude himself from serving in any advisory capacity to the PHS.

Sure, I could imagine the story of Charles Z. Graben, M.D., Ph.D. He probably worked hard for his A's as a pre-med. In the summer between his junior and senior years in college, he probably took a special course to prepare for the MCAT tests. He probably scored so high on them that the med school admissions people offered him a full scholarship to go into a combined M.D.-Ph.D. program. The theory behind those combined programs is that college grades and MCAT scores can identify future Nobel Laureates in Medicine at the age of 22.

I doubt that Graben had any trouble with the multiple-choice exams they give in med school. The Ph.D. classes were harder but he probably didn't take a full load of them. That's because the combined degree programs allow only six years for completion, including research for the dissertation. As likely as not, Graben was given an easy research project. And as likely as not, nobody ever taught him to solve problems by himself. A stand-alone basic research project is a lonely valley that you have to walk by yourself. Nobody can walk it for you. You have to learn by making mistakes, recognizing them as mistakes, and going back and correcting them. All by yourself. Doing independent lab research is like going into the darkened labyrinth to battle the Minotaur. You have to cast and test hypotheses, backtrack, and cast new hypotheses, all the time pulling out hair to make string so you can find your way back. I owed a big debt to my erstwhile dissertation advisor, Rob McGregor for shouting me encouragement but refusing to hold my hand. If he hadn't done that for me, I would not be able to call myself an independent researcher.

I doubt that they ever sent Charles Z. Graben into the labyrinth during his M.D.-Ph.D. program. Yes, I could imagine him now with his double-barreled degrees in his first job as Assistant Professor of Medicine and with nobody to help him wrestle the monster. I could imagine the failure of his first experiments. He probably had four days a week for seeing patients and one day a week for research. I could imagine the pressure he was under to send an optimistic progress report to the NIH. And yes, I could imagine him taking out a purple marker and drawing an extra band on a gel. Lots of Ph.D.s have done that sort of thing, too.

But I couldn't imagine Pete doing it.

I thought hard on the question. Was there any way that an old professor and his career technician could wind up fooling each other and publish a lot of irreproducible data?

Sounds coming through the wall began to disturb my thinking. Actually, the sounds were coming through a hole in the concrete wall, a few feet above the false ceiling. The lab next door had been torn up, but not reconstructed. The guys from the physical plant department were using it as a lunchroom and break-out room.

The guys were talking Spanish, blowing off a lot of jokes about *huevos revueltos*, scrambled eggs. And sometimes they said *tortilla*. Now was time to do some more work for "Scrambled Eggs." Maybe "Scrambled Eggs" would find some way to fix it. Maybe "Scrambled Eggs" would make Ready Plumbing's pipes stop leaking. They were sounding more hilarious by the minute. But why was this supposed to be funny?

Some day I would go over and shoot the breeze with them. During my pre-Rebecca years in Miami, I had spent a lot of time around Little Havana, picking up Spanish and consulting long-haired dictionaries. Yes, my Spanish could use some polishing up, but not today. I turned on WTMI and drowned out the scrambled eggs jokes with a little Mozart.

I sighed, and went back to work. Spent the rest of the afternoon poring through Pete's notebooks and summaries looking for evidence of fraud. Didn't find a thing. Old Pete Peterson was as honest as they come.

The only serious mistake that Pete had made was missing the boat. And he missed it several times. Pete had uncovered many important leads but had been slow to follow them. And other people rushed in and took the credit away from him.

Pete's first lost opportunity was in the early 1950s. Pete noted that the chemical industry was using peroxides to start free radical chain reactions that cross-link small molecules into a solid mass — plastics.

Pete figured that since there is hydrogen peroxide in the body, it might start a free radical chain reaction that would turn your proteins into a solid mass and muck up your tissues.

Well, Pete was right about the hydrogen peroxide, right about the chain reaction, and was even right about mucking up tissues in the body. But he was wrong about the muck being a solid mass. Aloys Tappel from U.C. Davis and several others showed that the damage was due to fragmentation of fats and lipids. And they showed vitamin E can intercept the reactive fragments and stop the damage.

Sure, Pete wrote a lot of papers on vitamin E and vitamin C effects on lipid peroxidation and free radical formation. He worked with rats and their organs and cells. But he never made any fundamental discovery. The scientific articles in Pete's file cabinets told the story of other scientists moving into the field and mining rich lodes of scientific ore.

Pete also missed the boat on the harmful effects of oxygen on all cells. Yes, what I had told the Unitarians about damage from oxygen in heart attack was right. Sure, the most dangerous time is when the clot is dissolved and oxygen-laden blood flows into the oxygen-starved tissue. But I got it wrong where Pete was concerned.

In his publications, Pete fought the idea tooth and nail. Yes, he understood that the mechanisms that fight rogue oxygen also need oxygen to work. But he didn't understand that a lot of oxygen damage occurs before the oxygen mop-up crew can get powered up.

Pete couldn't get away from thinking of oxygen as a good thing. Like the liberator of a concentration camp, he found it hard to understand that you can kill a man by giving him food.

So much of biology is like that — things working exactly the opposite of expected. When someone else discovers a new enzyme or "cofactor," he destroys your simple view of things.

Unfortunately, Pete Peterson had a tin ear for scientific nuance. He came out wrong on most of the big calls. After a while, colleagues started to ignore him.

Yes, Pete Peterson had been right when he said that there was gold in them there hills. But it took others to show how to mine it. And soon the hills were covered with miners and staked claims. And Pete Peterson went around making little excavations on the sides of the hills where the others were pulling gold out of mother lodes. It must have been frustrating to discover the range, only to spend the rest of your professional life sifting through other miners' slag heaps.

But Pete was an honest man. He had never tried to pass off fool's gold as the real thing. And his recent work, comparing different anti-oxidant drugs with each other, was solid. Thinking of the biography, I wrote down some adjectives: high-minded, a good spirit and a good sport.

But some notes written on the margins of colleagues' papers showed a darker side:

"That's what he thinks."

"Not so, my dear friend."

"A lot of bunk."

"Bullshit."

"Latest news from Mount Olympus."

Okay, Pete was crusty. Okay, he never made an earth-shaking discovery. But did he fudge data? No way!

So what the hell was Dean Weisburd really complaining about? Was it about Pete's speaking out on "sensitive topics" like sterilization of food by gamma irradiation? I searched Pete's file cabinet and pulled out a file labelled "Hamburger Experiments." It contained newspaper clippings describing how the meat-packing industry around Chicago was pushing for the use of gamma rays to sterilize meat. To one of these clippings, Pete had attached a note saying they would have to get FDA approval for this:

"They probably won't get away with it, because those anti-science people will protest and stop them. But those jackasses are all fouled up about what gamma irradiation is. They think they're putting radioactive chemicals in the food, but it never touches the food. The radioactivity comes out of a sealed source. Prepackaged food is moved past it on a conveyor belt.

"But the so-called scientists that are saying it's okay are just as fouled up as the jackasses that think they're going to be eating radioactive food. They're both wrong. How the hell do those so-called scientists think the gamma rays kill bacteria! By breaking up molecules and *causing free radicals.*"

He had underlined his "insight" three times, the last so hard that his pen had pierced the paper. There were several pages of doodles and whimsical notes about "Free Radical Burgers." He thought that free radicals would hasten the rancidity that comes with ageing. On the bottom of the page, in large letters, he wrote his expected result — "McRancid's."

He had done some experiments. He had irradiated a pound of hamburger and tested for free radicals and found some. The second experiment was apparently not completed. He had set up a hamburger sample to the gamma irradiation facility in the med school's basement that morning, and had removed it, and had put it in the lab freezer for later testing. I checked the freezer; the sample was there.

My mind wandered. I fell into daydreaming. Had Pete screwed up when he was down at the gamma irradiation facility? Had he gotten a lethal dose of radiation, whose delayed effects disoriented and weakened him so that he fell into the canal and drowned?

The phone rang. It was Ted Walden, calling to remind me about looking at the Oldsmobile, but actually trying to get me to firm up my decision on the biography project. He wanted to send a memo of understanding for me to sign. Hell, there was only one answer. Like it or not, I had burned my bridges behind me. The Patent Office job was lost. Rebecca and I needed the extra $20,000.

"Yes, Mr. Walden, I will take on the project. The longer I'm working here at Pete's desk, the deeper I am getting involved with him."

That turned out to be my understatement of the year.

SPAGHETTI TANGLE 9

I heeded Ted Walden's reminder and located Pete's 1956 Oldsmobile in the parking garage. It was in mint condition: red and white two-tone, glass free of cracks, metal dash and plastic upholstery in good condition. The big, heavy, gracefully rounded car with the large oval air-scoop grill and swept-back winged airplane as hood ornament awakened history-book images of post-WW-II America. They must have been optimistic, back then, to redesign their automobiles every year. I would find out what the automobile is worth today.

When I opened the door to our apartment, the air was thick with the smell of spaghetti sauce. Barbara was in the kitchen, presiding over one boiling pot, a sizzling frying pan and a strainer full of romaine lettuce.

"Welcome back, Ben." She put down the wooden ladle and took a couple of steps toward me.

I offered my hand before she could offer her cheek. She had always offered her cheek when Rebecca and I had bumped into her around the med center. But it didn't seem like a good idea to kiss her while we were alone in the apartment.

"Thanks." I squeezed her hand with both my hands to maintain distance. She offered her cheek anyway. It smelled of *eau de cologne*, not of volatile anesthetic. Her stiff, dark-blond hair looked freshly washed and dried. She was wearing fresh-from-the-drawer scrubs which sat nicely on her broad hips. I said, "Looks like they finally unchained you from your anesthesia machine at the O.R."

She laughed and raised her arms to suggest crucifixion. Then she raised them still higher and exclaimed, "Freedom, sweet freedom!"

Barbara's arms were muscular, but attractive. Her freedom gesture bared her midriff and lifted her breasts under the V-necked top. They would be the "high-slung, fully convex, turgidly suspended type" according to the classification system developed by my old Swarthmore roommate, Richard Bash.

I smiled back. "Congratulations. How many hours did they give you?"

"Twenty-four. And to celebrate my twenty-four hours of freedom, you are invited to an Italian spaghetti dinner."

"Only if you let me help."

I was glad to be able to focus on operations in the kitchen, decanting the frothing pot and stirring spice into the bubbling sauce. It helped me to get used to being close to Barbara in Rebecca's absence. Barbara is an attractive girl — a lot more attractive than she knows. Lots of girls are dissatisfied with what they see in the mirror and work with lipstick and eyeliner to improve it. I doubt that Barbara gives much thought to her rough-hewn, honest face. Her attractiveness comes from a total lack of pretense. It creeps up on you on the masculine side, like the smile of the Key Largo dive boat captain sitting at the Tiki bar, when you thank her for the good trip — and she invites you to pull up a stool and share a beer.

I wouldn't receive that type of smile from Barbara. She was engaged. The lucky guy was George Hammel, resident in surgery and graduate of Stanford University School of Medicine. He had a reputation for a wicked game of racquet ball. Barbara's angular, muscular body would be a good match for him on the court and on other playing fields as well.

Barbara completed the salad preparations briskly — a few brisk shakes to get the water off the leaves, a few brisk whips to mix the Italian salad dressing, and some spirited movement between the kitchen counter and diningroom table and — *voilà!* — there we were.

Not wanting to spoil our dinner conversation with the problems of my day, I took care to describe my situation optimistically.

After exhausting the topic of my return, it was time to hear from her. "Just think, Barbara, in only two more years, and you will be a board-certified anesthesiologist."

"Board Eligible," she corrected.

"So what are you going to do? Work in an academic medical center, or at a small hospital?"

"A small-town hospital sounds pretty attractive to me right now. I'm developing an allergy to academically affiliated hospitals."

The shape of a wrinkle on her forehead suggested this was something she wouldn't mind talking about. I'd oblige her while trying to keep the mood light-hearted. "What seems to be the principal *allergen*?"

Barbara's face clouded over. She exhaled with a groan, then took a deep breath. "There are *multiple* allergens, and I'm developing antibodies with cross-reactivity to all of them. The ones that give me the biggest rash are department chairmen who don't do cases and don't solve administrative problems, either. We've got two of them — the department chairman from Bryan Medical School and the chief of service for *Dade County General Hospital*. Each one is trying to do the other's job, and they spend all day battling each other from their offices."

I listened sympathetically while enjoying the meal. Hopefully, blowing off steam would be good for Barbara.

"And it isn't enough for us to run cases all day without a potty break. At the same time, we're supposed to be doing research so they can get their names on papers and so the program keeps its accreditation. And I'm getting allergic to our chief resident who's trying to enforce that system. I'm also getting allergic to a couple of second-year residents who are bucking for the chief resident position for next year."

"Yeah, I bet those guys are playing a lot of dirty tricks."

"Guys? They're *women*."

"I see." I threw a glance at Barbara's untouched plate. "The sauce you made is very good. And your spaghetti's very authentic — you left the strands long. Have some before it gets cold."

Barbara poked her fork into the curled bed of long spaghetti strands and drew her knife across it several times, like she was dicing carrots. I winced. It wasn't authentic Italian spaghetti any more.

"Look at the bright side, Barbara. In two years you'll be through with your residency. You will be an *attending physician*. You'll have a regular schedule and a regular salary."

" — Based on how many cases I do for those jerk administrators, calculated by a no-win formula that puts all the money into their salaries and into that damn bureaucracy in the Stillwell Building, with a big cut for the dean's office so they can run the medical school — or so they say." She caught her breath. "And to justify *my* existence, as if that isn't enough, I'd have to develop some damn anesthesia *research* program that I'd run on a shoestring and my own after-hours effort."

"Take a bite. The idea of dinner is to get *some* food in your stomach. It sounds like you should pick a small, non-teaching hospital. Maybe in a small metropolitan area along the coast."

"Yes. And be on call 24 hours a day, supervising a crew of nurse-anesthetists and making sure they don't get in trouble and someone dies."

What good a weekend in the Keys would do her!

She must have read my thoughts, or at least my face. She smiled back, teasingly.

"Okay, Mister Italiano from Newark with your suave, heartbreaking smile and your spaghetti all nicely rolled up on your fork. Tell me what it's really like to be a research assistant professor at Bryan Medical School."

My laugh came so percussively that I almost spat spaghetti. "Same crap as you have to put up with. Except that we have to write seven grant proposals before we even get started."

"Mmmm. It *is* good. The spaghetti, that is. Say, do me a favor, *Benjamino*. I forgot. There's a bottle of red wine on the counter. The corkscrew's in the center drawer."

I did what she said.

Barbara watched while I poured two glasses. "So what, exactly, is Rebecca doing up in Washington?"

I told her about Rebecca's bureaucratic stint and what I knew about evaluating health care needs for developing countries. This gave Barbara a chance to catch up with dinner. And the wine mellowed her out.

As I got to the end, Barbara collected me up with a glance over her wine glass — her second. "Rebecca's really into that stuff. Isn't she?" Barbara is pretty good at reading faces when she tries.

"Yes," I replied, neutrally.

"You know, she's really pretty lucky to have you."

I had to swallow before answering. "Yes, her mom keeps telling me I look like a guy called Frankie Avalon. He sang some song about Venus and starred in a 1950s beach movie. But I could never find the thing on video."

We laughed.

Barbara took another sip. "No, I mean she's lucky to have a guy with enough . . . mmm . . . who can believe in himself enough to go out and sail a thousand miles in the open ocean. I've never known a guy who was so self-reliant."

I started to tell her it wasn't such a big thing, and that I bet that she'd be good on a boat. Then her smile sneaked up on me — like the smile of the dive boat captain. I complained of a headache and withdrew to my room where I curled up with an *Atlantic Monthly*.

DOUBLE DUTY 10

Going to bed early helped get me off to an early start the next morning. But the Animal Rights people got a still earlier start. A dozen of them were marching around in an oval pattern in front of the steps of the med school, carrying high their stick-mounted cardboard signs bearing home-made slogans.

It was nothing new to me. They had picketed the med school at least once a month for as long as I'd been there. But this time something caught my attention: Annabelle Pemberton, the old lady from the Unitarian church — Pete's ex-girlfriend who wouldn't stay for his memorial service. She recognized me, too, and looked away quickly. Had Pete stopped to chat with her before crossing their picket line? I observed the demonstrators a while before going around them and entering the building.

Outside my lab, the physical plant guys were mustering for their first job of the day. Always looking for a chance to practice Spanish, I announced myself as their next-door neighbor and replacement for Pete.

"*Si, si, El Loco*," one of them responded. They didn't know that he had died. I told them about my biography project and asked for their recollections of Pete. They all said he was a good guy. They had chatted with him while smoking in the outdoor stairwells.

One man started to tell me that Pete had complained about a renovation but we were cut short when foreman called everyone back to work.

I went into the lab, said good morning to Mildred, flipped on the computer, and took stock of my situation. The science was on a even keel, local administration was under control, my chairman didn't care if I stayed or left, and the dean didn't like me. It was time to introduce myself to my fellow faculty members. No use waiting for Chairman Boyle to do it for me at the next faculty meeting. He would probably introduce me with a nihilistic joke that few would understand and nobody would find funny.

I spent an hour dropping in on my colleagues. Franz Gassler was my closest neighbor down the hall. The tall, large-boned Swiss scientist welcomed me as Pete's replacement, describing Pete as a good colleague that he could always count on. Franz was in his mid-thirties, had been in the department for seven years and was a tenured associate professor. He came from Zürich. He spoke with a strong German-Swiss accent with strongly rolled R's, drawn-out vowels, and gutturals, delivered at high pitch in a musical cadence. The overall effect was both quaint and friendly, like his broad, open face and shy eyes.

Franz studied secretion and capillary repair in lung. He was trying to understand emphysema and pulmonary hypertension.

Franz would have been the real target for the animal rights people because he experimented on dogs. But nobody saw much of his work. He performed it in an operating room behind the locked doors of the "veterinary core" located in the building's center. Access was controlled by magnetic I.D. card. The core had its own system of elevators, with the ground floor station near the dean's office.

I told Franz about doing a short biography for the Unitarians. I got the feeling that he would tell me plenty of stories about Pete once he decided that I was a good guy.

My next colleague down the hall was Hilda Beecher, a full professor. I told her that as a student I'd attended some of her research seminars on urine production in rat kidney. But I couldn't get her to discuss her research. When I told her about the biography project she frowned in disapproval. Why would she disapprove of someone promulgating anecdotes about Pete? Maybe she thought I needed to be warned against wasting time, because she immediately launched into a ten-minute monologue on how to write grant proposals. She aimed her advice at the importance of effective communication but she spent most of the time lecturing me about filling out forms. It made me feel like a third-grader kept after school to improve his sloppy penmanship. Dr. Beecher delivered her monologue in soft, sickly tones. While listening, I took stock of her. She couldn't have been a year older than 55, but she looked and acted an unhealthy 75: gray hair, pale skin and a pained demeanor. What she needed was a half hour's daily exercise out in the Florida sun. She already had suitable shoes for an exercise program: thin white rubber soled tennis shoes with red canvas tops. But she wore them in combination with thin white socks. And her floral print, one-piece dress reminded me of the old Sears catalogues from back in the mail order days. Maybe she'd picked up her style from her early professional years in Arizona.

No, I can't admit to having much affinity for Dr. Beecher. Could have overlooked her schoolmarmish qualities if she'd allowed me an open discussion of her rat kidney and urine experiments. I had to suppress the urge to ask why she wasn't studying the kangaroo rat. They live in the desert and are very sparse with their urine.

My next colleague down the hall was Ron Price, an assistant professor. He seemed a nice enough guy but couldn't talk with me much because he was busy injecting frog eggs with a human gene responsible for nerve excitation. A few days after the gene injection, a human nerve protein would appear on the cell surface, ready to produce electrical signals. By mutating the human gene before injecting it into the cell, Ron could produce a wide variety of human nerve proteins with different electrical signalling characteristics.

Assistant Professor John Falk and Associate Professor Susan Bligh were each in the middle of their separate experiments, and not available.

I found Instructor William Long was in his office and introduced myself. He was in charge of teaching human anatomy and cadaver dissection to the med students. The tall, middle-aged fellow wasn't particularly communicative, but I did learn that he had some sort of research program in the building's core, studying anatomical deformations resulting from tropical disease.

Having met my colleagues and having covered my flanks politically, I returned to my office and worked productively. Around one o'clock Carole Vandoren called. She said Ted Walden had asked her to give me a key to Pete's apartment, and could I please come right over and get it.

Ten minutes later I was there, knocking on the door. Carole Vandoren was wearing the same outfit that she wore at the lawyer's — the curve-hugging, heavy, red velvet dress that showed so much cleavage. But this time it seemed less provocative: A bad case of sunburn had reduced the contrast between fabric and flesh. I walked in, maneuvering around two suitcases.

"I'm moving out of here this afternoon. I can't stand the pipe smell." She gestured to a collection of pipes, sitting on a coffee table near the couch. "I didn't dare throw any of them away. I might be throwing away an important scientific relic."

I glanced around. The place didn't look bad at all. "You said the apartment was a mess?"

"Yes."

"You said there were magazines lying around?"

"I didn't say that."

"Weren't there a lot of typewritten papers lying around?"

"No."

"But you said there was a mess and you had to get a maid service."

"It was so muffy. It had to be thoroughly cleaned. I can still smell the tobacco residue."

"It won't bother me while I go through his papers. You haven't boxed anything or thrown any of them away, have you?"

"No."

"Fine." Now I could afford to chat with her. I looked down at the suitcases. "Where are you going?"

"I'm doing the Beach. I'll be at the Park Central Hotel on Ocean Drive. I'll stay there for two days, then go back home."

"When are you going to start sorting out Pete's personal things?"

She gave me a big smile, like we'd known each other for a long time. "That's what I want to talk with you about. I was wondering if I could . . . hire you . . . to do it. What I mean is, you do it and we could split the profits. I'm sure Mr. Walden trusts your judgement more than mine." Boy, she was turning on the charm. "I'll give you three thousand dollars to do it and I'll keep the rest."

"You'll keep twelve thousand dollars," I said.

"And neither of you will have to deal with me again. I'd just like to get this thing behind me. It will be easy if you do it. Mr. Walden likes you. He will agree with your decisions."

I thought about it for a while before answering. There wasn't that much to think about. We could knock off another $3,000 from Rebecca's student loans. "Okay, you have a deal. But I want to be able to call you up any time to interpret things, and to give me background."

"Yes," she said, without hesitation.

The more I thought about it, the better it was. I could get a lot of family history from her without seeming to be pumping her.

But maybe satisfaction didn't show in my face. She was pouting. "It makes me sick just looking at his stuff. Like some kind of goofy school where they never let you out. It's like those crazy 'Things of Science' that he would always send me when I was a girl with those long letters about the billions and billions of stars and how I was supposed to *do* things with those kits and had to save it all for him when he came for Thanksgiving dinner or Christmas."

The child who had to stay after school! Well, having been reminded of the feeling myself this morning, I could empathize with her.

I smiled. "I promise. If I find any Things of Science or copies of any old letters to you about science, I'll throw them out."

"Good," she laughed, dropping her head on my shoulder for a second. "Here's the key." Having successfully used her charm, she could relax. Now she was looking at me differently — like I was a real person. "I bet you've lived in Miami for a long time. Do you know the South Beach?"

"Like the back of my hand." This brought a smile. I shouldn't encourage her. "Like the back of my hand after waking up with a bad hangover," I added.

The smile faded. "So you don't go there now."

"Correct. Used to hang there before I got engaged. Don't have any time anymore. Spend all my free time maintaining my sailboat."

"You have a sailboat? Jacob and I have a motorboat. We go out on Lake Michigan every once in a while. Sometimes we motor to Suttons Bay for dinner. I've belonged to the Yacht Club for as long as I can remember." She studied me for a second. "Do you ever take your boat out for an evening sail?"

"It's anchored on the Potomac. My fiancée is up there with it."

"She's not that sleepy one in the green pajamas who answered when I knocked on the door of your apartment?" Carole inspected me with a conniving smile.

I, too, had to smile at the thought of Barbara, roused from a deep sleep, answering the door in her scrubs.

"No, my fiancée and I are just sharing the apartment with her, right now."

Carole reacted as if I'd just stated that water runs uphill. "I see." She batted her eyelashes, and behind them I could see the gears turning. "What are your recommendations for Miami Beach?"

"Well, it depends on what you're into." I took a couple seconds to imagine what was going on behind those inquisitive, light-blue eyes. "If you're into shopping, you might try Eve's Evenings for a couple light dresses so you can get around without overheating your nicely shaped body." She reacted well to the compliment. "Elevated rope-soled sandals would fit you well. Are we talking daytime or nighttime?"

"Both. I want to make the girls back home jealous."

"Then go to Wild Thing on Ocean Drive and get a two-piece bathing suit or a one-piece tanga that you can wear under your dress during the day. Then you can take a swim between daiquiris. You have your choice of salt water or fresh water. The Cleveland Hotel has a nice open-air bar beside a pool where you can take a dip. When you meet some girls from up north, get one of them to take a picture of you. Make sure there's always another girl in the picture too, so your husband doesn't get jealous when he sees it."

She was beside herself with enthusiasm. "Tell me about the night life."

"Liquid, at 14th Street and Washington is the hottest spot because it scores the most Madonna sightings. But you have to stand in line to get singled out. Take along ear plugs. You'll still hear the band and you can't talk anyway. All the communication is visual."

"What kind of people can you meet there?"

"People who think a lot about right now, and don't remember much about their yesterdays — people who are depending on you to take care of tomorrow." Carole didn't seem to understand, so I made it plainer. "People whose mouths are bigger than their wallets. On the Beach, élan is king."

She wrinkled her brow. "Any more good advice?"

"Decide beforehand whether you are going to buy your own drinks."

"Any advice on drinks?"

"Yes. If you're in a hot and heavy disco scene, never leave your drink unattended."

"Right. It might be stolen."

"Wrong. It might be supplemented."

"Supplemented?"

"Yes. With roofies . . . *Rohypnol* . . . a guy puts it in your drink, and you wake up several hours later in a strange bed."

But maybe that was what she wanted.

"Well, you don't have to worry about me on that. I'm pretty selective about who I hang out with. Got any more good tips?"

"Yes. Don't let them call you a Midwesterner. Tell them Michigan is a Great Lakes state."

"Sounds good."

I just hoped she would have sense enough to buy prophylactics *before* she went out for the evening.

I glanced at my watch and put on a frown. "Have to get back to the med school. I've got an appointment. Have a blast on the Beach."

She presented her cheek as I passed her to go out the door. I gave her a kiss on the cheek while touching her lightly on both elbows. She grabbed mine. "Ben, you'd make a perfect escort. Why don't you do the Beach with me tonight?"

For a second, I thought of "doing the Beach" with her in Pete's 1956 Olds. We could play it retro, like a couple of squares from a bygone decade. And if I drove the car to the right places, we'd probably find out what it was worth. But then, I thought the better of it.

"Sorry. I've got my work cut out for me here."

But I did carry down the two suitcases for her. She agreed to call me before leaving town.

While at the first floor, I dropped into our built-in Burger King. Didn't want to wake up Barbara. I probably should have returned to the lab, but curiosity about Peter Peterson's apartment got the best of me.

It wasn't voyeurism. It was my job as his biographer, for which I was being paid good money. To one side of the pipe-laden coffee table was a leather sofa; on the other side was a large wall cabinet with a VCR and a 27-inch TV. The cabinet held an extensive collection of video tapes, most of them self-recorded and hand-labelled. They were mostly nature programs and World War II documentaries from the Discovery Channel. But several were labelled "Television Interviews." I would look at them later.

Beside the tapes on the bookshelf I found the Dirk Pitt books by Clive Cussler that Pete's will had identified as "belonging to my scientific crusade." He must have had all of them. And he had books on naval salvage by Commander Edward Ellsberg. Also some books on famous naval battles of World War II and a few on espionage. But no mystery books, and hardly anything you could call intellectual.

When the shelves didn't yield his diary, the "great resource" which he mentioned in his will, I continued my search in the bedroom. On his night table were a woodsman's jackknife and a collection of sticks with carved-in designs. Did he whittle himself to sleep at night? Over the bed hung a picture of a buck raising his antlers amid snow-covered trees. The frame was hand-carved.

On a lower level of the night table was a naval magazine, and below it a stack of Playboys. Were these the magazines discovered laying around the apartment according to the rumors reported by Dr. Boyle? They sure as hell weren't objectionable. They were early 1960s vintage. Back in the old days those flat, fuzzy-focus shots might have gotten a guy worked up, but they were tamer than a lingerie ad in today's *Miami Standard*.

I continued the search in the three-drawer dresser along the opposite wall. It contained a full array of socks, boxer shorts, white undershirts and folded handkerchiefs, but no diary. I paused for a minute to inspect the home-made wooden candle holder that sat on the dresser. It stood one foot tall, about five inches wide at the base and two inches wide at the top. It was fashioned from a cypress knee, with flat sawed-off bottom, and round candle-hole carved in the top.

I didn't find the diary in his closet, either — just an orderly selection of clothes. The fanciest thing he had was a brown tweed jacket with arm patches. On the shelf over the rack was a photographer's bag with a couple of 35 millimeter cameras, a large telephoto lens and a couple rolls of unused film. The cameras were empty. The tall metal file cabinet in the opposite corner was my last hope. It contained no diary, but did show promise of containing the "other resource material, including my proofs," referred to in his will. Two drawers were filled with files. Actually, one was full and the other was half full. The folders slouched because he hadn't set the divider. The remaining two drawers of the file cabinet contained photo albums.

I looked first at Pete's file folders. They were filled with newspaper clippings, some scientific papers, and occasional hand-written notes. The folders were labelled with diverse topics, including "Animal Rights," "Right to Die," "Gene Therapy," "Human Cloning," and "Gamma Sterilization of Food." And there was a series of "Corruption" files: corruption in Miami, corruption in Miami-Dade County, corruption at the Port Authority, corruption at Miami International Airport, and corruption in the School Board. He had corruption from everywhere except the medical school itself.

The "Animal Rights" file was the thickest. It had material on animal rights demonstrations, and raids on university labs around the country. The files also contained letters to the editor by him, explaining why animal research is necessary.

Pete had a similar file on the Right-to-Life movement containing magazine and newspaper articles, and copies of his rejected letters to the editor. I would have rejected them too. His arguments were indirect and unpersuasive.

His file on the right to die was the next largest. It had scholarly articles on euthanasia from philosophical journals, and a lot of material on Kervorkian. Come to think of it, Pete did look a little like Dr. Kervorkian. And there were the usual letters to the editor, most of them rejected.

The files on organ transplantation consisted mostly of scientific papers. His file on human cloning was just getting started, with clippings on "Dolly," the cloned sheep. He had a couple pages of handwritten notes, probably draft letters to the editor, containing his favorite phrases, like "for the advancement of science and human knowledge."

And none of these clippings and notes to himself added up to a "crusade" worthy of recounting in a biography. It seemed that all he had done was champion the unpopular side of each of these issues.

I picked up the last file, ironically labelled as "Fan Mail." It was filled with letters written to him in response to his public pronouncements. The typical "fan letter" was handwritten with big loops and rounded letters, expressing, with misspelled words and awkward phrasing, complete disagreement with Pete's positions. Many were classifiable as hate mail. Three unsigned letters said that someone should do to him what he was doing to the animals.

Was this the essence of Pete's "crusades"? Performing a provocative, pseudo-intellectual dance in front of simple people who would respond with boos and catcalls?

Maybe it had been his good luck to have a heart attack rather than being murdered by one of his "fans." What was the actual cause of death, anyway?

I looked at my watch: 7:15 p.m. already! I had wasted the afternoon trying to make sense of a life, whose sole purpose was to tell everyone they were wrong, in the name of science. Well, I'd write the damn biography and get it over with. Where the hell was that damn diary?

Went back to the lab to shut down the computer. On the way back I took a meditation break at Wagner Creek. Saw the guard again but this time he wouldn't talk about Pete. Said he had orders not to talk about it until they "cleared things with the insurance company."

Went back to the apartment and heated up a can of camping slop.

11   FINDING MY PLACE ON THE TEAM

The next morning in the lab I spent half an hour staring at a blank screen. Finally, I hit *Shift F7*, *Caps Lock* and typed in "PETE'S CRUSADE." Then I hit *Enter*. It was the Wednesday morning of my second week in Pete's lab. I should have been doing science — instructing Mildred on a new project. But before me was the greatest problem — the one that had to be solved first: what to write about this goofball who wanted to go down in history as a great crusader? I typed in, "This will be a chronicle of Dr. Peter Peterson's crusades." Crusades for what?

Mildred poked her head in the door and complained about a leak under the sink. I told her to get someone to fix it. She told me there would be charges.

I typed in a description of Pete. Wrote a couple paragraphs. Followed it up with a short description of his apartment. Then, I skipped a page and set up a heading for each folder in his file cabinet back in the apartment: Animal Rights, Right to Die, Gene Therapy, Human Cloning, Gamma Sterilization of Food and Corruption in Miami, Miami-Dade County, the Port and the Airport. Now for the hard part: Could I find any evidence in his lab computer for a crusade on any of these categories?

I searched the computer's files, one by one, looking for the "summaries" which his will promised would be a "great resource" for his biography. I spent two hours looking and didn't find anything. Sure, there were some summaries on scientific topics like organ transplant, cloning, and so forth, but they were mostly notes — nothing that could be described as a great accomplishment and be included in his biography.

A few minutes before noon I put down the biography project. Enough time wasted. Now was the time for science. Just then Franz Gassler poked his big head in the door. "You are coming to the faculty meeting?"

"What faculty meeting?"

Franz slouched against the doorframe. "The special faculty meeting called for the so-called friendly visit of Robert Kotzen — Vice Provost and Assistant Academic Dean."

"I thought the Assistant *Academic* Dean is Robert Wriggler."

"No, he is the Assistant Dean for *Administration*."

"That's confusing."

"They are the 'two Roberts.' They are like Max and Moritz — the two bad boys from Wilhelm Busch. You cannot tell the two Roberts apart. And they are confused, too. Each one is trying to do the other one's job. Just remember that Kotzen is the bald one with the bow tie and Wriggler is the one with the long tie and a lot of hair. Both are overweight. Now come. I need your vote."

I got up and followed my new political ally. "You need my vote for what?"

"Kotzen is trying to take the dog lab out of the medical school curriculum, like he tried last year. Pete helped me fight him off. When you take over Peter Peterson's lab, you should vote like him. Pete didn't put up with nonsense."

Assistant Dean John Kotzen was sitting at the far end of the conference room table, next to our chairman, Harold Boyle. Kotzen was semi-bald, mid-sixties and was dressed like an Ivy League professor, with a blue blazer and yellow bow tie. His demeanor reminded me of a high-level government bureaucrat waiting to make a public announcement before a bank of TV cameras.

Next to Dr. Kotzen at the head of the table sat a man and woman, both suited up. Olga Hernandez, our departmental administrator, was sitting along the wall, looking uncomfortable. Our faculty were already seated. Franz and I took the two remaining places at the opposite end, near the door.

Boyle threw us an irritated glance and cleared his throat. Was he irritated with us as latecomers or was he displeased with having to make small talk with the guests? "As you know from the notices, this is a special faculty meeting, called because Dr. Kotzen has some things he wants to tell us."

Kotzen beamed a smile around the table. Franz was right: Kotzen was short and overweight. An extra 30 pounds was a distributed as a layer of subcutaneous fat, several millimeters thick and perhaps even thicker in his cheeks which stretched his narrow mouth and pressed against the thick frames of his heavy glasses. "Thank you for the time from your busy schedules. I want to introduce two members of the Bryan Medical team, whom you may not know. Ms. Irma Menendez and Ms. Kathlene Smith, from Central Administration."

How strange to have this outsider carry on like a host in our department.

The two guests of the guest nodded to us. Franz snorted.

Kotzen continued. "As all of you with research grants know, the National Institutes of Health, the NIH, has put out a directive that costs of photocopying and office supplies cannot be taken from the supply budgets of your grants, but should be paid by the medical school from overhead payments. However, we want you to know that we are negotiating with the NIH to allow you to continue purchasing your photocopies and office supplies from your grants."

Amazing! He had just told us that he was doing us a favor by making us pay for laser printer cartridges that the med school was already getting reimbursed for.

The frowns on my colleagues' faces told me they didn't like it either. But like Boyle, most of them were frowning at the surface of the table, and not at the guest administrators.

And still more baffling, nobody challenged Kotzen's statement during the few minutes that the matter was open for discussion.

Finally, Kotzen inspected us through his magnifying lenses and said, "In summary, until further notice from us, you can continue to charge photocopies and office supplies to your grants. And of course, physical repairs to your facilities will still require an account number."

Franz grimaced. "Like five hundred dollars for fixing the blinds?"

Is that the price I'd agreed to when giving Mildred the go-ahead to get the sink repaired?

Kotzen ignored Franz's comment. With an air of great deliberation, he thanked and excused the guest administrators. They handed us business cards on the way out. Then Kotzen stared at Olga. She got up and left with the guest administrators. Our chairman didn't seem to notice a thing.

Kotzen continued. "And for the second purpose of this meeting: You will remember that last year there have been substantive discussions about the dog lab, and its replacement. This problem has now become acute. As some of you are aware, members of the medical sophomore class are protesting our requirement that they participate in physiological experiments in the dog lab."

"Two members," Franz said quickly. "Two young men who have been getting nothing but C's and D's. They are troublemakers." He stated it as a matter of fact, slowly and methodically. Something about his German-Swiss accent seemed to lend credence to his words.

Kotzen stared back with expressionless eyes. Did he suffer from hypothyroidism? "It is more than two students. This apparently represents a growing majority of opinion within the medical class."

"From where do you know that?" Franz challenged.

"From a number of confidential sources."

Here was the ultimate bureaucratic answer. Pick the answer you want, call the source confidential, and then pat yourself on the back for maintaining the source's confidentiality — and shut up everyone else in the process.

It was amazing how expressionless Kotzen could hold his face.

"Presently, a majority of the students feel this way and I have been empowered by the administration to look into alternatives."

It felt like a seance. We weren't hearing words from a human being. We were hearing spirit voices from a distant administration. No colleague raised his voice in refutation. Why didn't the faculty pull together and fight off this raider?

Kotzen continued. "As most of you are aware, times are changing. It is necessary to develop increased sensitivity to the societal needs of certain groups. The U.S. is becoming more multi-cultural, and we must respect minority opinions."

Franz, the only ethnic minority member in the room, was drumming his fingers on the table. "I do not understand what you are saying."

"I am saying that it will not be possible to keep doing business as we used to. We must rationalize and *economize*. The dog lab will be replaced by a computer simulation plus an operating room experience, like they do at Harvard."

"That isn't going to save us money."

"Yes, it will."

"Have you done your homework?"

Kotzen puffed his cheeks and grunted something interpretable as "yes."

Franz interpreted it as no, and said, "Well, I have."

Franz stated that the dogs cost only $5,000 and the whole class could be instructed in one afternoon. He said that doing it by simulation would require 20 computers for $40,000 and $30,000 worth of software. "And I have tested the program, and can tell you that it does not do a good job of simulating the physiological reactions. So you have wasted seventy thousand dollars for something that will not work."

Amazingly, not one of my colleagues jumped in to support Franz. William Long, instructor of anatomy, followed the exchange with his eyes and wore a poker face. Assistant Professor John Falk was staring off in the distance, probably thinking about growing nerves in his Petri dishes. Associate Professor Susan Bligh seemed a thousand miles away, maybe pondering her smooth muscle experiments.

It was time for me to give Franz a hand. "I agree, completely," I said.

Hilda Beecher shot me a long-faced glance, like I'd spoken out of turn. None of my other colleagues reacted.

Kotzen took a second to rearrange his bow tie, using both hands. Bug-eyes and thick lenses shifted from Franz to me. "I thought this wouldn't be a controversial meeting, like we had last year. But you seem to have taken up the scepter." Was I now branded as Pete's heir for stirring up controversy? Kotzen looked back to Franz. "You don't need twenty computers. You can do it with one computer with small groups of students."

Franz answered slowly and methodically, arguing that it was impractical and that the Curriculum Committee wouldn't let them break up the class.

"So you are refusing to negotiate with the Curriculum Committee as a matter of personal convenience."

"No, I am just identifying an impossibility of logistics."

"They don't seem to agree with you at Harvard. They have done away with the dog lab, and they teach their students well. Each student is scheduled in the O.R. for one day."

" — where they probably don't learn anything. They can't see into the patient because the surgeon's head is already there. And if anything important is going on, then the resident has his head in there too."

"But they see it on monitors — blood pressure, heart rate, respirations, and oxygen pressure."

" — all of which the anesthesiologist is working full time to keep in the normal range. The students will not see any pharmacological challenge or cardiovascular reaction. They won't see how an injection of epinephrine speeds up the heart, or how an injection of acetylcholine slows it down." Franz's tempo picked up and his accent thickened. "The students will not see anything — unless the patient is crashing. And then the surgeons and anesthesiologists will be working on him so fast that the student couldn't keep up with them, even if there were someone around to explain it to him."

"To him? Not to his or her?" Kotzen asked.

Franz was visibly exasperated. "When I say 'him,' it means him or her."

"*Der Student!*" I said, putting the accent on the second syllable, with passable German pronunciation. When nobody responded to my joke, I explained it. "In German, the noun is masculine."

Bug-eye did not look up. "But the *students* might not understand that," he said, staring with dead eyes and giving no indication whom he was answering. "As I was saying, we must have heightened sensitivity. Times are changing, as the Harvard example is showing us." He delivered this pronouncement so slowly that it was painful. Probably thought he was expressing the gravity of the situation. "We can't keep on doing business as usual." Rob McGregor later told me this was one of the dean's favorite expressions.

For the last several minutes, Hilda Beecher had been listening with the type of pained expression you see in a laxative commercial. "I can agree that we must maintain heightened sensitivity, especially those of us in pedagogic positions. But if the change is going to be expensive, we should know where the money will come from."

The spirit voice answered that it would not be that expensive, and that the additional cost could be apportioned between the administration and the department.

Boyle grunted. His perpetual frown turned into a tiny smile. "Obviously this won't be solved now. It will require further discussion." Then he shook his head, and looked down, like he didn't want any trouble.

And nobody at the table said anything more. What a shame: so much brain power concentrated in one place, but hardly a word of common sense.

Franz announced, "I move that this special faculty meeting be adjourned."

"I second the motion," colleague Ron Price added quickly. People got up faster than Boyle could call a vote. As the nearest to the door, I was the first to leave. While doing so, I felt a pat on the shoulder. Franz said, "Thanks for your support, Ben."

"*Gern geschehen,*" I answered, using a vaguely remembered phrase from German at Swarthmore. I *was* glad to have been of service, even if it did put me on Robert Kotzen's shit list.

My stomach was growling and the urge to get out of the building was strong. I grabbed my brown bag lunch off my desk and headed for lunch where an old buddy saw my face and read my fortune.

"ADMINISTRATIUM" 12

I sat down for lunch in the mall area between the med school and *Dade County General.* Sat on a knee-high concrete wall with my back to the hospital. It faced the pedestrian plaza and a large expanse of grass which was crisscrossed by sidewalks and lined with gumbo-limbo trees. Across the plaza to my left was the med school, all 11 stories of it. And to the right of the med school was an enormous parking garage, almost as tall. Behind me was a small green area full of native scrub plants and home to feral cats and zebra butterflies.

The butterflies were in season and I didn't mind throwing the cats a few scraps from my lunch. It was a nice spot, away from my academic colleagues. What a shame: I'd had this job only a week and a half and was already bogged down in politics.

I unpacked a sandwich. Here, streaming in front of me, was real life — *Dade County General* patients and visitors, a cross-section of our metropolitan population — the walking wounded, the working poor, the recently arrived, the too-long-on-this-earth and the nurses and doctors who serve them. There was a mother with six children; a redneck escorting her sister with a bandaged arm; poor Latin Americans who asked me directions; scores of indigent patients and their relatives; and rehab patients arriving in wheelchairs, many of them self-propelled.

And some of the patients' wheelchairs were designed to *not* be self-propelled — with wheels too low to grab and turn. The legs of these patients were manacled with ankle cuffs and draped with a light blanket for privacy; the wheelchair was pushed by a uniformed guard from the Miami-Dade County Stockade. The injuries were often visible: a patch on the eye or a bandage on the head — probably wounds received while resisting arrest. But often the injury could not be seen, like a bullet to the arm or leg. The relations between the push*ers* and push*ees* were very casual and friendly. If you'd played me back a tape recording of the conversations, I couldn't even begin to guess who was who.

I unwrapped my second sandwich.

It was a humanizing experience to sit here watching patients and visitors stream by. Four patients were accompanied by two nurses who pushed their wheel-mounted IV rigs. They sat down at a pair of benches under a gumbo-limbo tree. One of the patients inspected its smooth brown bark, tore off a small strip where it was flaking off, and showed it to his nurse. Probably telling her it looks like parchment. Each of the IV poles held three bags. The solution in the smallest bag was the color of an artificial orange soft drink. I guessed that it was Adriamycin and that the disease was leukemia. Surprisingly, the guy had all his hair. Same for the other three. Considering their age and experience, the fellows were really good about not jerking their IV lines or tangling lines with their buddies. They all looked up as a low-flying jetliner flew over the med school building. Such things can be fascinating for a six-year-old.

And fascinating for me, too. The plane's length was equal to the distance between two spread fingers held at arm's length. That's about one-seventh of an arm's length. If the jet was 200 feet long, then it was 1,400 feet above us. That's high enough to satisfy the FAA, but still not a lot of margin for flying over a hospital and medical school.

I had never really contemplated our 11-story building from a distance before. Actually, it is 13 stories, if you count the two stories of penthouse on the northern edge. Although the penthouse had large plate glass windows conforming with the rest of the building, I guessed the two stories were not used as penthouses. They were probably architectural camouflage for a tower housing machinery for the four passenger elevators along the north wall. It had to be an elevator machinery tower; a similar tower for the elevators that served the veterinary core was undisguised. The two towers were connected by a catwalk along the side to the building.

Ben, you're such a nerd, doing engineering analysis of buildings on your lunch hour!

But whether for disguising machinery or storing spare parts, the rooms would have a nice view of the plaza and over the top of the parking garage to the neighborhood to the west.

A familiar voice shook me from my contemplation. "Well, if it isn't Ben Candidi . . . P . . . H . . . D!"

It was Lou, an old drinking buddy from Coconut Grove. Over the six years before I met Rebecca, Lou and I must have tossed down the equivalent of a dozen kegs at Captain Walley's waterfront bar. I stood up and slapped him on the shoulder. My touch released a light puff of sawdust.

"Hi, Lou. Just got back into town. Haven't had a chance to stop by Captain Walley's yet." It was important to reassure him I was still a friend, even though I'd left behind the hip life and was putting all my energies into professionalism. "Sit down for a minute and tell me how things are going."

Lou screwed up his face, and glanced at my button-down shirt and the photo I.D. badge hanging from my belt. "Where you been?"

"Washington, DC."

I sat down. Lou followed suit, but looked around uncomfortably.

"Pretty fancy."

"Rebecca and I were staying on the *Diogenes*, moored on the Potomac River. So close in we could see the Jefferson Memorial. Rebecca's still up there."

Lou pulled out a cigarette. "Were you close enough to peek in the White House window? Did you see Monica giving it to Bill?"

I laughed along with him. "No, but it seems that's all anyone was talking about in that town." I waited a couple seconds for Lou to light up and take his first drag. I took my own deep breath and challenged Lou to a round of barroom repartee. "Now Lou, you've always been ragging me with this kind of question, and now I'm going rag *you. What should we do with that guy?*"

Lou squinted at me over the tip of his cigarette, then glanced left and right to check if anyone might hear. "Well, if he wasn't doing such a good job, I'd say throw the slick bastard out. Frigging weasel word lawyers!"

We had a good laugh under the roar of an oncoming jetliner. Our friendship was renewed.

"Tell me, Lou, how's the carpentry business? Still doing a lot of townhouse work?"

"Doing a lot of office work."

I squinted back at him, as a request for clarification.

"Legal offices. If this here town's good at one thing, its cranking out lawyers. And each year, a goodly number of them strike it rich and want a new office. You remember me showing you my big lathe?"

"Right."

"Well, I got it working full time, turning out yards and yards of veneer. Glue it up on their wood panels and stain it right pretty so their offices look like they've been here since George Washington."

It was the high point of Lou's craft. I would not answer with a joke. "Great. I remember you showing me. It was a tricky business, lining up those panels, one over another, so they repeat the pattern in the grain of the wood."

Lou smiled to himself. "Yeah, it's good when you've mounted a good log and really got it working." He gazed far off into the distance.

"I hope you let those lawyers know it's a real art, and you're the only guy in town who can do it."

Lou wrinkled his nose and flicked his cigarette. "Hell, Ben, you gotta tell that to them right off, or you don't get *no* money outta them!" He slapped me on the back and we laughed again.

"So what are you doing here? I hope that Ida —"

" — no, she's at the shop, answering the phone. It's just that jerk I hired last week. He upped and cut his hand on the job, and now I gotta go and hold his hand for him before some damn lawyer gets to him first."

"Is it serious?"

"No, it ain't serious. But that didn't stop him from making a big thing of it and hollering and fainting all over the place. Like the Fire Rescue guy told him, all he really needed was to drink a *can of man*."

Lou threw his cigarette into the scrub bushes behind us and lit another one. "So what kinda work you doing here? You investigating someone?"

"I'm taking over the lab of an old scientist that died. I'm using up the last two years of his grant and trying to get a permanent position here."

Lou frowned and shook his head.

I continued. "But it seems that all I've been able to do over the last week and a half is to shovel shit out of his barn and to try to keep from getting mired down in local politics. The politics of this place is a real bitch, Lou." You have to tell it straight when talking to a friend. "I'm starting to kick myself for coming back here."

Lou smiled for a second, then got to his feet. He glanced to both sides, then looked at me, squinty-eyed. "You know that Ole Lou can keep a secret for his buddies. You didn't come back here for no lifetime job. They brought you back here for an *investigation*. Bet someone killed that professor and they got you figuring it out."

"No. A buddy on the faculty fixed me up in the job."

"Yeah, like your coroner buddy sent you back to school a couple years ago. Then the next thing we see in the papers that one of them scientists is arrested for murder."

"Sorry, Lou, but I told you I'm unable to talk about that."

"Yeah, because it's confidential — like you was telling Sam when he was fixing that guy's boat. And a few days later that guy smashes it up in the canal."

"I don't know what to tell you, Lou. Maybe I have a knack for getting into places where there's trouble."

"I'll Roger that." He locked eyeballs with me and said it as true as he could, one boatman to another. "Good luck, Ben. And remember to keep an eye out for the storm."

"See you at Captain Walley's."

As Lou walked away, I looked at the sky. Dark clouds were rolling in. I felt a cold down draft. A Burger King wrapper blew across the walkway. The pediatric leukemia patients were gone, but I was not ready to leave. Fifteen seconds was all it would take to reach the safety of the covered walkways. Fifteen quiet minutes was what I still needed to digest the morning's events.

Although he wasn't sure of himself around me, Lou was my friend — a real friend, not just a drinking buddy. All that's required of a drinking buddy is a glib tongue, a light heart, and the ability to keep track of who bought the last round. A friend is a good-hearted guy who will look out for you and keep you out of trouble.

Yes, Lou was right, even if he didn't know how or why. I was up to my waist in trouble. The big boss didn't want me here. His right-hand flunky was licensed to conduct one-man pogroms. My chairman couldn't defend me, and my only potential ally was an overgrown gnome who might win a few battles with Swiss charm.

How could I build a house of science at Bryan Medical School when they shifted the rules, the premises and the assumptions like sand on a barrier island?

Now, raindrops were falling on my head. I made my 15-second dash to the first convenient canopy and followed it to the med school. My route took me by the back entrance and loading dock area of the med school where an organ transplant station wagon was off-loading a long shrouded bundle onto a gurney.

Back in the lab, I asked Mildred for the details on the sink repair. She told me it would cost $475, chargeable to my grant. I told her to cancel the work order. I would repair it myself.

While checking my mail, I found a document that summed it all up. The hand-written note on top said, "From Franz to Ben." The document was a print-out from a web page: cyberhighway.com.

ADMINISTRATIUM
A new element has been discovered. Tentatively named Administratium, it has no protons or electrons, and thus has an atomic number of zero. However, it does have one neutron, 125 assistant neutrons, 75 vice-neutrons, and 11 assistant vice-neutrons. This gives it an atomic mass of 212.

The description continued in physicist's jargon, telling how the 212 particles were held together by a continuous exchange of memos, how this heavy element slows down every reaction it comes in contact with, how it multiplies itself and takes over hospitals, universities, mature corporations and especially government laboratories, always concentrating itself in the newest, best-maintained buildings, and how nobody has found a way to get rid of it.

It provided a good laugh just when I needed it. I walked over to Franz's office to thank him. He was analyzing a ten-parameter data trace from a dog experiment on his computer.

"Thanks, Franz, for giving me the Administratium article. The guy who wrote it just had to be a physicist . . . with that business about 212 neutrons making a lot of inertia."

"I think so, Ben. I have been trying to write one of these spoofs like a science fiction story. The bureaucrats are aliens who are *colonizing* us. They get their power by slowing us down and making it impossible for us to work."

"What about Olga? Does she belong to them or to us?"

"I don't know. It is hard to say. But before I forget, thank you again for the *Rückendeckung* — how do you say? — covering my back this morning."

"Glad to help. Tell me . . . what was Kotzen saying about a controversial meeting last year?"

A mischievous grin came to Franz's face. "Last year, Kotzen tried the same thing. I had no warning. Pete jumped in and argued with him and — how do you say? — pinned his ears back. He said that Kotzen was 'making an argument that only a jackass could make.' It was actually very funny to listen to."

"I can imagine Pete arguing on that subject. Apparently, he stirred up a lot of Animal Rights activists outside the school, talking about the need for animal research."

"I do not know so much about that, but I know Kotzen is all wrong. He quoted the med school's veterinarian as saying that it was hard to get the dogs and they are specially bred for medical research. But that is not true. The dogs we get are going to be killed anyway because they flunked their test."

"Racing greyhounds that run too slow?"

"No, they are dogs trained in Texas for use against prison riots. If they flunk the test — on when to charge and how to bite — the trainers kill them by lethal injection. We kill them too. We do not let them wake up after the experiment. But at least they were not killed for nothing. Everybody learns by making mistakes. And it is better to make mistakes on a dog than on a human being."

I agreed with Franz but felt sad for the dogs. To change the subject, I asked about Kotzen's background. Franz told me that Kotzen flunked out of Purdue University's veterinary school before studying medicine. After finishing his internship, he got an M.B.A.

I was curious about my new colleagues. "I can understand that Hilda Beecher gets off on telling everyone to hush up, but why was William Long so silent? I mean, if the dog lab gets thrown out, wouldn't cadaver dissection be the next to go?"

"They will not push him out. He understands politics and the dean likes him. He has a doctorate in undertaking and sits on an examiner's board for anatomy. He knows all the bones, muscles and nerves, so he can teach."

"This seems to be a very political place. What is the political key to survival?"

Franz answered me by raising his hand and rubbing his thumb over his forefinger to indicate money.

I pressed on. "What did the 'powers that be' think of Pete?"

"What does the cow think of a fly — of a gadfly? They tried to swat him. Sometimes they got him, sometimes they didn't."

"Tell me about when they didn't get him."

"When they outlawed smoking in this building and Pete kept on smoking his pipe — in front of the fume hood!"

"I can imagine that. Any more stories?"

Franz told me how Pete had stopped a copy machine that was set to make 1,000 copies of a blank page and then told the secretaries he was the Little Dutch Boy who stuck his finger in the dyke. Some of them didn't know the proverb. Franz grinned. "Certain people in Central Administration tried to make a big thing out of it. They also worried that a rich donor might hear him using bad language in the hallway."

"They were overreacting."

"Several months ago, the dean had him investigated."

"What for?"

"He was — how do you say? — tongue lashing an administrator from Central Administration. She made a complaint that he was physically threatening her. The dean said he would be suspended unless he went to 'sensitivity training' at Employee Resources. Pete said he did not threaten her. He just said she was lying about what she did with a request form he sent her a month or two earlier."

"Did he go the 'sensitivity sessions'?"

"I think so, but he did not like to talk about it."

Well, at least I had some anecdotes for the biography. I typed them into the computer while Mildred worked in the lab. Noontime events left me unable to concentrate on science. Feeling the need to do something useful, I crawled under the sink. The problem was a corroded J pipe. I could fix that, okay.

I put in a good day's desk work before going home where I found two big surprises.

My first surprise came around 6 p.m. when I checked the mailbox at the apartment and found a bulletin from the First Unitarian Church. It stated that I was doing a biography on Pete. It listed my address and phone number, and encouraged interested parties to send anecdotes and materials. Those Unitarians work fast.

My second surprise was from Barbara when I entered the apartment. She was dressed in a black pants-suit with an evening cut. She seemed very glad to see me.

"Ben, I have an extra ticket for the New Theater in Coral Gables. I'd like you to go with me."

I stalled for time. "What's playing?"

"Enemy of the People."

"Ibsen. Sounds interesting. But why aren't you taking George?"

She made a sour face. "I'm not taking him anywhere. He's ancient history."

"Ancient history?"

"Older than the play. Past tense. Gone. *Finito*."

"I'm sorry to hear that. Maybe you have a friend from the wards you want to take along."

"I don't have any friends *there*." She tugged at my elbow and took a step towards the door. "Now, come on. I know you like cultural things. If you don't come along, the ticket goes to waste. Come with me. I feel stupid going by myself. And we can talk during the intermission."

"Well . . ."

"I'm going right now. Come on! Grab a jacket."

I did what she said. Hell, I would have been unfriendly to refuse. We took the stairwell, four stories down to the parking garage level. Soon, Barbara was driving us south on 12th Avenue towards Coral Way. It felt funny, being taken out by my fiancée's girlfriend. It felt like a date. I toyed with the idea of setting up a boundary by restarting the conversation about George. No, that would be too cruel.

"How was your day in the operating room, Barbara?"

"Turned exciting around noon. Could have lost one. I just got off the case an hour ago."

As an anesthesiology resident, Barbara was training in a zero-defect specialty: A patient must never die in the hands of an anesthesiologist. A complete cardiovascular assessment must be made one day before surgery. The anesthesiologist is supposed to keep the patient's physiological systems balanced at all times — during the rapid descent into surgical anesthesia, during every minute or hour that the surgeon needs to work, and during the patient's emergence to consciousness.

It was like the physiological monitoring in the dog lab that Franz argued about with Robert Kotzen in the faculty meeting. If the heart is slow, you drip in more adrenaline. Pharmacologists call it epinephrine. If the blood pressure rises, you inject a vasodilator. It all has to be done carefully and skillfully, with no errors. Barbara's almost losing a patient was a serious matter.

I asked, "Did you get an idiosyncratic response from that patient?" Rebecca told me they use that term when things don't go according to the textbook.

"It was *idiosyncratic*, all right. About one chance in three thousand. Maybe one chance in twenty thousand for this defect. And I got the patient that has it! *Atypical plasma cholinesterase.*"

Little Havana was whizzing by, and the pages of my pharmacology book were whizzing through my head as I tried to recall the terms and guess what they meant.

"I don't understand. I know you need cholinesterase in your nerve endings to break down acetylcholine. But I didn't know you need the enzyme in your plasma — in your blood."

"You need it to break down the succinylcholine that we give to establish an airway."

I grunted and Barbara correctly interpreted it as a signal that she'd lost me.

"We usually start anesthesia with an intravenous push of thiopental. That knocks them out for a couple of minutes. Then we give them an IV injection of succinylcholine to relax the throat muscles so we can get down the breathing tube. We blow up the balloon around the tube so that they can't throw up into their lungs. Then we plug the tube into a respirator and let it do the breathing."

"Okay."

"You probably remember how succinylcholine works — overstimulating the sodium channels in skeletal muscles so they desensitize and shut down. The throat muscles belong to this group and a low dose of succinylcholine will relax them. Now if you overdose a patient with succinylcholine, you will stop <u>all</u> the muscles, including the diaphragm muscles. Then they can't breathe. It's as if an Amazon Indian shot the patient with a curare-tipped arrow."

It was nice of Barbara to simplify the terminology for my sake. Playing the teacher seemed to be good for her, too.

"So what was *atypical* about the plasma cholinesterase enzyme in your patient's blood?"

"His couldn't split succinylcholine after I injected it. You need the enzyme to get rid of the succinylcholine. The succinylcholine hung around the whole time. Even at the end of the eighty-minute operation, he couldn't breathe. I found that out after I turned off the nitrous oxide and isoflurane. I unplugged the respirator right after he regained consciousness and was telling him that I would be taking out the tube. He was staring at me but couldn't nod his head. He wasn't breathing. Then the tissue oxygen monitor started screaming and he started turning blue."

"What did you do?"

"I plugged the tube back into the respirator. I told him to be calm, and that everything would be okay. I could have used someone to calm *me* down."

"Sounds pretty scary. Did he put up a fight? Did he try to grab the tube out of his mouth?"

"No. That's just it. He couldn't move a single muscle in his body. It was scary for him. But what shocked me was all the trouble I had requisitioning the antidote."

"What was the antidote?"

"Fresh frozen plasma from a normal donor. I needed to give him one unit IV. It has the missing enzyme to break down the succinylcholine right away."

"But you did get the frozen plasma, didn't you?"

"Yes, but not fast enough. The blood bank didn't find pseudocholinesterase deficiency on their list of approved uses for plasma. And they were uptight about getting an informed consent from next of kin because of the possibility of HIV contamination."

"Bureaucracy is such a blessing."

"I finally got the plasma. The patient resumed breathing on his own, half an hour after I administered it. But I had to stay with him for three hours more. And here we are, now." She sighed, and smiled at me. "I ordered a workup to verify a low Dibucaine Number and Fluoride Number."

She recited the last two pieces of jargon with a touch of mastery — like her mastery over the car while rounding the corner onto Coral Way near Ted Walden's office.

"Yes, I can see that the episode was really stressful. Tell me, can a normal patient get in trouble if he is overdosed with succinylcholine?"

"Not really. Succinylcholine would stop his breathing, but that would make no difference because we have him on the respirator. It might take 15 minutes for the succinylcholine to get chopped up instead of the usual two, but we'd never notice it."

Barbara drove fast along the ficus-lined boulevard, smoothly changing lanes to get around slow-moving cars or to avoid cars turning in from the side streets of the middle-class Hispanic neighborhood. I could imagine Barbara in the O.R., smoothly turning the valves of her anesthesia machine and watching all the monitors, controlling the dive and ascent through the planes of anesthesia like the dive officer of a nuclear submarine. I knew my physiological systems would be in good hands if an ambulance ever brought me to her table.

It all added up to a different kind of feminine beauty. The kind that you see in Alaska, wearing boots, faded blue jeans and a heavy red-and-black plaid shirt. Feminine beauty expressed on the masculine side. Like the captain of the Key Largo dive boat. Too bad George wasn't sticking with her.

We emerged from the ficus tunnel. Barbara steered left, zipping us past the flamingo-pink arches marking the entrance of Coral Gables, and heading a couple of blocks south on Douglas Avenue. She pulled into a parking lot one-half block from the playhouse. It occupies a narrow two-story, flat-roof warehouse type building with a passably Spanish-Italianate facade. Coral Gables is a real stickler about architectural matters.

The theater's interior was off-off-off-Broadway functional. All surfaces painted flat black. They had a dozen rows of comfortable seats, bolted onto a plywood-covered, terraced metal scaffolding.

As the house lights dimmed and the stage lights sharpened, I sank into my chair next to Barbara ready to savor a two-hour helping of brain-food. I already knew the piece from my Swarthmore days. This time, I enjoyed it twice as much. The Miami actors treated the old Norwegian morality play with a lot of dignity. The actor playing Thomas Stockmann — physician and man of science — had the character down pat. He played it straight-laced while Stockmann discovered that the water in the "Baths" was contaminated and concluded that it was making the cure guests sick. The actor playing his brother and Burgomaster played convincingly, too.

My mind wandered, speculating on why Swedes and Norwegians were so concerned with morality. Did Northern European types have a special sense of morality? I remembered how incensed Franz had been with Kotzen's conniving in the faculty meeting.

Barbara seemed impressed with the play, too. But we didn't discuss it during the intermission. Like me, she probably felt intimidated by a lobby full of middle-aged people where every third man looked like a bearded college professor.

In the second act, I began to notice something I'd overlooked the first time back at Swarthmore. After Dr. Stockmann began preaching to the townspeople, he seemed less and less a hero. He overdid it. He couldn't see how anyone could disbelieve his "scientific truth." When he accused his brother and the town fathers of turning morality and righteousness upside down, I wondered if he hadn't turned himself upside down as well. He seemed all too glad to find other people's mistakes.

Then a funny thing happened. I started hearing Pete Peterson's voice:

"That's just what he thinks."

"What a lot of bunk!"

"Not so, my dear friend."

"Bullshit."

"Here's the latest news from Mount Olympus."

It was the nasty notes he had written in the margins of other people's scientific articles.

Telling people they are wrong may or may not be a heroic act, depending on your motivations and how you say it. In the privacy of her car, Barbara and I discussed whether the martyred Dr. Stockmann was a hero or a jerk. This got us into a discussion about the need for whistle blowers, which lasted all the way back to our living room. I was glad for the intellectual focus of our evening together.

Barbara stepped out of her heels. "Sit down. I have a bottle of

Chablis in the fridge. There's nothing on television and you don't have to go to bed, yet."

I hung up my jacket and sat down on the couch. Barbara came out with the bottle and two glasses. She sat on the opposite end of the couch and poured. She tucked a foot under a thigh and turned to me, presenting a glass.

"To the whistle blowers," she said, raising her glass in toast.

"To the interesting evening."

"To the first man or woman who is brave enough to blow the whistle on the Miami-Dade Public Health Authority. To the first person who blows the whistle on the division heads and administrative creeps who are taking shark-sized bites out of every billable hour I work."

"Hear, hear!"

We drank. I sipped mine; she took two hard pulls.

"To those of us who live at the bottom of the food chain," she offered, raising and swirling her glass, now two-thirds full.

I told her about Franz Gassler and his run-in with Assistant Dean Kotzen. We talked for a long, long time. Finally, Barbara fell silent, studying me over her third glass of wine.

"I'm sorry about your break-up with George," I said. In a way, my comment was thoughtless. In another way, it was really needed, right at that moment.

"Thanks. I'm just awfully disappointed in that guy." She licked a finger and drew it along the rim of her glass, in a circular motion. "I feel like the lost woman in that other play."

"A Doll's House?"

"No, that was just sexist oppression."

"Hedda Gabler?"

"Yes. I feel like . . . Hedda Gabler."

"I don't remember much about it, except that she had an affair with the wrong man, and it turned out bad."

"I don't remember the details, either. I just remember the feeling." She smoothed the black silk over her calf that was resting on the cushion, in the no-man's land between us. "I just remember thinking how lonely she must have felt that there was no man in her world that could appreciate her . . . that could understand her."

I understood. I understood too much. I would try to project optimism. "A modern woman has many more chances to find . . . I mean, it's a lot easier for a woman with expectations . . . for a woman of substance."

A slight smile came to Barbara's face. She reached for the bottle and replenished the glasses, my third and her fourth. "You can't be talking about my male colleagues. They can't stand a woman being on their level. There can't be any other explanation for it."

"Explanation for what?"

"That they're more interested in nurses than in us — the woman doctors."

"That's easy for me to imagine . . . but hard to understand."

"That's what I like about you, Ben. You listen. You aren't one of those self-centered males."

"Like I was saying, you'll find another guy. One that's worthy of you. I'll spot one for you."

"There aren't many good men out there. Not any *good* ones. The guys just want glossy girl. Their egos can't take a woman as an equal. That's why they'd rather mess around with *them*." She looked me in the eyes and pulled hard on her Chablis. "Rebecca is one lucky girl. She'd better take good care of you."

"I'm not such a good catch. I have to hustle day and night to bring in thirty thousand a year."

"Oh, I'm not talking about the money. I'm talking about knowing what you want to do. You know who you are. You believe in yourself. You stepped onto that boat and sailed up the coast to Washington. Rebecca would never have sailed the open ocean if she hadn't met you."

"But I didn't know what to do with my life before I met her." — And before I met Dr. Westley, I could have added. "I had wasted six years living on that boat, moored off of Coconut Grove and hanging around Little Havana."

"But you're a man. You can wait to settle down. I can't. I'm 29, and I have only six more years to find the right man, or I'll never have children. I've wasted three years with George. Now, I have to go back to my life before I met him. My life was such a soap opera when I was dating."

"My life was like an Updike novel," I replied. The statement could be interpreted many ways, but I had to say something quickly. Maybe Updike doesn't have a single interpretation, either.

Barbara had been inching closer for the last half-hour. I had to get myself out of that couch. It was either go to the john and return to the chair, or call it quits, altogether.

"Thanks for the nice evening, Barbara. The play was great, and I enjoyed our conversation."

I got up slowly.

She touched her lower lip to the empty glass. "Pleasant dreams, Ben."

My dreams did not start out pleasantly. They started with images of the med school and of Pete's apartment, accompanied by sickly and disoriented feelings. Sleeping on my back, I felt lost at sea, entrapped in a spiritual fog with thoughts sloshing around in my alcohol-benumbed brain.

I tried to summon an image of Rebecca. Slowly, like the sun burning through the fog, her protective spirit began to warm me. It was wonderful, how she sensed my longing and came to me, though a thousand miles away.

So deeply was Rebecca's essence imprinted in me, that I almost felt her weight beside me. Her gentle coaxing and fondling stiffened me. It grew like a wet dream that I couldn't stop, growing in passion with each heartbeat's throbbing pulsation, although my arms lay still at my sides. It grew so real that I heard her gasps and felt her breath on my chest.

"Ben," she whispered in synchrony with her movements. I reached out to explore her hips. My hands grasped their crown to aid her deep thrusts that were coming in obsessional rhythm. It could not be a dream. I roused to a live, throbbing female body above me — awaking seconds after the point of no return.

"Oh, darling!" I yelled, and erupted. Then, expended, I reached up into the darkness to pull her down and bring her lips to mine. But it was not Rebecca's thin arms that my fingers encircled. They were well-muscled arms that bent to accept my invitation. At that instant I realized it was Barbara.

"Darling," she whispered.

One quick thought, and I knew what to do. "Rebecca, darling," I moaned, "talk to me."

Barbara didn't answer.

I drooped. I exhaled. I threw my head to the side. "Oh, Rebecca, darling, where are you?"

Wordlessly, Barbara disengaged and returned to her room.

MED $CHOOL POLITIC$ 14

Thursday morning, the morning after. I started it off with a philosophical question: Is it really a sound, when a tree falls in a forest with nobody to hear it? Can you call it a crime, if there wasn't any victim? Did it even happen, if no one saw it and you deny it to each other and to yourself?

We did have breakfast together that morning — well, we had breakfast at the same time. She had her Special K and I had my corn muffins. The only thing we shared was a pan of boiling water, she for her decaf and I for my regular freeze-dried.

Tacitly, we agreed that it hadn't happened.

Barbara left the apartment first. I stayed long enough to search out what I'd hoped to find: her birth control pill holder. The spaces up to Thursday were empty and the spaces from Friday on were filled with pills. She was current; there was no need to broach that subject.

I went to the lab, where I received three phone calls. If they had come in a different order it would have been a complete disaster.

The first phone call was from Carole.

"Hi, Ben. I'm just calling up to say goodbye. I'm saying goodbye to South Beach. My plane leaves this afternoon."

"Well, I hope you had a good time."

"Yes, your advice was first-class. You should see my pictures. Naughty but nice. They're going to make the girls back home real jealous."

"Well, be sure the pictures don't make your husband jealous."

"No, I was always with Daphne. Met her at the News Café. She just got divorced from her husband in London."

"Well, good. When you get back, be sure to tell your husband who I am. Might have to call you if I need more information on Uncle Pete."

"Yes, but promise not to tell him about my doing the Beach."

"Promise."

"Say, how's the garage sale coming?"

"I haven't really gotten started yet." Suddenly, an idea came to me. "I was wondering. Would you have anything against my staying in his apartment for . . . say . . . a couple months? That's how long it will take to get the job done."

"No, its okay with me. I called the management today. Told them I was through with the place and that they should get in contact with the lawyer. And I just told *him* I'm leaving. Say, I hope you don't take more than two months to finish the job. I mean, we can use the money. Planning a trip to Hawaii."

"No, I should be able to get everything sold or placed in two months." That was more than enough time to put the thing with Barbara safely behind me.

"Okay. Keep in touch. Ciao."

The next call came from Ted Walden. He must have been worried about what was going to happen to Pete's stuff. I told him about my deal with Carole, and he agreed. He also agreed to my staying in the apartment for a couple of months. He promised to inform the building management and have the rent statements sent to his office. And he reminded me to check out Pete's Oldsmobile.

So, I was half-way prepared for the third call, which came from Rebecca.

"Hi, Ben. Just taking a coffee break and thought I'd share it with you."

"Thanks, darling. I love you. I was going to call you but . . ."

". . . But we need to save money? No, the e-mails were nice, but I want to hear your voice. I worked late last night, so I guess the University owes me one free long distance call. How have you been? How's the research going?"

"Could be going faster. Lots of bureaucratic hassle." I should have expanded on the topic to buy time because her next question was a killer.

"How are things working out in the apartment with Barbara?"

"Not well. We had a problem last night."

"Who made the problem?"

"Barbara."

"What's her problem?"

"Sleepwalking." I volunteered no further explanation, hoping the long silence would do the work for me.

"I see . . . And you didn't do anything to encourage her . . . her sleepwalking?" Rebecca seemed to be straining for patience with every fiber of her soul.

"No. Barbara was troubled. She has just broken up with George."

"I'm sorry for her." But Rebecca didn't sound it. "Did you comfort her?"

"Yes. From a distance."

"And? . . . "

"Damn it, she jumped me while I was asleep — in the middle of the night."

I heard rustling out in the lab, then the radio got louder. I took Mildred's hint and closed the door.

"And then?"

"Darling, it's hard to describe what happened. I was dreaming of you. As I woke up, I was calling your name. That's what drove her off."

"And? . . . "

I didn't volunteer anything. What I said was fair enough. If Rebecca wanted to know about orgasms, she'd have to ask.

"And all this happened the night before I decided to call you?"

"Yes. I swear to God."

"What are you going to do, Ben?" She sounded on the brink of tears.

"I'm going to move into Pete Peterson's apartment. It's eight floors up from ours."

She sighed. "Maybe I should have a talk with Barbara," she said, with considerable anger.

"Sure, but I'll have to talk to her first."

"Why? Does she have more rights that I?"

"No, but neither of us has talked about it. We've both been acting like it didn't happen."

"She doesn't know what she did?"

"She walked back to her room in a trance."

"Are you saying she has no inkling?"

"No, she knows something because she avoided me at breakfast. We avoided each other. We avoided each other like the two electrons in a helium atom."

Rebecca broke into a laugh. It started hysterical, then turned worldly wise. "Ben, sometimes you can be such a nerd."

"Believe me. This time, I was nothing *but* a nerd. But you are the one who has psychoanalysis for a hobby. Go ahead and analyze me any way you want."

Rebecca sighed. "Oh, Ben, I don't want to analyze you. I just want to keep loving you. It's just that sometimes you . . ."

"I bring it on myself with my roving eye." I was repeating back her analysis of another encounter. "And I'm subconsciously making up for a nerdy adolescence when I didn't find enough girls to hang out with."

"Ben!" She laughed.

Maybe I could rescue myself with humor. "Rebecca, your love has made me attractive in unforseen ways. And you know what my old Swarthmore roommate Richard Bash would say about that."

Rebecca laughed in protest. "How, when nobody loved him, he got desperate and he couldn't get anybody. And when he finally got a girlfriend, other girls followed him like flies buzzing around . . . around . . . a brick . . . *shithouse!*" She was out of breath from laughing. "Oh, darling, I hope I never meet that guy."

We laughed long and hard. I said how much I loved her and how much I missed her. She said the same things to me. Our whispered conversation lasted a long time, until we finally we agreed that we couldn't carry on this way at George Washington University's expense. We kissed and hung up.

Classy lady, my Rebecca. Subtle. And polite — like Mildred who turned up the radio. Rebecca knew where to draw the line. She left me a place to go. She nurtures my soul but doesn't invade it. I vowed to work hard and not disappoint her.

For the rest of the morning, I made good progress on Pete's scientific manuscripts. But my progress came to a halt at 3:00 p.m., when it was time to go to a General Faculty Meeting held in an amphitheater of the Cancer Center. Rob had said it was an important once-a-year meeting. I figured it would be a chance to learn more about medical school politics, thereby increasing my chances of long-term survival.

The sloping amphitheater could have doubled as a small concert hall. Most physicians came in white clinician's jackets and ties; most bench scientists came *sans* lab jacket and with open collars. The two types didn't mix much. Each formed little islands of their own type. I took a seat in the sixth row next to Rob McGregor. It was a good choice because he identified a lot of people for me.

There must have been an unwritten rule that the first five

rows were reserved for administrators and department heads. Most of those high muckety-mucks played the nonchalant late-comer game, strolling in slowly. One exception was a plump little old bald man with thick, rubber-soled shoes and a fast pigeon-toed walk. Rob said his job was keeping track of med school finances. Another exception was a tall guy, in his early forties, who entered with the stride and demeanor of a college athlete. He was the head of South Florida operations for the North American Hospital Group, a large multi-state HMO. Needless to say, he wore a business suit.

A short, stiff-faced, sixtyish guy walked slowly like he had just experienced one sour burp and was trying to suppress another. He wore a clinician's jacket and a red-and-black striped tie. Rob identified him as Irvin Koenigswasser, the head of the Miami-Dade Public Health Authority which controls all the clinical practice in *Dade County General.*

A guy with a moustache and dark sports jacket reminded me of a manager of a used car lot. My intuition wasn't bad: Rob told me he was the parking garage magnate for the Public Health Authority. He controlled all the parking garages around the medical center. Behind him came a guy who reminded me of a used-car salesmen — moustached, medium height, wearing a long-sleeved white shirt with no tie. He carried a beeper on the left side of his belt and a cell phone as thick as a walkie-talkie in his back pocket.

"That's Jerry Cartlick, our new security chief," Rob said. "He used to be in charge of parking garage security for the Public Health Authority."

Lizzy-Mae took a seat in the fourth row. Without a desk to lurk behind, the dean's old secretary looked unsubstantial. She leaned forward as she walked, looking from side to side as if cautiously making her way through a dry streambed. A clinician called out from behind us, "Hey, Lizzy-Mae. I don't see you on the Metrorail anymore."

She turned her head quickly, like a startled fox, and muttered an unintelligible answer.

But this didn't stop the friendly clinician. "Gone back to fighting the traffic all the way from Dadeland, now?"

"The traffic keeps getting worse and worse," she answered, with a pained expression.

Everyone sitting near Lizzy-Mae made some sort of gesture of respect, probably because she controlled their access to the dean. She was friendly to some, but not to most. Didn't seem to like herself much, either.

Rob must have been reading my thoughts. "Lizzy-Mae Wolf. Powerful woman. Establishing a dynasty."

A woman in her early twenties walked to the front row and started talking to the North American Hospital guy. She stood in front of him, next to the lectern, punctuating her words with exaggerated gestures and facial expressions. She had a broad forehead and a good head of thick black hair which made for a low brow. She was on the plump side, with a suggestion of double chin. Girlishly, she twisted her broad hips left and right and cast glances towards the audience.

"Who's that?" I asked Rob.

"Rosemary. Lizzy-Mae's granddaughter. She used to work part-time in Dean Weisburd's office, but now she is working in the P.R. office."

"Who's that thin Spanish-looking woman sitting down right now to the left of her?" She moved with strained grace, reminiscent of an ageing ballerina.

"That's Dolores Padilla. In charge of contracting and fiscal operations."

Her age could have been anywhere between an anorexic 30 or a well-preserved 60. "Looks severe . . . hair done up in a bun."

"Look, Little Britches, everyone's severe. I used to shelter you from these people. But now you will have to learn to swim with the sharks."

"Who did she bite?"

"Gave your predecessor a hard time, for one thing." But Rob didn't tell me what the grave-faced woman had done to Pete.

The noise level decreased quickly when Dean Weisburd entered the auditorium. He worked the crowd like a U.S. President entering for a State of the Union Address. He waved to some, slapped backs and shook hands with others, and gave lots of special attention to the people up front. He spent several seconds with Lizzy-Mae's granddaughter, then half-stepped around her to exchange a few words with the North American Health guy.

Once at the podium, Dean Weisburd attached a portable

microphone to the lapel of his white clinician's coat then spent half a minute staring out into the audience without saying a thing. Stragglers took their seats quickly.

"I think we should be getting started because we have a full agenda. Thank you for coming to this, our Annual General Faculty Meeting."

Last Monday's encounter had supplied me with plenty of motivation to watch and listen carefully.

"As you know, last year was a rough year. But I think that we can view the coming year with cautious optimism, thanks to your ability to take the bull by the horns and taking a good look at things, and tightening your belts where they needed tightening, and thanks to the careful projections of Ralph Rosen who has done what I must say is an enormous . . . no I must say *heroic* job of presenting our projections and our case to the people at our main campus in Opa-Locka and to a very tough-minded . . . but I should really say businesslike Board of Trustees who have the final say in these things."

It was the same type of oily mouthed performance I'd witnessed before. But Weisburd didn't stare, this time. His face scanned the audience, back and forth like a slowly oscillating radar dish at the airport. Undoubtedly, he was registering which objects in the audience returned "hard" or "soft" reflections.

For a quarter of an hour he slithered from one topic to another. During that time it became clear that he considered "health care delivery" to be the med school's most important function and that he didn't care much for Ph.D.s or laboratory research. If his speech had a *leitmotiv*, it was concern for money.

Next, the dean introduced his bald-headed financial guy. He waddled to the podium and spoke for ten minutes, presenting eight slides with histograms and pie charts. It might as well have been a beef stew chart, because he mixed together all the different types of money, hard and soft — student tuition and research grants and reimbursable and non-reimbursable patient care costs and Public Health Authority money. I doubt that anyone could sort it out, although he did cause a lot of scientists' foreheads to wrinkle with one statement: that decreasing overhead recovery on laboratory research grants was becoming a hidden cost of doing research.

In the question and answer session that followed, a disheveled, fortyish scientist from the Department of Biochemistry took issue with the "hidden cost" statement and complained that he was already bringing in 80% of his salary with Federal grants and that it wasn't possible to raise his percentage to 100.

Assistant Dean Kotzen stood up and did his best to refute him with a load of bureaucratic gobbledygook. Then an overweight man in a broad-patterned sport coat got to his feet and put his two cents in, saying that Florida Heart Association grants weren't good because "they cost the School money."

Rob whispered, "Robert Wriggler, Assistant Dean for Administration — Robert Kotzen's evil twin."

The second of the "Two Roberts," I remembered from my conversation with Franz.

Hell, if I were the Heart Association, I wouldn't want to pay those big overhead payments, either. After the two Roberts were done with him, the biochemist sat down, defeated.

Slowly, the dean's frown dissolved and the radar antenna returned to scan mode, sweeping back and forth across the hall. "We have been trying for a long time to secure a payment from the State for each medical student in our program — payments of the type already received by the University of Miami. As Miami's second medical school, we have not been successful. It would be good to talk to your local state senator or representative. You should know his or her name."

I guess he was saying that would put more meat in the stew, and that we would somehow derive nourishment from an expanded pie graph.

Another scientist who was sitting close to the biochemist raised his hand, and got the floor. He commented on the large physical plant expenses. And he thought a lot of the renovation and hallway painting were unnecessary.

The dean didn't interrupt, but indicated impatience by shifting his weight from one foot to another.

The faculty member continued. "And purchasing and accounting department expenses are high. Dr. Welshland calculated they amount to 25 cents on each dollar spent. And do we need such an enormous budget for security?"

In the front row, used car salesman look-alike Jerry Cartlick turned and half-rose in his seat. But the dean signalled him "no" with a shake of the head. "The Faculty Senate itself recommended tighter security two years ago. They were properly concerned about illegal access by animal rights activists. I think we can all agree that the cost of security is small compared to the loss of a lifetime's data like those poor scientists at the University of Minnesota last month."

McGregor leaned over and told me, "They say Jerry Cartlick has his home computer wired up to all the security cameras. Can keep track of every hallway without coming in."

The dean finished with a feisty smile. "Dr. Welshland is looking at me impatiently like he has a question."

All heads in the auditorium turned and triangulated on a point a few seats to the left of us. I had already noticed the tall, big-boned, white-haired man in the white lab jacket. He had been listening with a worried look and chewing on the corner of a folded handkerchief. He quickly removed it, rose, and cleared his throat.

"The Faculty Senate has addressed all manner of issues, from the fifteen cents per sheet cost of photocopies, to the enormous costs of administration." He spoke with an Australian accent. "All of our inquiries have been politely answered, and Central Administration has stoutly defended every questioned item. We have been unable to make headway."

Rob McGregor said, "Welshland used to be chairman of Microbiology. The Faculty Senate is his new hobby horse — that he's going to ride out into the sunset."

"But what I really wanted to ask," Welshland continued, "is about *existing* money. If we have exhausted all opportunities for being more efficient, then it is most important to hold onto existing sources of money. I read in the newspaper that a major donor is withdrawing support."

"Who's that?" I asked Rob.

"The guy who owns Cool Shades." It was a chain of kiosks selling sunglasses at every shopping mall from Palm Beach to Key West.

For a second, the dean looked very troubled. "Unfortunately, our project development officer is not here to respond. He is giving a speech in Boca Raton. But I must say that we have been very grateful for Mr. Edmunds' generous support through the years, and I realize that there are many worthy projects which are competing for his generosity, and that I can understand when the needs of some seem more pressing than ours, and it is my feeling, although I have not been able to talk to Mr. Edmunds and am only getting this second hand through our project officer who is not here, that this is only a brief interruption in support."

Dean Weisburd's radar worked hard while he negotiated this difficult passage. At the end, his eyes came to rest on Dr. Welshland, now seated, with the folded handkerchief near his face, the point touching his cheek.

"Our next item is a very short interim report on the status of our negotiations with the North American Hospital Corporation."

The dean introduced the tall, handsome guy, who stood up and described the deal. Their company would use some Bryan Medical School faculty, and Bryan would get referrals from them and it would produce all sorts of efficiencies, generating a symbiotic, synergistic, win-win situation that would benefit everyone . . . and we would live happily ever after. I guessed that was supposed to put more meat in the stew.

The physicians had so many questions that the remainder of the hour sounded more an HMO management meeting than a faculty meeting. I couldn't help wondering whether the North American Hospital Corporation was a white knight or a Trojan horse.

Finally, the dean looked at his watch and said, "We are well past the usual two hours. I would like to adjourn the meeting."

Dr. Welshland raised his hand and said, "There has not yet been a formal announcement, but it would be most appropriate to sadly announce that Dr. Peter S. Peterson passed away, two weeks ago. He was a good colleague. He will be missed by us all."

For a couple seconds, the dean seemed surprised and embarrassed. "Yes, I am sorry if his home department was slow in getting out an announcement. There are many who have said that Pete was outspoken, but let me be the first to say, because it really needs to be said, that his motivation was from the highest motives, and that we will sorely miss him in his role as conscience of the institution and for his willingness to lay matters on the table. I want to be the first to say that there probably isn't anyone in the medical center who wouldn't say that he's done a great job. I wish us all a successful year."

And what was I to make of Dean Weisburd's narrowing of eyebrows with every repeated phrase?

Rob said, "Don't worry, Ben. He's taking it out on Boyle . . . who probably doesn't even realize anything's wrong."

The dean scowled as he walked past us toward the exit. I pretended to be fumbling with my papers.

Okay, I now understood the School's politics: It was about money. And around this issue, Administration had split the Faculty into two camps. The physicians could generate their own money and would put up with an inefficient, gouging administration if it didn't hurt them too much. The lab bench scientists, who had a harder time generating their income, remained silent out of gratitude for being paid better than history professors.

The realization came as a shock. But a bigger shock came when I returned to Peter Peterson's apartment.

OUT OF THE BLUE   15

I popped into Peter Peterson's apartment to see what I needed to bring to make dinner there. I would spend the rest of the evening on the biography project and sleep there. A look through his well-organized kitchen showed that I would not have to bring utensils. I'd go to the other apartment and bring a head of lettuce, a couple tomatoes, and a few cans of "camping slop."

Just as I was going out the front door, it occurred to me to check out the bedroom to see if I needed a change of sheets. I hurried back to the bedroom, opened its door, and rushed in.

And then it hit me.

It hit me hard on the back of the head — wood — harder than hitting my head on a shelf — hard enough to make everything go black — hard enough to make a galaxy of stars that coned into a space-time warp that spun against the force of gravity. Luckily, my hands found my head before I hit the floor.

Someone swished past me as I lay there holding my head in blinding pain. Before I could open my eyes, running footsteps were echoing down the hallway.

"No accident — attacked by a man," came the diagnostic from my shocked cerebrum. "Escaping. You'll lose him in a few seconds."

I willed myself to my knees and crawled in the direction of the sound. Stumbled to my feet and groped along the wall.

A door slammed in the distance.

I ran through the front door, hitting my shoulder on its metal frame.

From the right end of the hall, I heard the fire door bang shut. Tunnel vision reported that I was accelerating myself down the hall towards the fire door. Put out my hands as I threw my weight into it. The shock turned on my lights. Reflex-driven legs propelled me down the stairwell, towards the sound of his escaping feet. Mine were hitting the steps at snare drum tempo. Slid my hand along the rail for a guide.

My brain wasn't damaged or I couldn't be doing this. And my body was finding rhythm on the stairs with 12 beats per flight, a quick grab at the post and a toss of the hip to reverse direction for the next flight.

Tempered rage was driving me and everything was white, like an over-exposed photograph. After scrambling down six of those dusty, fluorescent-lit switchbacks, wide-angle vision started to come back. I caught flickers of movement, three landings below. Our feet were pounding in unison. But after six more stories, I still wasn't making any progress.

"Stop, thief!" My shout echoed up and down the stairwell. Ridiculous, but I had to yell something.

We were now passing through garage levels, but he didn't exit there. He was taking the fire stairs all the way down to street level. I went for broke, going for three steps at a time. Finally started gaining on the bastard. Four floors to ground level.

Two floors more, and I snatched a look at him: late-thirties, white, tall, athletic, strong upper body, white shirt, blue slacks, black leather shoes. Dark hair under a blue baseball cap. The brim covered his face. Canvas duffle bag in his left hand. Must have been nearly empty, the way it was bouncing around.

"Stop, in the name of the Law," I shouted.

Two stories to go and I was a couple dozen feet behind him. Closed the gap right before the last landing. Now or never! My front thrust kick caught him between the shoulder blades. He stumbled and fell. Caught him in the face with a side thrust kick as he tried to get up. He sprang ahead and tripped all the way down the last flight towards the red, alarmed fire door.

I scramble-footed down after him, pulling my Cross pen from my shirt pocket. Makes a good fist extender when you plant it in the base of the palm.

I thought the man would go flying out the door. But he surprised me by turning suddenly and throwing a right to my face. I fended with my left, and threw a hard right, aiming my metal-tipped fist at his chest. The point caught his shirt, crossed in front of his chest and landed on pectoral muscle. My follow-through was good. Popped through fabric and skin, penetrating all the way to the knuckled hilt.

A split-second later, he knocked me silly with a left-handed roundhouse.

The alarm rang. The door slammed shut. The alarm kept ringing for a long time — almost as long as it took to lift my head from the dusty concrete floor. Coming so soon after the blow on the head, that punch in the face really laid me low.

Slowly, I propped myself up on my right arm and took stock of myself: Benjamin Candidi from Newark, New Jersey, Research Assistant Professor, Bryan Medical School, 305-244-9785, engaged to Rebecca Levis, M.D. Today's date: Thursday, September 24th. Presidents George Washington, John Adams, Thomas Jefferson, James Madison, James Monroe, John Quincy Adams, Andrew Jackson . . . .

Intellectual systems okay. But what a headache! Felt like he'd clamped it in a paint shaker and had thrown the switch.

Check motor skills for deeper brain damage? I shut my eyes and touched my nose with my left index finger. And now with the right finger? Looked down saw my right hand was still clenched in a fist — sprouting four inches of bloody Cross pen. It was the mechanical pencil, actually — fine-pointed, sharp as an ice pick. My fingers had made a good choice.

I set off the alarm again by opening the fire door for a look around. It opened to a narrow sidewalk along the street. The guy was gone — maybe around the building, maybe across 12th Avenue to the medical center. But over the exit door was what I hoped to find: a security camera.

I went around to the front entrance and reported the incident to the guard at the desk. He pulled out a walkie-talkie, squeezed down, and said some numbers into it. I tried to be calm. But time is only relative when your eyes have been transiting star-tunnels in hyperspace and when the guard's eyes are still glued to his motorcycle magazine.

"You have security cameras here. Stop the damn tape. Call the police, for heaven's sake."

"I have. My supervisor's on the way."

"*Supervisor?* I don't want any security guard supervisor. I want the real police."

He told me that they were the police. He said they were under Miami-Dade Public Health Authority Security which had jurisdiction around the medical center.

When the supervisor pulled up in a Plymouth Gran Fury jalopy marked "Public Health Authority," he gave me the same answer. The grumpy old troll told me they had jurisdiction by agreement with Metro-Dade, which owned all the land around the medical center.

He didn't think much of my bloody Cross mechanical pencil as evidence. He suggested I clean it up so it couldn't be used against *me* if they did find someone. He did pull out his radio and put out an alert for a man fitting the description I gave.

He grumbled some more when I insisted that he take a look at Pete's apartment. He made me explain why the door was open. He looked at the locks, latches and keyholes and said there was no sign of forceful entry. He walked through the apartment and said there was no sign of a struggle.

"Do you notice anything valuable was taken?"

It didn't seem like anything was missing. The TV was too big to carry off and the VCR was still there. The cameras in the bedroom closet had not been touched.

Old Grumpy followed me around. "My suggestion is that you go to the emergency room at *Dade County General* and get your head X-rayed, because you must have banged it into something pretty hard."

I found Pete's cypress-knee candleholder on the floor by the dresser. "This must be what he hit me with."

I winced when Grumpy picked it up with a bare hand. "Watch out! You'll destroy the fingerprints."

"Don't check for fingerprints when there's no evidence of forcible entry."

"This is an assault and battery."

He answered with a grunt, then spent a lot of time writing on a carbonless form. He handed me the yellow sheet. "It's all on here. My name and number are on the bottom. Suggest you go to the emergency room if you think you're hurt." He turned to leave.

"You will check the tape on the security camera on the Twelfth Avenue door."

"Sure."

I read the form as he waddled away. "Alleged burglary with no sign of forced entry and no evidence that anything's been taken. Mr. Candidi alleges he was hit on the head but no sign of physical injury. Confused but showing no sign of injury." Nothing about my description of the chase or the bloody pencil.

I ran out to the hallway, intending to force the slop-cop to write down everything I told him, but he'd already disappeared into the elevator. Well, the video tape should convince him.

Went back to the apartment and took a second inventory. Nothing missing. Only two things had been disturbed: Pete's candle holder and my head. If the intruder had come to steal, I must have interrupted him in the first minutes. And that seemed quite a coincidence. But I couldn't think of any other reason why he had broken in.

Actually, he didn't *break* in. The door was intact, so he got in by defeating the locks. Now anybody could have finagled the door knob latch with a sheet of flexible plastic, but the dead bolt was another matter. And I was sure that I'd locked it. So the intruder had either picked the deadbolt or used a key. After checking the face plate for scratches and finding none, I figured he'd used a key. I'd take the problem to the management.

The management office was a small room on the ground floor, across from the Burger King. Lucky that the assistant manager was still there. He was semi-bald and looked like he was in his mid-thirties going on his mid-fifties. I guess that can happen to a guy who has to work late every night on a thankless job. He knew about the arrangement for me to stay in the apartment. I told him about the intrusion, the chase and the unsatisfactory interview with security. I said, "There wasn't any damage to the door or any scratches on the locks. Big apartment houses like this work with a single master key. I'm wondering if your master key fell into the wrong hands."

He crossed his arms over his chest and said, "That's impossible."

Three rounds of cross-examination didn't bring any more information. And he argued that it was more likely that Pete had given someone else the key.

"In any case, I am requesting that the lock be changed."

"Yes, we would be glad to do that. I will put in a work order. It will probably take three days, and you'll be billed seventy dollars."

"That's pretty slow and pretty steep. I'll have to see if the lawyer will pay for it."

When I went on to complain about not getting a real cop, he gave me the same line of bunk about the Public Health Authority and Miami-Dade County. "Technically, you are on Miami-Dade County land right now."

I sighed. "Looks like I'd better work my way up the chain of command. Who is the supervisor's supervisor?"

"That would be Cartlick, head of Bryan Security." He noted my surprise and continued. "They take care of Medical School security, and the Miami-Dade Public Health Authority takes care of *Dade General*."

"Can you tell me why Bryan Medical School is involved in security for this building?"

"Because they own it. We're just the management company that they contracted to run the building."

"Yeah, I should have guessed . . . since their outpatient clinics and administrative offices already occupy one-third of the building."

I thanked the guy and walked across the lobby, where I ordered a "Whopper" with French fries to go. Carried the stuff up to Pete's apartment. I was also carrying a whopper of a headache. But I didn't dare take aspirin until I was out of the woods. Used the bathroom mirror together with Pete's shaving mirror to check the back of my head. No breaks in the skin. And it would have been more painful to touch if I'd suffered a fracture.

Presenting myself to the E.R. at *Dade County General* would probably cost me five hours and a non-reimbursable $500. Thought about asking Barbara to do an informal neurological exam, but decided the timing was bad. Did it on myself with what I'd remembered.

No asymmetry in the face. Both irises contracted in bright light. No sign of subdural hematoma, yet. If the bastard broke any blood vessels in my brain, my thrombin and blood platelets must have plugged them up.

I sat at Pete's little dining table in the corner of the living room and ate the Whopper while mulling over my situation. Maybe I should go to the E.R. at *Dade County General* and look for a muscle boy with a punctured right pectoral. But what would I do if I found a man matching his description? Summon a county flatfoot to interrogate him? Photograph him with one of Pete's cameras? And how many hospitals were there in the Miami area? No, it was best to stay home tonight.

And at which "home"? I went down to the apartment and brought back my toothbrush, bedding, a change of clothes and my laptop computer. I braced a tilted chair under the doorknob and loaded it with pans full of silverware. On Pete's answering machine, I recorded a message saying Pete had passed away. Business should be referred to Ted Walden; I would handle all messages concerning personal or scientific matters.

With that done, it was time to call the security supervisor and find out what he had learned something from the surveillance tape. I learned that he had gone home without leaving instructions.

I popped one of Pete's hand-labelled tapes into his VCR and ran it. It contained a 30-second television interview of Pete on a 6:00 p.m. news program. With a lot of hand-waving and rolling of eyes, he tried to explain to the reporter's microphone everything you need to know about cloning.

It took a long time to find those 30 seconds of Pete's glory, because he had taped the whole 30 minutes of the program, commercials and all. If I had wanted more punishment, there were a couple dozen more interview tapes, labelled with topics such as cloning, animal rights and "new drugs." Instead, I popped in one of his Victory at Sea tapes. A 30-minute episode of that old black and white documentary series helped me to imagine Pete in photo reconnaissance, fighting the Japanese in the South Pacific.

What a strange way to fight an enemy — with a camera. Curiously, the thought drew me to Pete's photo albums. There, I discovered that Pete's photos were well-composed, speaking much more eloquently than his words. His photos of tents, palm trees and bulldozers scraping runways from coral rock seemed more alive than the combat footage I'd just seen on the big TV screen. His still pictures had all the drama of the combat footage — the tom-tom beat of the carrier's anti-aircraft guns throwing streams of tracer and lead against the wasp-like descent of Japanese dive bombers.

As I looked through more albums, it became clear that all of Pete's photographs went to the essence of the subject — from the box camera pictures taken in his boyhood, to the numerous Everglades shots that he had taken recently. Strange that his cameras were not loaded now, ready for action.

Suddenly, I was very tired. I swabbed the mechanical pencil with a Q Tip which I placed it in a sandwich bag and stored in the freezer. I plugged my laptop into the telephone jack and sent an e-mail to Rebecca. I filled it with sweet nothings — sweet expressions of love, and nothing about the bad luck that came from stepping into Pete's shoes. Now, all that was left to do was sleep in his bed and hope that tomorrow would be a better day.

16   OH, SWEET JUSTICE

Praise the Lord! I woke up Friday morning and could remember all my presidents including Clinton. And no headache. What better way to start the day than to change the lock on the door of my new apartment? Pete's toolbox was under a pile of shoes on the closet floor. It wasn't very hard to find the right tools to remove the cylinder from the deadbolt lock. Took my bike from the other apartment and pointed it towards the nearest hardware store.

It was a pleasant enough trip, crossing Wagner Creek behind the building, following it along a parallel street, past the bungalows of the cheap lawyers, bail bondsmen and nursing temp services. I pedaled a few more blocks northeast through the Latin American neighborhood, waving to an occasional *ama de casa* and dodging the occasional yardbird. I pedaled north, passing a ma-and-pa-grocery that sold fresh eggs and live chickens, and arriving at the junction of 17th Avenue and 20th Street, the creek's subterranean headwaters.

The Allapattah Hardware store was just a few blocks farther north. Its multi-ethnic staff could say the words "key" and "lock cylinder" in many languages — including Spanish, Portuguese, Guyanan Dutch, French Creole, several varieties of island Patois and even English. They also knew the words for the monkey wrench and for the heavy-duty, chemical-resistant J-pipe that I selected.

And, most importantly for me, the staff was able to re-key my lock cylinder faster than the skateboarders and hiphoppers outside could get organized to steal my bicycle. I should have chained it *inside* the razor-wire perimeter fence.

On my way back, I made a sweep of the warehouse-commercial district along 20th Street. Here, Miami shows its entrepreneurial side, with warehouse stores specialized in such diverse consumer items as bikinis manufactured in Hialeah, straw hats from Nassau, ladies party dresses made in Brazil, S&M wear fashioned from authentic Argentine leather, and voodoo dolls, crafted in Haiti and topped with authentic shrunken monkey heads.

Maybe the monkey head totem was what I really needed to guard Pete's apartment. But I settled for a more high tech device, featured at an electronics export shop I knew. The salesman told me his doorknob-mounted alarm is very popular in Latin America, especially for business travelers who favor low-budget hotels. When the knob is turned or the door is jiggled, the gizmo's piezoelectrically driven crystal puts out an ear-piercing shriek that will throw even the meanest hombre off guard.

Who could call it a wasted morning? Reinstalling the re-keyed cylinder was easy. Installing the alarm to the inner doorknob was quite literally a snap, although it was an ear-splitting experience teaching myself how to deactivate it quickly.

The morning went splendidly until 10:15 a.m., when I went to the lab and dialed up the grumpy security supervisor. I asked him about the surveillance tape. The guy made me repeat my request, then stayed silent for a long time before answering. "Sorry. We didn't find anything on the tape."

He was hard to cross-examine. Yes, the tape was reviewed, but no, he couldn't tell me who reviewed it. It was a one-hour continuous loop, but he couldn't say what time they stopped it. Yes, he was sure it had been looked into competently, and if I didn't agree, I was welcome to talk to his supervisor, Jerry Cartlick.

That conversation left me running my fingers through my hair — quite literally. Touching the three-inch scar triggered memories of the clandestine investigation I'd done for Dr. Westley while a graduate student at the med school. And it reminded me of backlash from a couple of security thugs who did a not-so-clandestine investigation of me.

On Pete's shelves, I found a current school directory and directories for the last several years. Cross-checks of the pages confirmed that the thugs left the med school four years ago. Apparently, Dr. Alcibides, the previous dean, had done some housekeeping before stepping down. Jerry Cartlick took over a year later when Weisburd became dean. I remembered Rob telling me that Cartlick had previously been in charge of parking garage security for the Public Health Authority.

One last check showed that Grumpy wasn't listed in the old directory either. Apparently I was just dealing with fresh incompetence, and not with jaundiced corporate memory of Ben Candidi.

I dialed Cartlick's number and got his assistant, Ilse. Told her I wanted to complain about Grumpy's botched investigation. She gave me an appointment for 11:00 a.m.

The remaining three-quarters of an hour was too short to do anything but mull things over. It was long enough to wonder why the burglar's bag was empty. It was long enough to wonder if he had other reasons for entering the apartment. I started thinking about Pete's crusades — as ridiculous as they were — and wondered if the folder of hate mail in Pete's bedroom file cabinet had anything to do with last night's visit. Some of the letters were outright threatening.

Was it possible that Pete had not died of natural causes? Emerging from these thoughts, I noticed that my fingers were resting on the keypad of the phone. I punched in the number of my old mentor, Dr. Geoffrey A. Westley, Chief Medical Examiner of Miami-Dade County.

I owed the old expatriate Englishman a call, anyway, to let him know I was back in town. And my upcoming appointment would be a good excuse for holding the conversation down to one-half hour. His middle-aged secretary Doris picked up, and put me right through.

"Ben! So good to hear from you. What's the latest news from

Babylon? I'm missing all the juicy morsels. My telly's blown a tube."

His reference to the Clinton impeachment hearings rated a chuckle but his knowledge of consumer electronics called for a groan. "Try ABBA Radio & Video on Bird Road. Joe Kazekian still knows where to get vacuum tubes. He can repair your ancient phonograph, too."

My gibe probably went right over Dr. Westley's head.

"Oh, yes. Kazekian. That clever Armenian friend of yours who was so useful to Brian Broadmoore. ABBA? Is that what he calls his repair shop? After a primitive notion of God, I suppose. Sounds quite sacrilegious to me. I thought Armenians were more orthodox in this country. I have even heard that they make good Episcopalians!"

The Old Boy sure could revel in irrelevance! I imagined him pressing his pudgy, six decade old body back into his oversized leather swivel chair, telephone buried in a swatch of white hair, holding forth with enthusiasm while viewing multiple images of objects in his office through his brass and multi-faceted, lead crystal *dragonseye* ("Made in England, you know.") purchased at the Copper Kettle ("Very fine Episcopalians they are, John and Pamela ... very fine choristers, too!") as he engaged his intelligent but less cultivated partner in a multi-faceted conversation which, by rights, should last well into the afternoon.

I used every opportunity to keep the conversation on track. It took five minutes to dispense with the Patent Office, Rebecca's job and the *Diogenes*. My Bryan Medical School job description took another ten. This left me about five minutes to describe Peter Peterson and say I was interested in his death.

Then I popped the question. "The people around the med school told me he died of a heart attack, but I've never seen anything official. They found him floating in Wagner Creek, a canal by the med school. Could you do me a favor and see if your office did an autopsy on him?"

"Certainly. Do you suspect foul play?"

"Maybe. He was sort of a Don Quixote — always on a crusade. Most people just laughed at him, but he also ruffled a lot of feathers." I told Dr. Westley about the hate mail.

"Yes, I wouldn't mind looking into the matter for you. It would be off the record, of course, since a formal request would take several weeks to process and would be such a nuisance."

"Thanks." I gave him Pete Peterson's date of death and my phone number.

"Is there any other reason why you might suspect foul play?"

I told him about the unlawful entry of Pete's apartment just one day after Carole Vandoren had vacated it. I told him about the chase. He cut me off before I could describe how Grumpy botched the investigation.

"I don't know whether one is to be commended or scolded for chasing a burglar. The fellow could have pulled out a knife or a gun when he turned on you. Clever bit, though, using your metal pen. But the guard was right. You probably shouldn't keep the bloody pen as evidence. Your pen might become a double-edged sword, so to speak." He paused to emphasize his splayed pun, forcing me to respond with a half-hearted laugh. "Given the state of our present-day legal system . . . with rapacious lawyers swarming like a plague of locusts, blotting out the sun . . ."

Once the Old Boy got himself wound up in a biblical or historical analogy, there was no stopping him. But I had to, or I'd be late for my appointment with Cartlick. I ended the conversation, promising Dr. Westley to take his advice.

I hadn't visited the Security Office since getting my photo I.D. several years back. It was on the top floor of a converted 30-story apartment building located on the southwest side of the medical campus. It had the same mix of outpatient clinics and apartments as my building, but here they were all served by the same elevator. Access to the clinical floors was controlled by magnetically locked doors with small reinforced windows. Access to the residential floors was unprotected. I wondered if the residential tenants had any problems with lock-picking burglars.

I verified the security department's 30th floor location using the wall-mounted directory, then stepped into the elevator. My fellow passengers were a nurse and a gaggle of questionnaire-clutching elderly lady outpatients. They all got off at the "Women's Health Study" clinic on the tenth floor. The nurse inserted her card in the sensor, saving the ladies having pick up the wall-mounted telephone to get buzzed in. I thought of Dr. Taylor's sarcastic description of the four-million dollar project on the effects of dietary fiber on osteoporosis. Hopefully the ladies would get *some* benefit for their time spent in the study. Hopefully the study would record several scientific measurements on their blood, kidneys and bones.

I stepped out of the elevator at the top floor and walked up to the buzzer-activated door. My choices were the telephone or the magnetic card-reader. Would the magnetic strip on my photo I.D. still work? I detached it from my belt and ran it through the reader. The little red screen flashed, "entrance denied." So I picked up the telephone apparatus and punched in zero.

"Yes?" answered a female voice.

"Joe sent me."

My wisecrack was answered by a click and buzzing of the door. I entered and told Ilse behind the desk that I had an appointment with Mr. Cartlick. She got up and conducted me to his office.

Seated behind his desk, Cartlick didn't look much different from when he walked into the General Faculty meeting the day before. His desk was a large, rounded, tiered affair like the news anchors have on TV. My earlier impression of Cartlick as a used car salesman was reinforced when he came around to offer his hand, although his shake was a little soft. He wasn't very tall, maybe an inch taller than me. "Dr. Candidi, what can I do for you?"

I told him about last night's burglary and of my dissatisfaction with the "police report." I pulled it out and handed to him. I complained that the supervisor didn't stop the security tape before it was overwritten. Cartlick just sat quietly behind his desk, listening impatiently but without interrupting, regarding me with suspicious eyes that seemed to hover above his carefully trimmed moustache.

"I'm sorry, Dr. Candidi, but I can't alter the officer's report. Nobody is allowed to change a report. I wasn't there and I have no reason to believe his report was in error."

"You could take my statement."

"No, but you can write me a letter if you feel like it." He glanced at the top of his desk.

"Would you verify the bruise on my head?"

"No, you should go to *Dade County General* for that."

The guy was becoming cocky and combative. If I continued to assert my rights, this would probably devolve into a head-butting contest.

"I understand. You have done all that you will do." I said this while getting to my feet.

Cartlick got to his feet and extended a hand across the desk. While shaking his hand, I verified what I had suspected. The desk was terraced to accommodate small video monitors. There were four of them. They seemed to be switching from one location to another.

I couldn't resist taking a parting shot. "Yeah, I can imagine it is easy for a security tape to fall through the cracks when you have so many security cameras wired up around the medical campus."

He acknowledged my remark with an elevation of eyebrows and then let loose his own shot. "Dr. Candidi, while you are here, can you think of anything else we can do for you?"

"No."

He dropped his eyes to my waist. "You might want to update your photo I.D."

"Oh," I said. He got me there. The magnetic strip was probably out of date and the photo with the three-inch ponytail was sure as hell out of date.

Cartlick pressed the point. "We can also change the magnetic strip to show that you are *Doctor* Candidi and no longer a student. And we won't bother with an interdepartmental requisition or that this isn't a normal day for I.D. operations. Just consider it an apology for any shortcomings last night."

I was slow to find words of acceptance.

Cartlick called out the door. "Ilse! Please fix Dr. Candidi up with a new picture and a magnetic strip."

I told her I was working with animals and would need access to the veterinary core of the building. She fixed me right up. It was hard to stay mad at a guy who had just saved my department an estimated $50.

A few minutes after I'd returned to the office, Franz appeared in my doorway wearing an impish grin. "Time for the departmental faculty meeting."

It seemed like I'd gone to a heck of a lot of faculty meetings. However, eternal vigilance is the price of liberty — as Thomas Jefferson said.

"Be right with you."

Along the way, Franz told me that Assistant Dean Kotzen had

complained to the other assistant deans that Franz had dared to argue with him. "He said that I was taking over Peter Peterson's place as trouble-maker. Those were his exact words."

How did Franz manage to survive here? Did he have the ghost of William Tell for a guardian angel?

GRIPE SESSION 17

I entered the room looking forward to the chance to contribute to the democratic workings of my new department and to spend quality time with my new colleagues while eating a brown bag lunch.

We had only two agenda items. Assistant Professor Ron Price handed out the medical student teaching assignments. Luckily, my name was not on the list. Pete never had any assignments, either. I guess they didn't trust him in front of 150 medical school sophomores.

The next agenda item was a report from Professor Hilda Beecher on graduate student affairs. She lovingly described the progress made by our eight graduate students. She had a reputation as a Great Nurturer.

We cleared the agenda faster than our chairman Boyle could clear his paper plate of potato chips. He frowned and asked for items from the floor.

What followed was a gripe session. Ron Price complained about Kotzen's visit and how we would have to use our grants to buy "goddamn office supplies." Hilda Beecher grunted her objection to his profane language, and Boyle promised to bring up the question at the next chairmen's meeting with the dean. Yes, Boyle was a true philosopher-king, ready to let everybody speak his piece.

Next, John Falk complained how Administration was gouging the grants with high prices for everything from photocopies to boarding costs of laboratory rats. Beecher shook her head and said, "Now, now." Boyle made a sour face and said we couldn't change it any more than the weather.

Then Ron Price said he'd heard rumors that the dean was going to ratchet up the "production quota" for bringing in outside money, raising it from an unbearable 50% to an impossible 60% of faculty salaries.

Hilda Beecher reacted like she'd gotten a shooting pain. She told us that many proposals weren't funded because they were poorly written. If we would just mind our programs, keep our paragraphs well-balanced and make sure that every proposed experiment was clearly explained, there was no reason why our proposals shouldn't be funded.

Ron reminded Hilda that nationwide, every year, more scientists are competing for fewer grants. He said that a falling tide lowers all boats.

A frown came over Franz' face. He raised a hand and waited patiently for everyone's attention. "There is one thing that has never made sense, and it never will make sense." He spoke slowly, as if he were reciting the proof of a geometric theorem. "Let us accept that Dean Weisburd has less and less money to pay his faculty. Okay, that is accepted. He does not have the money. But then, why does he go around hiring new faculty? And why does he keep putting up new buildings that will require him to hire new faculty to keep them full?"

"We all know the answer to that one," Boyle answered, with a shake of the head.

I, too, knew the answer. The dean didn't care about the individual scientists; he just cared about the overhead money they brought in.

But Franz was not satisfied with an ironic answer. He was seeking a statement of truth and wanted a literal answer. "No, I cannot say that I know why he hires more faculty and builds more buildings." Franz settled his gaze on Boyle.

"You're starting to sound like Pete," Boyle said.

"I do not take that as an insult," Franz said with resignation. "Pete was always honest. Pete always — how do you say? — called a spade a spade."

Boyle said, "Pete isn't here anymore, so you have to decide among yourselves who's going to tie the bell around the cat's neck. None of you said anything in the General Faculty meeting the other day. And none of you said anything to Kotzen. And since I doubt that any of you are going to do it, I'll tell you what answers you would get. If you would criticize the dean's new buildings, he would say that buildings are what the wealthy donors like to give money for. If you would criticize his recruiting policy, he would tell you — indirectly of course because he can't come out and say it — that the new hires are star players who are good at getting grant money. He'd tell you that they more than pay for themselves with the overhead they generate."

If I started worrying about this, I would get depressed.

Ron Price picked up the gauntlet. "Yes, but we generate a lot of overhead, too. So what about giving some of that overhead money back to us? Where the hell is that money going?"

Beecher said, "Now, now, now! That is the dean's business, not the faculty's."

Boyle didn't lift his eyes from his paper plate. "You know where that goes. We all know where it goes."

It was strange how abruptly Beecher's and Boyle's remarks stopped the discussion. No one said another word.

At Administration's command, we would have to bring in more money. It was the dean's money and we had no say about it. We could grumble to each other, but it was taboo to complain to Administration itself.

Would our world plunge into chaos if any of us broke the taboo?

Suddenly, I realized that the discussion was over and I hadn't said a single word. No, Ben, it was right for you to stay out of it. You have enough problems already. Just put Pete's money to good use for the two years and then get out.

Boyle declared the meeting adjourned. When I got up to leave, Boyle detained me with an outstretched arm. "Ben, there will be an organizational meeting for a Program Project Grant proposal, coming Monday. They're trying to put together a group of researchers working on ageing, with special emphasis on Alzheimer's disease. The people from the Project to Cure Stroke will probably get the lion's share of the money, but you should give it a try. You should be able to come up with something about anti-oxidants, if someone hasn't thought about it already."

How nice of him to be looking out for me.

"Thanks. It sounds good. I'll go for it."

"I thought you would. I told Dr. Luke McDougal to expect you. He's the designated organizer. The first meeting is next

Monday afternoon. You should bring a two-page summary of your proposed project."

Back in the lab, I thought a lot about the project while fixing the leaking pipe. I took off the old pipe, lined up the new one, and went next door to borrow some plumber's compound from the physical plant guys. It gave me a chance to speak some Spanish. When I asked them why the estimate on the repair was so expensive, one of the guys cracked a scrambled eggs joke and told me to ask Ready-Serve Plumbing.

The repair took me less than half an hour. I presented Olga with Allapattah Hardware Store receipts, totalling $72.50, including the wrench. She said that Administration might deny a reimbursement because the store might not be an approved vendor. I said they should cut me some slack because I was new here.

Although it was the worst of times, it was also the best of times. Back at my desk, I spent four exciting hours brainstorming on how Pete's work dovetailed with my past work on the protein phosphatase enzyme and cellular control. I planned dozens of exciting experiments that would clarify the effects of bad-guy superoxide and hydroxyl free radicals on my enzyme. I drew up protocols for measuring malonaldehyde, ubiquinone, glutathione peroxidase and even the cellular energy level. Yes, I would be able to hand in a good proposal for the Program Project on Ageing next week.

My brainstorm was interrupted a few minutes before five o'clock by a phone call from Dr. Westley.

"Ben, I am calling back with the information you requested. We did perform an autopsy on Dr. Peterson. The information in the file indicates he died a natural death. The autopsy revealed no sign of foul play."

"What was the cause of death?"

"It would appear to be a fatal arrhythmia leading to unconsciousness and then drowning, although there was less water in the lungs than one would expect from a typical drowning."

"So the examiner chose arrhythmia because other causes were absent. Was there any positive reason to suspect arrhythmia?" It was an aggressive question but I had to ask.

Dr. Westley cleared his throat. "Sudden onset arrhythmia is a common cause for cases of sudden death among 74-year-old men. From the absence of a clot, the examining M.E. deduced that it was not a coronary occlusion. He ruled out foul play because there was no sign of a struggle, no broken neck, no sign of strangulation, and no petechial hemorrhages."

Dr. Westley laid in a pause.

"By way of reminder, a petechial hemorrhage is the bursting of small blood vessels in the eyes and skin that is observed in strangulation. When the veins of the neck are compressed, the heart is signalled to pump harder, and extremely high blood pressures are produced. All these signs were absent."

"Could it have been possible that someone hit Dr. Peterson on the back of the head?"

"The M.E. would have seen trauma. The autopsy was done by Xavier Martinez, one of my best medical examiners. And we were especially cognizant of the question because of the information in the police report."

"Could it be possible that Dr. Peterson received a lethal injection?"

"As in an assisted suicide?" he answered, impatiently.

"No, I didn't mean a voluntary I.V. injection. I was thinking of an intramuscular injection. Like someone walked up to him and stuck a needle in his arm."

At first, Dr. Westley did not answer. All I heard was a train of high-pitched grunts, accompanied by a rustling of paper. "A multidrug screen was performed. It came out negative."

"And there were no needle marks?"

More grunting and rustling. "None was noted."

"So we can rule out an injection?"

This time, Dr. Westley's high-pitched prevocalizations were louder. They covered a wide range of vowel sounds before landing and strengthening on the consonant m. "M . . . m . . . may I learn the basis of your persistent inquiries?"

"I don't know. It's just that Dr. Peterson was so outspoken on so many controversial issues — against animal rights, for abortion and for assisted suicide. He got a lot of hate mail. He was a lightning rod for controversy. If one of these groups — "

" — these lunatic fringe groups can certainly be violent. When one stirs up violent emotions, one might expect a violent death — violent, as in *gunshot*. But I can assure you that Dr. Peterson's death was by no means violent. And as for the incident in your apartment, obviously you surprised a burglar. These things happen ... Oh, dear! Doris is making signals that I am needed elsewhere. Sorry, I have to ring off. Perhaps you could come to my apartment, some time, for a nip of sherry." (Click)

Mildred had already left. It was time to call it a day. A Friday. Time to call it a week. So much time spent, and so little progress. And so much that it didn't make sense. Was Pete Peterson really nutty enough to think his rants and ravings were a crusade?

I searched again. I spent another hour rechecking his hard drive, file by file for anything resembling a crusade. I found absolutely nothing that would justify his use of the term.

Before turning off the computer, I composed a love-and-kisses e-mail to Rebecca, censoring all hints of frustration. What a frustrating week it had been. The harder I tried to tie up the loose ends, the more new ones came popping out.

18   FAMILY AFFAIR

I went back to Pete's apartment. Against Rebecca's advice, I cooked a fast dinner of "camping slop." I ate it glumly, considering what to do with the evening. Usually Friday nights were for going to a movie with Rebecca. I longed to call her, but couldn't bring myself to pick up the phone. There was too much up in the air — too much that I couldn't explain, even to myself.

I couldn't treat myself to a movie while the Pete Peterson biography project hung over my head. I compromised by staying home and watching the remainder of the two dozen video clips in which Pete made his pronouncements for the 6:00 p.m. and 11:00 p.m. news.

This time I viewed them efficiently. I fast-forwarded through the tape until his big head filled the screen. Then I backed up and listened to the story. It was always a local station's work-up of a national story — lung transplants; human genes injected into pig embryos to make pig hearts transplantable into humans; Kervorkian's latest assisted suicide.

First came the network's footage. Then the local newsguy or

gal poked his or her microphone in Peter Peterson's broad, heavy-boned face for a 30-second sound bite. The bites were as smooth as what comes out of a wood-chipping machine. Sentence fragments stuck out like splinters — too raw to swallow, although the reporters did their best to sugar-coat them.

Sometimes the reporter would summarize by calling the question "controversial," then let Pete dangle. Sometimes they described him as a "maverick professor from Bryan Medical School." In one case they used a 30-second sound bite from a local physician, followed by a 10-second goofy-bite of Pete so they could comment that the topic was "full of controversy."

What a shame, those TV interviews! It was a shame because many of his comments were grounded in common sense. If only he had used shorter sentences. If only he could have stopped going off on tangents. If only he had held his head still. And why did he always glance directly into the camera?

No, he was just a convenient fool for the local TV news people when they needed quick reaction filler. None of his clips ever made it to national television. His story never made the "big time" — to quote that curious expression he used in his will.

But I kept working and transformed Pete's sound bites into five pages in my laptop computer.

Next to his video tapes, I found a trove of hand-labelled audio tapes of Pete's appearances on talk radio. Unfortunately, these tapes were not as easy to fast-forward. Each tape started with about 30 minutes of calls and discussion of a controversial topic, often biomedical. Then came Pete, for a minute or two. Then I had to listen to another half an hour of contributions from other callers.

Sometimes Pete called the station to correct misinformation from a previous caller; often he was responding to someone else's ridiculous statement made half an hour earlier. The shock jock sometimes agreed with him, but more often tried to make a fool of him.

On radio, Pete's opinions did sound more like a crusade. If his impassioned comments on these diverse topics had a common denominator, it would be a crusade for common sense and against mendacity and stupidity. He even might have achieved a certain eloquence if he had not been so quick to criticize others.

By one o'clock in the morning, I had 20 pages of quotes. Time to call it a night.

Saturday morning, I was back on the job, going through his personal stuff. His photo albums did the best job of telling the story of his life. The high school annuals showed me what it was like to be a teenager in the 1930s. In his closet I found two shoe boxes full of letters which showed a very human side.

But I never did find the diary mentioned in his will.

I created files in my computer for the phases of his life: early childhood, adolescence, young adulthood, military, college and later life. I spent hours filling the material into the right section. By late afternoon, I had roughed in 60 pages.

Pete was born in Grand Rapids, Michigan on May 20, 1924. He went to school there, through high school. In the earliest album, obviously arranged by his parents, black and white photos were held carefully by triangular corner mounts pasted on black paper. Underneath, the pictures were labelled and dated in white ink. The pictures told many stories — of Pete and his brother Tommy fishing in the Grand River in the summer and sledding in John Ball Park in the winter; of their proud, formal father and loving mother; and of their narrow, two-story Victorian house on Knapp Street. Young Pete always looked so protective of little Tommy who was one year younger.

Pete attended Union High School. He did not play any sports, although several pictures revealed him an enthusiastic softball player at picnics. The Union yearbook showed him playing bass drum in the marching band. From the way his fellow students signed his senior yearbook, it was clear that he was a good Joe. One student held him in higher regard. "I'll wait for you," wrote Linda McClure, in a flowing, rounded hand. She had elongated the M of her last name and closed it at the bottom to suggest a heart.

Linda had also signed his annuals for his junior and sophomore years, but not his freshman year. I looked her up in the index and found her picture — dark blond and pretty. She was the type of girl you would think of when you see a big, red valentine in the drugstore. She was a year behind him in school.

Pete graduated high school on June 7, 1942, six months after Pearl Harbor. On the next day, he enlisted in the Navy. He shipped out to basic training a few days later. He was trained as a photo reconnaissance interpreter and was then moved to the Pacific Theater.

The story of Pete in the Navy was told in the collection of

letters from the two shoe boxes. He wrote faithfully to his mom, dad and Tommy. The letters were written on flimsy "airmail paper" and folded into small envelopes that they used back in those days. He must have taken them back after his parents died. They were filled with understated descriptions of Navy life, first on shore and then on a carrier.

In the later part of the war, Pete was assigned to the Marines, moving from airfield to airfield during the island-hopping campaign. He said little about the actual fighting. A couple of times, he apparently did, because portions were cut out by the censor. I found a lot of anecdotes about military life. Each letter ended with an assurance that he was taking care of himself and to not worry.

More revealing were the occasional letters from Linda and the carbon copies of letters he had sent to her. He repeated the messages to his family, but often referred to the "promises I made that night at the prom." He signed them, "Love, Pete."

Linda's letters were full of teenage banalities. She signed them with, "Fondly, Linda." After graduating, she got a job as a cashier in a cafeteria. Several months later she wrote that it would be hard to keep up the correspondence. It was the last letter. On that envelope was written, in Pete's hand, "From the girl who married someone else."

Pete's bookshelves were full of material on the Second World War — books on the naval battles, memoirs and handbooks cataloging battleships and airplanes — probably 50 books in total. Folded and tucked in a handbook on military aircraft, I found a dozen typewritten pages. It was the start of a memoir, apparently written several years after the war. The page showed a strangely designed, two-engine fighter. Its fuselage was stubby and tailless. The engines were mounted on each side of the wing. Their housings extended all the way back to form a double tail which surrounded the fuselage but did not touch it. The book said it was a P-38 Lightning, a fast pursuit plane with an unmatched top speed and rate of climb.

On the inserted, yellowed pages was written the story of First Class Petty Officer Peter Peterson's flights in this plane. He had ridden on photo reconnaissance missions. His job was to control the nose-mounted cameras after the pilot "dipped the stick." He described how his cameras "picked up the scared looks on the Japs' faces as we came screaming down out of the clouds." The missions were to probe island defenses before sending in the Marines for an amphibious assault. It was an enthusiastic description, written in a good-guys-versus-the-bad-guys spirit. I would use it verbatim. What a shame he hadn't written more.

One year before Hiroshima, Pete was transferred Stateside for service at the Great Lakes Naval Training Center near Chicago. When the war ended, he was a chief petty officer.

In 1946 Pete went to the University of Michigan and studied chemistry. He finished in four years, then studied biochemistry at Washington University, in St. Louis. I found his master's thesis on the bookshelf. The work was on an enzyme important to carbohydrate metabolism. The M.S. degree was granted in 1952. He stayed on at Washington University to extend the work, receiving a Ph.D. in 1956.

He came to Bryan Medical School in 1958, as the third man in their biochemistry department. His main job was to teach the medical students biochemistry. He also set up a lab to continue his enzyme studies. This led to his anti-oxidant work which I had already reviewed.

The photo albums from his Miami period revealed some social life but no close relationships. There were photos taken of groups — beach picnics with students and pictures of colleagues. But there were no girlfriends or lady friends. The shoe boxes contained no more love letters.

The albums contained some shots of his niece Carole as a little girl, sometimes at play and more often standing in front of her mother and her father, Pete's brother Tommy. Carole had the same broad forehead and blond-headed good looks as her mother, just like Pete's teenage sweetheart. Carole was always looking into the camera. Strangely, the parents always seemed to be looking to opposite sides.

Was Pete a born bachelor or did things just turn out that way? Only one girlfriend, then off to war as a teenager. He fell in love with science, but never again with a woman. In fact, his only interest in women seemed to be those vintage Playboys under his nightstand. To me, their "girl next door" centerfolds looked more like the woman living down the hall. How flat, those reproductions! How unconvincing, the colors! Today, those pictures are laughable — those living room poses that hid the pubic hair behind strategically placed easy chairs and hid the nipples behind lamp shades. In the most risqué of the bunch, the model had improvised a bikini top using a man's tie. I guess that was pushing the limit, back then. Much more interesting were the black-and-white action photos showing the same woman at work as a secretary or bank teller. Pretty gutsy for a woman to model nude back then. Most interesting were the "Vargas Girls," those pure creations from ink and paint, so stylized, statuesque and unapproachable. Were these the qualities that most appealed to Peter Peterson?

So where's the beef, man?

Were these the magazines that Boyle said they had found laying around? And who had seen them and spread the rumor? They couldn't be referring to the Proceedings of the Naval Institute which Pete had cut up and organized into binders. I had trouble imagining the apartment as a mess.

Pete was a man of no vices. Judging from his collection of pipes, knots and whittled sticks, he kept his hands busy and everything shipshape.

With my laptop computer now brimming with about 100 pages of material, I decided it was time to round out the picture by interviewing Carole. On Saturday mid-afternoon, she should be home. I punched in her number in Traverse City, Michigan.

The phone was answered by her husband, Jacob Vandoren. He sounded at least 10 years older than her, and spoke gruffly. Maybe he didn't approve of *any* man calling her from Miami, even one who spoke deferentially with an adolescent tenor voice.

"It's for you, Carole. Someone in Miami who calls himself Candidi."

In the background, I heard her muttering an explanation involving "Uncle Pete" and "lawyer."

"Yes, Dr. Candidi. You are probably calling about Dr. Peterson's things." She sounded oh so formal.

Jacob was still grumbling. Maybe this guy's doctor should write him a prescription for Viagra. Maybe the prescription should include a second honeymoon at Niagara Falls.

"Yes, Carole, I have made good progress in getting his things organized. And I have been working on his biography."

"Yes, it is good that you have been making progress. What can I do for you?"

"I have some questions about Pete. Do you have time?"

"Yes."

I mentioned some of the things I had learned that morning. Then I popped the question. "Did Pete ever have a serious girlfriend?"

"No. I don't think he did too well with women. He was too goofy."

"So there was never a girlfriend you knew about?"

"I once heard something . . . that he might have had one as a teenager. But I don't really know anything about it."

"Was he close with his brother — your father?"

"I think they used to be. But after Pete came home from the war, something came between them."

"Do you have any idea what it could have been?"

"Pete was a big war hero, and he let everyone know about it. Daddy was 4-F, and was never drafted."

"What did your dad do after high school?"

"He moved up north and got into the lumber business. Then he settled down in Traverse City and married my mother."

"When was that?"

"It must have been in . . . 1943."

"What is your mother's name?"

"Linda."

"Was she from Traverse City?"

"No, she was from Grand Rapids."

"Did she know your father in Grand Rapids?"

"I don't know. She never told me too much about herself as a girl."

"What was her maiden name?"

"Linda McClure."

Pictures of the blond highschool girl and Carole's blond-haired mother fused into one. A complicated jigsaw puzzle self-assembled before my eyes. I tried to continue in the same tone of voice. "Would it be possible to talk to your father?"

"No, he died three years ago. Cancer."

"I'm sorry. Would it be possible to talk to your mother?"

"She wouldn't be able to tell you much about Pete. He hardly ever came to visit. And now she has a lot of trouble talking. She had a stroke last year and we had to put her in a nursing home."

"I'm sorry."

Jacob was muttering and grumbling in the background.

"Excuse me a minute." Carole laid down the receiver. Jacob was saying he'd be going out on an errand. He said Carole shouldn't stay on the phone too long. It sounded like she was following him to the back door. When she returned to the phone, Carole sounded a lot less formal. "So how are you doing, Ben? That's a real nice city you're living in."

"Yes, but I'm sure Traverse City is awfully nice, too. Especially in the summer. I just have a couple more biographical questions."

"Okay."

"You don't have any brothers or sisters."

"I had a brother. But he died before I was born."

"What did he die of?"

"Some kind of respiratory infection. I don't know. They didn't have so many antibiotics in those days. He was four."

"When was he born?"

"Some time in the middle of the war."

"Second World War?"

"Yes," she answered, hesitantly. "Mom and Dad didn't talk about it much . . . Can't we talk about something more pleasant? It's raining, here. How's the weather down there?"

"Great. Did you make the girls jealous with your tan?"

"Yes, and how! Your advice was *so* good — where to shop for the right clothes and everything. I had such a great time. I'd really like to come down again. Maybe we could find some reason . . ."

"Sure, bring down your husband this time."

"I wasn't thinking of it *that* way." She said it light-heartedly.

"But *I* was." It was hard to project a jocular mood while telling her "no way."

"Ben, dear, the only way I could get *him* to come down would be for fishing."

"Sure. Tell him the Watson Island Marina is full of boats that will take him out trawling in the Gulf Stream for forty dollars a night."

"Yes, that would keep him busy," she said with disgust. "Look, I really have to go, now." Charm had not worked and she was offended.

"I just have one more quick question. Did Uncle Pete tell you lately that he was working on anything that could be described as a crusade?"

"He was always on a crusade."

"No, I mean some special crusade, like what he mentioned in his will. Like what I am supposed to write a book about. Because I can't find anything noteworthy — just a lot of spouting off about cloning and experimentation with animals."

" — and how science is going to save the world."

"His will mentioned a diary. Did he keep a diary?"

"If he did, I didn't see it in the apartment."

"Did you throw away anything in his apartment?"

"No, just an ashtray full of ashes and stinky old pipe cleaners."

"Did you find a lot of things lying around?"

"No, just some of those navy magazines. I put them back on the coffee table."

"And you never found any file folders lying around or any drawers open or things lying on the floor."

"No. What are you getting at?"

"I'm tearing my hair out, trying to find any evidence of any project of his that might qualify as a crusade."

"I don't know about anything like that. He was a loony." Impatience was setting in.

"And you don't have any papers from him that might help to explain what he was talking about?"

"No," she said, loudly. "Ben, dear, you are a very handsome guy. And I know you can be very charming, when you want to. But when you keep on going with this Uncle Pete stuff, you are almost as bad as him. It makes me want to scream. Now be a nice boy and work hard on giving away those things in his apartment so we can get our money."

"I promise."

"And if you want me to come down and help you . . ."

"No. I can handle it myself."

"Then do it. Bye." (Click)

LAURA 19

I had an outline and 100 pages of copy. And the story made me sick. I pictured the gangly teenager skating alone on frozen ponds in the winter and discovering love in the springtime. How cruel when winter returns in April. Blossoming love was placed in limbo when he answered his country's call. While he was risking his life, his sweetheart ran off and married his brother. The blossom was frozen down to the stem cells, never to bloom again. He returned a prisoner of war: a boy war-hero and male spinster, imprisoned in a bipartite soul, rendered incapable of self-examination and condemned to an ever-tightening spiral of goofiness and spite, culminating in a bogus crusade.

There was nothing useful in that damn bedroom file cabinet. I jerked the middle door open so hard that the files tipped into the empty space in the drawer. Okay, I'd just look through this junk one last time. Once more, I went through the files on animal research, cloning, organ transplant and found nothing new. There was only one file I had overlooked and it contained only two sheets of paper. It was a poem, written in forced rhyme and doggerel cadence. The poem seemed to be inspired by "Birdie, birdie, in the sky; dropped some whitewash in my eye." Except that Pete didn't even spell "Birdie" correctly. He spelled it "Burdie."

The poem seemed to be about discovering a bird nest and taking pictures of birds in their nest until one "Burdie" dropped whitewash in his eye. Then there was something about piling the family into a "Tin Lizzie" and taking a ride.

He fancied himself a poet, as well?

That did it. I snapped. Had to get out of this apartment. Had to expel the silly old man from my mind. I walked to the window and looked out. There might still be a couple more hours of light left in the day. Changed into swimsuit under my shorts. Wrapped a pair of swim goggles in a towel and put it on the rat-trap carrier of my bicycle. Wheeled the bike out of the apartment building and rode down 12th Avenue. The waters of Biscayne Bay would wash clean my body and mind.

But pedal as hard as I could, the spirit of Pete followed me all the way through Little Havana. What sickened me most was that damn tin-eared literal-mindedness — that inability to think intuitively or imaginatively. I bet he couldn't tell that the girl didn't really love him. I bet he couldn't tell that his colleagues regarded his research as run-of-the-mill.

Science is a profession where it isn't enough to prove the other guy wrong. Anybody can take an accepted theory, rewrite it in bold letters, and then throw a lot of stuff up at it to show that it doesn't work in every case. To do your work properly in science, you have to think up your *own* new hypothesis and then start throwing cowshit against it *yourself*. Only after your work survives every bullshit test you can think up, *only then* can you announce it to the world.

In science, it isn't good enough to stand up on a chair like a ham actor — like some 19th century Swedish doctor — and cry out that the water's not pure enough. You can't make yourself look good by making someone else look bad. And there's no room for sarcasm. By its very nature, science is a humbling profession. Pete had no right to mock others' aspirations or their "revered theories."

Literal-minded Peter Peterson couldn't float a new theory any more than he could float in Biscayne Bay with a millstone around his neck.

In the heart of Little Havana, I passed a familiar restaurant. Its sign showed a decrepit knight on a swaybacked mare, and a servant on a donkey in the background. Quixotic! That was the best I could say about Pete. A simple-minded man on an obsessional quest for grandeur.

But I didn't get rid of him so easily. Images of Pete pursued me through the Roads Section, past Ted Walden's office and all the way out to the Rickenbacker Causeway. I locked the bike to a tree right before the broad-arched bridge leading to Key Biscayne, and went for a long swim. The sight of other people helped remove the goofball from my mind. Along the narrow strip of sand and tree-lined asphalt, Cubans, Nicaraguans and a host of other nationalities were barbecuing and playing loud radios in their parked cars. Women and children were lying in hammocks strung between Australian pines.

I waded through the sea weed and turtle grass toward the sun, now setting over the Vizcaya Mansion. The sun's reddish glow reflected from the tall cumulus clouds that had built up over downtown skyscrapers to my right. Oh, what I would have given for my green-eyed lady to be standing next to me now, water dripping from her straight black hair, the reddish glow on her cheeks

I'd waded two hundred yards out. The warm water was up to my waist. I knelt, put on my goggles and pushed off, immersing myself in the same water that was floating the *Diogenes* a thousand miles to the north. Was Rebecca on board?

It was a baptism of sort — a reconnection between soul and body through a healing ritual known as the Australian Crawl. Sun-warmed sea grass flowed under me. Each stroke of my arm into the grassy bed released trapped warm water that massaged my stomach and legs. Each stroke created a *schlieren* effect in the warmed salt water, distorting the grassy bottom as if viewed through wavy plastic.

I swam ever harder and faster, parallel to shore. I didn't stop until my chest hairs had filtered a kilometer of sea water. How good it was to pump the lungs with fresh, moist air; to pump blood through my heart; and to drain the lymph and the bad humors that had been collected all day in the dead man's apartment.

Finally, after the sun had sunk behind the trees, I waded back and dried myself off. Nobody seemed to notice while I exchanged my wet swimsuit for Fruit of the Looms. I put on my khaki shorts and shirt, mounted my bike, and rode in the direction of home. The thought of a can of beans at Pete's place slowed me down while nearing Little Havana. Black beans with yellow rice, *frijoles con arroz*, and with pork cubes seemed like a better deal.

I chose one of those restaurants with a sidewalk service window where you can savor a *café cubano* while standing. Inside, it had a line of small tables, sandwiched between a counter with rotating stools and a long mirrored wall. The open-faced *muchacha* working the counter smiled as I entered, so I took a stool. After a couple of minutes, I was flirting with her in Spanish. Neither of us took it serious — it just helped to pass the time — and the cook in the back didn't seem to mind. In fact, we livened up the place enough to attract a lot more customers. I left a good tip under the plate. Paid up front where the old-fashioned register sat on the glass case filled with opened boxes of cigars.

Returning to Pete's apartment in no mood to work, I flipped on his TV and scanned the cable channels. I settled on American Movie Classics which was showing a black and white flick called

"Laura." The host said it was made in 1944 and was one of the original examples of *film noir*. It wasn't bad for a film that was half a century old, although the plot was simplistic and the detective spent too much time in the presumed victim's apartment, looking at her portrait and wallowing in pity.

The theme song did a good job pulling it through. It was a complicated, dreamy piece played by a full orchestra, with a lot of lush coverage by the violin section. The arranger switched tempo from ballad to waltz and back to ballad, giving it a mercurial feel. The music stayed with me as I lay down and fell asleep.

That evening must have rejuvenated me because early Sunday morning I was attacking the Pete-project with gusto. By noon, I had 130 pages of narrative. By late afternoon, I had integrated his P-38 airborne reconnaissance memoir with the quotes from his letters and his photos of the airfields. After two more hours, I had selected and captioned enough photos to cover his whole life. As goofy as he was, he sure had an eye for a good picture.

With good conscience, I was able to quit around five that Sunday evening. I jogged around the neighborhood, returning in time to fix a real dinner which I ate while watching Sixty Minutes. Afterwards, I was in no mood to be touched by an angel or even to be Angela'd. I killed the T.V. and pulled from the shelf one of Pete's Clive Cussler books, *Inca Gold*. But then came second thoughts. The book might prove interesting and cost me 20 hours to finish.

Instead, I picked up the controller for Pete's stereo tuner and pressed the power button. Button Number One was set for public radio, WLRN. Number Two was for an oldies station, and Number Three was for a 24-hour news station. I went back to the public radio station.

I recognized the program's sign-on music right away. A puff and a chuff, and the clanking of metal, and I could almost smell the oil-doped water vapor of released steam as Ted Grossman's Night Train pulled out of the station. The guy played a lot of big band stuff — the music that helped the G.I.s fight World War II.

After a couple of choruses of "Night Train" came Ted's deep New York style voice. "The next few cuts we'll be featuring 'Laura,' one of the great songs of all time. We'll start with a radio transcription from a 1945 broadcast, then we'll play the famous version from Charlie Parker with Strings, then we'll play a wonderful rendition by Bill Harris, that great jazz trombonist who lived in Ft. Lauderdale. Of course, this wonderful song was written for the film of the same name."

What a coincidence. Had the guy been watching AMC along with me last night?

The first selection had the feel of a live, A.M. broadcast. The band started with an eight-bar introduction, carried by alto and tenor saxes, lined by silvery clarinets semi-harmonizing in upper register. They built to a climax, then stepped down to make way for the vocalist, who sang the first verse of the ballad in a sincere baritone.

He sang that Laura was a haunting *deja vu* that plays tricks on your memory, catching you by surprise. And that she gave your very first kiss to you, and she's only a dream. Scenes from the movie played before my eyes — the upward-facing shot of the portrait and the detective's rummaging through the drawers and closets. Funny, the power of the music to evoke feelings and frame memories.

Slowly, the ephemeral Laura was replaced by images of Linda, Pete's teenage sweetheart. These were followed by images of a gawky 18-year-old in the sailor's uniform and by the 1940s calendar girls who followed the men to war.

Then it came to me: Here *I* was, just like the detective, wallowing in a dead person's apartment. I was wandering around Pete's apartment at slow fox-trot tempo, in sync with the wistful Laura tune played in four-four time. Awkward! Square! That's what Pete was. As square as the frame of that kitschy picture hanging over his bed.

The strings did an interlude and the band switched the song in waltz tempo. Funny how dropping one beat per measure made the song so natural, so elegant. I couldn't imagine Peter waltzing with Linda under the reflecting globe. I could only imagine him stepping on her feet with an indecisive fox-trot.

The music was telling me what to do: Cast off inelegance. Cut corners on the biography project. Finish it off in a couple of weeks. Take his books to a nice little used bookshop on Miami Beach. Same deal for the furniture. Recycle Peter Peterson for the good of Mankind. Collect the money from Ted Walden. Move back in with Barbara and hang the piezoelectric alarm on my bedroom door. Better to have a sleepwalking nymphomaniac scratching on my door than to have a goofy ghost from the past walking through it.

But for some reason, the Laura theme had waltzed me into Pete's bedroom. I came to a halt at the file cabinet — that damn file cabinet where I'd received the blow to the head. That damn file cabinet with the drawer full of bogus crusades. Was there no escaping this jerk?

Filling with anger, I once again jerked open the middle drawer. The files lay on their sides. That's when the thought occurred to me: If Pete ran a taut ship, why hadn't he tightened the spacer mechanism to keep the files from falling over? I checked the spacer mechanism. It was fully adjustable.

Then it hit me as hard as the cypress candleholder: The drawer wasn't half full. It had been half emptied!

And if true, that would change everything.

20   GRANTSMANSHIP

About 10 hours later, I got a chance to act on my suspicions. It was Monday morning, the first day of my third week on the job. It was around nine o'clock and I was walking to the medical school. And there they were again, blocking the front entrance, marching around in a tight oval pattern and handing out their leaflets: animal rights demonstrators.

Yes, there was Annabelle Pemberton, Pete's old girlfriend and enemy from the Unitarian church. Did any of the marchers resemble the guy who hit me on the head? No, but that didn't mean he didn't belong to the group. Maybe he decided to keep a low profile around the medical center for a week or two.

It was time to check them out. I hurried back to Pete's apartment and pulled the bag of photographic equipment out of the closet.

Screwed the telephoto lens into a 35 millimeter camera and laid in a roll of film. Hurried back and took up station by a tree planter about 50 yards from the demonstrators. With 18 people in the group and 20 shots on the roll of film, I got everyone's face at least once. Got an especially good full face shot of one of them on my 20th click. Then I noticed he was coming towards me. I sat down on the concrete wall of the planter, repacked the camera in the bag and then pretended to be studying a sheet of paper. Turned my badge around so my name didn't show. As he closed in on me, I pulled out the mechanical pencil and started scribbling.

"You taking pictures of us?"

I looked up and studied the guy's rough face for a couple of seconds. He was about my age and twice my size. Heavier build than the guy who hit me on the head. Looked like he lifted weights every night and hadn't lifted a book since high school. And now he was standing over me like he wanted to get physical.

"No, I was taking pictures of the building. Going to send them to my fiancée up in Washington. I'm working here now."

My answer might have thrown him into confusion, but his hands were still balled in fists. "Looked to me like you were aiming at us."

"No, I was more interested in the sixth floor where my lab is."

"You working with animals?"

"No, I'm doing a project involving urine samples from steroid abusers. You part of that animal rights demonstration?"

"Yeah. You think something's wrong with it?"

He was looking for an excuse to hit me. If he did, I'd fend with my left and go for his stomach with a loaded right.

"No. But I am wondering why you are standing over me like this."

He took a step back but then stepped forward again. He said nothing, so I filled in the gap:

"And I'm not in the right mood for conversations with strangers today. So look . . . What did you say your name was?"

"I didn't say."

"Then let's leave it at that. My business takes me this way, and I'll bet yours takes you back that way. So *adios*. And please don't follow me or I'll run over to that guard and complain."

I scooted my butt a couple of feet along the planter before

getting up, turning my back on him and walking away. Fifty yards later, I glanced back before putting my pencil away. The lout was still standing there — pondering the logic of our conversation, I guess.

After bringing the camera back to the apartment, I returned to the medical campus. Retrieved an animal rights handbill from a trash receptacle. It listed a meeting for the coming Wednesday evening at the Kampong in the south end of Coconut Grove. Maybe I would pay them a visit.

Entered the med school building from the other side this time. After sipping a cup of coffee at my desk to steady my nerves, I started work on the two-page summary for the program project grant proposal on ageing. With gusto, I whipped into shape my ideas on how free radicals might be affecting the protein kinase and protein phosphatase enzymes important to cellular control. I would look for effects in blood samples in elderly patients, and correlate them with antioxidant and vitamin levels. My brainstorm was under control; my proposal might lead to an important discovery. Ben Candidi wasn't a vulture picking on a corpse. No, this proposal would be the rebirth of Pete's work — a Phoenix bird reborn from its own ashes.

Three hours later, with several copies of my two-page proposal in hand, I ventured out through the med school's back entrance and went to my spot for a leisurely lunch among the patients and butterflies. The noisy animal rights demonstrators were gone, but jetliners still thundered by. The lull between them was filled by the low-level hiss of the air conditioning cooling tower mounted on the med school's roof. It was up there somewhere, behind the pseudo-penthouse for the elevator machinery.

The tranquility was also broken when a car alarm went off inside the eight-story public parking garage next to our building. The garage did a lot of business. At ground level there was always a line of cars outside, waiting for the ticket-dispensing machine, and inside, another line waiting to return the ticket and pay the fee.

A rescue helicopter flew over the parking garage and landed on the roof of the Ryder Trauma Center. By the parking garage entrance was parked the Channel 8 van, ready to dispatch a camera crew to the hospital and capture the medical phase of the life-and-death struggles resulting from gang-bangs, drive-bys and plain old traffic accidents. Mounted atop the van's hydraulically operated pole, its microwave antenna was a veritable signal flag for these events: half-mast for paramedical emergency and full-mast for death.

What a tabloid T.V. station! Why weren't they filming the minor disturbance that was now taking place at one of the parking garage's collection booths? Having finished lunch, I walked in that direction. A dilapidated Chevrolet was sitting, dead, in one of the toll slots. A woman with a heavy bandage over one eye sat in the front passenger seat, with a couple of thumb-sucking toddlers in the seat behind her. The driver's seat was empty. The father was outside, arguing with two guards, half in Spanish and half with gestures. The collector sat in her booth, reading a soap opera magazine.

One of the guards didn't know any Spanish, and the other one kept telling him, "*No pagas, no salas.*"

Apparently, they'd been telling him this for a long time — that he couldn't exit without paying. Now they were threatening him with arrest if he didn't back up and repark his car. I asked the man selling flowers by the automatic teller machine what was the story. He said the man didn't have any money with him. When glass broke and got in his wife's eye, he packed her and the kids in the car and drove to the E.R. as fast as he could. Now he had to pick up his other kid from pre-school or there would be a hefty fine. The parking garage would not take an I.O.U.

I asked the attendant why the E.R. didn't stamp the patient's ticket. She said they don't do that. The LCD display showed a fee of $8.00. I pulled the money from my pocket and gave it to her. She pushed the button that raised the gate. It took a while before anyone else realized what was happening.

"*Mi regalo a usted,*" I told the man. "*Le deseo una pronta recuperación a su esposa.*"

An eight-dollar present from a stranger wishing his wife's recuperation was a big surprise. He thanked me so profusely that it was almost embarrassing. He refused to leave until I had given him my name and address for repayment.

While walking to my meeting, I thought about the backwardness of the situation I'd just corrected: A county hospital serving low-income people charged $8.00 to park their cars. Private Baptist Hospital and Mercy Hospital let you park for free.

❖❖❖❖❖

Ten minutes early, I walked into the first meeting of the "organizing committee of the Program Project Grant on Ageing" feeling well-prepared. But a dozen people were better prepared. They had already staked out every place around the big table. Most were biding their time shuffling papers while some engaged in small talk.

Luke McDougal, Ph.D., the designated director, was sitting at the head of the table. I walked up to him, introduced myself in a soft voice and handed him my two-page project summary. His welcome aboard was as friendly as a hollered invitation to join a campfire in the Smoky Mountains. But his deep-set eyes regarded me slowly and suspiciously. And his greeting quenched small talk around the table as effectively as a if he'd pitched a bucket of water.

McDougal brought a pair of half-cut reading glasses to his pudgy face and inspected my two pages for as many seconds. He looked like a hard worker and a hard drinker who was getting too little exercise. I took a seat in one of the chairs lining the wall and shuffled my own papers until the small talk rekindled.

A couple of middle-aged scientists at the table — a casually dressed male and a well-dressed female — were carrying on a line of small talk that identified them as high-status individuals: members of a Federal grant proposal review committee, a "study section."

Her research was in immunology. He sliced brains from patients who die with Alzheimier's disease, put them under the microscope and counted the "plaques and tangles" of nerves.

"Dr. Candidi, maybe you have an extra project description for me." While taking my seat, I must have ignored this man a couple of chairs away. "I am Hong Yung," he said, smiling and extending his hand.

He was compact, athletic, handsome, and probably 20 years my senior. After one glance at the thick stack of index cards bulging the pockets of his white jacket I knew he was a clinician.

Dr. Yung shook my hand and accepted my project summary with a twinkle of the eye. "It is better to sit here than at the table. There is more room." He spoke in a soft voice, accent-free. "And it is easier to leave if the meeting doesn't pan out."

He must have been in the U.S. for a long time.

I replied softly. "Yes, writing grant proposals is like panning a stream bed to find a vein of gold."

"That's why I do not rely on them for personnel — just for equipment." His face was proud but his eyes were friendly.

"What sort of research do you do?"

"Using magnetic resonance imaging to evaluate the effectiveness of treatments of stroke — in real time. Watching the clot dissolve." He was reading my summary as he talked. "I see you were trained as a pharmacologist and are working on antioxidants. I need to find a way to deliver the antioxidant *tirilazad* through a catheter. The company gave up on it because the things they had to use to dissolve it were too toxic to the patients. Someone told me there is a pharmacologist in town with a *lecithin-coated microcrystal system* that can be used. Do you know anything about it?"

"No, but it sounds interesting."

Dr. McDougal called the meeting to order and described the program. The National Institutes of Health was going to fund four program project grants for ageing around the country. Dean Weisburd wanted Bryan Medical School to get one of them and he had designated Dr. McDougal as the coordinator of the grant proposal.

We could ask for five million dollars a year. Our group proposal should combine laboratory studies with clinical studies and patient care. Twenty different institutions around the country would be competing for the four grants.

I figured a one in five chance on a group grant is better than a one-in-seven chance when going it alone.

Within five minutes, the people around the table were arguing about how to carve up the five-million-dollar pie. I didn't see why that was necessary. If the 18 of us would agree to divide up the pie evenly, everyone would get about $140,000 useful dollars a year and *Administratium* could take it's half — $2.5 million. But all men and women weren't created equal according to the colleagues around the table.

To be fair, it wasn't out-and-out squabbling. They argued indirectly, professing a lot of special knowledge about what the NIH study sections were funding. Their argumentation was like a pillow fight conducted in slow motion, according to rules which forbid you to strike your opponent frontally while looking at him or her.

An effective blow seemed to require the delivery of a half-dozen bureaucratic buzz-words in a single sentence.

The winners seemed to be five physicians from the Department of Psychiatry. They belonged to a clinical group that was treating geriatric patients and they already had grants from Miami-Dade County to provide "counseling services for indigent elderly."

Allied with the psychiatrists were a couple of statisticians who probably worked for them, and a nutritionist who administered questionnaires to nursing home patients. On the fringes of this alliance were the brain slicer and the lady immunologist, whose name was Judith Cass.

McDougal followed the discussion with slow, appraising eyes. He took no initiative as moderator, and did nothing to help others to participate, although Dr. Yung had raised his hand several times.

Finally, Dr. Yung's pager went off. He held it up to read a number. He started to get up but then sat back down. A minute later he was leaning my way and handing me a business card.

"Maybe you can visit me in the laboratory tomorrow noon. We can have a chat. If I get tied up with a patient, Barry can show you around."

I promised to do so. The next time I looked, he was gone.

As the discussion around the table focused on "equitable but viable sharing of resources," Judith Cass nominated herself to head up a committee to "screen" us for membership in the group.

McDougal rebuffed this as encroaching on his turf. "You basic researchers should get yourselves together and form areas of research concentration."

Obviously, it had been a mistake to come to this meeting without having any alliances in place. As Judith Cass ranted on about the danger of Alzheimer's research becoming "an amorphous area," I rehearsed a ten-second sound bite that would defend my project.

Judith Cass repeated her argument at a high rate of words per minute, thumping the table to make her alliterative point. "All we need is one fatal flaw and that could be fatal to the fate of the *whole* proposal. And we'd be finished — *finito!*"

Abruptly, all conversation came to an end. This seemed miraculous until I identified the cause: Dean Arnold Weisburd. He was standing in the doorway, surveying the room with a benevolent smile. After a few seconds, Dr. McDougal said, "We've essentially wrapped it up. Would you like to say a few words to us, Arnie?"

Dean Weisburd raised his hands and shook his head in mock self-dismissal. "I really don't want to disrupt your meeting. I just wanted to wish you success with the application." His eyes slowly went around the table as he talked. "I just want you to know that Luke has been doing a tremendous job coordinating the wide-spread activities of our outpatient monitoring studies. This program project grant will increase our coverage around the medical center."

He made a circular gesture to describe the real estate all around us.

"Over the years, the new project grants and center grants, like this one, have provided visible evidence of our commitment to community health. Every time we convert a new floor and staff it with physicians, their well-trained assistants, and let us not forget the ancillary sciences like nutrition and pharmaco-metrics . . . we demonstrate this School's true commitment to health care delivery in this community."

The nutritionist perked up at the mention of her specialty. The dean returned her smile, then shifted his gaze to the Alzheimer brain morphologist.

"And not to forget the backup of basic scientists like Phil who is doing a great job, one slice at a time."

The brain slicer shook his head in embarrassment. As an afterthought, he laughed with the rest of them. Maybe his brain was not hard-wired for humor.

Dean Weisburd's eyes shifted to the hyperexcitable immunologist.

"Judith, I know that we have disagreed on a few things, but let me be the first to say that there will always be a place for neuro-immunological studies, just as I think that there should be a place for study of molecular immunology in a clinical setting . . . just as much as there is a need for clinical mentorship, and indeed guidance of physician-scientists in this rapidly developing field."

It was almost painful to watch Judith Cass strain to figure out what the dean was telling her to do. I guessed that he wanted her to spend more time helping the physicians. The dean's eyes moved from one to the next as he worked the room in the counter-clockwise direction, tossing out or spinning his tidbits of praise. Within a couple minutes he had covered everyone at the table.

Then the dean's eyes landed on me. "Of course, we must always be vigilant with special reference to the integrity of our data and be sensitive to the possible impact of raw, unfiltered, unevaluated lab-bench data on clinical practice. However, I have always been the first to say that we should always be looking for cutting-edge basic research projects which impact on medicine, *if* their impact will positively affect health care delivery."

I worked hard at maintaining a neutral demeanor. Here he was, pulling the same stuff on me as before — implying that something was wrong with Pete's data. I met the dean's eyes with a neutral gaze, pretending to consider his generalities to be reasonable. McDougal was nodding his head like the dean was making a lot of sense. The other basic scientists didn't seem to react one way or another.

Then, the dean addressed everybody, telling us that the grant proposal was important, that he had great faith in Luke McDougal, and that he would be ready to support us, at a moment's notice, by picking up the phone to answer any Federal bureaucrat who might call to probe his commitment. He would even place phone calls to South Florida's congressmen if there were any sign that the grants might not be distributed equitably between the different regions of our country.

So there it was: The dean had said he was 100% behind us — behind some of us more than others.

After the dean left, Luke McDougal said his final words. "Now you candidate investigators be sure to turn in your biographical sketch pages and submit a minimal budget."

A tight crowd formed around McDougal. No use trying to compete with my elbows right now. I would have to learn some more local politics before going another round with this group.

But I must have hungered for some type of good news, because I went to Rob McGregor's lab. Rob didn't seem too busy. He greeted me with a smile.

"Rob, I went to a try-out for a program project grant headed up by Luke McDougal. Got the cold shoulder."

"I hope you didn't make a big thing of your connection with Pete."

"No. But why?"

"McDougal didn't like Pete. He could never get over Pete's phone call."

"Phone call?"

"Yes, a phone call — that was broadcast over the radio. McDougal was interviewed on a public radio call-in show, talking about 'problems with the aged population in South Florida.' And then Pete calls in, identifies himself as a Bryan professor, and starts arguing with him about some damn thing. The argument made the papers, and it messed up McDougal's fund-raising campaign."

"What did Pete argue about?"

"Something about which projects Bryan was spending money on. McDougal has a lab with a couple of HPLC machines that can measure drug concentrations in blood. He's a big help to those physicians who want to do human testing for drug companies. Now, he's finagled things to the point where he is actually helping run their studies. Let me give you a piece of advice, Little Britches."

"What's your good word of advice, Baloo?"

"Cool it on this Pete business. I've been getting bad vibes from a number of people. Don't go around telling any more people you're working on Pete's biography. It's a waste of time, even if you *are* getting paid for it. Look, Pete was a nice guy in his own way, but he's dead now. Best thing's to forget about him and start working on your own identity. Now, you got any leads on integrating your project with that ageing grant proposal?"

I described my proposal to measure free radical products, vitamin C levels, and vitamin E levels blood samples in elderly.

"That should fly if you have a physician collaborator. Who's it going to be?"

"Well, I talked briefly to Dr. Yung. He's using diagnostic MRI for disseminated stroke and neurodegeneration. He seemed pretty nice."

"Yeah, pretty nice like in 'nice guys finish last'."

"What do you mean?"

"He doesn't have any NIH grants. He's an old-fashioned physician researcher. He doesn't go after grants to cover his salary."

Rob said that although Dr. Yung did excellent work and had many publications, he didn't have a good enough track record for getting Federal grants. Rob explained how you have to be engorged with grants to be considered worthy to receive new ones. The idea made me sad.

"It looks like I'm stuck, Rob, because I don't think any other physician at that session would make a good collaborator. What do you suggest I do?"

"For that grant proposal? At least get yourself under someone's protection."

"Who do you suggest?"

"You'll probably have to make some kind of a deal with McDougal. Like making him a 'collaborator' if the project is funded, and putting his name on your first several papers. He's the pet Ph.D. of the chairman of Psychiatry, so you might have to give him honorary authorship, too. Might seem revolting, but that's the only way that you'll get access to geriatric blood samples."

It was not the time to tell Rob I was feeling discouraged. And now I had no basis for complaining about the dean's latest between-the-lines comments on Pete. I went to my office and worked half-heartedly on one of the unfinished manuscripts.

Towards the end of the day, I broke off and did an Internet search on the market value of 1956 Oldsmobiles. At www.myclassiccar.com, I identified Pete's car as a Rocket 88 four-door hardtop. Everything checked out, down to the conical tail lights. I e-mailed them a query, and Joey Randolph messaged back that it would be valued between $6,000 and $10,500, depending on whether it was in "very good" or "show-winning" condition.

I was about to leave for the day when the phone rang. It was Rebecca.

"Ben. I just got off work. You didn't call all weekend and . . . frankly . . . I was a little . . . *worried.*"

"Don't worry. I moved into Dr. Peterson's apartment like I said I would. Left Barbara a note. It isn't going to happen again."

"But . . . when you didn't call I was worried . . . that you . . . didn't care enough to call me." Her voice cracked.

My throat was tightening as I blurted it all out. "I'm sorry. It's just that I wanted to call back with good news . . . and I don't have any."

"But you could just talk to me, anyway."

I didn't want to tell her about the hit on the head. She would probably say I should have gone to the hospital. I didn't want to talk about the emotionally exhausting biography project and how the missing files were raising my suspicion of murder. And I wouldn't tell her about my encounter with the animal rights lout. The only thing I could tell her about was my scientific work.

"Ben?"

"Yes."

"I know it is hard for you. But tell me what is bothering you."

Uncanny, how she knew. And no way to fight it.

"Okay, I'll open the floodgates and hope you don't get washed away."

"Try me," she coaxed. Then she imitated my command voice in the cockpit. "Both anchors firmly planted, sir!"

"You're right. A lot has been bothering me. It seems that all I've done is go to waste-of-time faculty meetings and get bogged down in local politics. And the dean doesn't like me."

I told her about the interview.

"Maybe you shouldn't take it too seriously. It's probably just a male dominance thing. He will probably forget about what he said in a couple of months. He'll see that you are putting out good work. Tell me about your work."

I told her all about the experiments.

"And are you planning new projects?"

"Yes. In fact I went to an organizing meeting for a program project grant proposal on ageing. I have a proposal to measure free radical products, vitamin C levels, and vitamin E levels in red cells in elderly. I expect the free radical levels to be up when the vitamin levels are down. I want to relate this to my protein kinase and phosphatase enzymes."

"Wonderful!"

"Except that everyone in the project has his turf staked out and you have to join a gang to survive."

"I see."

I described my feelings about the meeting. "Clinicians rule the roost. Laboratory science interests are being represented by a hypertensive immunologist — a real bull in a china shop."

"What's his name?"

"Judith Cass."

"I see."

"Dresses like an anchor on the eleven o'clock news and has an attitude and an attention span to match."

"I know what you mean. I hate it when women play that game. And I understand your problem. You need an alliance. Maybe there is a clinician that you could . . . bring into the project as a collaborator."

"There is one. His name is Hong Yung. He does MRI on strokes.

He asked me about delivering an anti-oxidant drug in cerebral thrombosis."

"Wonderful!"

"Except that his beeper went off in the middle of the meeting and we didn't get to talk. And Rob tells me he doesn't have Federal grants."

"So?"

"It seems that you have to be engorged with grants to qualify for new ones. It's a strange system."

And Rebecca couldn't help me with that one.

I told Rebecca I loved her. Got pretty emotional. We both did. She said that if I didn't feel right about Miami, I should come back to Washington.

But no, as much as I loved Rebecca, I was too proud to go back to Washington and work as a post-doctoral in someone else's laboratory.

We closed with a final I-love-you.

I went back in the apartment where I ignored Rebecca's advice and ate dinner from a can. But I did take her advice on being kind to myself. Put on a unstructured white jacket from my pre-Rebecca days and pulled the keys to the Oldsmobile from the night table's drawer. Grabbed Pete's gray fedora. It was too big for my head, but it looked nice sitting on the seat beside me. The old buggy fired up on the first try. I put on a debonair mood and suppressed all guilt. I was killing two birds with one stone: taking the night off and testing the South Florida market for Pete's 1956 Olds.

It turned a lot of heads at the drugstore where I dropped off the film. And it was a big hit, too, with the South Miami Beach street crowd. I cruised around slow and popped into an empty parking space whenever I found one. Got out and leaned on the front fender, pretending to look at my watch like I was waiting for someone.

The car received a lot of expected nostalgic interest from stylish sixty-year-old couples. It probably reminded them of the first time they made it in the back seat. There was a lot of interest from my generation, too, particularly for its value as a head-turner and pick-up tool. Before the night was over, I had turned down three girls — and five guys. And the buggy was a real smash with the waiters and valet parking people.

The evening would have ended on a high note if I hadn't remembered to check Pete's mailbox back at the apartment building.

I almost threw out the letter with the three pieces of junk mail that hit Pete's box that day. It was addressed "To Current Occupant" but didn't look like a mass mailing. It was stamped rather than metered, and it bore a curious return address: "Eubie Careful" followed by a post office box number in Homestead, Florida. The message inside kept me up half the night:

> Your poking around is going to get you in alot of
> trouble, if you don't stop it now. So be advised to
> put your muck shovel down for your own good.
> — Watcher

It was upsetting enough to keep me glancing over my left shoulder in the empty elevator. Checked out the whole apartment before closing the hallway door behind me. Turned the deadbolt and set the alarm before giving the letter a second look-over.

It was done in 12-point Courier type using a laser printer: no more traceable than a gangster's message with letters cut out of a newspaper. It started in the center of a page of copy paper — left and right justified to a one-inch margin. The envelope was also laser-printed. I took another look at the name above the return address: Eubie Careful. *You be careful.*

This one was different from the hate letters in Pete's file folder, those awkwardly worded, handwritten missives addressed, as often as not, to "Perfesser Peterson at the Bryan Medical University." Sure, this one had misspelled "a lot." Sure, its reference to a "muck shovel" added a bucolic touch. But this writer had a word-processing computer and knew how to use it. And this writer knew where I lived.

This writer was no dumpster-diving psychotic and no survivalist living out in the Everglades. This one probably knew that I was doing Pete's biography and was worried about what I might find. This one probably had a support group with members capable of raiding this apartment and bopping me over the head.

Pete's death was no accident.

Who were they and what were they trying to keep me from finding?

I ran down the list of suspects. The Right-to-Lifers could

produce a laser-printed letter, but would they have killed Pete? He didn't perform abortions, he just argued for them. And how would my "muck shovel" threaten them?

The same reasons eliminated people who were against organ donation or human cloning.

I thought about suspects who were uncomfortably close to home: people around the medical school, or people Pete had known. These were the people who knew that I was doing Pete's biography. Here the "muck shovel" fit. But it was hard to imagine that Pete had pissed off anyone around the med school enough to have the person murder him. Should I be suspecting the dean or Dr. McDougal? Should be suspecting Mildred? Bless her devout soul. Or should I suspect Ted Walden's secretary?

Now the animal rights activists and the Unitarian woman — they were good suspects. They were passionate in their cause and Old Annabelle Pemberton may have been passionate about Pete. Had Pete ever ridiculed her and her cause on the med school steps? Did Old Annabelle have a key to Pete's apartment, maybe dating back to the time when they had been hot and heavy? Could she have put poison in his pipe tobacco or injected him while he was sitting by the canal?

The back-off and muck-shovel language would fit Old Annabelle well. She knew about the biography project from the church newsletter, she recognized me last week when I walked past her demonstration, and her lout friend probably went right back and told her he'd caught me taking pictures yesterday.

I went to the other room and retrieved their leaflet. "Animal Advocacy" is what the group called itself. It listed some good works — like helping the Humane Society to advertise pets for adoption, doing volunteer work at their shelter and supporting an educational campaign to increase the use of neutering and spaying. But it also listed political education about medical and commercial use of animals.

And it listed their next meeting as Wednesday — tomorrow! No, make that today because a glance at my watch said it was two o'clock in the morning. Suddenly I felt weary. Just two weeks after coming here to start a new career, I had semi-anonymous enemies and was getting dragged down by a dead man's unfinished affairs.

❧❧❧❧❧

Six hours later, arriving at the lab, I took a hard look at Mildred. No, not a suspect. She was just her usual placid but steady-working self. But I did decide to keep my sandwiches locked securely in my desk.

Mentally, I put away my muck shovel and took out my pitchfork. Time to make hay while the sun shines. Four good hours to give it all to science, shaping one of Pete's manuscripts into publishable form. A few minutes before noon, I hurried off to my appointment with Dr. Yung.

I didn't need to hurry because he wasn't there. But Barry, his career technician, was nice enough. He showed me their hematology instruments that measure blood coagulation and changes in blood platelet metabolism. He told me about the intracellular markers and said they would be glad to collaborate with me on the protein kinase and phosphatase enzymes. Tall, gaunt and balding supertechnician Barry had the type of enthusiasm you see in a good high school science teacher. At the end of our five-minute chat, he took me to the corner and introduced me to a tall guy who was working at the laser flow cytometer.

"Dr. Candidi, this is Mr. Howard Edmunds."

We shook hands. I remembered his face and half-remembered hearing his name before, but couldn't place him. His age was in the mid-fifties and he had the quiet and dignified comportment of a church organist.

"Mr. Edmunds works here every Tuesday."

He wore a photo I.D. identifying him as a volunteer.

"You picked an impressive laboratory," I said.

"Yes, Dr. Yung's lab is quite impressive," he replied.

Something in that exchange of words seemed to block further conversation. I begged off, saying that I really had to get hold of Dr. Yung concerning a grant proposal. Barry gave me directions for the Magnetic Resonance Imaging facility.

The MRI was in a separate building. My lab jacket got me past the front desk without challenge. I found Dr. Yung in a control room. Through its large window, I looked down the mouth of the cavernous machine that swallows patients whole. Dr. Yung was looking at an image displayed on a monitor and was giving a technician instructions on fine adjustments.

He didn't notice me at first. In fact I wasn't sure exactly when he first noticed me. He just started talking to me slowly without looking away from the monitor.

"You see, Dr. Candidi, we are looking at a patient who has just suffered a stroke. Thrombotic stroke. In some places the vessels are blocked and the blood flow is stopped. In others, it was stopped but has been restarted."

The brain image looked like a cross section of pomegranate. Dr. Yung moved a pencil over it as he talked.

"What we see here is mostly the difference between cell membrane and water — the magnetic $T2$, they call it. It tells us something about where blood is moving and where it is blocked. But the image is too fuzzy. This area is disrupted. It will probably die. The area next to it is at risk. It is getting some collateral circulation but it is hard to tell how much . . . What we really need is a physiologically acceptable agent that will sharpen these images . . . that will tell us where the nutrients are moving . . . so we will really know what is happening to the metabolism inside these nerve cells."

He sighed and fell silent for a few seconds.

"We need to know where cells are dying, right now, so we can adjust the therapy. The statisticians would say that's just a 'surrogate measure,' but I see it as the death of a healthy cell. Cell death, that is always the question, whether you are studying stroke or general loss of brain function with ageing."

Dr. Yung said nothing more for a full minute. The semi-darkness of the room and the gravity of his words, delivered in a low voice, had an almost hypnotic effect. He had just defined the objective of a grant proposal that we could make together. The physician had asked the bench scientist for help. What could the bench scientist deliver?

I struggled for an answer. "The manganese ion is paramagnetic and shortens the $T1$ of water. I'm not sure about the $T2$. Wherever it goes, it should change the MRI image. I remember from college chemistry that it can wipe out an NMR spectrum at concentrations of around one-tenth millimolar. It might not be toxic at that concentration. You would have to inject it in the carotid and get time-resolved images to see which tissues it penetrates rapidly. That would tell you which regions are getting oxygen and nutrients. If manganese is toxic, we could look for a chelated form."

"That sounds very interesting."

"Has anyone tried manganese ion?"

"I am not sure. But there is a gadolinium-DTPA complex. We will have to do a literature review."

A nurse approached. "Dr. Yung, Dr. Smith has a patient in G-3 he wants you to see."

"Excuse me. I'll be back in ten minutes."

But Dr. Yung didn't come back in ten minutes. And he didn't come back in half an hour, either. But I didn't hold it against him. He had suggested a research problem for me. And I talked to the technician running the machine and learned a lot of useful facts about "T1's," "T2's," "spin-echo," and "flow-sensitive gradient echo."

But I wouldn't have waited the half-hour if I had known what was in store for me at the Department that afternoon.

CHICAGO CALLING 22

The big surprise was waiting in the departmental mailbox — a letter to Pete from a Professor Kurt Hammerschlag of the University of Chicago.

> Dear Pete:
>
> I just wanted to remind you of your presentation for the Social Responsibility Subgroup at the annual meeting of the Biophysical Society here in Chicago, two weeks from today. As always, we will be meeting on Tuesday evening, the second day of the conference. As we agreed on the phone last month, you will give a 30-minute progress report and update on your local efforts on behalf of social responsibility.
>
> I am also looking forward to visiting your scientific presentation at the poster session, earlier in the day.
>
> With best wishes, Kurt

I wasn't worried about Pete's "social responsibility" spiel, whatever that was. But the news of having to make a scientific presentation knocked the wind out of me. I hurried up to Mildred, with the letter in hand.

"Did you know that Pete was scheduled for a scientific presentation at the Biophysical Society in less than a week?"

"Yes. He goes to the meeting every year." She was quite calm.

"We have only four working days to put together a poster presentation. How am I supposed to know what goes in it?"

"You can check in the volume of abstracts. I saw it on your desk when we were discussing experiments last week."

And she was right. The book was there and Pete's abstract in it: "Protection by melatonin from hypoxia/reperfusion injury of liver cells." It was the same story as in one of the unfinished manuscripts.

After spending two feverish hours going over the data with Mildred, it became clear that we had 80% of what was needed for the presentation. The missing 20% was mostly repeating experiments so that every result was observed at least five times. I also thought up some new experiments for cross-checking Pete's conclusions. Made a list of things to do and gave it to Mildred.

I called Gisela Schloss Birkholz at Blue Lagoon Travel and asked her to book me an inexpensive flight and hotel for the Chicago meeting. Had her put it on my American Express card. I would get it reimbursed from the grant.

My next step was to tell the bad news to Pete's friend, Dr. Hammerschlag. I picked up the phone. It took a long time to get an outside line after dialing "nine." The med school's automated system also took a long time to place the call. Funny, I thought, the times that things pick to go wrong.

"Hello?"

"I would like to speak to Dr. Kurt Hammerschlag."

"Speaking." The word was uttered with the patience of a professional who has dealt with all sorts of strangers and was adept at putting everything into the right category. There was no trace of a German accent.

"This is Dr. Benjamin Candidi, calling from Dr. Peter Peterson's lab."

"Yes. Very good." He sounded like a baritone who did most of his speaking in tenor range. Well-enunciated. Sharp. Was it carry-over from a German grandfather? "Tell me, how is Pete? I should speak to him. I hope he got my letter."

"That is why I am calling."

"Yes?"

"It is my unpleasant duty to tell you that Pete passed away two weeks ago."

"Oh, no!" The line was silent for several seconds.

"I have been hired to finish the work on his grant and to take care of his affairs."

"What! Poor fellow. Poor old Pete. What happened?" His immediate response of genuine surprise followed by an expression of loss identified Dr. Hammerschlag as a true friend of Pete. Lies, rationalizations and intellectual analysis always take much longer.

I told Dr. Hammerschlag how Pete was found floating face down in Wagner Creek and that he'd apparently been sitting on the rail, smoking his pipe. I deliberately avoided talking about the cause of death. After I finished, the line was once again silent.

"Was it a natural death?" he asked, cautiously.

It wouldn't hurt to soften him up a bit before questioning him on this "social responsibility" thing. I gave him a clinical answer. "Since the coroner didn't find external injuries or sign of a struggle, he attributed it to natural causes. He guessed it was a fatal arrhythmia."

"Fatal arrhythmia? Sudden discoordination of the heart. Natural causes, then? Well, at least . . ."

At least what? Hammerschlag was silent for a long time.

"The authorities called it drowning during a heart attack, but I don't think they ever ruled out murder. Could you imagine anyone wanting to kill him?"

Again, a long silence. "Well, you know that Pete was a controversial fellow. I mean, he was involved in a lot of controversy. And you know that there are a lot of crazy people out there. Especially in Miami."

Sure, blame everything on Miami.

"Can you imagine any kind of controversy that would make someone want to kill Pete?"

"No," Dr. Hammerschlag said, "I wouldn't know anyone who would want to kill Pete, and certainly not anyone who really knew him. The poor fellow."

Time for another tack. "Although I am picking up Pete's scientific work, I don't know what he'd prepared for his 'progress report and update' at the Social Responsibility Subgroup meeting which you are chairing."

"No. That's okay. We will make due without his presentation. But what a loss. He was one of our most active members."

"It sounds like an important topic. Can you tell me a little about your Subgroup?"

"Oh, it isn't by any means as *grandiose* as it sounds. We are just a dozen Society members that get together on Tuesday nights of the National Meeting, in whichever city it happens to be in, and discuss . . . issues. Like the issues of communicating candidly with the lay public."

"Yes?" I coaxed.

"Like issues of responsibility of industry. Like issues that are internal to science — like ethical conduct questions in study sections. Like the grant review process itself. Like the responsibilities of local institutions, themselves. Like thinking globally but acting locally."

It was quite a litany of *likes*. I said, "I'm interested in these issues, myself."

"Good. I invite you to attend our meeting, especially since you are . . . associated with Pete."

"Thank you. And for right now, can you tell me which of the *subtopics* you mentioned Pete was most interested in?"

"Subtopics?"

"Yes. Relations with the lay public, responsibility in industry, NIH study section abuses and responsibilities of the universities themselves."

At first, Hammerschlag seemed a little surprised to hear my terse recitation of the subtopics. Then he laughed. "Well, Pete was always interested in public relations, although his results were a mixed bag. Regarding industry, you probably know of his concern about gamma irradiation as a method for sterilizing meat."

"Yes," I said, remembering his files of clippings and the notes on his frozen hamburger experiments.

Hammerschlag warmed up on the hamburger topic, like we were settling down for an in-depth scientific discussion. "You know that the industry already has FDA approval to gamma-irradiate poultry. It kills salmonella bacteria which is a big source of contamination, given the way they wash chicken carcasses in packing plants."

He told me that industry was seeking approval use low-level radiation to sterilize ground beef, and although there is no danger of radioactive contamination because the cobalt sources are sealed, Pete was concerned about free radical production.

He told me a lot of stuff I already knew, then he concluded. "Free radical chain reactions in irradiated food could — at least theoretically — be a problem, especially if the product is allowed to age. You do know that Pete was planning experiments with frozen hamburger and steaks, don't you?"

"Yes. Do you think the industry felt threatened?"

"By Pete? No, I think his work in this area was too . . . *preliminary*."

"Can you tell me about your subgroup's concern about the university's responsibilities."

"Oh, yes." With these words, Hammerschlag's voice dropped to baritone. "We all cooperated on that topic." He was speaking very slowly, now.

"What sort of issues did you cooperate on?"

"Uh, uh. On issues of . . . *procedure*. On procedure with respect to university and public assets. Attempting to think up some general guidelines in the face of a complete absence of policy, other than limited accounting guidelines of OMB auditors." He made it sound like this issue was distasteful and the discussion was over.

"What types of guidelines did your subgroup think up."

"Oh, I don't know if we came up with anything *earthshaking*. No Hammurabi's Code for administration of science funds for the next millennium. Perhaps I could show you some of our summaries at the meeting. We actually worked more on individual cases . . . like physicians publish their case reports in the medical journals. We talked about *cases* with each other. Pete was quite active."

Did this guy have an aversion to straight answers, or was he just habitually slow to come to the point. Everything else about him seemed so crisp and precise.

"Can you tell me about the case reports that Pete presented to your group?"

"No, no. You are taxing my memory. I cannot remember a

specific case. But we can talk about it with the other members when you come. Dr. Candidi, can I ask why you are interested in this aspect of Pete's career?"

"Some of his friends at the Unitarian Church have asked me to work up some biographical material to include in a . . . memorial book . . . that they are keeping."

"Yes, yes, Pete was a good Unitarian. It's a great rational religion. I'm a Unitarian, myself."

"Yes, I'm becoming an admirer of that religion, also. Great crusading religion — crusading for the truth."

"I'm sorry to have to break off, Dr. Candidi, but I have a two o'clock lecture. I am looking forward to meeting you here."

I let him go. His subgroup meeting in Chicago — that's where I'd get the lowdown on Pete's "crusade" for scientific social responsibility.

And I returned to my own scientific crusade, working all day and well into the night to get Pete's data into shape. Funny how time flies when you are working against a deadline.

Caught my next breath of outdoor air on Wednesday morning, while out on the bike doing a couple of errands. It was a pleasant ride along Wagner Creek then along the Miami River, traveling past river-front fish wholesalers and outdoor restaurants. The Scottish Rite Temple marked my turning point. A few blocks from this formidable, lion- and pyramid-topped stone edifice was the headquarters of the Miami Police Department.

I went to their Freedom of Information Office on the first floor and ordered the police report describing the discovery of Pete Peterson. I learned how to do this from *Contents Under Pressure*, a detective novel by Edna Buchanan. The clerk said a copy would be ready the next afternoon.

On the way back, I stopped at the drugstore where I'd dropped off the film. Among the telephotos of the Animal Advocacy people were excellent shots of Pete's ex-girlfriend and the lout who had threatened me.

By 10:30 a.m., I was back in the lab working up the graphs to pin up on the posterboard at the meeting in Chicago. By mid-afternoon I was sure that everything would be ready before the plane took off.

Now, to tie up some loose ends: I wrote a 100-word obituary

of Pete and e-mailed it to the Biophysical Society with the request that they publish it in their Journal or promulgate it via e-mail distribution list. Writing the obituary was easy, but sending it off took a long time. I had a lot of trouble getting a modem connection. The med school's phone system was now accepting my computer's dial pulses so slowly that I had to go back into the modem program and insert a lot of commas to create pauses.

And the line itself was working at only half the normal baud rate. It took a long time to download abstracts from the Medline website. In fact, the line never did work right from that day on.

My experience that evening was not optimal, either.

MISSION IMPOSSIBLE 23

That night I was on a mission.

Place: The Kampong compound — a large stone-walled property that slopes from ficus-lined Ingraham "Highway" down to the shore of Biscayne Bay. The one-time estate is now a nature preserve, planted with countless varieties of tropical tree and shrub.

Time: 8:15 p.m. It had just gotten dark.

Mission: To learn something about the Animal Advocacy group.

Their meeting was well underway, and I was standing behind a large clump of bushes, listening in. They were set up on the porch of one of the buildings, with folding chairs arranged in a semicircle. Under a naked lightbulb, an old man was holding forth on the topic of resolutions for their organization's national meeting.

Pete's ex-girlfriend, Annabelle Pemberton, was sitting on the end. The lout wasn't there, and I didn't see anyone resembling the guy who hit me over the head in Pete's apartment. Old Annabelle had a lot to say during the meeting. The more I listened to their talk about slaughter of fur animals, crowding of food animals and mistreatment of performing animals, the more I could feel their humanity. But their local actions had nothing to do with these things. They should be going after the greyhound owners and breeders. They should be stamping out cockfights. They shouldn't be demonstrating against us, the one group that was doing something for the health of all animals — whether furry or human.

The naked lightbulb provided just enough light to compare my telephoto mug shots with the people before me. A lot of first names popped out during their discussion, and before long I had 11 of them written on the backs of the corresponding photos.

Before the meeting broke up, I would walk to their parked cars by the entrance and take down a list of the makes and license numbers. And I would wait on the bike path by Ingraham Highway, and identify each of them as they drove out the narrow entrance. Get their license number and you have their name and address.

The more I listened, the more I felt sorry for this little group. Sure, they felt bad for animals, but the roots of their problems were deeper than that. Life is full of all kinds of injustice and cruelty; it's dishonest to project all the sorrow on helpless animals; there are a lot of helpless humans, too.

As much as I had wanted one, my parents never let me have a dog. And as an adult, it had been impossible, living on the *Diogenes*. But if I did have a dog, I would have the vet implant one of those identifying chips so if he ever got lost, the pound people would get in touch with me. If animal rights people were behind that invention, I'll give them a lot of credit. It seems a lot better idea than trashing a university lab.

Maybe I could get Dr. Westley to pull some strings for me and find out if anyone in this organization had been arrested for getting physical. Like the lout. I could imagine him getting into an argument with someone, and then building up an uncontrollable rage. He'd get his moral support from the old man, Old Annabelle and other middle-class members of the group. They were authority figures . . . with the power to convert self-pity and warm feelings of cats and dogs into —

— He almost wrenched my arm out of its socket when he grabbed me. "What are you doing here?" he yelled. "Oh, its *you!*"

It was the lout and he had me by my left arm. He jerked it up behind my back.

"Get your hands off me. You have no right. This is the Kampong and —" Constitutional rights have no meaning when a bully has raised your wrist to your shoulder blade and when he's looking for an excuse to hike it up several inches more. I should have let go of the photos then.

Annabelle called through the bushes. "What's the matter, Chuck?"

"This creep's spying on us. The same one." He grabbed my left ear and rushed me around the bushes and toward the porch.

My right hand was free. Maybe I should have pulled my mechanical pencil out of my pocket and let him have it in the thigh. But maybe the group would tell him to let me go, anyway.

He manhandled me to the front of the semi-circle. Annabelle exclaimed, "Oh, no!"

The old man stuttered something.

Chuck the lout let go of my ear but kept my arm locked with his right hand. He snatched the photos. "Look what he's got here. He took spy pictures of us."

"Spy pictures?" Old Annabelle swooned. This gave Chuck all the moral authority he needed to hoist my arm another excruciating inch. He handed her the photos. The old man and a couple of members moved in to get a look.

Maybe I could talk my way out of this mess. "Let me go! This is a free country. I didn't break any law."

But nobody was going to help me. They just stared at the photos in wide-eyed fascination. And a middle-aged man was coming around to lend Chuck a hand. His wife put out a hand to stop him.

I caught her eye. "Call the police. I'm being assaulted." She didn't move. I repeated the words, screaming at the top of my lungs.

"Don't let him go," Old Annabelle yelled.

"Here, I'll help you," said the middle-aged man. He helped Chuck shift his grip on my tortured arm to his left hand. The two men flanked me like guards around a prisoner.

My ear was smarting. Now was time to reason with them. I turned my head to Middle-Aged and said in a low voice, "Please stay out of this. You haven't done anything wrong, yet."

I turned my face to Chuck on the right. Locked eyes for a second, to let him know I meant business. Then looked away to deny him a focus for his rage. I relaxed my body to gain some slack. Tried to keep my tone matter-of-fact. "If you take your hands off of me this second, I won't press charges. Otherwise, I'm charging you with —"

His answer was a brutish hoist that might have popped a socket. But I had premeditated a response. I jumped high and caught him in a right-handed headlock that supported my weight. This brought our bodies together and trapped his torturing hand between us. I threw my right knee forward, and snapped the leg back. My heel must have struck his crotch with emasculating force, because his arms immediately loosened and he started to fall over. I caught him in the mouth with an up-thrust of the left knee as he went down. He rolled on the wooden floor, writhing in pain.

Middle-Aged made a move on me. I repulsed him with a low-strength, flat-footed thrust kick. "I said you aren't part of this. Let's keep it that way."

I turned to face the crowd. Showed them two flattened palms at shoulder height. Tried to stay calm but spoke very fast. "I'm Dr. Benjamin Candidi of Bryan Medical School. I'm here as a private citizen. I am not armed. The Kampong is affiliated with David Fairchild Gardens and is now open to the public. I am not guilty of any sort of trespass and I have not threatened anybody. I was assaulted and battered by this man."

My words drove them back. Keep it up and I might even gain the upper hand.

"You're all witnesses to that fact. I asked you for help and none of you lifted a finger to help me. In fact, two of you gave this man orders to hold me. That makes you both accomplices to this man's criminal acts."

They were dumbstruck. I lowered my hands and rubbed the wrenched shoulder.

"I have told you who I am. Now, I demand to know the name of my assailant."

The lout was still doubled up on the floor. The answer eventually came from the wife of Middle-Aged: "Chuck. Chuck Luber. But he didn't mean any harm."

"Do any of you deny that this man assaulted and battered me, wrenching my arm behind my back and pulling my ear?"

It was amazingly silent except for Chuck's groans. I'd still have to watch out for him.

"Then I will ask you to not compound the felony with theft," I said, making up my legalisms as I went along. "Please give me back my photographs."

People started giving them back to Old Annabelle. It was clear that she was the one who wore the pants in this family. She handed them over and then stepped back into the crowd. She seemed to be gathering strength from them. She stared at me, incredulously. "But why? Why did you take pictures of *us*?"

Counting the photos gave me the needed seconds to think out my next steps. The next few seconds would be a priceless, one-time opportunity. I drew a big breath.

"I have been gathering information on you because I believe that your organization planned and engaged in actions against my deceased colleague, Dr. Peter Peterson, who was an outspoken advocate of animal testing at the medical center. I am gathering proof that you targeted Dr. Peterson as an enemy of your cause. Three weeks ago, Dr. Peterson was found floating face-down in a canal behind the medical center."

They reacted with shock and confusion.

"And I believe that actions of your group are responsible for putting him there."

Denial came quickly from many people.

"No."

"Never."

"We are non-violent."

"We demonstrate peacefully."

The reaction was so spontaneous that it had to be real.

"You demonstrate peacefully, like Chuck was demonstrating on my arm?"

The old man said, "Nothing like this has ever happened before."

Old Annabelle was in tears, but I couldn't give up on her. Memories of an old, black-and-white Perry Mason film gave me inspiration.

"You did it, Annabelle Pemberton. You walked up and did it when he was sitting on the fence by the canal bank."

"No," she cried.

"You were the one member of the group who had access to him. You used to be his lover. You went to the Southeastern Unitarian conference with him. But he didn't love you anymore. And you hated him for speaking against Animal Rights."

"No." She was crying. The others were staring at her, apparently surprised about her connection to Pete.

"You walked up to him and injected him with a syringe full of poison."

"No."

"And he fell into the canal and drowned because he couldn't rescue himself."

"Never," she shrieked. "It's true that I loved him and he couldn't love me. But that was years ago. I haven't seen him outside of church for years."

The old man put his arm around her. "Is that why you didn't want to go to our demonstrations at the medical center?"

"Yes, that's why," she whimpered. "It was too painful to see him."

The old man drew himself up and faced me. "I think this has been quite enough."

I sensed the group pulling together. I also heard a siren in the distance. It was either get out of here quick, or face a sticky situation.

"I'll see if this is enough. I'll see if any of your fingerprints on the photos match the fingerprints on the threatening letter mailed to me at Dr. Peterson's apartment."

I turned to the lout who was now sitting up, holding a handkerchief to his mouth. "Mr. Chuck — I don't remember your last name — do you think that I assaulted you or used unnecessary force to escape your grip?"

He clenched and unclenched his fists while looking up at Old Annabelle, who was still sobbing. The old man signalled Chuck with a shake of the head. Chuck was smart enough to read it. "No, you were just trying to get away."

"Good. And do any other of you think that I have committed an illegal act?"

Nobody answered.

"Then I hope that we can lay this matter to rest."

I turned on my heel and walked away. When I got past the bushes, I broke into a run. Had to slow to a walk when I reached the front entrance, because a patrol car was coming in with red and blue lights flashing. I gestured towards the house around the corner and he speeded towards it. Unlocked my bike from the sprinkler pipe and rode off as fast as I could.

I zigzagged through the overgrown streets of Coconut Grove running parallel to Douglas Road. Didn't come off the adrenaline rush before I got north of U.S. Highway One. Ten minutes later, a squad car stopped me in front of Books & Books. Could I run into the famous literary bookstore seeking sanctuary? No, I dismounted and walked over to squad car's window. Luckily, he just wanted to tell me it's illegal to ride a bike on the sidewalk in Coral Gables.

Back at the apartment, I found a note slipped under the door. It was a notice from the management company stating that I had an unauthorized lock on the door, and this was not allowed by the fire code and insurance regulations.

I would write them a sassy letter tomorrow — providing no policemen knocked on the door and hauled me off tonight.

MENSA RECONNECTION 24

Nobody was waiting to arrest me when I returned to the lab the next morning. Hard work helped to keep my mind off the foolishness of the previous night. But trouble, albeit vicarious trouble, was still with me. While leaving for lunch, I fell in behind two security guards escorting a man down the hall. It seemed strange how closely they flanked him. He was acceptably dressed and seemed mild-mannered. A couple of scientists from the Project to Cure Stroke were following a few steps behind.

The guards conducted the man out the door, then left him. Outside the building, the scientists approached him and began to apologize. The woman scientist said she'd just learned that the man's company would need to become "vendorized." It might take four months before they could buy from him again. The other scientist promised to tell the med school purchasing agents that the company was selling reliable tissue culture medium at the lowest price. Both scientists apologized for the security guards' interference with his sales calls.

After eating my brown bag lunch on the plaza, I returned to the lab and printed out the figures for the poster session at Chicago. I glued them to pieces of stiff posterboard, giving them one-inch frames. The maroon border lent the data a certain dignity.

Now for a new project. I spent most of the afternoon doing an Internet Medline search on stroke and MRI, coupled to "indicators." It was my attempt to answer Dr. Yung's challenge to come up with a way to improve the visualization of blocked arteries in the brain. The Medline search itself was something of a challenge — to my patience. The modem transfer went so slow that I was tempted to go back to Pete's apartment and plug my laptop into his phone line.

Around four o'clock I received an interesting call from Ted Walden.

"Dr. Candidi, hopefully I am not disturbing you at your work."

"No."

"And I hope what I have been asked to tell you does not disturb you."

"What?"

"I received a call from Annabelle Pemberton today. She apparently drew the connection between us after learning that I was Pete's attorney . . . and that I had appointed you to do Pete's biography."

"Yes." I tried hard to keep my voice neutral.

"At the end of our conversation, she asked me to relay a message to you."

"Yes."

"A most curious message."

"What was the message?"

"That she could not have killed Pete because she was at a meeting of the Unitarian Women's Alliance on the evening of his death."

"Well, thank you."

"Could I ask why she would want me to pass on such a message to you." He asked politely but insistently.

"Yes, you may ask. But I assume you asked her the same question. How did *she* answer it?"

"Just that you had visited her Animal Advocacy group meeting and had stated that you thought Pete might have been murdered."

"Is that all she said about the evening?"

"Yes."

Then we would leave it at that. I shut the door so that Mildred would not hear me, then told Walden my reasons for thinking that Pete might have been murdered. I told him about the intrusion in the apartment and the anonymous warning letter.

"Annabelle said she was at the Women's Alliance from 8:00 p.m. until after 11:00 p.m. And she can account for an additional three-quarters of an hour when she drove another member home in Perrine."

Perrine is in the southern extreme of Miami-Dade County.

"Please let her know that I was wrong in suspecting her. That probably goes for the rest of her animal rights group, as well."

"I'll tell her." Walden waited a long time before resuming. "Isn't it improbable . . . to speculate that Pete was murdered."

"Did he ever tell you about the hate mail?"

"No." And in the next few minutes of conversation Walden made it clear — without really coming out and saying it — that he thought Pete was just a harmless screwball who didn't have any real crusades. Walden just wanted me to finish up the biography and clean out the apartment so the conditions of Pete's will would be fulfilled. He put no stock in my conspiracy theory nor in my revelation that the file drawer was half-emptied and not half-full.

I wasn't too disappointed by Ted Walden's response. What else could you expect from a guy who lets a ficus tree overgrow his house?

I returned to the apartment and wheeled out my bike. Tonight, I would kill three birds with one stone: Get exercise with a nice ride down to Coconut Grove, eat a decent meal, and reconnect with my old friends and acquaintances from the Miami Chapter of the Mensa Society. The link had not been severed; I had just missed most of the meetings for a couple of years.

It was a nice ride through Little Havana and down to the Chinese restaurant on the edge of the Coconut Grove tourist district. As always, our group had reserved the long table near the large plate glass window looking out on Grand Avenue. They were a pleasant bunch: Harold, an acupuncturist; Susan, an expert at the art of Rolfing and therapeutic massage; Brad with a Ph.D. in musicology, currently working in the classical CD section of Spec's Music; Joanne who is into Zen and makes a living painting Coconut Grove street scenes; Marty who runs a bicycle shop on Coral Way; Mike who works in an auto parts store; Bruce who designs computer games; and Rachel, who is somewhere between 50 and 60, is between husbands, and plays piano bar and Bar Mitzvah gigs for a living.

Luckily, a few seconds after I slipped into a chair, the waiter came to take orders, thus saving me from having to play the role of a long-lost Chapter member. I had no handy explanations for what I'd been doing the last two weeks.

Actually, the Chapter had lost much of its verve since psychiatrist Arnie "Livewire" Green had settled down and stopped throwing parties. My tablemates represented the hard, persistent core of the Chapter who trumpeted the Society's proclaimed vision: "For those who rejoice in the exercise of the mind."

A Mensa-pervasive corollary to the above-mentioned credo, to which I subscribe, is that people who don't like to exercise their minds should be more ready to listen to those who do. But I've slowly come to realize that the world cannot be run on thought experiments and pure intelligence, alone. And I've given up pissing into the wind.

After the waiter brought our drinks, small conversations began to coalesce into a group deliberation on whether we should have roundtable discussions on pre-chosen themes. A couple of us were drinking beer, one was drinking wine, and the rest were drinking tea or soft drinks. Our opinions on roundtable topics were no less varied.

Ten minutes later, with nothing decided, Mike started waving his hand in the air. "Can I have the floor? I really think we should draft a joint, public pronouncement and send it to Marilyn, in the name of the Chapter."

"Not that again," Bruce protested. "We talked about that last time and nobody wanted to do it."

Mike was getting red in the face. "It's *not right* what she is doing. When she gets away with something like that, it gives the whole Society a bad name."

I was curious about what this Marilyn had done. Working in an auto parts store, Mike shouldn't be shocked by anything.

Bruce kept up Marilyn's defense. "Look, she is writing as a private person. There's only one line in her column that mentions she's a member of the Society."

"With the highest I.Q. — or so she says." Mike made a type of grimace that I hadn't seen since grade school. He was turning shrill.

"She's writing that stuff in *Parade Magazine*. Therefore, she has misinformed millions of people. There has to be some way to correct her. There really should be some way to correct her *before* she publishes those things. There should be a review committee. Maybe, we should be that committee."

During the long ensuing silence, curiosity got the best of me. "What did she publish wrong?" Frowns and groans around the table told me I shouldn't have asked.

"She got the statistical distribution of male and female puppies wrong!" Mike frowned. "She gave everyone the wrong answer! For the simple case where there were only four puppies!" He looked around the table for affirmation and didn't find any. "And there she is, on the *front cover* with those dogs, with three white and only one black! It is misleading. She's telling everybody that it's going to come out that way more often than two white and two black!" The guy was beside himself.

"But she didn't *say* that," Bruce said, with irritation.

Mike pulled a photocopy from his back pocket and said, "Here is exactly what the question was: *Your dog has a litter of four: Is it most likely that two are males and two are females?* And here is her answer: *Nope! The most likely split is three males and one female, or three females and one male.*" Mike curled his lip while quoting the last sentence.

"We've been over it before," Joanne said, gazing through the beaded curtain to the street, crowded with cars.

"And I showed you the binomial expansion." Mike quickly rattled off the expression $(a + b)^{**}4$ where a is the probability of male and b is the probability of female, with $a + b = 1$, and so forth. He was frustrated beyond words.

I tried playing the moderator. "I agree that she was either wrong, or careless with her language — her use of 'or.' And it's certainly misleading to people who aren't used to thinking —"

" — and I e-mailed her, and I didn't even get an *answer*." He turned his eyes to the cracked ceiling as if beseeching Heaven.

Harold the acupuncturist inserted the first pin. "Our Chapter is not going to sign your letter. If you want to do it, you have to do it yourself."

"But she is saying these wrong things in the name of the *Society*." Mike was close to tears.

Hoping to hide my embarrassment for the little guy with the whiny voice, I focused on the tattered photocopy, hiding my face in the process. Marilyn's wording *was* tricky and misleading. It was one hell of a bum steer for a poor guy who makes a living by loading boxes in a warehouse — for a poor guy who tears advertisements out of *Parade Magazine* and sends in a hundred dollar money order for a Franklin Mint replica of a 1956 Chevy or an angel-faced plate for his wife's birthday.

Hell, two male pups and two female pups is more probable than three males and one female. Three females and one male is a separate case. I was starting to get pissed off, myself. First off, it stands to reason. And second, I can prove it with mathematics if I have to. And if you try to tell me I'm wrong, I'll call you a yellow-bellied sapsucker. I agreed with the auto parts salesman.

At that instant I knew how Pete felt on his crusades.

It wasn't fair when someone sets herself up as a goddess of intelligence and then abuses people's common sense with a trickily premised question.

I raised the article and offered a face-saving pronouncement. "Well, I do have to admit, Mike, that her definitions are very *Clintonian*."

"Yes! Like his definition of sex!"

Gazing across the table, over Mike's head, Bruce made his own pronouncement: "Your argument is not going to be any stronger even if you do get all eight of us —"

He halted in mid-sentence. A slim, medium-height dark blond coming through the door with a brisk but lanky walk provided a good excuse for changing the subject.

" — Alice! Glad you could come."

I knew Alice McRae and I knew her style. Hurried but not harried, she waved to us all. "Sorry to be late. The County Commission meeting ran late." She walked briskly up to the table and slid into an empty place. She looked around the table with a Tomboyish smile, spending an extra second on me.

Bruce picked up the role of talk show moderator. "Tell us, what will be the big story in the *Miami Standard* tomorrow morning?"

Alice didn't miss a beat. "That the County Aviation Department will be indicted for construction kickbacks . . . and that the mercury will plunge to minus thirty degrees right here in Miami. In other words, it will be a cold day in Hell." Those last words came out with a trace of Georgia accent.

The waiter started bringing our meals. Without breaking his concentration or her conversational rhythm, Alice interjected an order — a dropped egg soup and hot tea. We all listened while she batted the ball back and forth with Bruce. She had more than enough style and élan to make the second string on Channel 8 News. She looked good in that loosely fitting gray business suit. You might say she was functionally attractive — moderate height and bone structure, no fat, and enough loosely attached muscle to make her a good jogger.

It was a functional charm that let her rub elbows at city hall without getting dirty. True, a few specks of mascara had migrated from her lashes to her eyelids and some powder had clumped on one cheek. But it had been a long day. It just wasn't her style to go home and remake herself into a nocturnal beauty. Her style was to drive straight over here and get the scoop on our meeting — or at least a scoop of ice cream.

Brad the musicologist joined in. "We were just getting around to planning the themes for our next meetings. Maybe Mike could make a list of discussion points, and we can talk about it next meeting."

"I will," Mike said. "And I also think that we should go around the table and give everyone a chance to say what they are doing. Alice just told us her story. What about you, Ben? You haven't come for a long time either. The last I heard, you were in training at the U.S. Patent Office."

I told them about giving up the job to take over Peter Peterson's lab. I told them how Rebecca was staying on in D.C., living on the *Diogenes*. Alice tossed her elbow over the back of her chair to face me. I told them about writing Pete's biography.

"So, you are really stepping into his shoes," Susan said.

"You might say that."

"Was he famous?" asked Harold.

"No, but he got his proverbial fifteen minutes of fame every once in a while. It was enough fame to keep him working hard in a tough career." I glanced at Mike. "Hell, everyone craves recognition."

"So why does this Dr. Peterson warrant a biography?" Harold asked.

"His estate is paying for it. What has any of us done to warrant much attention?"

Harold and Susan didn't have anything to report about their last month, but Bruce did. He was going to form a new company called "Internet Security," piggybacking on the computer store where he worked. He had written software for a simple burglar alarm system. It consisted of a digital camera, triggered by the type of motion detector that switches on spotlights over garage doors. Both would be connected to a personal computer.

He glowed as he made his pitch. "You see, most people have a personal computer at home and modem connection to the Internet already. So all I do is sell them a digital camera and the cheap motion detector. If a burglar breaks in, he sets off the motion detector which clicks the digital camera which sends the picture to the computer. The computer dials your phone at work and tells you there's been a disturbance. Then it gives you the photo, either by a direct FTP, or as an attachment to an e-mail message at your Internet access provider. If you see a masked man in the picture, you call the police."

"Pretty good," Mike said. "Have you tried it out?"

"Yes."

I got into the discussion. "You'll have to test it out under a lot of conditions before you can sell it."

"That's just it. I want you all to volunteer to test it at home or work."

Mike said he would check with his boss at the auto parts store, and Marty volunteered his bicycle shop.

As the dinner progressed, the mood around the table became warm and fuzzy. We spent the last few last minutes reading our fortune cookies out loud. As people were getting up to leave, Alice caught my eye, signalling that she wanted to talk. That didn't surprise me; I'd sensed it the moment she arrived. She navigated around pulled-out chairs and departing Mensans with an interesting mixture of feminine grace and masculine directness. She set herself down next to me like we were scheduled for an interview. All that was missing was a notepad. Such is Alice's style of social navigation. She always takes the direct approach.

I knew Alice's direct approach from when I first met her, over my third drink at a Mensa Christmas party a few years back. Rebecca had gone back to New York for the holidays. This was before our commitment had solidified. Alice had used an interview style with me then, too. Well, it had started out as an interview.

Alice brushed crumbs from the edge of the table, planted an elbow, and rested her head on her hand. "I'm glad you're back in town, Ben."

"Thanks. It feels like home."

"It feels good to be back in Miami? And you're not going to become a patent examiner?"

Funny, how a drunken flirtation can generate long-term spin in a couple of people. The little gyroscope inside keeps spinning and pointing for months and years. There's not much energy in the spin, but you can read it out as surely as Dr. Yung's magnetic resonance imaging machine reads proton spins in your body's blood and tissues. Read out the spin for a non-destructive image of the heart.

"No. I won't become a patent examiner." Not wanting to encourage a news story charade, I let her dangle with that.

"No loss to the world. You're too imaginative for that kind of work. You should be cooking up your own inventions."

Resisting a feature story charade would be harder.

"You're right. First, I have to set up a stable research program."

"And you're going to walk a mile in the dead scientist's moccasins?" She lifted her voice in jest and challenge. With charming effect she tossed her head, sending a wave through her mid-length hair. Her hair required no further effort from her to return to its natural position. Alice knew how to compromise between the demands of glamor and the everyday.

"You've already heard that from me," I thought. But a flash of inspiration furnished me with a milder and more useful reply. "Tell me, Brenda Starr, did you know Dr. Peter Peterson of Bryan Medical School?"

She laughed. Her eyes sparkled like the comic strip heroine's.

"I didn't know him personally. Wasn't my beat. But he was in the news every few months, and I guess the Op-Ed people got a letter-to-the-editor from him every week. He was a real concerned citizen."

"Did his concerns make anybody nervous?"

"I doubt it. I just figured he was a crackpot."

"I've been toying with the idea that someone killed him."

"That could happen to anyone. This is Miami." She made a firing pistol out of forefinger and thumb. "What's your coroner friend say? The one that you did the undercover job for." I cleared my throat and she corrected herself. "I mean your coroner friend that some people still think you did an undercover job for."

Alice was holding a three-year grudge because I wouldn't help her put a story together. No matter that the story would have blown my cover and would have invalidated the case Dr. Westley was building. Alice and I had never talked about it since.

"Dr. Westley said the examination of Dr. Peterson revealed no wounds or blunt force trauma — no sign of a struggle. He was found floating face down in Wagner Creek. The examiner on the case called it a heart attack. I'm waiting for the police report. I've requested it under the Freedom of Information Act."

"You'd make a good reporter, Ben."

"That's a compliment, coming from an ace. I'm figuring that if someone killed him, he did it with poison. I really should be saying 'she.' The last person seen with him by the canal bank was an unidentified old woman."

"You could have the body exhumed and look for poison."

"Yes, but Dr. Westley doesn't think much of the idea. And it will require a court order and permission of next of kin. Right now, I need a better choice of suspects and motives." I caught myself fingering my left ear.

"What makes you think anyone killed him?"

I told her how Pete had mouthed off about everything and had called it a crusade. I told her about the hate mail, the illegal entry, my suspicions that files were missing, and the anonymous threat.

Alice said that Pete's statements on the cloning of human embryos and on the right to die wouldn't mobilize any organized group. She discounted the Right to Lifers because they don't demonstrate in Miami and we've never had an abortion clinic bombing. She rejected the animal rights group.

"Sure, they demonstrate against the University of Miami Medical School and against Bryan Medical School. But you know yourself that neither institution was ever broken into."

"True."

"Where they broke in was at Washington State or Oregon. But I don't think they ever hurt any scientists, to say nothing of killing one."

Alice smiled at me. The girl was sharp. The best-focused girl in our Mensa Chapter. And not unattractive, either.

"Ben, let's look at this like a scientist — a criminologist. You think someone poisoned him?"

"Yes."

"How?"

"Either sneaked up behind him and injected him, or fed it to him."

"Let's work it backward from there. The poisoner had to be intelligent and motivated. What are the possible motives? Protecting herself or himself after Dr. Peterson did something that threatened them. What kind of threat would make them want to kill him? An opinion is not enough. It would have to be a threat to someone's money or career. Or maybe betrayal in love. Could he have been seeing any Coral Gables matrons who have jealous husbands?"

I smiled at the thought of Old Annabelle as a Coral Gables matron. "Pete wasn't attractive to women. Too goofy for them to take seriously. His only women were the centerfolds in old *Playboy* magazines."

"Okay, we forget about passion. Was he a threat to anyone's money or career?"

I told her about Pete's frozen hamburger experiments.

"Good. Anyone else that he was a threat to?"

"Well . . . to Bryan Medical School. Actually, it would be more of an embarrassment to them. All those called-in comments on talk radio. And all those awkward 20-second appearances on Channel 8."

"I can believe that. I once heard that our Medical Editor got a call from some higher-ups at Bryan saying that they didn't want him quoted in the *Miami Standard*."

"Good. Thanks for the lead."

"But embarrassment alone wouldn't be a reason to kill him."

"You're right."

But interference with someone's revenue stream might be a motive for murder. And that would fit with the intrusion in his apartment, my theory of missing files and the threat letter. I would ponder that when I got home.

"Thanks, Alice. You've been a real help in thinking this through. I really do owe you one."

A smile formed and then disappeared from her face.

"You owe me *two*. You didn't give me the scoop when that chairman of pharmacology was poisoned."

Nature has no greater fury than a charming woman reporter whose request for inside information is scorned.

I said, "We both know there is no way I could have helped you back then."

"*Touch*é."

"As I was saying, I really owe you one."

A smile glowed behind caked makeup. Alice turned her chair, pulling it a bit closer in the process. "Interesting that you were up in Washington at the Patent Office. Did you know I had a six-month fellowship at the *Washington Post*?"

"No. That sounds great. Sounds interesting. I bet you learned a lot about the city — geographical and political. How did you like it?"

"Oh, it was so interesting. It would take *hours* to tell you all about it . . . following the footsteps of Woodward and Bernstein. Say, I have a good bottle of wine in the fridge. I just bought a condo on Brickell Avenue. Love to show it to you. Why don't we pick up the conversation there?"

She said it so casually, so lightheartedly.

"I can't."

"Sure, you can. It's not too far from here. The balcony looks out on the Bay."

"I can't."

"Or you won't?" It was nine parts of disappointment and one part of rebuke.

"Okay. If I have to choose between the two words, it's *won't*." It was hard to look her in the eye. "It's just that —"

" — your mind's still up in Washington." She said it so softly.

"A piece of my heart, too."

Her eyes dropped to the table. "You love her."

"Yes, deeply. Too deeply to betray her . . . which is exactly what I would do if I went with you to your apartment."

Alice jerked her head away so fast she startled me. She looked at the basket containing the fortune cookies. She took one, removed its cellophane wrapper and broke it open. With exaggerated deliberation, she read the strip of paper. She frowned and tossed it into an empty teacup. Then she held the cookie over it, crumbling it to dust.

"Where do you keep her picture?"

Alice's question caught me by surprise. "Here in my little brown address book . . . together with my driver's license and credit cards."

Alice opened her purse and took out a little gold-plated case. She removed a business card and wrote on the back.

She handed me the card. "Put this in there with her picture."

It read, "Rain check, for a rainy day." I pulled out my little brown book and inserted the card.

This time she locked her eyes on me. "I'm a thick-skinned woman. I don't bruise easily. But with you, I couldn't stand to be a three-time loser. Promise me this: The first time Dr. Quinn Medicine Woman really slips up and does something unforgivable, you tell her. And then, I want to be the second person to know. You hear, now?"

"Yes."

"Promise?"

"Cross my heart."

I could promise her that. If I ever lost Rebecca, it would take me a thousand years to tell anyone.

I walked Alice out to her car and validated my promise with a kiss on the cheek. She returned it with a kiss on the lips which I kept under control by holding her at half an arm's length. She didn't drive out of the parking lot until I mounted my bicycle.

Funny, that I'd just confided more of the crazy Pete story to Alice than to my own fiancée.

On the ride home, I thought about a lot of things: about the extremity of Mike's indignation with Marilyn's mistake on the front page of *Parade Magazine*; about the nature of indignation; about whether Northern Europeans are less tolerant of human short-comings than Southern Europeans; and whether some people have enhanced perceptions in the moral dimension, seeing sharp edges where others just see a fuzzy picture.

I pondered E.O. Wilson's suggestion that we might have a gene for religion. And what about a gene for righteous indignation? I remembered the Robert Frost poem about good fences making good neighbors. I tried to remember the words to "Choose Something Like a Star." I thought about unrequited love; about old-fashioned heros; and about patience. And I thought about science and lives dedicated to the study of Mother Nature who yields a true secret once a decade.

I thought about Pete's ill-fated quest for grandeur. Was a new insight as good as a discovery? Was a compelling argument as good as a new insight? And was a tireless harangue as good as a new insight if supported by moral authority?

How had Pete been earning his moral authority in his last couple of decades? From working past the normal retirement age? From working out of habit?

As I rolled the bike through the door of Pete's apartment, I realized that I'd been pondering everything except the most important question before me: Was there a killer at the med school? How did he or she do it? By poisoning Pete's food? By spraying or injecting him while he sat on the fence by the canal?

26   BABY, IT'S A WILD WORLD

It became clear to me the instant I rolled my bike across the threshold of Pete's apartment. I had to decide between two choices: either toss out my not-a-natural-death theory, or start looking for a murderer.

My fingers returned to my scalp.

My feet took me to the file cabinet. My weak, impatient side was taking over. I could kill the theory by disqualifying Pete as a goofus. I pulled open the middle drawer and removed the document that could do it for me — the goofy poem. I reread it.

ODE TO BURDIE

One day I turned my eye to the sky,
And something so curious I saw up on high.
Moving silhouettes did betray,
The return to the nest at the end of the day.

Just chance that the clouds blocked the sun's setting rays,
That block the Burdie nest with firey red glaze.
Just chance that that instant Old Pete looked up in the skies
And what he first saw, he couldn't believe his eyes.

Just luck what was caught in the lightbulb's glow,
Was blown up on the wall like a Jap lantern show.
An instant's enough for Deadeye to see,
And Old Pete's an expert in photo ID.

Quick home Old Pete hurried for his camera bag,
Towards heaven he scrambled over rebar and slag,
Over the hootchie hutch, the Burdie nest,
He took the best shots of his life, I must confess.

Funny Burdie in the sky,
Loves dropping whitewash in everyone's eye
But no one hollers, no one cries
It's not so bad 'cause cows can't fly.

But Pete will take potshots at sacred cows,
And climb the Himalayas if the Dalai Lama allows,
Taking shots of birdies with their mates.
More fun than in the jump seat of a P-38.

So bring out the tin Lizzie, let's go for a ride
Take along mom and the grandma, and sugar daddy Clyde
Tin Lizzie'll last forever if you don't burn out her clutch,
And she'll drive you to the door of the hootchie cootchie hutch.

Damn! The theory survived. This time the poem seemed purposeful. Or was it just purposeful *voyeurism*? There was nothing

to see out the apartment's windows except for the Veterans Administration Hospital, a block away. Maybe I'd have to suspend judgement until I'd checked out Pete's do-gooder group in Chicago.

I mulled over the poem until my thoughts were interrupted by the ring of the phone. I picked up and answered.

It was Rebecca! "What's with you, Ben? You don't sound yourself. You sound kind of down."

How could I tell her about my theory?

"Sorry, Rebecca. I love you. But I am kind of down. A lot of things are coming up all at once. Like in three days I'm going to have to get on a plane to Chicago."

I told Rebecca about the Biophysical Society meeting. She asked all the right questions, but seemed preoccupied with something else.

"You sound a little down, yourself, darling."

"Yes, to be truthful, I was calling so you could cheer *me* up."

"What's getting you down?"

"I'm really missing you. It's getting lonely up here. I know it was right for you to follow your opportunity, but it's getting hard for me, not knowing what we are going to do."

"I feel the same way. Wish I could tell you that my new job is a big success . . . or even a total flop. Either way, we'd know what to do. But there are too many questions up in the air for me to even make a prediction. There's a lot of damn politics here."

"I know what you mean, Ben. All the politics that you have to put up with just to *keep* the job. You know what I did the other night? I went to a cocktail party thrown by one of the world health bureaucrats. And do you know what we did all night? We listened to a couple of policy wonks. And then we *networked*. The bureaucrat floated ideas on us, pretending that she had just read them or heard them from another policy wonk. And you know what? They were all *wrong*. And they didn't really have anything to do with world health. It was about rearranging the darn bureaucracy."

"Makes you want to puke, doesn't it?"

"That's the way I felt. I was thinking of saying 'no' to the second year of the fellowship, and coming down to join you in a couple months. Why do they need *me* to prepare reports that no one is going to read. I'm thinking about getting a job in an E.R. in some hospital around Miami. Everyone calls a 'scutt job' — but I'd be making money for us."

"I love you." My voice cracked.

"I was thinking how I'd show them — doing a good job counseling, and connecting every child abuse case with a social worker and following it through. Phooey to policy wonks and their career statisticians. I'd do my own statistics. I started daydreaming about putting anthropology into action . . . maybe even writing a book about it."

"Rebecca, you'd better think twice before giving up on your Washington gig. You'd lose your contacts for the grant proposals you want to make. You shouldn't give that up for me . . . not with this lousy job at this lousy place."

"Lousy place?"

Yes, Bryan Medical School — the lousy place I shouldn't have returned to, the lousy place that Rebecca shouldn't be sacrificing her career for.

"I'm seeing it a lot differently than when I was a student. I'm seeing it like a guy who has to make bricks with no straw. I'm drowning in a sea of *Administratium*."

"Administratium?"

"Parasitic bureaucracy," I replied.

Streams of minor irritations had been dammed up for weeks. Now the floodgates were opening. Words flowed out in a tirade. I complained to Rebecca about Bryan Medical School's fixation on overhead money. I complained about the dean's unctuous impromptu speech at the grant proposal meeting. Complained about the expensive clinical endpoint studies eating up all the money. Complained about having to do my own plumbing repairs to spare unnecessary expenses to my grant.

"Rebecca, they don't care about scientific discovery. They just care about getting an extra fifty dollars every time I order a hundred-dollar bottle of something. And they are probably extracting kickbacks from the company selling me the bottle."

"Kickbacks?"

"It's the only way to explain it. Just a few days ago, some administrator ordered security guards to throw a guy out of the building for selling culture medium. The damn guards threw him out of the building! Threw him out of the damn building! For what? For going around to the different labs and offering a good price on tissue culture medium. They threw him out because he wasn't an 'approved vendor'."

"No, that doesn't sound fair."

"As if the bureaucrat knows better than the scientist."

I rattled off half a dozen complaints that I'd heard since taking the job — of the administration forcing scientists to buy things at higher-than-market prices, of $40,000 lab renovations done by outside contractors.

"Kickbacks is the only way that to explain it." And as I said the words, a thought came to me: The murderer may have been engaged in kickbacks.

"I know it sounds bad, Ben, but maybe you shouldn't let it upset you *so* much."

"Okay." End of conversation. I had no basis for discussing a murder theory with Rebecca tonight. Hell, I couldn't even tell her about the nonsense with the Animal Rights people.

"I'm sorry that I couldn't cheer you up, Ben. Let's talk about something else. Tell me about your biography on Dr. Peterson."

"That project is over half-done. Guess I've earned an honest ten thousand dollars so far. But to be perfectly honest, this whole Pete Peterson thing is making me sick."

"Why?"

How could I tell her without getting into the theory?

"It's his goofiness that's the real problem. It's wearing off on me."

I told her about Pete's goofy call-ins to the radio talk shows, about his goofy appearances on the local TV news and about his quixotic letters to the editor. I told her how he had pissed off physicians at the medical center, had pissed off the dean, and had been getting ready to make trouble for the meat-packing industry. I finished by telling her that he was a crackpot loner with delusions of grandeur.

"He's something like the man who built the Coral Castle . . . and had a crazy theory on electricity and magnetism."

Rebecca's comparison was so brilliant that it left me wordless.

"You remember when we visited the Coral Castle, don't you, Ben?"

"Yes. And your comparison is right-on."

Yes, I remembered Coral Castle, down in Homestead where U.S. Highway One leaves the mainland to jump along the Florida

Keys. The Castle is a walled enclosure formed by 4x4x7 foot coral blocks stacked maybe 15 feet high, built single-handedly by a man named Ed Leedskalnin. He had quarried the enormous blocks from coral bedrock. He had hoisted them with the help of cables, pulleys, and I-beam tripods that he had grubbed together from junkyards. He'd called it the Eighth Wonder of the World.

He died there as an old eccentric some time in the 1950s. But he was probably a certifiable nut case even before he came to Florida. I remembered the goofy stuff inside the enclosure — the oversized furniture carved from stone, his "throne room," and his elevated planets and crescent moon — nutty enough to impress any hick that drove through there in 1938.

"But I don't remember anything about Ed Leedskalnin doing anything with electromagnetism," I said.

Rebecca turned insistent. "Sure you remember his electromagnetism theories. You made fun of them." She giggled. "You've got to remember reading the sign in his electrical laboratory — you called it a pigsty — describing his electrical experiments."

"Right!"

"And his collection of bottles wrapped with stove wire?"

"Yeah, with no insulation. He probably thought he was making solenoids. They couldn't have worked. They would have shorted out."

Now Rebecca was laughing, almost out of control.

"Remember how you made fun of his *pamphlet*?"

"Yes." I laughed.

"And how he *proved* that all the physicists are wrong and that everything is really made up of *magnets*."

"Yes." My chest started heaving. "He was trying to sell them by mail for one dollar — in 1938."

"And you remember how you were reading it out loud in the gift shop. And the people started looking at you so funny that the man almost asked you to leave."

"Yes." In a split second it came back to me.

Rebecca was giggling into the phone, hyperventilating and cracking up. "Come on, Ben. Quote me . . . the theory! You're always so . . . good . . . at theory."

"Well . . ."

"Come on, Ben. We're a thousand miles away from each other.

You've got me laughing. It would be better than phone sex. Come on, Ben. Do it to me! Read me the pamphlet in front of all those people."

It came back to me in a split second. I used a twangy voice. "From this you can see that physicists are basing their thoughts on *non-existent things*. In fact, all matter and everything everywhere is held together by the North Pole and the South Pole of individual magnets."

It had been a year since we'd laughed so hard together, both of us out of control. Every time I stopped, Rebecca just laughed harder.

Now she was hysterical, gasping for breath between words. "Do you . . . remember . . . what you said about his . . . hanging . . . leather chair?"

His living area was about ten-foot square, in the crude stone turret above his "laboratory." There was a stone bed with a straw-filled mattress. A screen-cage hung from the ceiling. I'd joked that it was a Faraday Cage for electromagnetic experiments. Actually, he used it to keep cockroaches and mice out of his bread and ham. Next to the case hung the chair — a broad, red-dyed, leather strap arrangement suspended from the ceiling by chains. To an innocent eye its design would resemble a swing seat for very young children.

I was having trouble breathing, myself. "Yes, I remember . . . the chair. I said it looked . . . like something that belonged . . . in a San Francisco . . . S&M parlor!"

Rebecca was giggling in uncontrolled frenzy. Finally she managed to stop, and took two heavy breaths. "Ben, you slay me!" She was imitating a *femme fatal* in an old movie we'd seen together.

I affected a lifeless "Munster" voice. "No, I wouldn't slay you just yet. First I'll drag you down to the courtyard and take you by force on the *Feast of Love Table*. Then I'll draw and quarter you on the Florida-shaped table. Then I'll drip your blood in the *Moon Fountain* and stuff your twitching body in *The Well*. Then I'll check to make sure that the North Star is still in the iron bar cross-hairs of the *Polaris Telescope*. Then I'll sit on my throne in the *Throne Room* and think it over for a while. And before going to bed, I'll say the rosary in the *Repentance Corner*."

"Ben . . . Stop it. I can't breathe!"

We must have laughed together for five minutes, our laughter interspersed with deep breaths, moans and I love you's.

"Ben, you cheered me up so. Are you happy?"

"Yes."

"Try to stay that way. And remember that I love you." (Click)

And I did try to stay happy, chuckling at my mental images of a couple from the Bonnie and Clyde era driving down a dusty U.S. Highway One at 40 miles an hour, then slowing and stopping the Ed Leedskalnin's self-proclaimed Eighth Wonder of the World — his Taj Mahal — and photographing each other with an old-fashioned camera.

The Coral Castle doesn't pull them in like that anymore. The last Coral Castle picture I'd seen was on a CD cover, as a funky backdrop for Vanilla Ice.

I started brooding again. Rebecca's comparison of Pete Peterson with Ed Leedskalnin ran too deep. Both men had been jilted and both had set out to do "great works." Leedskalnin's great work was a monument to a love that never was — to his young Latvian bride who jilted him on the eve of their wedding. The sixteen year-old bride decided he was "too old and too poor." He worked on his monument single-handedly, for decades.

Well, at least Pete wasn't quite that crazy. He didn't build any stone chairs for his "sweet sixteen" and for his "mother-in-law to be." He didn't carve any "marriage bed" or bed for their unborn child.

I remembered the old photographs of Ed standing proudly in suit and tie before his creation. With his small stature, his small nose, and with his chiseled features carrying such a serious expression, he reminded me of Ross Perot, the man who wanted to be President.

With my mind so unsettled, I would have to read myself to sleep. I pulled from the shelf one of Pete's beloved Clive Cussler tomes, *Inca Gold*, one of the emblems of Pete's crusade, according to his will. I read my way into the Peruvian expedition, the Shining Path guerrilas, and the divers trapped in the mountain cave. The book conjured vivid pictures of saponified bodies and Dirk Pitt's daring underwater rescue.

But even on the pages of this book, Pete Peterson had found a way to irritate me. Every second line, the page was punctured by a pin prick. I imagined confused, distractible old Pete trying to hold his place and keep his thoughts organized with the help of a sewing pin.

I fell asleep in the middle of the guerilla counterattack on the ancient Inca fortress.

Turbines whined outside. Acceleration pulled me back into the seat. Funny, how three days can go by in an instant. And as the Miami International tarmac blurred and receded and we climbed for the clouds, I looked back on all that I'd accomplished:

— Readying a dozen graphs, figures and tables mounted on stiff maroon poster board sitting in an art folio now safely tucked in the side of my window seat on the portside of the airplane; and

— A dozen trips between the library and Dr. Yung's clinic where we bent my ideas around the current dogma on imaging stroke by MRI and figured out how to express them as a testable hypothesis; and

— Three pages of carefully worded text describing my proposal for testing paramagnetic drugs and metal chelates as MRI contrast agents; and

— Two hours of checking with Administration on fringe benefit rates and making sure our budget was right; and

— Getting emergency approval from the "Human Use Committee" to use blood samples from Dr. Yung's patients.

I had done my best. My science was good, and I had taken all the bureaucratic measures necessary to guard my flanks.

And I had even made some progress on the conspiracy theory. It was no surprise when my reply to the anonymous letter came back, "address unknown." The police report seemed to rule out robbery. Pete's watch and billfold were found on his body. His pipe, ashes, and spent matches were found under the fence where he had been sitting.

And I had looked into Pete's frozen hamburger experiment in the basement gamma radiation facility. After I got the guy from Radiation Control to show me the facility, I was convinced there had been no radiation accident. The facility was foolproof. When the worm gear starts lifting the gamma radiation source out of its lead chest, alarms start beeping and red warning lights start flashing to tell you to get the hell out of there.

No, I hadn't figured out how Pete died, but I had figured out how to sell his 1956 Olds — and for a good price. I'd taken it to Classic Chassis. Nice touch, wearing your Miami Beach outfit, taking along Pete's fedora and putting on that *shtick* about how "Uncle Pete" should have given it to you. That droopy-eyed, poker-faced dealer called Ted Walden with an offer faster than you could walk to the nearest payphone to advise him how to handle it!

Enough is enough. You did good, Ben. Time to stop worrying and let American Airlines do it for you. Now kick back and relax.

We were flying high over the tops of the clouds towering over the Everglades. Off to the left, the sun was setting on a woolly virtual horizon. We were heading north to Chicago/O'Hare.

When the flight attendants came along with the drink cart, I took out a five-dollar bill. You earned that gin and tonic, Ben. You've been a good "junior faculty member," a good professional colleague, a good future husband, and even a good Mensan. It really wasn't convenient to let Bruce spend all that time on your computer, installing his home monitoring software and testing out the digital camera and his modem and Internet connections. But when a fellow Mensan invents a security system that will cost less than $300 and will work on any half-decent PC, you take the time to play guinea pig. You're a good guy, Ben. Drink up, kick back, and let this baby take you to Chicago.

The drink smoothed out the wrinkles on my brain. I shut my eyes, knowing all would turn out well, and didn't open them again until awakened by changing pressure in my ears. Caught my first view of the Windy City as we descended over a line of tall buildings and a half-mile-wide band of railroad tracks. Then came an endless expanse of two-story wooden houses, closely spaced like rabbit hutches.

It was a sleepy walk in the airport, and a sleepy ride in the van that took me to the Hyatt Hotel near the McCormick Place Convention Center. The map showed it close to the south of downtown along the South Shore, but north of the University of Chicago.

They rolled my plastic, and I rolled into a $260 bed where I had a $50 sleep. Woke early the next morning and hurried to McCormick Place, beating the crowd to the registration lines. Wrote a check, got my program book and badge, and walked past the monitoring guard into the cavernous exhibition hall. Found my corkboard #357 at the end of the fifth row. Took out my maroon-framed squares and rectangles and pinned them to the board, creating an attractive arrangement of figures, tables and discussion points. Large letters on the top presented the title and the authors, Peter S. Peterson ‡ and Benjamin Candidi. At the bottom right, marked with a ‡, I thumbtacked a 60-word biography of Pete.

Slowly, the walls of the exhibition hall began to echo with the sound of a waterfall which increased in strength with the babble of hundreds, then thousands of scientific conversations. Slowly, the hall was filling to capacity. Many scientists passed before me, some quickly glancing from my number to the program book and back as they hurried to find another poster, and others strolling leisurely and actually reading our title.

My first real "customer" came around 10:30 a.m.. He was a fortyish guy in a tweed jacket, with a scarf around his neck, and wearing thick-soled brown shoes. He carried a cloth bag that said "FASEB Meeting, 1985." He looked up and read our title. "Ah, a melatonin effect on oxidative damage. That looks interesting. Maybe you can give it to me in a nutshell."

I pointed to my first figure that showed the free radical targets we were studying, and ran down the mechanisms to damage, and showed him some gel electrophoretograms demonstrating molecular fragmentation with oxidative damage, and how melatonin protects against it. Then I took him to the right side of the poster and showed him five "bullets" recapitulating our findings and discussion points.

The guy seemed to be interested in the work. He listened politely and asked a probing question every once in a while. When I got to the end of my spiel he chuckled, broke into a condescending smile and said, "So you're working with Old Pete?"

"I'm finishing up his work. I'm sorry to say that Pete died several weeks ago."

He reacted with surprise followed by embarrassment, and finally with a deliberate frown, probably meant as an expression of condolence. "I'm really sorry to hear that. Pete was one of the last of the pioneer biochemists."

We talked for another five minutes. And between the lines this guy told me what I already knew from my review of Pete's scientific papers. Pete had discovered gold dust in the stream beds, but had never found and mined his own vein of gold.

The guy's final words summed it all up: "He was the last of

the rugged individualists. Some of the things he did and said were pretty whacky, but you always knew that Pete was honest."

And that pretty much summed up the dozen comments I gleaned from the poster's four dozen visitors. I wrote them down:

"Pete came across like a crackpot, but down under he really loved science. And he hated it when people tried to hide weak science behind a glossy presentation."

"An old-fashioned, no-nonsense scientist. Couldn't get any nonsense past *him*."

"I remember the time when they almost laughed him out of the meeting room. Sometimes he would really put his foot in it. But when he got onto something, when he thought there was something out there, he wouldn't let go until he gave it a good looking over. And a lot of times he was right."

"Pete never made the big time. It was a shame. He had a lot of good ideas, but he couldn't keep focussed. He was a little too ambitious — hopped from one project to another. But he made a lot of useful contributions."

"Pete was rough-hewn. He was real prickly."

"You know, he was really the one who discovered free radical damage, but he wasn't able to get his lab in high gear, so he got crowded out. And it didn't help him any, being wrong on the reperfusion injury mechanism."

"It was hard knowing how to cite his papers, because he always had so many statements I disagreed with mixed in together with the data I wanted to cite."

"He was a maverick. He always stood up for what he believed in. He was a scientific Barry Goldwater. Got a lot of flak that he didn't deserve."

The news of Pete's death brought tears to the eyes of two scientists — one a woman, the other a man.

By the end of the day, four dozen people knew that I was working in the area of oxidative damage and two dozen of them knew I was Pete's successor. And I knew that talking and thinking all day can wear you out.

That evening was the National Lecture, given by one of the inventors of "combinatorial chemistry." I learned about techniques that let you synthesize and test chemical compounds for drug activity hundreds of times faster than before.

I made good use of the second day of the meeting. I visited every poster and slide presentation having to do with free radical chain damage. I caught up on the latest findings on protein kinases, the subject of my dissertation. I was feeling darn good about science.

Had dinner that night at a Polish restaurant where I was served by a Russian waitress. Then came the session I had been waiting for: the meeting of the Social Responsibility Subgroup.

The program book's listing led me to a mid-sized ballroom of my hotel. The room was set up for a symposium. A large projection screen dominated the wall up front. To the side of the screen was a low movable platform with a lectern and a draped table with four microphones. And before me was an acre of chairs, the stackable kind with hooks on the sides that held them close together in tight, regular rows. I walked up the center aisle towards the platform.

Nine people were sitting in the front, near the center aisle. Four sat in the front row, widely spaced; the rest sat together, one row back. Except one sat way up front of the first row, facing everyone. He had obviously unhooked his chair. The assemblage reminded me of the meeting of Animal Advocacy group.

As I approached, the man up front waved to me. His badge said Dr. Kurt Hammerschlag and he looked as I had pictured him: fiftyish, unexpressive face with formal demeanor, non-athletic but not overweight, dressed in a tweed jacket and brown leather-topped, rubber-soled shoes.

"Dr. Candidi, I presume. Welcome."

His compatriots turned in their chairs, both curious and glad to see another person ready to join their group. Dr. Hammerschlag introduced me as Pete's successor. I took a seat in the front row, a couple of spaces from the man sitting on the end. Hammerschlag said their meeting was suffering from competition from a presentation from Representative George Brown from California. The congressman had a lot of influence on science appropriations and was an outspoken critic of any basic science that doesn't produce commercial applications.

While explaining this, Hammershlag looked occasionally to me. Was I making the group self-conscious? In the front row, an elderly scientist nodded her encouragement back to Hammerschlag and threw all-inclusive glances at the scientists sitting around her.

Hammerschlag gestured in my direction. "Pete had prepared

an extensive presentation on institutional ethics questions. Dr. Candidi told me he was unable to find Pete's script or any notes he was working from. Thus, we will have to regard Pete's work as his Unfinished Symphony. He was a great crusader who will be missed by us all."

"Hear, hear!" said the lady scientist. Almost everyone vocalized some form of affirmation.

"What do we have on the program?" asked the tall guy in the second row. His voice sounded like a cross between Henry Fonda and Kermit the Frog. His name tag said he was from the Department of Chemistry of the University of Oklahoma.

Hammerschlag said, "I have prepared some material on communicating with the lay public. I have also compiled all of your inputs for a set of draft guidelines for maintaining ethical standards and providing fair reviews during service on study sections. I think that it is every scientist's right to receive a fair review of his or her grant proposal. I do not think that the National Institutes of Health has gone far enough with this. This should leave at least forty minutes for your individual contributions and matters arising."

The Oklahoma chemist confirmed the plan with a nod. I didn't see anyone's hand in the air volunteering to fill the forty minutes.

Hammerschlag segued into his a presentation on the NIH grant proposal review process. His major point was that grant reviewers should be rewarded for spending more time reviewing a proposal. He also believed that the quality of an applicant's previous work should be given greater weight in the decision process. He criticized the NIH's rating scales for "injecting statistical noise into the process."

The lady scientist asked how the group would address institutional accountability, now that Pete had left us. She invited me to join their group.

I stood up and turned to face them. "Yes, I would like to come to your meeting next year. But you must realize that I am a newcomer to academic science, and didn't have much weight to throw around for any cause. I have been asked by some of Pete's Unitarian friends to do a short biography on him, particularly on his crusades for social responsibility. It would help me a lot if you all could tell me what Pete was doing in the area of *institutional accountability*."

I stared into a collection of blank faces.

"I searched hard through his files and his rooms and couldn't find any notes for this talk he was supposed to give."

The faces looked pained and eyes averted.

"In fact, I couldn't find any notes from Pete on this subject at all."

Now, everyone was looking away. Was I turning an evening's entertainment into an evening of punishment?

"It would be very helpful to me . . . while you are here . . . if you could tell me what type of work on the subject of institutional responsibility Pete was actually *doing* down in Miami and —"

" — Alex," the elderly lady interrupted, "you are the group's secretary and you have been keeping notes."

"Yes," said a scientist from Oregon, "I have some notes from Pete's presentations at previous meetings. Think I have some hand-outs, too. I'll be glad to send them to you."

"Yes, thank you," I said. "And in the mean time maybe each of you could — while we're here now — tell me something about what he was doing down there."

Everyone fidgeted in embarrassment. Two people said some nice things about Pete, but it wasn't any public outpouring like at the Unitarian memorial service. And I learned nothing about any crusade.

"Could I ask each one of you to write a one-page reminiscence for Pete's biography?"

Everyone quickly agreed — and quickly agreed that the meeting was adjourned. And they spread out like a bundle of electrons, each going his separate way, almost faster than I could get down their names and addresses.

Yes, that group had told me *something* tonight. Yes, I had received information on *them*. The pack of watchdogs hadn't barked tonight. And that was significant.

The next day brought eight solid hours of great science. I took in a lot of good sessions. Wrote 20 pages of notes and five pages of new ideas.

That evening, I wound up at the Improv, catching a comedy act by Larry Miller. He's that fairly young guy with a mostly bald head who played the demanding doorman on *Seinfeld* and once played an intelligent, teasing psychopath on *Law & Order*. At the Improv, he did a real self-deprecating *shtick* about his previous married life and about being a good neighbor. He pulled a lot of hard laughs by dragging us through rough examples. The guy has a hell of a lot of insight.

I sat at a long table with some people around my age — two married couples from Indianapolis and a couple of women from southern Illinois. Towards the end, members of the audience asked Larry Miller to do the piece about how women and men look at each other differently. I nearly burst my sides, laughing at his impersonation of a man watching a nude dancer. He compared the man to a crippled lion watching a gazelle. The Chicago crowd gave a standing ovation to their hometown boy who made good.

One of the southern Illinois girls said that their hotel had a good piano bar, and maybe I wanted to catch a set with them. I declined politely. One thing might have led to another.

The next day, the Society had only a morning poster session. By that time, I was pretty conference-worn and unenthusiastic. Maybe it was the effect of the propane residue in the exhaust of the fork lift trucks maneuvering behind the curtained boundary, removing the crated company exhibits.

After an hour, I quit and took the Metra Electric Train to the 59th Street station. It is near the Lake shore, and serves the Museum of Science and Industry, and the University of Chicago campus. With a 7:00 p.m. O'Hare departure, I could certainly afford a couple of hours at the museum. Around noon, I grabbed a hotdog from an outside vendor. It was a mild, sunny day with a pleasant wind off the Lake. I strolled to the Oriental Museum. Dr. Westley had once told me they had a good Egyptology collection. They also had a store with a nice collection of Egyptian necklaces. I bought one for Rebecca.

By two in the afternoon I was museumed out. I strolled along the grassy expanse of the Midway Plaisance, admiring the Gothic buildings on either side. After a couple of blocks, something deflected my course to the right, and I wound up inside an enormous quadrangle. And there, in the northeast corner, it caught my eye — a three-story ivy-covered Gothic building with a spire and pointed roof. The Kent Chemical Laboratory.

My feet took me through its oaken double doors and to the directory. And there it was: "Prof. Kurt Hammerschlag, Office Room 305; Laboratory, Rooms 306-308."

The realization came over me slowly: I wouldn't get any damn notes from the Oregon professor. It wasn't an accident that I'd wandered over here. It was no more an accident than when aimless wandering in Pete's apartment had led me to his bedroom file cabinet. Prof. Kurt Hammerschlag wasn't half-assed. He was half-hiding the story.

I climbed the two flights of wide stairs, and went down the hallway to his office. Hammerschlag's name was painted on a frosted-glass of his wooden door which stood one-quarter open. He seemed glad to see me, and invited me into his long, narrow office. Deciding to begin low-key, I told him about visiting the museums and strolling through his beautiful campus. Told him how impressed I was with the University of Chicago and how it felt like a real university.

Hammerschlag said that Clarence Darrow had described it as the Athens of the Middle West. We talked about education and the liberal tradition. This made it easy to bring up the Social Responsibility Subgroup. For several minutes, we bantered generalities back and forth like a helium-filled beach ball. Then I saw an opening and used it.

"What I can't get a handle on is what Pete was actually doing under the heading of institutional responsibility."

"Yes?" Hammerschlag said cautiously.

"I'm sure it will be a lot easier to describe orally than for us to exchange notes and letters. Could you tell me privately what he was really saying in your subgroup meetings?"

I had to repeat the question many times and many ways to get a partial answer. Hammerschlag was a reluctant witness, just like in our phone conversation. He stalled, saying that the issues were sensitive. They were most sensitive in private medical schools which depend on "soft" Federal money to pay their faculty. Yes, the issues were financial. They were sensitive because they involved faculty/administration relations.

Slowly, I got Dr. Hammerschlag to say that the issue was lack of faculty power. At his school, where there was a strong faculty government, the profs were able to hold their own against the administration.

"But Bryan Medical School has weak academic traditions and a weak faculty senate, which will do essentially nothing even in the face of the greatest inequities." I sensed a wisp of emotion.

"Am I correct in guessing that Pete had a lot of criticism of Bryan Medical School?"

"That would be an understatement."

"What did he say? I can find nothing in his files."

"He had a broad range of criticisms. I cannot remember the specifics."

Obviously, the specifics were distasteful to Dr. Hammerschlag. I would have to tease them out of him, taking best guesses and starting with the questions that were easy to say yes to. "Would the criticisms include low quality of administrative service?"

"Yes, very much so."

"And of charging things such as plumbing repairs to the scientist's grant?"

"Exactly, it was this type of issue." He frowned and squinted. He must have been surprised that I would know this.

"And inefficient use of outside contractors for this type of repair?"

"Yes, that sort of thing."

Now for a more sensitive question.

"Did Pete's criticisms include a demand for accounting on Federal overhead payments to Bryan Medical School . . . in relation to the above?"

"Yes, he was quite interested in the question."

"Did he complain about administration restricting purchases to a list of approved vendors, forcing the scientist to pay top dollar?"

"Yes, he was interested in such issues."

The more weighty the question, the more cautious was

Hammerschlag's agreement. Now was the time to go for broke.

"Pete was investigating fraud within the institution and fraud by the institution, wasn't he?"

Hammerschlag rocked back in his wooden swivel chair. Its spiral spring made a loud grating noise. "I wouldn't go so far as to say that."

Hammerschlag kept looking towards an open book on his desk like he wanted to pick it up and start reading.

I'd have to lighten up on Bryan Medical School for a while. "How far did Pete get along with his idea that gamma irradiation of meat was a health hazard?"

Hammerschlag cleared his throat. "You must know if he had preliminary experiments. My impression was that it was in the idea stage."

"That's the impression I got, as well. Do you think he talked to the companies that do gamma irradiation?"

"No, I don't think so."

"Where are they located?"

"A couple of them are located north of Chicago, actually."

"Can you tell me their names?"

"No, I can't remember. I don't think Pete really spent much time or effort on that idea."

Now, to get back to Bryan Medical School.

"So his watchdog activities at his own institution were more important."

"Yes."

"Could you give me any more examples of institutional abuse that Pete reported to your group?"

"No, I can't remember. Could I ask why you are so interested in this?"

"I'm being paid by Pete's estate to write his biography. If he had really sunk his teeth into something, I need to know. If he was just whipping up a lot of foam, I need to know so I don't create a false legacy."

Hammerschlag was looking at his watch like he wanted to invent another two o'clock lecture. "What I remember best was his discussion of *principles* and *approaches* to the problem."

"Could you give me an example?"

"He talked about the Freedom of Information Act and Federal law on waste, fraud and abuse. He said there was some legal opinion that private universities have a responsibility to the State because of their tax-advantaged position." He looked at his watch. "I have an appointment in fifteen minutes and I really . . ."

"I'm sorry to be keeping you. But if nobody can give me any evidence that Pete was a great crusader, I sure as hell won't describe him as a crusader in the biography."

"And no one at Bryan Medical School can help you?"

"I haven't found anybody, yet."

"Do you know Dr. Donald Fleischman from your institution?"

"Yes. He gave lectures to us when I was a student."

"Don is recently retired, or I should say has been forcefully retired. Perhaps he could help you with local information. I also remember Pete saying he was getting a different sort of help from a young man who worked with computers at the school." He inhaled audibly and looked away. "I am running out of time, now."

While moving to the door, I threw out a final question. "Did Pete ever tell you that he was threatened because of any of his inquiries?"

The question caught Hammerschlag by surprise. "No, I do not believe so, although he did tell me that he got a lot of hate mail from other groups — Animal Rights, et cetera."

Turbines whined. Acceleration and gravity were pulling me back into the seat again. Chicago spread before me like a collection of matchbox houses, then transformed into a textured gridwork under the setting sun. The skyscrapers diminished into Lego blocks and the southern tip of Lake Michigan curved beneath us like on a satellite image you can pull down on from the NASA website.

The drink cart made its way to me somewhere between Indianapolis and Louisville. I asked for a gin and tonic. Certainly my brain had earned an hour or two of warm fuzzies. It had spent the last three days trying to see things more sharply. Despite Hammerschlag's smokescreen and jitter in his social responsibility group, my visual data enhancement algorithms had produced a sharp image: of Pete reporting to them on corruption at Bryan Medical School and of them cheering him on.

And now, in the solitude of my airliner seat, my brain was playing back fuzzy images from the med school's general faculty meeting: of the pudgy financial expert who watched the big money, of the two Roberts who managed streams of overhead money, of Jerry Cartlick who managed the security tapes, of the moustached parking garage magnate, and of Lizzy-Mae's plump granddaughter showing off her fat thighs near the podium before the dean went up there and turned on his radar.

Yes, I could cut and paste these images to create a story of a kickback ring, of uniformed men communicating on walkie-talkies during an illegal entry, and of a faceless bureaucrat running off an anonymous threat letter on a laser jet printer.

And I could paste into the guard's description of Pete's last hour by the creek the image of an old lady or a woman who could pass for one. Could it be contract expert Dolores Padilla? Chief secretary Lizzy-Mae? Or even Professor Hilda Beecher? She was such an expert at hushing up her colleagues.

Although the images were strong, I had too many of them and too many ways to combine them. And I had no real evidence. But I had a warning. From now on, I'd play it dumb and low-key.

But here in the plane I was safe. Now was time to let the alcohol dissolve the sharp edges and fluff everything up. Somewhere before the Tennessee border I had the flight attendant bring me another drink.

Alcohol closed my eyes but couldn't stop my brain, which started playing in-flight movies. The first were crudely cut, black-and-white cinematic images of a gawky old Swede, reminiscent of an Ingmar Bergman film. Then came a cruel comedy sequence with an awkward little Charlie Chaplin struggling to work in a soft-money factory without getting mangled by the wheels, belts and gears. Then I was in the back seat of a WW-II fighter, screaming down through the clouds as fast as the twin propellers could pull us, bearing down on palm trees and almost making out excited faces of the enemy.

The flight attendant woke me, requesting that I put up my tray table and seat back. The warehouses and the Palmetto Expressway came up awfully fast. We landed with a jolt. I never really woke up while trudging through the terminal corridors and baggage claim, nor during the cab ride to Pete's apartment. The doorknob-mounted alarm was intact. I hit the sheets and slept for the remainder of the night, too tired to dream.

OF PATIENTS, PATIENCE AND OLD MEN

Mildred was glad to hear that our work was well-received in Chicago. She was also glad I was back to help her with problems that came up in the experiments. Afterwards, I took my coffee break at the snack bar on the second floor. From now on I would be careful about food and drink. Ditto for all communications. While I was down there, I dialed the number for Donald Fleischman, Ph.D., Professor Emeritus. He was home. Yes, he remembered me. And, no, he wouldn't mind me stopping by around two o'clock to reminisce about Pete.

I returned to my desk and put together travel reimbursement claim which I hand-delivered to Olga. She looked at it and frowned. She said it probably wouldn't be reimbursed because it wasn't put it through in advance, and because I hadn't used a School-approved travel agent. To cite the policy, she pulled out a four year-old memo from Dolores Padilla in Contracts and Fiscal operations.

I explained about having little warning and asked her to plead my case to Dolores Padilla. Back at my desk, I replayed my mental image of severe and oldish-looking Dolores Padilla from the General Faculty Meeting. Could she be the one that Franz said had complained about Pete to Security? Could she have been the woman by the canal?

If the reimbursement was turned down, that wouldn't be such a bad thing. Then I could make an appointment with Dolores Padilla and check her out.

After a couple hours of work at my desk, I received a call from Carole Vandoren, asking, in a friendly manner, when I would finish disposing of Pete's things so she could get paid. I told her I was hard at work. I asked her again whether she had taken any papers out of the apartment. She assured me that she had not. I claimed a desperate need for biographical material and asked if she could take another look around her house.

Before leaving to see Dr. Donald Fleischman, I had just enough time to check my e-mails, read through the memos from the administration and throw out a seven-day accumulation of junk mail.

Mildred had left me a note to call Bruce, but I figured he could wait. I left the building, planning to go back to the apartment for lunch.

Out on the plaza I saw Dr. Yung. He was sitting on a bench under a tree with a wheelchair-bound patient. His ward looked tall, heavy-boned, muscular, and quite athletic for his 70-some years. The man was staring blankly at the shrub garden.

Dr. Yung recognized me immediately and signalled me to come over.

"Dr. Candidi, how you been?"

The twinkle in his eye and wrinkle on his flat forehead told me it was a friendly greeting. The proud set of the rest of his face was only a product of culture and upbringing. Too bad that I had no time for a scientific discussion right then.

While shaking Dr. Yung's hand, I mentioned being away for the Biophysical Society meeting.

Dr. Yung said, "Let me introduce you to Mr. Boltner. He is a very important man." He turned to Mr. Boltner and said his next words much louder. "Mr. Boltner, this is Dr. Candidi. He is a very promising young scientist."

Boltner raised his eyes from the shrub garden and looked at me for a second. To leave any impression, I would have to focus a smile on his face. He searched my face for several seconds, raised his right hand, and tried to say something. It came out garbled. I took his hand and squeezed it gently.

"I am very glad to meet you, Mr. Boltner."

His right hand had very little strength. His left arm hung limply.

"You know that Mr. Boltner is a famous businessman and engineer," Dr. Yung said, loudly and slowly. "He designed the superconducting coils on our MRI. And now Mr. Boltner's machine is telling us how to make him well again."

Boltner's eyes returned to the shrub garden and followed a zebra butterfly.

"Stroke?" I asked, softly.

"Disseminated thrombotic stroke," Dr. Yung said in normal volume. "We are titrating with TPA and streptokinase using the MRI to monitor clot dissolution." He turned to Boltner and raised his voice. "Mr. Boltner is my most important patient."

These words aroused Boltner. He squirmed in his wheelchair. Dr. Yung noticed, and put his hand on Boltner's right shoulder.

"And my most important patient is going to get well very soon."

Boltner sighed and seemed to relax.

"You take care of your patient like the old-fashioned physician," I said.

"And Mr. Boltner also takes care of me." He said it loud, and slow. "Mr. Boltner has financed my laboratory for over ten years. I owe him a debt of gratitude."

"So that's one of the reasons why you don't worry so much about NIH grants."

"NIH grants are a waste of time," Dr. Yung said, returning to a conversational tone. "If a doctor really wants to do research, he just has to take the time to do it. Sure, he will lose a little salary because he cannot bill so many patients. I think it is wrong for doctors to try to make the NIH pay a portion of their salary. NIH money should only be for their technicians and equipment."

"Do you put in for NIH grants?"

"I try to get them for the laboratory, and sometimes I am successful. But I cannot count on them. The NIH study sections are too political. I am lucky that I can count on Mr. Boltner . . . and just do the work."

"That seems like a novel approach. Do you have other big private donors?"

Dr. Yung studied me for a few seconds before answering. "Yes, I have a very big one."

"How did you meet him?"

"He gave big money to Bryan and I got some of it. And later I got a lot more."

"How did that work?"

"He visited my lab and Barry showed him around. Then he asked if he could use one of our instruments for his business."

"Is he in the medical equipment business?"

"No. He sells all types of sunglasses. He wanted to know which ones are better. Barry showed him how to put sunglasses into the spectrophotometer and test them."

"Right. It will measure light absorption as a function of wavelength. Bet you could do polarization as well." Hell, the instrument is just a glorified light meter.

Dr. Yung smiled. "Soon he was coming to our lab every week with boxes full of sunglasses and testing them."

"Doesn't sound like your usual donor."

"He's not a tuxedo donor who talks only to the dean. He is a hands-on donor. He has his own lab jacket. He comes to the lab once a week and spends all day, helping calculate the data. He has enough patience to be a scientist."

One fast spin of my cranial hard drive and I had it: It was Howard Edmunds, the dignified man who Barry introduced me to. And he was the owner of Cool Shades.

Couldn't ask Yung too many questions, but I just had to know.

"At the General Faculty Meeting, someone said a big donor had been giving the Medical School lots of money and then he stopped."

Dr. Yung hesitated before answering. "The donor was going to give thirteen million dollars, but he stopped at three million when he found they were spending his money on all kinds of junk. Now he chooses the projects himself and deals with the scientists directly."

And this donor was Mr. Edmunds.

"What kind of junk did the med school spend it on?"

"Renovations, special office equipment and expensive computers, and on consultants and administrators' salaries." Dr. Yung glanced at his watch. My questions were probably making him uneasy.

I looked at my watch, too. I was running late and wouldn't have time for lunch at the apartment. "Nice talking to you, Dr. Yung. And I guess we will be talking soon about our portion of the Program Project Grant Proposal."

"Oh, didn't you hear?"

"No."

"It didn't pan out. I guess they didn't bother to tell you. I heard the bad news when I called to see about making some changes in the budget. Luke McDougal pulled the plug on it. He withdrew the proposal."

"Withdrew the proposal!"

"He was at a cocktail party in Washington. The Program Manager said the word was that Bryan Medical's proposal was too expensive. Said that it had too much nonessential stuff. So McDougal told the Program Manager he would withdraw the proposal."

"Just like that?"

"Yes. But I heard from some other people that his part of our group proposal was under consideration in another program anyway. The Program Manager told him he can't have both."

"Thanks for letting me know. I wasted 40 hours on that proposal."

"Don't look so sad. You still have a good idea. You can write an NIH Career Development grant application." He hesitated for a second. "Maybe we can find a hands-on donor who would be interested." He spoke loudly, now. "Or maybe Mr. Boltner will be interested, after he gets better." Mr. Boltner stirred and Dr. Yung patted him on the shoulder.

I rushed off to the Metrorail Station and waited 20 minutes on the open-air platform for a southbound train. I always enjoy that high-speed ride at treetop level, skirting the downtown, the Brickell Financial District and Coconut Grove. Got off at the University of Miami Station in Coral Gables and satisfied my appetite at the Burger King where I crossed U.S. Highway One.

Prof. Emeritus Donald Fleischman's house was a four-block walk along Maynada Avenue. It was a modest, 1930s vintage, one-story, extended bungalow located on an expensive side of the street where the backyards adjoin a side-arm of the Coral Gables Waterway.

His wife answered the door and led me to a crowded backyard where the professor was tending orchids. Several well-developed live oaks provided shade and support for his pet plants. Between the oaks was a maze of trellises and shelves bearing more orchids and tropical plants. At the end of the property, a weathered gazebo marked the edge of the canal. From my vantage point, I couldn't see the water. The only indication of the canal was the rough, bromeliad-lined coral ridge where his backyard neighbor's property began.

At this point, the canal was probably 25 feet below us and 25 feet wide — just sufficient for transit of those modest-sized cabin cruisers you see docked by the Holiday Inn near U.S. Highway One.

It felt strange, speaking with the professor away from the lab bench. But he seemed to be thriving here, as if he had simply moved his laboratory activities outdoors. His rustic straw hat flapped gently when he nodded his large, ovoid head. His pudgy body seemed to quiver with enthusiasm as we made small-talk about science.

He poured me a glass of iced tea from a pitcher on a work table, then went back to inspecting his plants as we talked. We went very lightly over my days as a graduate student in the Pharmacology Department where he had researched and taught. I mentioned the Biophysical Society meeting. Then we talked about Pete and my biography project. He warmed up to me with an anecdote about Pete playing volleyball at a departmental picnic on the Crandon Park beach. All the while he kept busy spiffing up his orchids. Half of them reminded me of pansies and the other half looked like necrotic genitalia. Every once in a while, Dr. Fleischman cast a swift, searching glance at me over his half-cut glasses.

"One thing I wanted to ask you, Dr. Fleischman, was whether you knew anything that Pete was doing recently that could be described as a crusade. He used that word in his will."

Fleischman threw another glance and said, "Pete had many crusades."

"At the Biophysical Society meeting, the members of the Social Responsibility Subgroup told me that Pete was conducting a crusade on institutional integrity. They said he had a lot to say on the subject. The trouble is, I can't find any notes in his apartment, or in his lab. They said you could help me by remembering specific issues."

Fleischman was staring at a small tincture bottle in his left hand. He removed a medicine dropper and fed an orchid five drops. "Who said this?"

"Dr. Hammerschlag from the University of Chicago."

"He did, did he?"

"Yes."

"Did Dr. Hammerschlag identify an area of institutional integrity Pete was working on and that I would remember?" Again his eyes darted over the tops of his glasses. Luckily, I had just raised the flowered glass to my mouth.

Time for a wild-assed guess. "Yes. It was the misspending of scientific funds to pay outside contractors for expensive, unnecessary renovations. It was about discrimination against low-bidding vendors and insistence on use of high-priced, slow vendors for simple commodities like desks and file cabinets." I looked back up at him. He had been staring at me all the time. "And Pete was also concerned with the possibility of kickback schemes in the purchase of over-priced computers from local vendors," I added, for good measure.

Prof. Fleischman's smile reminded me of the time I had delivered the right answer in one of his lectures. "Have you studied German?" he asked.

"Yes. Two semesters, back at Swarthmore."

"Good. Dr. *Hammerschlag* seems to have lived up to his name," Fleischman said. "*Er hat den Nagel auf den Kopf getroffen.*"

That sent me back to my Swarthmore German class: Hammer . . . had . . . nail . .. head . . . meet? Hammerschlag had hit the nail on the head. "Great! And I was hoping you might help me with specific instances, and . . . might name some . . . individuals on whom Pete was focussing his attention."

"*Nein, der Richter hat es verboten.*" The look on his face reminded me of when he had teased the class along to solve a problem.

"*Richter?* That would be knight."

"No, knight is *der Ritter. Der Richter* is a judge." Getting the upper hand brought a smile. "*Der Pfeifer hat gepfiffen.*"

I must have been slow at putting it together — judge and whistler — because Fleischman was beaming down at me. "So you don't know that I left the University, fighting it tooth and nail?"

"No, I didn't."

"First, they decided it would be cheaper to not have me around. They tried to force me out. Pretty dumb of them, the way they did it. They took my minority access grant away from me. Then they said I wasn't doing my job right because I didn't have a grant. And they used that as an excuse to reduce my salary. But when I showed my lawyer some files I had been keeping, he was pretty interested. And after a couple rounds of pretrial negotiation, we came to an agreement. And part of the agreement is that — *Der Pfeifer kann nicht mehr pfeifen.*"

Damn! I could get no more information from him. He had threatened to blow the whistle on the med school for financial malfeasance and they had come to terms. A gag order was part of the settlement.

I crossed my fingers and asked one more question.

"Dr. Hammerschlag said that Pete had a helper. A guy who knew a lot about computers. Would you be able to tell me his name?"

This brought an enigmatic smile to Dr. Fleischman's face. "I heard about a guy in Biomedical Communications who helped him with a project. I think his name was Melvin Armino."

"*Danke schön*," I said.

Fleischman moved to the door, indicating that this would be all. "*Sie sind ein guter Student.*"

Yes, I've always been a good student.

When Dr. Fleischman saw I didn't have a car, he insisted on firing up his 1974 Toyota Corolla and driving me to the station. I felt sorry for the once-famous scientist, the discoverer of the sodium pump in mammalian cells, having to drive such an old car. He told me that he was the only orchidologist who knew something about cellular ion pumps. He made a joke about orchids needing stamina in their stamens.

Back at the med school, I dropped in on Biomedical Communications. One of the guys told me that Melvin Armino was now working for a Silicon Valley company called Plethora.

I went back to the lab and looked in our records for the name of the guy who had worked for Pete, setting up software on his desktop computer. The name came as no surprise: Melvin Armino.

I plugged my laptop into the telephone jack and dialed up my Internet access server. No more crusade-related work on Pete's desktop computer from here on. I searched for Plethora on the World Wide Web. As a state-of-the-art software company, Plethora had a name-search feature on their page. I got Melvin Armino's address and sent him an e-mail.

> Hi Melvin:
>
> I'm Ben Candidi. I am sorry to tell you that Peter Peterson died a few weeks ago. I'm finishing up unfinished work in his lab. I'm also trying to put together a few pages of stories about Pete for his friends at the Unitarian Church. I'll be in Silicon Valley in a couple of days, and was wondering if I could talk with you for half an hour and hit you up for a couple of anecdotes.
>
> — Ben Candidi

A few minutes after logging off, the phone rang. It was Rebecca, upset and needing advice.

Rebecca was having trouble with the boat. Water was leaking in around the propeller shaft and the float switch wouldn't turn on the bilge pump. I told her to use the manual switch and reminded her of how to tighten the stuffing box. The conversation was short because she was anxious to fix the problem before it got dark.

Mildred had just left for the day. I called it a day, too.

Around the automobile entrance of *Dade County General*, I caught sight of a strange yet familiar phenomenon: a handful of cops working up to a driving frenzy like a bunch of automobile-fixated high school Harrys.

My second glance showed they weren't real cops. They were Bryan security officers, two in marked cars and another three in private cars — five adolescents in a party mood. It was all so trite — the ones up front looking back; the flash of headlights from the ones behind; the couple of revolving flashes from the marked car up front; the key-down on the P.A. mike of another. And the one farthest behind, taking it all in, was none other than Jerry Cartlick.

They broke loose in a most predictable way: Number One jumping forward nimbly, followed by Number Two hugging his rear bumper in the turn, while Numbers Three, Four and Five hurried to catch up. Jerry Cartlick looked proud of his boys as he accelerated over the zebra stripes.

A black and lime-green Society Cab stood at the curb, pointed in the same direction. With a flash of inspiration, I jumped into the back seat so fast that I startled the driver. "Follow those cars. I'll double the fare if you stay with them."

The guy did what I said. Any cabbie in his upper thirties had probably seen and done it all before. The sign by the meter said he was Leroy Johnston. After the first block, he turned his attention to me. "Why's it so important to you, man. They didn't steal nothing from you, did they?"

"No, they were supposed to take me along, and they forgot."

"Yeah, I heard that one before," he said, in a slow-spoken, world-weary, incredulous baritone.

Everything went fine for several blocks along 20th Street until we caught up with Cartlick who was stuck behind a red light. "So now we's caught up with him, you want me to give him a beep?"

"No!"

"No, somehow I didn't think you did. So you just sit back and reach in your pocket and start pulling out your money, and Ole Leroy will follow your man like a pilot fish sticks to a shark."

"Thanks."

I reached into my pocket and showed Leroy my money clip. And Leroy showed me he was even better than he let on. He didn't match Cartlick's jackrabbit starts, but he was a fast runner with a good eye and excellent timing. He never let a red light or a slow truck get between us. A few blocks south of 79th Street on Biscayne Boulevard, Cartlick took an abrupt left into a side street. Leroy handled it well. He just glided along, overshooting the mark, but turning adroitly in a half-empty parking lot.

"You can catch up with your buddies in there," he said, gesturing towards a windowless bar carved out of derelict motel. "Name of your place is the 'Eaton Don.' And the meter says eight dollars."

"We'll make it twenty. No, let's make it twenty-five, and you go in there pretending you want to make a phone call and check them out."

"You gotta be crazy, you little motherfucker," he exclaimed, his baritone transforming into excited countertenor. "I wouldn't take a hundred to touch the *door handles* in that place. You go in there and check out them fudge-packers yourself."

"Hold on! I didn't know *that*. I didn't mean nothing."

"You think for nine extra dollars I'm going to go in that fairy bar and check out them fairy-fucking, drip-ass excuses for a policeman — you outta your mind."

"Hold on, Leroy. It's cool. I really didn't know. Here's the twenty. Just wait here for a couple minutes."

I went around to the parking lot behind, and checked out the cars. I recognized the three private automobiles and wrote down their license numbers. Two of them had the guy's I.D. cards on the dash. Ditto for one of the marked cars. The other marked car had a nicely pressed uniform shirt hanging in the back, with the name sewn on the pocket.

Leroy was still waiting at the curb when I returned. He was considerably calmer, now. He had set the meter back to zero.

"Could you take me back to the medical center?"

"Sure."

"And sorry for jiving you about why I wanted to catch up with them. I didn't think you'd go for it if I told you the truth."

"Sure."

By the time we were back at the med center, the meter said eight dollars. Leroy said I could give him another five and we'd call it even. As suggested by the top hat, cane and gloves on the cab's logo, Leroy was a real gentleman. I made it twenty.

It was a well-spent forty dollars — my round trip to the Eaton Don. Not only did I get a forty-dollar joke on Dr. Westley — how some Americans were profaning the name of one of his famous English "public schools" — but also, I got one-thousand dollars of insight. Cartlick had a little circle of friends who read a different type of magazine than most of us. Not that there was anything wrong with it, as Jerry Seinfeld used to say. There was nothing wrong with it unless Cartlick's special interest group was doing things that were detrimental to the medical school . . . things that weren't legal. Could one of his drinking buddies be the intruder in Pete's apartment?

I was back at Pete's apartment heating a can of Dinty Moore beef stew when Rebecca's second call came in. She had tightened the stuffing box and stopped the leak. Busted her hands with the big monkey wrenches while doing it, but was proud of herself. And I was proud of her, too. She had also renewed the contacts on the float switch in the bilge. The pump worked after she "palpated" the wire — those were her words — but then the wire got hot and she burnt her fingers. I told her the wire was rotten and to buy a new float switch.

With all the excitement with the pump there was no chance to tell her I was thinking of going to California. It would have been hard to explain to her anyway.

We said our I-love-you's and hung up, and I sat down to dinner. I chewed on the Dinty Moore beef cubes and I chewed on the situation at the med school. Kickbacks and corruption were the explanation. That explained why they made it difficult for new suppliers to get "vendorized." Protecting the suppliers who were kicking back. It explained why the physical plant guys joked about Ready-Serve Plumbing getting all the work. It explained the $40,000 price tags for the $10,000 lab renovations.

And it explained the 15 cent photocopies. Of course this one required a little more administrative finesse because the discrepancy was so obvious. So when the Australian guy in the Faculty Senate starts questioning it in public, just roll your eyes and shake your head like he was born yesterday. After the meeting, take him aside and explain, Yes, the med school is skimming, but only for the good of medical education. The poor med school desperately needs a bigger piece of the Federal grant dollar.

The Australian probably accepted the argument. And from then on, he had to accept everything.

Pete didn't accept the argument, so they branded him a troublemaker. Did they encourage a senior administrator to complain to Security that Pete had threatened her? Did Security humiliate Pete, like the tissue culture medium salesman they escorted out of the building? Doloris Padilla, that's who must have complained about Pete. And she was in charge of outside contracting.

Who else might have been in on it? My whirling brain retrieved images of the cast of characters occupying seats in the front rows in the General Faculty Meeting. I saw all of them, including the parking garage magnate who collects eight dollars from everyone who drives to *Dade County General* and the HMO executive tapped into the billing power of Bryan physicians.

Pete's anti-corruption crusade probably threatened every one of them. Ergo, any one of them could have killed him or contracted the job out. Ditto for the two-foot gap in the drawer of Pete's bedroom file cabinet and the bump on my head.

What a shame that the only person who could bring me closer to the truth was on the West Coast.

Being too excited for TV, radio or reading more from Pete's pin-pricked *Inca Gold*, I went down to Wagner Creek. I leaned on the railing and looked in the water.

There, I was touched by an angel.

"He flow in and he flow out." The voice had a Jamaican accent and came about 20 paces behind me.

I turned my face from the creek and looked back. He was a big guy, jolly and content, with plump skin but with a good layer of muscle underneath. He was broad around the middle, but his stomach did not sag. He took me in with a friendly smile that got friendlier as he perceived that I didn't understand.

"De tide."

"Right," I answered. "Of course, the tide. It flows in and flows out. Like the *doctor wind* and the *undertaker wind*."

Now his smile seemed brighter than the moon. "It be a long time since anyone say anything about de doctor and de undertaker, mon."

"The doctor wind comes in with the morning and the undertaker wind goes out with the night."

"Now how do you know that?" He leaned over the rail beside me and looked down at a wavy image of the moon reflected in the creek. The moon had risen high above the elevated Metrorail station to the east; water was flowing up the creek, languidly but insistently. A metallic loudspeaker voice warned passengers to stand back as a northbound train pulled in.

"I know Jamaica. I spent some time with my girlfriend in Montego Bay when she took her clinical rotation there. We learned a lot about Jamaica."

I started to explain who Rebecca was but he cut me off.

"Oh, that has to be the little lady with the black hair and the nice smile that I used to see around here. And I used to see her at *Dade General*. Where is she now? I hope she is still your little lady."

"Yes, she still is, but she's up in Washington right now. You have a good memory."

"When they look so sweet, they are not hard to remember. But I always remember everything I see. I never forget a face. But the names of the drugs and diseases, that is another thing."

We both laughed.

We exchanged first names and fell into conversation so casual that it felt we'd known each other for years. Elliot was a respiratory therapist at *Dade General*. At the moment, he was waiting for his "old lady" to swing by and pick him up. He had lived in the building for a couple years.

"You make a good Jamaican when you come out and listen to the water every night," he said.

"I come down here to think."

A Styrofoam cup floated by, momentarily eclipsing the shimmering image of the moon.

"Yeah, that's what that old man that died . . . that's what he say, too, when he come down smoking his pipe. But I think Old Pete spend most of de time throwing matches in the water."

"Pete Peterson. I knew him. He always had trouble keeping his pipe lit."

"Yeah, I always tell Pete he not burning the right stuff."

Visions of Pete and Elliot passing a back and forth a ganja pipe were too much. For a few seconds our bodies shook the rail in concerted laughter.

"Hey, Elliot, you didn't tell me you were *that type* of a respiratory therapist."

We shook the railing still harder. Finally, I said, "It's too bad Pete's not with us. They tell me he died of a heart attack down here."

"Yeah, Pete was a good man. Like I tell the officer, I was maybe the last man to see him before he fall in."

My heart skipped a beat. "Can you tell me what you told the officer?"

"I come down for my lady to pick me up. Pete was sitting on the rail smoking his pipe like usual. I would have gone over to talk to him except he was talking with someone already."

"With who?"

"Some old lady. She was talking to him."

"What happened?"

"They were just talking for a few minutes while I was waiting for my lady."

"They were just having a friendly chat?"

"At first it look like they were arguing, but then it looked like they were just talking. Or maybe she was talking and he was listening."

"Where was she? Where was he?"

"Like I say, Pete was sitting on the rail. And she was standing at the rail, beside him. Behind him."

"So what made it look like they were arguing?"

"Pete stopped smoking his pipe. He turn sideways and start moving his hands and talking louder."

"And what was the woman doing?"

"She stepped back. I can tell she was arguing."

"What happened then?"

"They were quiet and he turned towards the canal and started lighting his pipe again."

"And what then?"

"Oh, I think she was closer to him like they were still talking."

"And then?"

"He moved his arms like he was losing his balance, but then they got busy with something."

"Like they were reading, or doing something together with their hands?"

"No, like they were looking for something on the rail. Then Pete step down and look on the ground like he lost his matches. And the old lady was looking too. Then Pete got back up and started lighting his pipe and the old lady hurried off like she was afraid to be missing her train."

"What did Pete do next?"

"I don't know. I went up to the apartment to call my lady to see if she be late. When I came back down, Pete wasn't there."

"How long did it take to make the call and come back down."

"Maybe five minutes."

"And what happened then."

"My lady was down here in the car to pick me up, and I didn't see anything more. When she brought me home, maybe three hours later, all the police and ambulances were here."

"Do you know the old lady?"

"No, but maybe I see her around here."

I asked Elliot to wait for a few minutes. I rushed to the apartment, retrieved the photo of Annabelle Pemberton, and showed it to him.

"No, it wasn't this lady. But this lady looks like her. You know, skinny and short. A little bit shorter than you. And gray hair. Looks like a missionary." He smiled. "I just know I see her before."

"Could she be living in this building?"

"No. But I'm sure I've seen her around the medical center. Why do you want to find her? You think she did something bad?"

I had been so lucky with Elliot up to now.

"No, but maybe she could tell me if he was complaining of chest pain."

"Or pain in his left arm?" The guy knew the warning signs of heart attack.

"Right! You said the old lady was hurrying off to catch a train. How did you know she was catching a train?"

"I don't know. I can't remember. Maybe I just thought that. Or maybe I saw her waiting on the platform." He gestured to the elevated Metrorail station.

Elliot's girlfriend pulled up.

I said, "If you see her again, could you find out who she is and call me?"

"No problem."

I stayed there by the fence, thinking, for a long time, while the moon rose high and the "doctor tide" slackened. Would I stay here thinking for the three hours the moon would take to pass overhead, release its resonant tug, and abandon control to the "undertaker tide"? How far had it carried Pete's body?

I was lucky to have talked to Elliot, a guy who was conscious of the wind, the tide and the people around him. Funny how growing up in an industrialized country renders us insensitive to these things.

What Elliot had witnessed was consistent with the old lady injecting Pete in the arm or buttock — or placing a nerve agent on his skin — or spraying any sort of poison in his face. Of course, it couldn't have been just any sort of poison, because Dr. Westley said that nothing had come up on the multi-drug screen. But Pete's enemies came from a medical school. Some of them might have knowledge and access to drugs or agents that would not be picked up by the instruments in Dr. Westley's laboratory.

I added an item to my list of things to do: use Pete's high-powered camera to take telephotos of certain short, skinny, gray-haired old ladies around the medical school, then show them to Elliot.

I went back to the apartment and read myself to sleep from Pete's *Inca Gold*.

Thursday morning proved a busy day. Before sitting down to breakfast, I plugged in my laptop, checked my e-mail and retrieved a piece of good news.

From: mel@plethora.com
To: ben.candidi@netrus.net
Subj.: Greetings

Hi Ben,
Yes, I heard the bad news about Pete. Sure, you can come by tomorrow or Friday and I will tell you some stories. I should be at Plethora the whole day, or otherwise the guys will know where to get me.
— Mel

I clicked on "Reply" and wrote that I'd be there tomorrow. I also clicked on the attachment Mel had sent. It was a map showing how to get to the company from San Francisco. I also got an applet that made the Plethora logo dance on the map. It was a "horn of plenty" bulging with fruit.

I called Gisela Schloss Birkholz at Blue Lagoon Travel and placed an order. With Germanic efficiency she repeated back my preferences.

"San Francisco, arriving no later than ten tomorrow morning. And can I assume we are trying to save money on this one, Ben?"

"Yes."

After a couple of minutes of clicking, she was offering me a round-trip special on a red-eye to San Francisco that night with an open-ended return. Gisela also fixed me up with a rental car promotion, and a motel convenient to the airport.

I sent Rebecca an e-mail saying that I would be in California for a day or two consulting with one of Pete's collaborators. I would bring her in on this thing when I had the whole story.

When I called Ted Walden, he was out of the office. I told his secretary that I urgently needed complete information on any checks that Pete had written to Melvin Armino.

I went to the lab and spent the rest of the day working hard, ignoring a pile of mail and some messages. Working hard would keep me from feeling bad about taking the next day off. I told Mildred I'd be gone, but didn't say where.

In the middle of the afternoon, Ted Walden's secretary called to give me the news: Over the last year, Pete had written personal checks to Melvin Armino totalling $6,370.

I would take that California trip.

The turbines whined again, around ten o'clock that evening. And a low image of a high moon blinked on and off as we flew over the reflecting pools, wet grasslands and hammocks of the Everglades. Concentrating on the hum of the engines, I willed myself to sleep. No gin and tonic tonight. Tomorrow, I must be fit.

Five hours later, I caught the moon's reflection on San Francisco Bay. The pale orb was still at a high angle. Flying at three-fifths of the rate of the earth's rotation, we had given the moon a good run for the money.

As we came abreast of the Oakland Bay Bridge, the pilot dipped the port wing. A few minutes later, I was saying sleepy goodbyes to him and his crew. I trudged to the baggage level where I found the correct rental car desk, pulled out my plastic and signed my name. Piloted my economy car down U.S. 101 until I found my motel and repeated the plastic ritual. Finally, I could slam the door shut, turn on the air conditioner against the road noise — and flop.

⚜⚜⚜⚜⚜

Sitting on my wrist, nestled against my ear, my Timex Ironman did what I'd programmed him to do. It wasn't enough sleep, despite the time change. Soon, I was doing what I'd programmed myself to do. Pulled on a comfortable pair of Dockers, a polo shirt and a pair of canvas slip-ons. Staggered to the door and made a run on the complimentary coffee and jelly rolls before heading for the ramp for southbound U.S. 101.

California drivers seemed precise and unforgiving — a lot different than I expected for a state with such a laid-back reputation. The land seemed to be made of dry dirt stuck between rocks. It was overgrown by dry yellow grass, concrete, asphalt, houses shopping centers and office buildings. After twenty-some miles, it was time to take the Palo Alto exit and zig-zag according to the instructions on Plethora's map.

The company occupied a three-story orange brick and glass

building on the side of a broad hill. It was set off from the highway by a long expanse of green grass. They must have been keeping it alive with a sprinkler system. I parked my car in a large lot and made my way up a long rising walk, past their corporate recreational facility. A dozen guys and a few girls, all about my age or younger, were playing volleyball on the sandy court. A foursome of girls was playing tennis on one of the green-painted asphalt courts.

Pretty early in the morning for that, I thought. What a different world. And such open, trusting faces. Inside the building's main entrance was a guard station. Told the guy I'd come to see Melvin Armino. He phoned upstairs and then told me Mel wasn't there. He had no idea when Mel would be back, but suggested asking the guys outside since they worked on his team.

I took a second look at them on the way down. All were dressed in shorts, tee shirts and tennis shoes or sandals; some were athletic but many were pale.

I hung around on the sideline. It was a lively game. The three girls were quite good-looking, and played well, too. Among the guys were a couple of spikers who also didn't mind throwing themselves into the sand to rescue a ball driven below knee level. One of them threw up a lot of sand at a keyboard and monitor set up by the sidelines. The guy standing next to it kept his eye on the screen and sometimes called out the names of modules what were running.

Once, he called out "Alpha 3, production," and everyone cheered, and stood around for a second.

I called out, myself, before they got the ball back into play. "Hey, has anyone seen Mel? He told me to stop by today."

"What's your name?" one of the spikers yelled back.

"Ben. I'm from his old place, Bryan Medical School in Miami."

"Come play on our side," said a guy from the other team. "We're a man short."

"Gotta see," I yelled back.

"Mel's out, making a run," said the guy at my side. "Probably won't be back for two hours."

"Well, maybe you could tell me where he is going jogging and I'll catch up with him."

Lines were moving quickly along his screen, and he didn't look up. "He's not jogging. He's on an abalone run. Getting topping for pizza. Tradition. Like when a big job is ready for production."

He yelled to one of the players, "Jane, it's working through your objects, now."

Jane switched places with the guy. She studied the monitor for a couple of minutes, which gave me a couple of minutes to study her. She was blond and very good-looking, in a bouncy, well-muscled sort of way. Her white gym shorts were a little too fluffy and her gray Everlast halter was a little too tight to suggest a perfect figure, but I got the feeling that when she took it off and came out of the shower her proportions would seem just right.

"You say you were with Mel in Miami. You a programmer, too?"

"Biomedical science. Ph.D. type. A lot of lab bench science."

"Cool. But you didn't grow up in Miami. I can tell. Bet you're really one of those Northeasterners. New York or Boston, maybe?"

"Newark." I said it with a strong Jersey accent that made it sound almost like "New York."

"Cool," she said again. She said it California style — two syllables, lots of enthusiasm, and an unselfconscious pause at the end. "You get around." She tossed her head, throwing back her thick, sweaty hair, and catching a face full of California sun.

"Yeah, been a whole lot of places. What are you guys doing there, Jane?"

"First day we are testing the system on site. It's a bank job in San Antonio. Fast optical scanning of checks, cash balance and that kinda stuff. It's running heavy on my modules right now so I'm keeping track of it. You going to be here long?"

"Depends on what Mel says. I'm trying to find him. Your friend said he's on an abalone run and won't be back for a while."

"Yeah, but I can get him for you." She walked over to the windbreak fence and picked up a canvas bag. She pulled out a cellphone and punched a speed dial button. And she beamed up a real nice smile which I had to return. Her eyes returned to the monitor, but she moved closer to me. She traced an arc in the sand with a pointed toe.

"Say, Mel. Your old friend Ben is here to see you. Wants to know where he can meet you." She listened for a minute. "Yeah, north end of Pescadero, like always. Yeah, I'll give him directions."

She smiled. Was it what Mel had said or what she saw in the monitor?

She hung up and gave directions that would get me to U.S. Highway 101, headed north. "Take Highway Eighty-four. When you get to the ocean, go two miles south to Pescadero State Beach. Then look for Mel's red Mercedes convertible parked on the road, on the north end. You can't miss it. His license plate says 'Mr. Chip.' Look for him down in the pools."

"Thanks, Jane," I said as I started to leave.

"Hey, make sure you come back with him. Bet you've never tasted abalone. You're coming back?" She threw me a glance that let me know she was serious. "Promise?"

I couldn't promise, but I might need to call her again for more help to find Mel. "Right. But give me the number of your cellular, just in case."

She gave it to me.

The westward drive on Highway 84 was pleasant, starting with rolling hills covered with brown, dry grass, gaining elevation and leading into a redwood forest with deep canyons and hairpin turns, then descending through artichoke fields and dirt, rock and grass-covered hills down to the Pacific. The view from the coastal highway was spectacular.

Mr. Chip's Mercedes was just about where Jane said it would be, parked on a scenic overlook. I saw his towel among the stones and boulders of the crescent beach 40 feet below. The coast was a series of broad indentations, each hundreds of yards wide. Broad-fronted waves rolled through the scattered, outlying rock formations and into the semicircular basin where they swayed the submerged kelp before crashing into the rocky shore. After scanning the surface for a long time, I spotted the red tip of Mel's snorkel and the pattern of spray when he blew it out. Sometimes his face mask flashed in the sun.

He was working a line of semi-submerged boulders several hundred yards out. Although shielded from the three-foot waves, there would still be a danger of getting smashed against the rock by the back surge. He held his breath like a pro. Twice, I counted 90 seconds between when his fins went up in the air and the blast of spray from his snorkel that marked the dive's completion. After a quarter of an hour, he started making his way to shore.

Carefully, I descended a steep, narrow, rocky path and sat on a boulder a few yards from the spot where Mel had left his tennis shoes and folded towel. He made his approach to shore face down, breathing through his snorkel and timing his landing to the waves. Had to admire his skill and agility, getting out of those oversized flippers between waves and climbing four feet of rock and boulder.

He walked up to his spot and regarded me, wordlessly, while laying down a tire-iron and a net-bag with two giant abalone. He took off his weight belt and inflatable flotation vest. He was moderate height and build, but the black wet suit gave him an imposing look. He widened his stance and gestured for me to come.

A look at his face confirmed what I had guessed from his name — that he came from the same Italian gene pool as I. With his dark, wrap-around eyebrows, Mediterranean nose and black olive eyes, he would have fit well in Sicily. He pulled off his rubber hood, revealing a full head of straight, thick, black hair. "You came all the way out to California to talk to me about Peter Peterson?"

"In the neighborhood."

"Really?"

"Yes. Pete died a few weeks ago."

"Yes, you e-mailed me."

"I'm taking over his lab."

"That's what you e-mailed."

"You see, I'm also being paid to do a biography of Peter. He specified it in his will."

"Yeah, that's what you e-mailed me." Melvin Armino was a damn tough customer for a guy my age.

"I want to talk about your work with him."

"For your biography?" He regarded quizzically.

No bullshitting this guy. I'd have to give it to him straight. "I think he was murdered. He pissed a lot of people off. Animal Rights, Right to Life, or maybe someone at the med school." I would keep cool about the med school for right now. "There were threat letters. And someone broke into his apartment while I was working in it."

The guy showed absolutely no surprise at any of this.

"Are you connected with the police?"

"No. I used to work in the county M.E. lab, but I'm doing this on my own."

"Are you working for any private security outfit?"

"No, I'm doing this on my own."

"Tell me the name of Peterson's tech and all the profs in his department."

I rattled off the names. Armino stared at me. His olive-black eyes were impenetrable.

"You've come from Florida to California to tell me you think Pete was murdered."

"Yes." I tried to hold his gaze to prove my sincerity.

"Are you carrying any kind of electronic device?"

"No."

"Prove it to me."

"What?"

"Strip to your shorts and jump in the water. Hold your head under for thirty seconds."

I was wearing red patterned Jockeys — not my usual white Fruit of the Looms — so I couldn't protest on the grounds of dignity. I kicked off my slip-ons and took off my shirt and pants. I climbed over the ledge and surrendered my stomach to the chilly Pacific. Three waves washed over as I held tight to a boulder, communing with the abalone and kelp for what must have been 30 seconds. When I resurfaced, it took all my conscious effort to convince myself that I really was breathing.

It took no conscious effort to figure out what Armino had been doing in the meantime — going through my pockets and looking through my little brown book. While climbing out, I mashed a big toe and cut my leg.

Mel Armino smiled at me. "Refreshing, isn't it."

"Yeah, you should have lent me your wet suit."

He offered me his towel. "Okay, I can believe you are working for yourself. You wouldn't have taken the dip if it was a job. But how do I know you aren't going to make trouble for me? I'm not working in that dump anymore. I've got a good job here. I'm making three times what I did there."

A dump? He disliked Bryan Medical School. I was glad to find one handle on this monolith. But his eyes were still unfathomable. I finished drying off, taking care to not bloody the towel, and gave it back to him.

He dropped it where his shoes were sitting. "What do you think happened to Pete?"

"Someone killed him but made it look like a heart attack."

"Why?"

"Because he pissed someone off."

"You said that before." His eyes stayed solid; his cheek quivered.

I'd cast around and see if his replies would bracket the target. "It could have been one of the contractors. They were ripping off the University, charging inflated prices. Pete was getting ready to complain. It probably got back to them."

Arimino smiled, almost derisively. "Complained about the contractors, huh." He reached down to his shoes and pulled out a pair of sunglasses which he put on.

"More likely he wanted to expose a ring of crooks working inside the med school's administration."

"Okay. What kind of evidence do you think he had?"

I was still shivering. "Documentary evidence of every damn type of corruption."

"How do you know that?"

"Because he compared notes with a colleague named Hammerschlag from the University of Chicago."

Armino smiled at this. "That guy didn't give you *my* name."

"No, but Prof. Donald Fleischman did. He got his butt kicked out of Pharmacology. He and Pete had been fishing in the same hole." Armino's forehead wrinkled. I had him worried. "But Fleischman didn't come right out and say it. He answered me with a lot of German that he thought I wouldn't understand.

"You are guessing."

"You could call it that, except for three things. *Number One*. A couple feet of files missing from the file cabinet in Pete's bedroom. *Number Two*. The whack on the head I got when someone decided to make a return visit to his apartment." I paused and locked my eyes onto his sunglasses. "And *Number Three*. Personal checks totalling six-thousand, three-hundred and seventy dollars written by Peter Peterson to Mel Armino."

"And what do you think that means?"

"That he paid you to do some serious hacking."

"Why aren't you saying that I did some serious tutoring?"

"Sure, that's how it started. The first four-hundred dollars for setting him up in Windows and showing him how to use it. But then you guys found out you had something in common. You can't stand waste, fraud and abuse. You can't stand kickbacks." The monolith now showed a couple of cracks. I went for a long shot. "You couldn't stand seeing them spending four-thousand dollars with a local computer shop when you could order them the same computer on the Internet for one-thousand, five hundred."

Armino looked to the cliff and to his equipment and back, like he wanted to pack up and get out of there. "That would make anyone sick, wouldn't it?"

"Maybe so, but you'd be surprised how few people would try to do something about it . . . at that dump of a med school. But you did. You hacked into their records, and found where the money was going. And then you hacked in some other places, too."

Armino clenched his fists for a second, then pretended to be exercising his fingers. "You can say anything you want. What do you want from me?"

"When they killed Pete, they removed and destroyed all that information. I want to pick it up and run with it. I need your copy."

"Do you think that if a guy did all that hacking, that he'd keep a copy so they can go after him when the shit hits the fan? Going into a university's password-protected files is a crime, even if their fire walls are made of rice paper."

"You don't have a copy?"

He shook his head. "But you did describe pretty good what a guy could do."

"So the data would probably be on a diskette. What do you think it would look like?"

"It wouldn't have to be anything special. Just a small file with some check numbers, dollar sums and some people's names. Maybe there'd be another file with the names and locations of certain data in the university computer."

"But I've looked everywhere, and I can't find it. They stole it back. Do it again, for Pete's sake."

"First off, this conversation isn't taking place. Second, that's a lot to ask of a guy who isn't in the university system and doesn't have a password anymore. And if what you think is true, then the bad guys are already wise."

"Tell me who it was, and what to look for."

"So you can take the information to court. Then I would get

subpoenaed because they want to know where you got the information? I get enough legal excitement already, every Wednesday night, watching *Law and Order*."

"It would be the same deal you had with Pete back in Miami."

"No, it wouldn't. Would you believe that he was fanatic enough to swear that he did the hacking himself?"

"But —"

" — This conversation didn't take place. It's time for you to get in your car and drive off. And watch your ass when you go back to that swamp. If anyone asks me what we talked about today, I'll tell them I got pissed off when you accused me of poaching abalone. I'll say that you don't know shit about the rules."

"Mel, I read you loud and clear." I couldn't push him any harder and keep him on my side. "Just tell me one more thing. Pete wrote some crazy poetry about birds nesting in a 'hootchie hutch' — crazy stuff like that. Do you know anything about that?"

Armino tried hard to suppress a smile. "If you want to get into that, there's a guy named Marvin Rabinowitz. He has an outfit called Mechano-Med. But don't tell him I sent you."

"Thanks." I put on my clothes and walked up the steep path to the highway. Didn't look back until I passed the crest. Mel gave me a naval salute, and I saluted back.

I drove up coastal highway several miles north and stopped at a little diner that could have been a setting for a 1950s movie. Got a hamburger and then strolled down to the rocky beach. Sat down and listened to the roaring of the waves and thought about a lot of things:

Thought about how I'd just wrestled with my identical twin on that rocky beach between a cliff and kelp bed. I couldn't blame him for not wanting to put a $100,000 a year California job in jeopardy for a failed crusade of an old idealist who'd lived in the swamp too long.

I thought about clean money earned by a tightly knit team of nerds. I thought about how nice it is to have a job where everyone wins.

I pictured a loose-fitting pair of white shorts and tight-fitting halter top. I reached in my breast pocket for the scrap of paper bearing the California girl's number.

And I pictured my idealistic physician soul mate stuck in a gooey web of Washington policy-wonking parties.

I made two wishes, then tossed the paper into the sea. Then I picked myself up and drove back to the airport.

After I was securely ticketed for an early evening flight, I put coins in the slot and got hold of Miami-area directory assistance. They gave me the number for Mechano-Med. I dialed them up and was answered by an excitable but helpful Girl Friday, New York variety. As soon as I persuaded her it was important and personal, she patched me into her boss, Marvin Rabinowitz.

"Hello," Marvin answered.

"Hello, I'm Ben Candidi, a friend of Pete Peterson, calling from California. Gee, that was bad news, him passing away. Some of his Unitarian friends have asked me to write up a few anecdotes about him. I'm going to be in town tomorrow. Could I stop by and talk with you?"

"Sure. Any friend of Pete is a friend of mine. Come any time. We're here all the time."

I hung up and surrendered my body and soul to American Airlines.

Maybe, in the future, the whole world will turn into one big airport, with everyone connected to it like a big life support system, where you can walk miles and miles without going outdoors, where you can get your meal and a present for your sweetheart, paying with plastic, and where you are never more than a few yards from a TV set that broadcasts the distilled essence of what you need to continue living successfully, until it is time to heed the prim and pretty woman who calls your aisle number so you can walk down the jetway and ensconce yourself in a soft chair that you'd really like to have in your living room — if only there were some way to get your feet up — and you leaf through their magazine that offers the distilled essence of everything in such inspirational tones that you have a genuine feeling of accomplishment for having ascended to 35,000 feet.

I worked hard at sleeping as we raced westward, towards the moon and the sun, and towards tomorrow's appointment. At what must have been Pensacola, I felt the plane turn south. Once I opened my eyes for Tampa Bay, and later for the lights of Naples. Then we swung left and my half-open eyes saw moonlight reflecting obliquely from patchy ponds of the Everglades. Soon "lake communities," shopping strips and finally warehouses were rising to meet us and our wheels laid rubber on the tarmac.

An eventful day came all too soon.

Three hours sleep in the apartment was just enough to enable my brain to grudgingly respond to my watch's piezoelectric alarm. The cerebellar rejuvenation was adequate for the mechanics of shaving, but it took me a while to recognize the guy in the mirror. My stomach wasn't ready for the two bran muffins but the coffee went down easily. It started taking effect towards the end of my long cab ride to Dania.

Mechano-Med's address was in a warehouse community located between Interstate 95 and the AMTRAK tracks. There were rows and rows of warehouses, many converted for specific commercial purposes. The diesel engine repair warehouses had large bay doors and chain hoists. The showroom warehouses were fitted with picture windows to display oriental carpet or Scandinavian furniture. But most were of standard design, fronting only a small door and window, each protected by a steel door that could be secured by a heavy padlock.

Mechano-Med's only identification was a white-on-black sheet-plastic sign which was lag-bolted into the cinder block wall, a few feet over their front door.

The cab driver was nice enough to stick around while I pushed the button and waited until they buzzed me in. I entered a small reception area where several metal chairs were crammed around a small coffee table. A large display stood in the corner. It was one of those portable, fabric-covered types that you see at trade shows. The tacked-on cards and photographs described implantable orthopedic devices.

"Come on back." It was yesterday's voice — female, New York, and encouraging.

I walked a couple steps down a narrow hallway to the first office.

"You must be Dr. Candidi. I'm Marcey." She smiled up at me. The sign on her desk said Marcey Zinn. Her hair was black and bouffant, her nails were mahogany and long. Her lashes were also long and heavy with mascara, accenting sympathetic eyes. Her topside feminine assets jiggled nicely behind her tight silk blouse as she rose from behind the desk. She was wearing snug-fitting, tapered jeans and medium-rise heels. After a glance at photos on the wall and then back to her, I figured she was in her high forties and proud of having successfully launched two college-age kids and having maintained an hourglass figure.

"Let me see if Marvin can see you." She said it softly while sliding by. She turned her face to the end of the hall and yelled, "Marvin, your Dr. Candidi's here to see you."

Her announcement had enough volume and saw-toothed modulation to carry all the way down to the machine shop, but a mumbled acknowledgement came from the next office.

Marcey smiled at me and said, "Marvin's in his *oarfus* next *doah*." There's something backhandedly charming about a New Yorker going out of the way to be nice. While moving on, I thanked Marcey with a smile which, I hoped, would also camouflage my amusement. I had no trouble finding my own way.

Marvin's office was identical to Marcey's, except that his wall was covered with framed certificates and black and white photographs. A suit coat hung on a coat pole behind him. One of the certificates was a Master of Engineering from Columbia University, dated 1956. The photos showed him shaking hands on podiums and demonstrating mechanical devices at trade fairs. Some of the photos were taken many years ago, judging from the cuts of the suits.

When I entered, Marvin was hunched over his scuffed wooden desk working on a mechanical sketch. He looked up at me like I'd just asked for help unloading a truck full of boxes.

"Hi, I'm Ben Candidi. I'm the one who's doing a short biography on Pete Peterson."

"Yeah. You told me that when you *coraled*." He looked like he sounded: heavy, half-bald, and old for his sixty-some years.

It wouldn't be smart to push him too hard. I glanced at his diploma on the wall. "Did you come here after Columbia in '56? That's when Pete came here — in 1958 from St. Louis."

"Yeah, we came here around the same time. Used to make bets about who'd be the last to go." He looked down, and laid a heavy hand on a stainless steel roller bearing assembly. "Upset me a lot when I heard. Too late for the funeral. Don't hear much from Bryan Medical School."

Out of sight, but not out of the loop, Marcey put in her two cents worth. "Didn't hear much from them on the last three invoices we sent them, either." Shrill and nasal, it carried well from one office to the other.

Marvin Rabinowitz shook his head. "We still do work for some of the doctors there . . . when they call up in the middle of the night because their liquid nitrogen freezers have gone on the blink. Or when the tissue processors don't work right anymore. They escort us into the building, and we fix them up. We get them to sign for it, and then Marcey sends them a bill that they don't pay for a year."

"Yes, I heard that they are giving independent vendors a hard time. I heard that everyone has to be 'vendorized'."

Marcey's answer ricochetted down the hall faster than the word left my mouth: "*Vendorized, schmenderized* . . . FENDERIZED! They just run you over!"

Marvin acknowledged her point with a tired shake of the head. Obviously, he'd seen it all, and heard it all, and had a lot of spirited conversations with Marcey *via* their hallway intercom.

"So you came here to talk to me about Pete. Fine. We can talk about him. Want to see the shop?"

I was glad for that. "Yes. They tell me you have made a lot of medical inventions."

Rabinowitz got up slowly. As if cued telepathically, Marcey approached from behind. "Can I get you some *korfie*? Cream and *sugah*?"

"Yes, please."

A minute later, Marvin and I were standing, cups of coffee in hand, in the middle of his machine shop, talking about his medical devices. The coffee was strong and so was the smell of the thread cutting oil. A Latin-American guy was running a lathe, and a Haitian was scrubbing something with a wire brush. Another guy, whose ethnic background was hard to guess, was lowering some steel parts into a chrome electroplating bath. He had a poorly trimmed, blond beard and was wearing a wrinkled shirt and worn-out blue jeans.

Marvin was bellied up to a work bench. "What we are specialized in, at this workshop, is simple mechanical devices that can be implanted around bone. Things that the surgeon can screw in to hold troublesome fractures together. Or better yet, devices that can be screwed on, to take the load off a damaged spine."

He picked up a piece of black plastic that was the length of a bent little finger, but more flattened. Each end was widened and bore two counter-sunk screw holes.

"You see, the things you screw into the spine will work better if they are made from smart materials that can give and flex with your body. We're working with space-age composite materials from NASA. We've got a Cooperative Research and Development Agreement to work on it." He pressed the device between three stubby fingers. It seemed to flex a couple of millimeters. "We're helping to take the load off. Well, at least that's what our collaborating surgeon says."

The bearded guy didn't seem to be listening, but he kept track of us with intelligent eyes. The guy at the lathe was half-listening as Rabinowitz spoke. He was short, muscular and had a Mayan face. I guessed he came from Central America. Rabinowitz glanced at him like he was part of the conversation, but didn't introduce him. Over a small desk near the lathe hung a certificate stating that Alonso Fernandez was a certified black belt instructor in the art of Tae Kwon-Do Karate. It had to be him. I guessed that Alonso was Marvin's partner and second-in-command in the shop.

I asked, "Are some of your inventions ready for clinical trials."

"This lateral extender is being tested in *doaghs*. We're saving a lot of German shepherds from being put down for hip dysplasia." Lovingly, he cradled the device in an open hand.

"So I guess you are looking to license a big medical device company that can bring it out in humans."

"Our surgeon is going to do his own trial and we're going public. Got a brokerage house in Boca Raton that's going to offer our stock on NASDAQ."

"Tell him about the stereotactic device," called the now-familiar voice from offstage.

Rabinowitz smiled. "We're working on a lot of stuff."

"Can you tell me about how you came to Bryan Medical School and some of your experiences with Pete?"

"Sure."

While Rabinowitz told me his story at Bryan Medical School, Marcey came around every once in a while to listen in and top off our coffee mugs. The two were married to other people, but they had enjoyed a close working relationship for the last 20 years.

Rabinowitz had been in charge of biomedical instrument repair at Bryan Medical School since 1956. He had kept everyone's refrigerator, shaker and incubator running. He also did a lot of electronic repair until integrated circuits replaced vacuum tubes. He spoke in a tired monotone and dropped his voice at the end of every sentence. He dropped his eyes, too.

When I asked about Pete, Rabinowitz said he was a good guy but didn't volunteer much more. Our conversation reverted to Rabinowitz' experience at Bryan Medical School. He had collaborated with some research physicians and had given Bryan a number of inventions, including radiation positioning devices used in cancer diagnosis and surgery. At the end of the description, his eyes sank to the floor.

"Then, four years ago, the dean decided that it would be better and cheaper to have the scientists get service contracts or to use outside contractors." He took a long sip of coffee. "And then we came in one day to find out that we didn't have our jobs anymore." He half-turned, and replaced the space-age bone implant on the workbench.

"Tell him how Assistant Dean Robert Wriggler did it," shouted Marcey, from the water cooler on the other side of the shop.

"It wasn't a very nice way," Rabinowitz said, shaking his head sadly.

In shrill tones, Marcey supplied the missing details. "Four security guards came in and told us they had orders to throw us out of our *oarfus.*"

I shook my head in sympathy and exaggerated disbelief. Rabinowitz shook his head, too, but as if to say it was water over the dam.

"Did they ever do anything like that to Pete?"

Marvin's offstage prompter didn't let him miss a line. "Tell him about how they sent him to the psychiatrist!"

I nodded back to her, hoping to bring her on stage.

Rabinowitz said, "One year he had twelve thousand dollars left over in his budget, and they used it to pay for a renovation of his lab that he was supposed to get for free. They did it by moving around components of his salary. Pete got real mad when he found out. Stomped down to Research Administration and demanded that they pay it back. Said it was a Federal Grant, that he was the Principal Investigator, and that what they did behind his back was a Federal crime. He didn't get past Dolores Padilla. She said she'd gotten 'prior approval' on it and it was done, and there was no changing it."

Marcey had moved in closer. "*Prior approval*! Drag-you-through-the-fire approval!"

Rabinowitz continued. "Dolores Padilla said she wouldn't talk about it anymore and told Pete to leave. He said he wouldn't leave until he could talk to someone about whether that was legal. Then she called Security, and they came and yanked him out of her office. Then she filled out a report that he was threatening her and the dean wrote a letter and made him go to a psychiatrist to get his head examined." He glanced at Alonso Fernandez who had been listening in all the time. "You heard about that one, Al."

"Yeah," Alonso said. He laid down his coffee mug and came over. "That old *tortillera*. If she did that to me, that place would really be needing our spinal implants."

Tortilla? Spanish omelet? Scrambled eggs? Was that what the physical plant guys had been making all those jokes about? But no time to think about that, now.

I gestured to Alonso's karate certificate. "I see you're a black belt." If I could just keep this group together long enough to tell me the whole story. Rabinowitz needed his prompter and a cheering section to keep going.

"What happened then?"

Alonso picked up the story. "Pete went to the head-shrinker and passed his mental exam after three tries. Didn't pass it with flying colors but he passed it. Word was that he was just *poco loco*. You know like when a guy gets too serious about some things that it doesn't pay to get serious about . . . because those things are not supposed to be good for your health."

Could I get him to firm up this statement? "You mean like in one of those old movies where the gangster tells a guy to take a couple weeks' vacation for his health?"

"Yeah, like don't mess with us because we're the Cuban mafia that's running this place." Alonso Fernandez laughed and put up his hands as if to hold me back. "Hey, Dr. Ben, don't look at me like that. I'm not one of them. I come from Costa Rica."

"So they've got a Cuban mafia made up of administrators —."

Marcey jumped in. "They aren't all Cuban. What about that big blond that the *tortilla* bitch is in bed with? What about Kotzen? What about Wriggler?"

A sarcastic little smile appeared on Rabinowitz' face. "They're an equal opportunity mafia. They take anyone who will work with them."

"Did Pete know about the mafia?"

"Yeah, he knew about it."

"Did he do anything about it?"

Marcey picked up the ball. "Four years ago, when I was still working there, he brought his records down to me. I *taurght* him how to read those Report 70s. He studied them every month, religiously. And he made sure he got them on time. They never pulled one over on him again."

"Did he do anything else to stop the mafia?"

Rabinowitz eyeballed me for several seconds. "And who did you say told you to come here to *torque* with us?"

"I got your number from Mel Armino. I knew him from the Southeastern conference. And there was a death notice from Ted Walden. I'm just looking for new stories, to round out the picture. I'm learning that Pete was a real crusader. From what people have been telling me, Bryan Medical School really needs to be shaken up. I mean in California they . . ."

"That school is too rotten to shake," Marcey rasped.

Rabinowitz concurred. "The only thing keeping it from falling down is the crooks holding hands."

I had to keep the pump running. "There must be a lot of ways to make illegal money in a medical school besides ripping off scientist's grants and shaking down vendors."

"Yeah," said Alonso. "Like opening up a candy store."

"Candy store?"

"Yeah, you know, like all types of candy. Selling the physician's free samples. You wouldn't believe all the shit they had on that list they gave me when I first came to work there."

"Who gave you the list?"

"Some guys from Receiving. But I don't want to name no names."

Marcey said, "They're still selling you naprosyn."

That comment didn't help. Alonso frowned.

I smiled and said, "I hear it's the best for sports injuries — like sore joints from karate. Lot better than ibuprofen. No side-effects and no abuse potential." I turned to Rabinowitz, and glanced to Marcey. "But I guess the candy store was pretty penny ante stuff."

"Nose candy is more expensive," Rabinowitz said.

"Tell him about the cadavers," Marcey said.

A glance from Rabinowitz told her that was too much. But after several seconds silence, he told me anyway. "You see, medical schools have to deal with all kinds of things coming from all kinds of countries . . . if you know what I mean."

My mind was racing. Mules. Body-packers. Every day, human beings risk their lives swallowing a dozen greased prophylactics, each loaded with 50 grams of cocaine, and getting on planes to the U.S. If one of the prophylactics breaks, the smuggler loses one mule and a half kilo of coke.

How much more humane to stuff the coke in a corpse that's already dead. And with all that formaldehyde, the dog couldn't sniff it. And the Customs people won't look at a corpse going to a medical school. Just a group of honest doctors doing medical research.

Thinking had probably slowed my answer. "Yes, I can imagine all kinds of things coming from lots of different countries."

We exchanged glances.

"But you didn't hear that from us," Alonso said.

"No, I didn't hear it from you. But Pete was working on uncovering these things, wasn't he?"

The phone rang, and Marcey went to answer it. *Please, guys, don't clam up now.*

"Pete was working on something," Rabinowitz said.

"And any one of these could have made a lot of trouble for him if they found out he was getting into it?"

Rabinowitz said, "Yeah, those are third-rail issues. Like Social Security. Touch it and the shock will knock you on your ass."

"There is just one more thing. Pete wrote a crazy poem that I'm having a lot of trouble figuring out. It mentioned a 'hootchie hutch'."

Marcey called from her office. "Marvin, it's the lawyer. He wants to talk about the contract."

Before leaving us for the phone, Rabinowitz smiled to Fernandez. "Tell him about the thirteenth floor," he said.

"There was some talk about a secret room on the top floor, but

I don't know any more." Now he was acting like it was time to get back to work. Okay, this was plenty of information for one day.

I thanked Fernandez and waved to the Haitian and the other guy on the way out. Marvin was in the middle of a spirited telephone conversation on details of a licensing agreement. I thanked Marcey for her help. She called me a cab. It came so promptly that the only new thing I could learn from her was the identity of the silent guy with the blond beard: Igor, an "apprentice" from Moscow.

On the long cab ride back, I pondered Marcey's last words: "Mel Armino *coral'd* and said you are a good guy . . . and a smart guy. Now you watch your step around that place."

Funny, that she knew I was from Bryan Medical School but still went along with my charade about coming from California.

Funny, how I had to go all the way to California to find the people willing to tell me that I would find vermin under the log — and that the log would crumble if the termites stopped holding hands.

The intuitive part of my brain knew that I had enough information to piece together the who, why and how of the murder of Dr. Peter Peterson. But the logical part of my brain was on the verge of malfunction. Sleep deprivation. Couldn't put more than three things together at one time.

Memory wasn't working well, either. I struggled to recall the exact words of Pete's crazy poem about the birds and the hootchie hutch. The expression reminded me of the lyrics of a blues song. Maybe I should go straight to the apartment and restudy the poem. And what was the slang meaning of *tortilla* and *tortillera*? And scrambled eggs? Both Alonso Fernandez and the Physical Plant guys had used it on Dolores Padilla. Did she have egg on her face because she was accepting bribes? She was a prime suspect. She had motive and she probably had opportunity. And she even looked like an old lady.

Half-way down I-95, I almost fell asleep. I told the driver to take the next exit. Told him to get into the Burger King drive-through. It was against all that I stood for — running an eight-cylinder motor in a one-lane traffic jam behind a fast-food pickup window — but my body needed nourishment.

I tried to rest my tormented brain while eating my hamburger and fries as we rolled south on I-95. Big thunderheads were forming west of Miami and Hialeah. An orange Search and Rescue helicopter was flying south, parallel to the highway. The helicopter must have been picking up one hell of a charge from moving so fast through the electrically charged air. I remembered the scene in *Red October* where the man on the submarine's conning tower touched the man who was being winched down from a helicopter. The kilovolt jolt knocked him over the side.

Marvin had suggested the Medical School was a delivery point for drug smugglers. He had called it a "third-rail issue" — touch it and you are dead. Had Pete caught them bringing in cocaine in cadavers from South American? God! William Long in our department was working with cadavers. And he knew I was working on Pete's biography. Maybe the 13th floor penthouse by the elevator machinery was where they unpacked the bodies.

Or was it Pete's exposé of kickback operations? It couldn't be only Dolores Padilla. There would be a lot of co-conspirators, like the two Roberts. Cartlick and his buddy-boys had to be in on it. They would be in on any kind of deal. It's always helpful having the cops watch your back.

The helicopter was way ahead of us. I remembered when the Bahamian dive boat captain pointed to the thunderheads moving in and gave us two choices: run for home now, or stay at anchor in a storm for the rest of the day. The Bahamian Brit swore that he would never run when lightning is in the air.

But lightning can also strike you while at anchor. I remembered thinking about this while anchored several miles from a thunderstorm in the Bahamas. The air seemed to crackle like high tension wires in a fog. And the *Diogenes'* rigging was singing, though the wind was still. It was a strange, persistent hum around middle C. And it stopped immediately when lightning discharged five miles away. Then the hum came back again. After this happened again and again, there could be only one conclusion — my boat was part of an electric circuit between polarized water and angry clouds.

Too fascinated to go below, I had moved to the center of the cockpit, crossed my legs under me and put my arms across my chest. Should I have bought one of those rounded charge diffusers and bolted it to the top of my mast?

Pete probably didn't believe in charge diffusers; he had sharp edges; he was a lightning rod for controversy. And I had shown my sharp edges around the med school, too.

As the cab approached the medical center exit, the helicopter maneuvered to land on the roof of the Ryder Trauma Center. No question there was a charge imbalance between earth and sky. I could feel it in the air. The intangible evidence was humming — the half-empty file drawer, the sideline cheers from the orchidologist, the smirky-faced denial by Mel Armino, and the barrel full of rumors from Mechano-Med. The lump on my head started to throb.

But what to do? Anchor or keep on moving? Go back for a nap in the apartment so you can take stock of your situation with a rested brain — or go straight to the med school and spend the day acting like nothing had happened? Either way you might get hit. Somehow, the call of the lab was stronger. I gave the driver directions for the med school. I paid him and got out.

As I walked through the two glass doors and showed my badge, I heard crackling in the air — the crackling of a security guard's walkie-talkie.

33 DOCTOR WILL SEE YOU

"Good that you are back, now," Mildred said when I walked in. "A lot has happened."

"It always does. Give me the bad news first."

"I don't know if it's bad or good. The dean's secretary called for you yesterday. I told her you were out of town."

"Say what she wanted?"

"No. You also had a call from a 'Bruce from Mensa.' He was very insistent."

"Yeah, I've been letting him use my computer as a test bed for his pet project. It can wait. Now, what else?"

"Yesterday, a Mrs. Vandoren called. She wanted to tell you she found some very important things from Pete. She said you would want it right away, but she didn't know how to send it and maybe parcel post would be too slow. She really wanted to send it FEDEX and have us pay shipping."

"That's fine."

"I thought it would be. But I had to talk to Olga about it. She called Central Administration for permission."

"Great."

"Well, here it is. Came at ten-thirty this morning." She pointed to a FEDEX box, small document size, under my desk.

Good. I would check it out right away.

"And . . ."

"Yes, what else, Mildred?"

"Well, excuse me for bringing it up, but I have been having a lot of problems with the experiments."

"What kind of problems?"

That was what I needed: a scientific discussion to calm me down . . . to diffuse the ions. After we had talked for half an hour, the phone rang. I should have had Mildred pick it up.

"Mr. Candidi. This is Lizzy-Mae."

"Yes, this is *Doctor* Candidi. What can I do for you?"

"Dean Weisburd would like to speak to you."

"Fine. Put him on."

"In his office."

"Okay. When?"

"Now."

"Okay. What about?"

"He would like to talk to you."

My brain was whirling. I looked at the computer and down at the telephone. I was still groggy and wasn't ready to talk to him about anything. I didn't know how deeply he was involved in the criminal enterprises going on in his medical school. But I couldn't find an excuse to put it off. Seconds were ticking. The old witch did nothing to break the silence.

"Okay. I'll be right down."

Hell, I'd just made the wrong choice.

Was there anything I could do? Anyone I could talk to? I dialed up Dr. Westley. His secretary Doris answered. She said he had stepped out for a while. Could she take a message?

"Yes. Please take this down. The situation with Peter Peterson is becoming very serious. I received important new information by FEDEX today. And I'm being summoned to the dean's office right now."

She read it back to me. "Is there anything you would like to add?"

"Yes. If I don't call back in one hour, ask him to — Heck, I don't know what I should ask him to do."

I hung up. Wrote Ted Walden's name and phone number on the FEDEX box, then packed it under my arm.

Mildred was still waiting outside my door. "Is there anything I can do for you?"

"Yes. I've just been summoned to the dean's office. And when he's done with me, I'm coming straight back here. And if I'm not back in one hour, I want you to come down and get me. You can say something came up."

"But — "

" — it has to do with Pete. I can't tell you any more, right now."

I grabbed my tape recorder from the desk top and ran out the door. I ducked into the stairway and hurried down to the Pharmacology level. Ran into Rob McGregor's office, surprising him in the process.

"Look, Rob. I need a favor. Please hold onto this box. It contains some very important documents." I pointed to the name and number. "If anything happens to me, make sure this guy gets it."

"But Ben —"

" — I can't talk. I've just been summoned to the dean's office. I don't know what he wants, but his secretary Lizzy-Mae made it sound damn important. I'll come right back as soon as he lets me go."

I was out of there before he could protest. Now there were three people who would miss me if I didn't come back. My brain was working better now. Must have gotten a shot of adrenaline because my heart was racing.

Half-way down the hallway, I had second thoughts. Maybe I should ask Rob to come along with me. It would keep the dean from opening a second round of veiled threats. But with Rob there as a witness, the dean might refuse to hear about the rats in his woodpile. No, wait! You can't tell him that. Put up your lightning diffuser. Keep it low key. Let him reveal himself.

I took the elevator to the first floor. Walked past the brassy wall of donor plaques, past the overly manned guard station with the crackly radio, and through the double doors to the administrative section. Walked past the magnetically locked doors guarding the "veterinary core" and service elevators. Turned down the narrow, plastic-lined hallway with the spongy floor material.

I walked past all the dean's doors that nobody was allowed to enter. Switched on the tape recorder and shoved it deep in my rear pocket. Turned in at the peon entrance. Walked into the waiting room.

I announced myself to the two receptionist/secretaries who played handmaiden to Lizzy-Mae. "I am Dr. Candidi. I was called down here to talk to the dean."

One of them looked up from her fingernails and picked up the phone. In a hushed voice, she gave Lizzy-Mae the word.

The witch's voice came out through the diagonal. "Yes, I will take care of it."

She didn't come out right away. Apparently, she told her handmaidens they could leave for lunch because they both got up and left. I positioned myself on the couch in order to watch the hag across the diagonal. She fumbled in her desk drawer and ignored me for five minutes.

I spent the time thinking what I might say to the dean if he came on hostile — and what I would say if he were friendly. I wouldn't show any cards, in either case. Must have been engrossed in my thoughts because Lizzy-Mae startled me when I first noticed her just a couple of feet away.

"Would you please come in."

"Sure."

I followed her through her office and into the dean's office. He wasn't there. She circled around behind me. Something about that woman put me in a sarcastic mood. Would she invite me to sit in one of the upholstered chairs around the coffee table, or in the Spartan visitor's chair in front of the dean's desk? During the few seconds I loitered, Lizzy-Mae gave me no cues.

And what the hell was the purpose of the steamer trunk along the wall? Was the dean going to blow town? Using my sassiest body language, I plunked down in one of the upholstered chairs. I half-turned to keep Lizzy-Mae in sight.

"So here I am!"

"Doctor will be here in a few minutes. Would you like a cup of coffee."

Laying on that doctor stuff, again?

"No thanks. I will just be a patient patient and wait for *the* doctor."

Hell no, I wasn't going to drink anything prepared by her. My eyes followed her as she crept back to her office.

I reached in my pocket to make sure the tape machine was still recording. The next time that woman dropped the word *the* before *doctor*, I'd ask her if they'd trained nurses to say it that way back in the 1930s.

She returned to the room and walked towards me. "Doctor has ordered a light sedation." I was halfway out of my chair before she could get close, but I was surprised how quickly she pounced. The jab caught me in the right shoulder before I could take a single step. It felt like a sharp prick.

She hugged my back like a bobcat as I tried to scramble away. Dislodged her with a back-handed left to her face. She just stood there, squared off against me, holding a ten milliliter syringe. It looked half-emptied. My shoulder stung. I touched it and felt a knot.

She watched me with quick eyes, like a cornered fox.

For some reason, my words came out politely. "You can't do that. What did you inject me with?"

"No, please, Mr. Candidi. Please don't make a disturbance. You have made too many disturbances already." She made it sound like we were in a clinic.

"What's in it? Give me that damn syringe."

"No. Just wait quietly until Doctor comes."

Now, I saw it clearly. She was the old lady that killed Pete. And now she had used her poison on me.

I took one step forward and smashed her chest with a front thrust kick. She fell backwards on the steamer trunk.

Now I knew why the trunk was there. It was my coffin.

The syringe dropped to the carpet. Lizzy-Mae went for it on all fours. I caught her on the head with a forward stamp-kick. It stunned her, or maybe worse. I grabbed the syringe.

I flew out the door and ran up the tacky hall. At the end of the hall, a guard moved to block my way.

"Mr. Candidi, you will be detained for making a disturbance."

He was reciting practiced lines.

I kept up my rush until the last couple of yards. Pretended to stumble. Dropped my left shoulder and rolled. Caught his nose with an upward palm thrust as I snapped out of the roll.

He had leaned over to grab me, but he grabbed his face instead. When I hit the double doors he was already on his knees. Ran fast, past the "veterinary core" and through the second set of doors. Slowed down while making my way past the guard station, blending into a crowd of med students that was streaming in.

Had to get away — find someone to rescue me — get to the phone on the second-floor. I tried to open the door to the stairwell. My right arm wouldn't work to grab the handle. And my legs were weakening with every step up. The poison was leaching out of my arm and into my system. In a matter of seconds, all muscle control would be gone.

Pulled change from my pocket. Dodged through a group of med students to the pay phone mounted on the wall. A med student, probably a sophomore, was using it, deep in conversation. I couldn't get her attention.

"Please hang up and dial nine-one-one." I held up the syringe. "I've been injected with poison."

She shook her head and looked away like I was a nutcase. I held down the switchhook to disconnect her. "Please help me."

She just stood there staring at me.

I held the syringe in my teeth and snatched the receiver with my left hand. Heard a dial tone. Punched in Dr. Westley's number. The recorded voice said to deposit 35 cents. Fed in the coins.

A big guy was coming up on me fast with balled fists. He looked like a second year med student who was into body building. "Need someone to teach you manners?"

It was hard, getting the syringe and receiver into one hand.

I pleaded. "Help me or I'll die. Please!"

"Hey, look at his badge. He's faculty," someone said.

A crowd was gathering.

"Medical Examiner's Office," Doris answered.

"Doris, get me Dr. Westley immediately. Emergency."

"He's right here. I'll put him on."

The Old Man was so painfully slow. I must have looked horrible because everybody was watching me but avoiding my eyes.

"Ben, I can understand your occasional impatience but —"

" — Shut up and listen! The dean's secretary, Lizzy-Mae Wolf has just injected me in the arm. I'm losing muscle control. Probably the same poison she used to kill Pete Peterson. I'm dying — outside the med student's lounge — on the second floor." My speech was slurring.

The syringe slipped from my fingers. My right arm was useless. My left arm was going numb. My legs, too.

Body-builder was standing close by, no longer a threat but no help either.

"Get someone here to save me," I said into the phone. "Call nine-one-one," I yelled to the crowd. To keep from sliding down, I jammed myself into the space between the wall and the phone.

Dr. Westley's voice seemed so faint. "Doris, on a separate line, please. Dial nine-one-one, Fire Rescue to Bryan Medical School, student lounge on the second floor. Ben, try to describe your symptoms. And breathe deeply."

And that was just it. I couldn't breathe. The world was turning gray. Westley's voice was slipping away. And so was the phone. Helping hands softened my fall. I could feel the pain of my wrenched arms but I couldn't move them. Couldn't move my legs either — like my body was buried deep in sand.

Gray turned to black. My body was falling to the bottom of the sea like a lifeless rock. Oh, Blessed Mother, hear my prayers while I can still pray. Deliver my soul to Heaven.

"Resuscitation! Two-man team." It sounded like the medical sophomore who'd been using the phone. "Ed, call Fire Rescue. Then call Anesthesiology for a breathing tube and an Ambu Bag. He's cyanotic."

Loud, excited conversation, but so distant. Life was still in me, but deep in a hard shell like an abalone. Sensations billowed through me like waves on a beach. Warm flesh was pressing against me. A moist wind blew in, raising my chest. Then it went out with a sigh. Something was infusing me with strength.

Black turned into gray. Moist flesh was rendering a kiss of life. Slowly, gray turned into a textured sea. From a sea of tan emerged a tilted pair of eyes. They stared down at me under a stringy black curtain. Oh thank you, Blessed Mother.

She pulled back. The sea of flesh transformed into a sea of faces. My angel spoke. "Roger, are you getting a pulse?"

"Pulse sixty but strong."

I couldn't make out her face through the blinding fluorescent lights.

"Come on, guys. I'm doing the breathing for him. Give me observations! Discussion! "

White was turning to gray.

The moist wind returned with a full-mouth kiss. My lips felt clammy. Fuzzy gray images resolved into crisp black and white — and then to Technicolor. What beautiful blue eyes!

"Vital signs!" she commanded between breaths.

"Pulse is sixty and strong. Heart sounds are normal for high exertion." It was Body Builder.

"Fasciculations. Leg and arm muscles rippling," said another.

"Cyanosis disappearing," said another.

And I still couldn't move.

Angel skipped a breath. She moved her head back and stroked my lashes. "What's his name?"

"Benjamin Candidi, Ph.D.," one of them called out.

"Don't panic, Dr. Candidi," Angel said. "Your breathing muscles are paralyzed. Arms and legs, too. But I'll breathe for you as long as you need it. If you can hear me, blink"

With all my might, I tried to blink. She bent down and put her mouth to mine and blew.

"Appendages limp," called a male voice.

Angel interrogated between breaths. "Probable toxic agent? Anyone."

Body Builder answered. "Profound muscle relaxation with no breathing. Must be muscle relaxant — whopping dose of Valium or dantrolene."

"No," Angel said.

"But it couldn't be tubocurarine or succinylcholine. If he got that, he couldn't have walked in here. That stuff paralyzes in 30 seconds."

Angel kept up the breathing and the interrogation. "Where's the injection site?"

"Here it is in his arm," answered a nasal male voice. "Probably deep intramuscular."

"Clear, watery fluid in syringe," added another.

"Intramuscular tubocurarine or succinylcholine," said the nasal male.

Angel stayed in control. "Rule out tubocurarine. Doesn't cause fasciculations."

"Buddy, can you hear us talking?" asked Body Builder

"He can't speak," said the nasal male.

Angel spoke. "Dr. Candidi, blink if you can hear me."

I tried with all my might. It was hard. The agent must have relaxed my blinking muscles, too.

"Good, Dr. Candidi. Now we are going to ask you some questions. Blink once for yes; blink twice for no. Okay guys, ask your questions."

"Were you at the hospital?"

I squeezed them shut twice, as hard as I could.

"He said the dean's secretary injected him," Body Builder said.

I blinked once.

Another guy chimed in. "Is that what you said? How in the hell can that be?"

I blinked once and prayed they all wouldn't talk at once.

A new voice said, "His badge says he's in Physiology. Maybe he had an accident when he was injecting an animal."

Damn!

"Hey, he's blinked twice. He's saying no."

"But that doesn't make any sense. Hey, buddy, is today Wednesday?"

I had to think for a long time before blinking no.

"Is it Thursday, the 26th?"

I blinked yes.

"Well, he got that right."

Body Builder came back on line. "And you say that the dean's secretary, Lizzy-Mae, attacked you with this syringe full of succinylcholine?"

I blinked yes.

The next speaker silenced the crowd. I couldn't turn my head to see him, but I recognized his oily voice.

"No! He told it to you backwards. He tried to attack Lizzy-Mae with a syringe. And I've given the guards orders to take him into custody. Now!"

Angel lifted her face. "You cannot. He can't breathe. He will die."

"I'm the doctor, here. Fire Rescue will intubate him. Now get away from him, and the rest of you get out."

"I'm sorry, Dean Weisburd. He is my patient. I will keep breathing for him until he can breathe on his own."

My world was turning from white to gray. My face prickled like needles and pins. Angel couldn't breathe for me if she had to argue with him.

"Miss Mary Atkins. You're only a medical sophomore. It will be two years before you will have your first patient."

"Ben Candidi," she said to me. "Are you my patient?"

I blinked once, with all my might. She dove for my lips and the moist wind returned.

"He said yes," several students said, all at once.

The dean assumed a command voice. "That's insubordination. Mary Atkins, you're washed up. Guards, remove this woman."

Body Builder didn't let a second go by. "You touch her, and you're dead meat. Mary's my fiancée."

"Everyone who doesn't have any business here, out!"

"Stay here, guys, and see the case through," Body Builder said.

Weisburd screamed, "Guards, bag that syringe and secure the area."

The next voice spoke in high register with an unmistakable English accent. "You will touch nothing. I am Dr. Geoffrey Westley, Chief Medical Examiner of Miami-Dade County. By that authority, I designate this area as a crime scene, along with several other areas including your office and the office of your secretary, Lizzy-Mae, if that is indeed her real name."

The only answer was murmurs, grumbling and footsteps.

"He's the guy that gave us the lecture on forensic medicine," one voice said.

Westley did not respond; he commanded. "You remaining guards — Fuentes and Miller. As security officers deputized by Miami-Dade County, you are duty-bound to follow my instructions. Fail to do so and you will be charged with obstructing justice."

I tried to get up.

"Look, he's moving."

Dr. Westley's voice took on a familiar lecture-hall quality. "It is consistent with an intramuscular injection of succinylcholine, as you have deduced. By now, all the succinylcholine has left the injection site. The plasma esterase in his blood is degrading the compound to harmless choline and succinic acid. Thus, his acetyl-choline-activated sodium channels are free to resensitize. Voluntary muscle function will return shortly. I predict that he will be sitting up in five minutes and will be rampant in another ten."

Thanks for finally telling me.

"Ben, I know it has been hard for you. 'Twas hard for me to watch and listen to that bloody scoundrel without twitching a muscle. Ben, I'm going to ask you a few questions. Now you are sure that this Lizzy-Mae injected you with the contents of that syringe?"

I blinked yes.

"Is it correct that you did not prepare the syringe, yourself."

I blinked yes.

"And had this Lizzy-Mae called you to come down to her office?"

I blinked yes.

"Good. This will suffice for arresting this Lizzy-Mae. Was Dean Weisburd in the office?"

I blinked, no.

"Very well. And I see he has absconded with his little squad of security guards. We will content ourselves with questioning him. I must leave you, Ben, in the capable hands of your young colleagues. Students, you are all to be commended. Take good care of your first patient."

And they did. The Old Man was right about everything coming back fast. Breathing came first. Then my arms and legs started doing what I told them. My first voluntary act was to thank my angel, Mary Atkins. Tried to sit up, but she kept me lying down for a long time. She said I had to be careful because my muscles had dumped a lot of potassium into my blood.

"Why did this happen?" Mary's fiancé asked.

I told them that Pete had been investigating corruption at the med school, and how he died suddenly. I told them how I'd taken over Pete's lab and the biography project. "They must have found out I was getting wise to them. Then Lizzy-Mae injected me, just like she injected Dr. Peterson."

"And Dean Weisburd is in on this?" asked the guy with the nasal voice. "I can't believe it."

"Couldn't have happened in his office without him being in on it," said another.

"When I started working here, he gave me a big warning to not follow up on Dr. Peterson's work. I was just too dumb to read between the lines. Where is he, now?"

"The dean went to the elevators in the veterinary core," said a guy in the back.

Maybe the dumped potassium was good for my brain because my mind was whirling. The dean didn't need those elevators to get back to the office. He needed them to get to the 13th floor. To his penthouse on the roof — his "hootchie *cootchie* hutch." As in "hootchie cootchie man." The place that the Mechano-Med people knew about. The place memorialized in Pete's doggerel verse. The place where "Burdie" Weisburd, the white bird, had nested. The place that "Tin Lizzy," as in Lizzy-Mae, would take you to.

I struggled to my feet.

BATTLE OF THE HOOTCHIE COOTCHIE HUTCH

34

At first, Mary and her fiancé tried to restrain me.

"I've got to stop him," I said. Everyone followed me.

My legs worked, but like a pair of rubber stilts. My magnetic card worked on the doors to the veterinary core. A dozen people followed me in. We crowded into the freight elevator and I pushed the button for the eleventh floor. At the top, the doors opened to a large space with a high ceiling.

"What are we looking for?" the students were asking.

"They call it the penthouse. The hootchie cootchie hutch." No, I'd have to do better than that. I remembered Pete's magazines. "The *Playboy Club*."

They looked at me skeptically. Group enthusiasm was ebbing. I'd have to make up a story. "It's the place they made all those jokes about in the Senior Class Play, a couple years ago."

That did the trick.

I looked up the high walls and found two doors. Both were 12 feet over our heads, accessible only by a steep metal stairs and catwalk. The door on the east side was centered over the elevators; the other one had to be on the western wall of the building. That had to be the false penthouse that I had seen while eating lunch on the plaza.

I half-climbed, half pulled myself up the stairs towards the west door. It was unlocked. I opened it and was struck by a wave of hot, moist air. Outside, I was struck by vertigo. A low-railing metal catwalk extended some 24 feet to a door on the side of the penthouse. On the right was a 12-foot drop to the building's roof. On the left was a 12-story drop to the plaza below.

Thunder was rumbling from tall storm clouds west of the airport.

Holding tightly to the door, I peeked around to the left. The top of the parking garage was almost on our level. A roofing crew was using it as a staging area for repairs on our building. On the far side of the garage they had stockpiled rolls of roofing felt.

The top of the elevator machinery room of the parking garage was right at my level. I noted the rebar ladder leading to its roof. That was what Pete had climbed to take his first pictures.

There was only one way to go. On rubbery legs, I wobbled towards the penthouse, trying to keep from looking down. At the end, I braced a knee against the low railing and leaned over the side to look at the large window of darkened plate glass. Opaque by day and transparent by night. Yes, you would be able to see inside at night when they had the lights on. And I saw a rebar ladder that Pete could have used to climb to the roof to get some more photographs.

I was almost knocked over the side when the door opened. Out came Dean Weisburd, carrying an oversized attaché case. I moved quickly to block his way.

"This penthouse has been designated a crime scene. It contains material evidence to a murder."

"Get out of my way, you lying troublemaker."

"You are under citizen's arrest. Hand over that briefcase and follow me."

"You have no right. It's my briefcase."

I grabbed the briefcase as he tried to dash past me.

"Let go, you little bastard, or I'll push you off."

"Surrender the briefcase. It contains material evidence in a murder."

It started as a tug-of-war. Crowded in the doorway, the med students watched, as dumbstruck as I. Weisburd was pulling with one hand and hitting me with the other. I had to hold on with two hands and they were getting weaker by the second. Mary was right. When your muscles dump potassium, it leaves you as weak as a kitten.

Slowly, Weisburd's strategy started taking shape. He pulled hard on the handle with his left and hit me with his right. He hit me with a flat hand around the head, but used a balled fist to punch my throat. I did my best to hold two corners of the briefcase with both hands. I couldn't afford to lose the moral high ground by hitting back. But I squirmed, wormed and pulled, trying to keep him off balance.

At an instant when my back was to the 12-story drop-off, he gave an enormous shove. I almost went over the side. Now, his strategy was turning lethal. But I hung on like a bulldog. He kept hitting me and jerking away. I maneuvered my back to the shallower side. I could survive a 12-foot fall onto a tar-paper roof.

The first of us to weaken was the briefcase. First, a latch sprang open. Then the two halves came apart enough for me to insert four fingers on one side, getting a better grip. It was just in time because my forearms were cramping and his jerks were becoming more violent until . . . .

. . . the briefcase tore open and left my grip and . . . in slow motion . . . went sailing over the edge, in the hands of a corrupt medical school dean . . . who fell with it . . . down 12 stories, streaming a trail of paper squares that fluttered like falling leaves . . . obscuring my vision of his horrible landing . . . which was announced to my ears with a sickening thud . . . that could mean only one thing: that his body had undergone instantaneous, spleen-busting, heart-stopping deceleration.

There I stood, trembling, too dizzy to look down. Were the people below pointing fingers at me? Slowly, I turned to the medical students still crowding the door.

"Please, tell me I didn't do it," I shouted. But nothing came out of my dry mouth. I took two steps towards them and my legs gave way. Down I came on my knees, on the steep side, holding the rail for dear life.

My firm grip on the rail gave me the courage to look down on the confusion below: the antenna of the Channel 8 van, rising on its telescopic pole; the camera crew running to the point of impact; and the ant-like scurrying of the crowd. They were grabbing up the little squares of paper like they were 100-dollar bills from an overturned Brinks truck.

What, I asked myself, made the paper squares so valuable? Then, I saw the answer lying right in front of me on the catwalk — two Polaroid photographs. Amateur porno shots. One was a sideways shot of a bare-chested Dean Weisburd making a rear entry between broad buttocks. The other shot was also of canine coupling, but it was taken from the front, close to the instant of ecstasy, judging from their faces. Hers looked strangely familiar — the broad forehead, the pudgy cheeks, the widely spaced eyes and coarse black hair. No, it couldn't be . . . yes, it was . . . Rosemary, assistant in the publicity office and Lizzy-Mae's granddaughter!

Lizzy-Mae had not killed for money. She had killed Pete to keep him from showing photos of her granddaughter and her "Doctor." To keep a lid on the ugly secret, she even tried to kill me. But she didn't blame "Doctor." She still worshiped him.

Hissing and crackling of two-way radios heralded the arrival of two policemen with orders to "secure the rooftop." One of the med students started telling them it wasn't my fault. Then, we all ducked as a helicopter flew directly overhead. It slowed, and hovered over the parking garage. One policeman's walkie-talkie started squawking about "the subject in the parking garage."

Deep inside the garage, red and blue lights were flashing. They spiraled higher and higher inside the eight-tiered concrete structure. The wail of sirens and the screech of tires were plain to hear, even over the thudding of the chopper blades. And now, beside me, the securers of the rooftop were radioing to advise that the roofing crew would be imperiled when the subject arrived at the top level of the parking garage. Please have the airborne unit advise them to get their butts out of there.

It felt like everything was happening in slow motion: the loudspeaking helicopter herding the workers to the safety of their trucks, the pursued car careening around the corner and accelerating up the last ramp to the top, and the chaotic arrival of the screaming pack of squad cars.

Had the excitement so sharpened my eyesight or was it the

effect of the drug? I saw Lizzy-Mae, sure as day. Her head was forward and low; her back was hunched. As she turned her car and accelerated towards us, I could even make out her white knuckles on the steering wheel. She had nowhere to go.

Her pursuers were scattered behind their squad cars along the top entrance. Between them, they were forming a picket of drawn pistols and pointed shotguns.

Lizzy-Mae screeched her car around in front of them. Maybe this was a practice run for ramming them. Their first shot shattered her side window. This, she answered with a squeal of rubber and a rush of acceleration. Was she trying to outrun the bullets? She must have been doing forty when she rammed the pile of stacked roofing felt. Like a Matchbox Car on a ramp, it lifted over the pile, over the retaining wall, flipping as it arched into the distance behind the parking garage. For an amazing four seconds it was out of sight. Then came the crushing boom of a 60 mile-an-hour head-on collision and the sound of steel grinding to a halt on concrete. Seconds later, an eight-story fireball reported that the fatal stunt had been performed on a full tank of gas.

Could I really believe my eyes? My right hand rose to my chest to pinch myself. And there I found a better assurance of reality. It was my little brown book in my shirt pocket. I withdrew it, removed the rubber band and opened it. There nestled between the last page and back cover were two things I sought: my picture of Rebecca and Alice's card. I kissed the one and removed the other. I went up to a medical student who was talking into a cellphone and asked if I could make an important call.

I was so shaky he had to dial the number for me; she answered on the third ring.

"Alice, this is Ben. I promised you I'd call, and here it is."

"You're leaving her?"

"No, Dr. Quinn, Medicine Woman, is alive and well. But Arnold Weisburd, dean of Bryan Medical School, just fell 13 stories. Channel 8 is crawling all over the site with cameras. But I'm saving the biggest scoop for you — for you and the State Attorney."

I told her to come to my office as fast as she could.

Dr. Westley got to me before the Metro-Dade plainclothes men. He took down the students' statements that Weisburd's fall was his own fault. Everyone agreed that all I did was hang onto the briefcase.

When the pair of Metro detectives came, Dr. Westley assigned one to complete the interviews on the roof and told the other to come along for my debriefing. I took them to Rob's office. It was empty, but the FEDEX box was still under his desk. When we got to my office, Alice was already there.

I gave Mildred a minimal explanation and asked her to lock us in the lab and not let anyone in. I took the phone off the hook and sat everyone around my desk. I suggested that Alice tape-record while Dr. Westley, the detective and I make an oral inventory of the box. It was then that I remembered my own tape recorder in my pants pocket. It was still running, almost at the end of one 45-minute side. I turned it off and handed it to Dr. Westley as evidence.

We opened the FEDEX box. It contained a bundle of letter-sized envelopes, one diskette and a hand-written note to me from Carole:

> Dear Ben,
> I opened these shortly after Uncle Pete's death, but didn't realize they could be important until after your last call. So here they are.
> Ciao,
> Carole

I took the rubber band off the bundle. Each envelope contained several typewritten sheets. On the front of one envelope was written, "To Be Opened in the Event of My Death, Peter Peterson," followed by the date that was about three months ago. The other envelopes were similarly labelled, spaced several months apart and covering the last two years. Apparently, Carole had opened them after Pete died, and after finding that it wasn't giving her any money, put it away and forgot about it.

The most recent letter told the story best:

> Dear Carole,
> Maybe you will think I'm being melodramatic again. I'm sure that sending you all these letters has made you curious. But what I've been doing isn't exactly legal, so I want to keep it secret as long as I'm alive. If I die of natural causes, I don't

want my life work to go to waste. And if they kill me, I sure as hell don't want them to get away with it.

I might just be imagining things, but it seems like things are getting dangerous. I remember a time over 50 years ago when they told me I was just a fraidie cat for imagining things. They said the island was secure. But one night a Jap snuck down from the hills and slit the throats of three guys sleeping in the C-2 barracks.

These bastards here are just as sneaky, so after you open this one, go to my code book and see if I wrote any more. It's Clive Cussler's <u>Inca</u> <u>Gold</u>. It's easy to read. Just start at the first page and write down every letter that's got a pin-prick under it. It's a good trick that I read about somewhere. Thought it was fitting to use Clive Cussler for it because that man really knows how to tell an adventure story. Dirk Pitt's my biggest hero.

Now for my adventure. In a few weeks, after I figure out how to do it, I'm going to go public with the story I've been piecing together. The longer I've worked here the rottener things have got, 'til a decent guy can't stand it anymore.

Well, first things first. Any service company that works here pays kickbacks. The plumbing company, the electricians, the carpenters. The one that's running it is Dolores Padilla. She's in charge of purchasing and contracts. She has a couple of friends in the Physical Plant who work with her on it. To get the contract they have to pay Dolores Padilla 40%. The way it works is they pay for "bookkeeping services" to a company called Contruría Piedad that her cousin owns. They tell me the name is a good joke if you know Spanish. The cousin sends the companies an "invoice" and they pay like it's a legitimate business expense. And then the cousin turns around and writes a check for all the rats in the medical school who are going along with that. And guess who gets the biggest slice of the evil pie — Burdie!

But I'm getting ahead of myself. The diskette that I put in this envelope has the details on two years worth of this slime. I worked a long time organizing it. Actually that's been my only hobby, lately. For each case where they kicked back, it gives all the information. The data's organized into tables. Each row is for a separate med school purchase order, the corresponding bill from the company, the matching kickback check to the cousin, and the checks she wrote to the culprits. Real interesting how the kickback always comes to 40% and how constant everyone's slice of the pie is. Both those "assistant deans," Wriggler and Kotzen, are in on it. Jerry Cartlick gets a big slice for enforcing "security" and arranging to beat up any outside vendor that complains.

Why didn't anyone ever wonder why they use so many outside contractors, and they won't even let their own physical plant people buy tools? Or why they want to milk everyone's grant to redo the window blinds and they're always looking for an excuse to renovate a lab? And why they won't let a scientist use his own travel agent? Last year, the kickbacks came close to five million dollars.

I've had to hack pretty hard to get all that information, and that's all I'm going to say about it. I stand by it, and if uncovering this crime is against the law, then I'll take all the blame.

But that's only part of it. Mike Sims sells pain relievers and steroids and even narcotics around here like the Tutti-Frutti Man. All he needs is the three-wheeled bike and a soda-jerk hat. I enclose a photocopy of his list of flavors. His Popsicles are free samples that the drug company representatives donate to certain high muckety-mucks on the clinical faculty here. They give it to him wholesale, and he sells it retail.

But if you want to see some real drug action,

come around here at night. Wait for the organ donor station wagon to come back from Miami International Airport where it meets a flight from Colombia. I had always wondered why Dean Burdie was so interested in autopsies of people who died of "tropical diseases" in South America, especially since he never published a paper on the subject. Took me a long time to figure out that they were packing up to half a kilo in those stiffs. I guess that a dead "mule" that's pickled in formaldehyde is a lot easier to watch than a live one.

I couldn't get check numbers on that operation because they are dealing with cash. But I did get a lot of photographs of the guys that are in on it, and the guys they are turning the stuff over to. The photos are in the enclosed envelope and are labelled. I also have notes from my surveillance. Dr. William Long from Physiology was always around when they were doing it, but I don't think he was really in on it. I think they were keeping him around for a fall guy in case a Federal agent would follow the station wagon home.

But I guess my trickiest photography was of old Burdie in his love nest. You could almost call it child molestation, when a 58-year-old man messes with a 20-year-old, and I've got a mind to tell Lizzy-Mae about what he was doing with her granddaughter Rosemary. But she probably won't believe me. She worships the ground he walks on. Did she think Burdie was paying her granddaughter $37,000 a year for her typing skill?

It was bad enough what Burdie used to be doing with Daisy, Lizzy-Mae's daughter, but she's turned to the bottle so bad that her liver won't hold out more than another year or two. What does Burdie think he is? God's gift to women? Seems like it wasn't good enough to whack up a big score with his tally-whacker. No, he just had to go for a two-fer and make sure he'd dipped his stick in both of them.

Not that the granddaughter's any spring chicken. I sure learned a thing or two from her that first night when I was sitting on top of the parking garage's elevator shack watching them through my telephoto lens. I clicked off shots 'til I ran out of film. The other nights I got a better perch on the roof of their hootchie cootchie hutch and leaned over the edge to get my pictures.

I hope I won't have to use the photos of Lizzy-Mae's granddaughter with Burdie. I'm just planning to keep them in reserve, in case Burdie starts playing tough and sends around Jerry Cartlick and his boyfriends. Twenty years is still pretty young for a girl to be doing that kind of stuff — giving mouth jobs like a Tunisian whore (pardon my French). Twenty-year-old girls were pretty foolish back in my times, too. Just let them be foolish and maybe they will see the light and mend their ways.

Anyway, if I die, give this to my lawyer, Ted Walden, and ask him to do what he can do to blow the whistle on those rats. They are pocketing money that was given for science. In my book, that's worse than stealing from the church collection box.

Love,
Uncle Pete

After we had all read the first page, Alice had taken over, reading us the rest out aloud. As I listened with closed eyes, it seemed like Pete was sitting next to me, talking.

When Alice came to the end, we were silent for a while, looking at each other.

I was the first to speak. "I guess Pete did warn Lizzy-Mae about what her granddaughter was doing. And Dean Weisburd had his security people snoop in Pete's apartment. And when they told him what Pete had collected, he gave Lizzy-Mae a syringe full of succinylcholine and told her to go to it. She injected Pete when he was sitting on the fence by the canal."

Dr. Westley nodded. "It fits the facts quite nicely. Sgt. Ramos, I suggest that Dr. Candidi make two copies of the letters and diskettes. I suggest that you bring the originals directly, minding chain of evidence, to the State Attorney. Dr. Candidi will retain one copy and Ms. Alice McRae will retain the other."

He turned to Alice. "I would suggest that you coordinate your news stories with the State Attorney's office. They must first have an opportunity to formulate their indictments."

"Yes."

Dr. Westley raised a bushy white eyebrow. "But if the State Attorney proves too slow, there would be nothing wrong with your getting a little ahead of them."

Dr. Westley turned to Det. Ramos. "Am I correct in assuming that we have finished our business with Dr. Candidi?"

"Well . . . not really, Chief. When this guy was fighting with the president of this medical school and he goes over the side, it calls for a little more explanation."

"Ms. McRae, could you give us a few minutes alone. Ben, please give Det. Ramos your statement."

I told him my side of the story. Then I told him the whole story, starting in the dean's office.

"You also attacked a security officer."

"He had orders to detain me to make sure I would die. I got past him with a palm thrust to the face."

"You came close to killing that one. They have him in an O.R. at *Dade General*, trying to pull nose cartilage out of his brain without causing any more bleeding."

"When he wakes up, you should arrest him for attempted murder."

"You'll have to go over there and identify him for us."

"Shouldn't be a problem, with his busted nose." I thought for a minute, and added, "I bet I can identify something else wrong with him — a puncture wound in the right shoulder. Just healed."

I told the detective about the incident with the burglar in Pete's apartment and how Security refused to investigate it. Det. Ramos agreed that he had his work cut out for him.

I copied the diskette onto the hard drive, and then made a copy for Alice. Dr. Westley said he would walk down to the departmental office and make the photocopies of the letters.

Outside in the hallway, Mildred was holding off quite a crowd. "Ben," she said, "your friend Bruce from Mensa called the office.

He asked for your e-mail address because he has an important message he wants to send you. He was very emphatic."

I left the others and locked myself in the lab. I clicked on the Internet access server and typed in the password for my e-mail account. Bruce's message was the next to the last.

> From: Hi-IQ@herald.infi.net
> To: ben.candidi@netrus.net
> Subj.: It worked but be careful
> Hi Ben,
> My security system is working fine and it's discovered something you've got to know about. A couple guys have been coming around in the middle of the night and messing around with your computer. I have attached a couple digital pictures. You can get the rest of them by http'ing to my website under /~ben.htm. They are time-date coded. One of the guys is wearing a security guard uniform.
> Here's the info you'll need to complain: The computer is programmed to use the digital camera and a motion detector between midnight and seven in the morning. When it senses a change, it stores pictures to memory and sends them to me as an e-mail attachment.
> They might say they were visiting the Hustler site, but I think they were hacking. See for yourself.
> — Bruce

I clicked on the five attached *jpg* files and saw he was right. The pictures showed Jerry Cartlick and a guy in a guard's uniform. I looked up and located the digital camera and motion detector. They were between a couple of rows of books on Pete's shelf, positioned well to cover most of the office and some of the outside lab. In most of the pictures, the scoundrels were peering into the screen. Some of the pictures caught Cartlick going through papers in my desk drawer.

My mind whirled as I remembered typing into that computer my analysis of Pete's crusade. Every day, they had tracked my progress on the road to realization. And they had intercepted my e-mail messages. That was probably why my modem couldn't work faster than half-speed. And they had obviously listened in on my phone calls. They'd bugged my office for sure.

I clicked on Bruce's website and I found the unlisted subdirectory. As I clicked on the time-date-titled hypertext links and the pictures of the nocturnal visits scrolled before me, I fell into a hypnotic trance. I snapped out of it in a nick of time. Jumped out of the chair and turned to chop his neck.

But nobody was there. I had been hearing things. It was too much for one day; my senses were becoming unreliable. Time to find someone to take care of me. But first, I had to download one last e-mail:

> From: abalone@hotmail.com
> To: bcandidi@mailserver.bryan.edu
> Subj.: Sticky subject
> Hi Ben. Greetings from California. Thought you might want to check out a website at your school: http://www.bryan.edu/cellanatomy/porn.htm Lots of people are busy cloning it.
> — Your friend Abalone

The site was served by our department's computer. I bet that Mel Armino still knew the passwords that control computers around here. I http'd to the site. The title popped up:

"Dean Weisburd and his secretary play 'Bill and Monica' in Penthouse Lovenest at Bryan Medical School."

As the picture slowly filled in, from top to bottom, I thought about our collective fascination with porno — a cooperative fascination that moves pictures so quickly. A Miamian scoops it off the street, digitizes it and sends it to a Californian who turns around and inserts it in the Miami institution's webpage. I bet they were bragging about the stunt.

It was a picture to kill for. And soon, hundreds of thousands of people would have copies.

A wave of nausea came over me. It must have been a delayed reaction to the succinylcholine. My stomach heaved, pushing a stream of bile acid up my throat faster than I could close it. On weak legs, I raced to the sink where I lost my fast-food lunch. To the accompaniment of dry heaves, I rinsed my mouth and gargled.

35 FINAL CHAPTER

Long-period swells rocked me gently. The smell of salt was strong in the air, now carried in by a cool easterly breeze. Gone was the river-algae smell of the Potomac River and the Chesapeake Bay. We had passed Cape Charles and had sailed through the main shipping channel, past the Chesapeake Bay Bridge. Ninety degrees to starboard was Cape Henry. The *Diogenes* was slicing green water at six knots, pointing into a 20-knot Atlantic easterly. Oncoming waves were too low and widely spaced to produce any bow spray that would moisten the cockpit.

Weather forecasts were favorable. Abnormalities in the water flow in the far North Atlantic were holding back the arctic air, giving Washingtonians a week of September temperatures, and were giving the *Diogenes* a two-week window to head out into the Atlantic and dash south. Nature was being kind to us.

Portside, a large container ship was overtaking us. Pointing into the wind, the *Diogenes* was so steady that the autopilot had little to do. At six knots, we would hold this course for about nine hours to get the desired 50 miles of sea room before changing the tack to the southeast. Best to give Cape Hatteras a wide berth — the Gulf Stream, too, when your destination is in the southerly latitudes. The Little Bahama Bank is a pleasant destination and the Abacos will be a nice place to throw out the hook.

Although the North Atlantic Oscillation had transformed November into September, it had not stopped the sun's daily slippage to the south. It was now at a low angle in the west-southwest, warming my back as I sat behind the wheel of the *Diogenes*.

The container ship gave two thunderous blasts, signalling its intention to overtake me on the portside. I pulled the air horn out of the cockpit's side pocket and gave two honks to signal my agreement. While returning the horn to the side pocket, I did a quick inventory: hand-held VHF radio, one-million candlepower spotlight, and flare pistol. These are important tools when you have to negotiate with the big boys at night. They might overlook my radar reflector's passive return and might miss our 20-watt red, green and white running lights. In a couple hours, it would be time to ask Rebecca to switch those lights on.

It had been a hectic week in Washington, getting the *Diogenes* ready for the sea. Before that, it had been a hectic two weeks in Miami — days filled with statements to the police and conferences with State and Federal attorneys, with a police detective at my side every waking hour. But it had been important to work quickly, keeping up with the rat race — the race between the rats of the med school mafia to turn each other in.

It had been amazing how quickly they caved in. First came a wave of lower-level administrators volunteering "just-discovered" information on wrongdoing by their higher-ups. Theirs were the crimes of silence. They had received "overtime bonuses" and "merit raises" to look the other way. Next, came a wave of pre-indictment bargaining, where the State Attorney traded sworn testimony for grants of immunity, and plea bargaining for the perpetrators of the more serious crimes.

It was interesting to see the power structure of the medical school mafia working backwards. It was like a counter-surge where lightning seems to shoot from the ground to the sky, following its own ionization trail. It zig-zagged up to Dolores Padilla who is now facing 10 years. Bank records of Contruría Piedad made a trail to Assistant Deans Wriggler and Kotzen. The Board of Trustees immediately suspended them from duty, pending outcome of criminal charges. Several of the contracting companies that were paying kickbacks agreed to stiff fines and restitution payments to avoid criminal prosecution.

The cocaine smuggling investigation was still wrapped in secrecy. All I knew was that William Long was whisked from our department under police protection and that Jerry Cartlick had disappeared.

Alice had a field day with exposés on the kickbacks and bribes. Her investigative work showed that a lot of charitable gift money had been diverted to administrative perks and salary raises. The dean had even pocketed one of the scholarships. Alice was a star reporter, but it wasn't her work alone. My biggest surprise was learning that Mr. Howard Edmunds of Cool Shades had been conducting his own investigation of how charitable gift money had been spent. He had used his own auditors together with information he gathered during his working visits to Dr. Yung's lab. He had developed a good informant network using technicians and departmental administrators. Now, his auditors were working in the open. A number of major donors were demanding return of their money.

It was gratifying how the spirit of reform spread to other parts of the medical center. After Alice ran a story on the parking garage scam, Channel 8 did a story called "All You Need is 8." They interviewed low-income patients to show that the eight-dollar fee was a hardship. They had some nice shots of the Coral Gables mansions of the directors of the Miami-Dade Public Health Authority who were running the scam.

The spirit of reform spilled over to *Dade County General*. Attending physicians gave the investigators anonymous tips on their department heads and some administrators. The Feds were interested in over-billing. Bryan Medical School's deal with North American Hospital fell through. But this did not stop donors from asking for return of donations they had made for CAT scanners and computerized ultrasound machines.

In my spare moments, I had wondered whether Mr. Cool Shade's investigation could have forced these reforms if Pete hadn't taken up his crusade and died in the process. The answer had to be "no." The inequities between heaven and earth would have been dissipated slowly; there would have been no flash of lightning. The blitz required the sacrifice of Pete Peterson — the lightning rod for controversy, the guy with sharp edges.

And public exposure of mere graft was not powerful enough to drive the counter-surge. It had required blood, guts and porno — Channel 8's pictures of red concrete and photos from Dean Weisburd's porno show. Those pictures were hot items, swapped like digital baseball cards between hundreds of personal websites and geek pages from here to Malaysia. I shook my head at the thought of it all.

"Stop mulling, Ben. Get it out of your mind." Rebecca was standing in the companionway, regarding me with a "general practitioner look." Oh, how she can read my thoughts!

"I wasn't mulling."

"Yes, you were. You've been frowning for the last two minutes, so buried in bad thoughts that you didn't even see me looking at you."

She knows me better than I know myself.

"I can't help it." I shook my head and busied myself with cranking in the jib line one more inch.

"We've got two months, Ben — paid vacation for you, leave of absence for me. But it isn't going to be any fun if you spend the whole time mulling."

"Sorry, but I'm always thinking. It's been a lifelong habit."

"Then think about where we're headed. Margaritaville." She smiled and sang the verse about changes in latitudes and changes in attitudes.

I smiled back, but it didn't last long. I blinked and touched the corner of my eye, removing a drop of saltwater that had not been splashed up by the *Diogenes'* bow.

"Oh, Ben. I'm sorry."

I caught her glance before fixing my eyes on the binnacle. She sat beside me, putting her arm around me.

"I'm sorry. I said the wrong thing. I know that post-traumatic stress is hard. Let it all out."

I exhaled deeply. The pent-up emotion escaped through my mouth. "It just makes me sick . . . them, all of them . . . using rapid growth as an excuse . . . like that ficus tree growing all over Ted Walden's house . . . dropping all that trash . . . all that blackmail, graymail and greenmail." My words probably weren't making much sense, but I was sure feeling something. I took a deep breath and said it loud and clear. "They have the ethics of a pirate ship."

Rebecca moved over and hugged me, kissing the back of my neck, exposed by my bowed head. "I feel the same way, too. About the corruption. I now feel ashamed to tell people that's where I got my medical degree."

I couldn't stop. "Everybody knew about it, but nobody did a thing about it. Like our chairman and his gallows humor. Like that schoolmarm, Hilda Beecher. She knew the bad guys had taken over Main Street, but all she did was box our ears and tell us to mind our P's and Q's."

"I know, Ben. It's hard for people to stand up. There were times when I should have stood up, myself — like that cheating incident when I was a sophomore, where the dean didn't punish the guys who were cheating. He used the incident to get back at the prof who was organizing the course. It made me so sick."

"Why is it that as soon as a guy gets a position of power, he goes around flaunting it — selling it."

"I don't know, Ben. Maybe it's just a male thing. No, women are just as much at fault. Look at those three generations of women — grandmother, mother and daughter. They went along with it. They probably rationalize it saying the chief must have his way for the good of the tribe. Maybe what it takes is for a warrior — like you — to feel insulted and do something about it."

A confusing mix of emotions left me unable to say anything for a long time. "It wasn't me. It was . . . P-P-P . . . Pete. And he had to die for it."

A high-pitched trill roused me from the depths of self-pity. It came from the front of the boat and took us both by surprise. We figured it out on the second ring. I hurried to the main salon and I zipped the diving bag containing my clothes and water-sensitive possessions.

"It's mine and I'm taking it," I yelled to Rebecca. I grabbed the cell phone and said, "Hello."

The voice on the other end was instantly recognizable from the first syllable — a syllable delivered with such idiosyncracy that all the fiber optic networks, satellite uplinks, microwave translators, and cellular networks in the world couldn't distort it. It began with a mildly percussive "b." It continued with a short "e" carried at high pitch in perfect resonance. And it ended with a gentle dip of the "n." . . . "*Ben*," it said.

"Dr. Westley!"

"From the flapping jib, I perceive that you are underway on your boat."

I made a face. "Sure, Dr. Westley. I will tend to it as soon as we finish this conversation."

"I will be quite brief. I thought you would like the results of the autopsy. It took some time to arrange for the exhumation. Luckily, the undertaker did not spare the formaldehyde. All tissues were quite well fixed. Of course, succinylcholine may be completely hydrolyzed by now, but we will try to find it anyway, using a new, improved Swedish method — ion pair extraction followed by GC-Mass Spectroscopy."

"Good."

"Be that as it may, we did find a needle track in the left buttock, which would be consistent with any sort of lethal injection. Its position and orientation were consistent with an upwards jab to the accessible portion of a buttock of a man sitting on a fence."

"Great."

"Also, we did a histological analysis of the muscle tissue, using a corresponding sample from the right buttock as a control. We found evidence of disorganization in the muscle's striation pattern, consistent with long-term fasciculation."

"Good."

"Thus, I have rendered a judgement that the death was consistent with your theory — succinylcholine injection. Together with your interview of the Jamaican respiratory therapist, we can picture the death as follows. Our Florida Cracker version of that most evil James Bond villainess, Rosa Klipp, approached Dr. Peterson from the side and engaged him in conversation. She injected him from behind, and then acted as if he had snagged himself on a splinter. This explains his agitation, and stepping down from the fence. She stayed with him until it was clear that he wasn't going to cry for help. Then she absconded."

"I can imagine that."

"The Jamaican respiratory therapist now remembers seeing her standing on the Metrorail platform, looking down. He remembers wondering why she remained there when the train came and went."

"Great."

"The timing would be consistent with her telephone call to Dean Weisburd. We subsequently subpoened telephone records. It would seem that her motive for the murder of Dr. Peterson was loyalty to the dean. Her motive for trying to murder you was the same and to protect her granddaughter from exposure."

"Right."

"You will also be interested to know that an arrest warrant has been put out for Jerry Cartlick. He skipped town, you will remember. Besides his central role in the cocaine smuggling, he was an active planner of your murder. The guard who tried to detain you made us clear on that. Incidentally, I had no idea you were so skilled in the martial arts. It took the ENTs the better part of the day putting his sinuses back together. You fractured his ethmoid bone, you did. A bit harder and it would have been a cerebral hemorrhage. But not to bother, for we persuaded him to sign a document releasing you of all civil damages — for this, and for the other incident. We obtained a perfect match between his DNA and the DNA swabbed from your bloody pen after your stairwell altercation. I must say, Ben, you are quite the ninja."

"Thanks."

"At any rate, we also persuaded the chap to sign a document detailing the murderous intent of his boss, Cartlick. That scoundrel is probably setting up a new identity in Latin America . . . or pursuing his true identity in the bowels of San Francisco."

"Thanks, I was afraid of reprisals."

"No, it is quite beyond that. They would need reprisals against the Federal government. This little Himmler had quite a video command post at home. He was able to watch the med school. He had blackmail videos on the dean, and a lot of other people. Funny how much fornication goes on within institutions behind closed doors, after hours. But this chap's particular fornication seemed to also be his Achilles tendon, although his tastes were of a different variety — I hesitate to say 'flavor' — than most of us folks. Suffice it to say, he belongs to a *most* bizarre fraction of the outer five percent. His police pretensions did put a different twist on it, with handcuffs, et cetera. That, alone, would have been enough to make . . . . . . institution dismiss the queenie . . . . on the . . . of common decency and taste . . . although . . . . . . when they . . . a cabal . . . Sodom . . . Isle of Lesbos . . . "

"Dr. Westley, I agree with you wholeheartedly, but your signal is breaking up."

"Very well. My love to Rebecca. Godspeed." (Click)

I deactivated the phone and put it back in the diving bag. It wouldn't do us any good out in the Atlantic. From now on my GPS unit — my longitude and latitude-reading Global Positioning System receiver — would be our most important hand-held device.

Rebecca was looking down on me from the steering station. "Dr. Westley sends his love," I called up to her.

"That reminds me, when I downloaded this morning, I noticed there was an e-mail for you, in care of me. It was from an *Alice*."

Rebecca hadn't completely forgiven me for what had happened with Barbara. Happily, George had realized what he was throwing away and had gotten back together with Barbara.

I swallowed hard before replying. "Great. Alice is the reporter who kept the ball rolling. What . . . what did the message say?"

"I didn't open it. The subject line said 'for Ben.' Just thought you'd want to take a look at it while you are down there."

"Good idea. Thanks."

I pulled the laptop computer from the bag and unzipped its case. Turned it on and retrieved the message. It consisted of ten high-spirited lines of greeting with so much squeezed in between the lines that I was glad Rebecca hadn't opened it. Funny how many girls will go for a guy in the hours and days after his publicized heroics. My old Swarthmore roommate, Richard Bash, had a reptilian theory on the phenomenon.

I blocked and deleted all the text down to the last line, which had something I could use. "I remember how you compared Dr. Peter Peterson to the Coral Castle guy. I attach a 1951 picture from our archive."

I clicked on the attachment, and the hard drive started sending a black and white picture to the screen. Horizontal lines began filling in, top to bottom. First came the 23-ton crescent moon, sitting high above the "throne room." Then came a patch of wispy hair, and a high forehead, over smiling eyes and an indented mouth that looked like it would have smiled too if there had been enough teeth. It was an old, wrinkled, leathery face. His head occupied the diagonal between the high crescent moon in the background and his demonstratively extended hand in the foreground.

Yes, his face reminded me of a desiccated Peruvian mummy, but in that face I could read the pride of creation and the triumph of persistence.

It was not for me to lament a wasted youth, when its thwarted energies had sublimated into a crowning achievement in the last decade of life. Such was the legacy of Edward Leedskalnin.

And this would be my lead-in to the story of Peter Peterson, Ph.D. I closed my eyes to mentally scan his photo album, and found the picture that summed it up. Pete was wearing a white lab jacket and standing in front of Bryan Medical School.

Yes, I could now work with inspiration, sitting at the autopiloted helm and peering into the greenish glow of a computer screen on the midnight watch. Now, I had the theme around which to organize those 130 pages of biographical data. Now, I had the title for his biography:

"Pete Peterson's Crusade against Corruption in Academic Medicine"

About the Author

Dirk Wyle is the pen name of Duncan H. Haynes, Ph.D., a 30-year veteran of biomedical science. He studied at the University of Pennsylvania and in Germany and has served as a medical school professor, conducting research in abnormal blood coagulation and drug delivery. He invented a drug microencapsulation technology which lead to the founding of three companies employing approximately 65 people. He retired as a professor in early 2001.

Dirk Wyle has a passion for fleshing out the skeleton of the traditional mystery with the muscle and sinew of biomedical science. His stories (*Pharmacology Is Murder*, 1998; *Biotechnology Is Murder*, 2000; and *Medical School Is Murder*, 2001) take place in authentically rendered medical centers and drug companies. His free-spirited protagonist, Ben Candidi, accepts the dual challenge finding the murderer and discovering what made him (or her) do it in the first place. Considering guns to be overused devices, Dirk gives literary preference to methods that could fool a coroner but not a dedicated mystery buff.

Dirk has received the Icon Award from the National Writers Association (S. FL chapter), he is a member of the Mystery Writers of America, and his *Pharmacology Is Murder* was selected as the Best First Mystery of 1998 by Joe's Detective Pages.

Dirk invites your visit to http://www.dirk-wyle.com. He is hard at work on the fourth and fifth books in the series.